D0724141

Charming the Shrew

Laurin Wittig

[signature: Laurin Wittig]

BERKLEY SENSATION, NEW YORK

CHARMING THE SHREW

A Berkley Sensation Book / published by arrangement with
the author

PRINTING HISTORY
Berkley Sensation edition / May 2004

Copyright © 2004 by Laurin Wittig.
Cover art by Leslie Peck.

For information address: The Berkley Publishing Group,
a division of Penguin Group (USA) Inc.,
375 Hudson Street, New York, New York 10014.

ISBN: 0-425-19527-9

BERKLEY SENSATION[TM]
Berkley Sensation Books are published by The Berkley Publishing Group,
a division of Penguin Group (USA) Inc.,
375 Hudson Street, New York, New York 10014.
BERKLEY SENSATION and the "B" design
are trademarks belonging to Penguin Group (USA) Inc.

PRINTED IN THE UNITED STATES OF AMERICA

10 9 8 7 6 5 4 3 2

For Mom
Jane Magruder Watkins
who taught me to follow my own star

Acknowledgments

I would never have come this far without the unflagging support and awesome brain power of my critique group: Elizabeth Holcombe, Karen Lee, Courtney Henke and Catherine Anderson. Thank you, ladies!

Special thanks go to my dear friend Pamela Palmer Poulsen, who's always there to cheer me on and help me untangle the thorniest plot problems, and to Anne Shaw Moran, who coached this southern-bred woman on the details of serious snow.

As always, my love and thanks to my family, Dean, Samantha and Alex, who make it possible for me to spin my stories.

Prologue

❦

December 23, 1307, Inverurie, Scotland

*R*obert the Bruce, king of Scotland, shouldn't be dying.
Tayg Munro tried to understand this strange twist
of fate as he huddled near a stingy fire, wrapped tightly in
his plaid against the bone-chilling cold of the Scottish
winter. Smoke from the army's cookfires drifted, leaving
a faint gray haze both within and without the palisaded
walls of the nearby fort. He could just make out the rise of
the motte, a huge earthen hill clad in dirty drifts of snow,
upon which sat the timbered tower where the king lan-
guished, growing ever weaker.

Despite the death of Longshanks, Edward I of England,
in midsummer, and despite the relief afforded by Edward
II's disinterest in war, Scotland's fate had not yet been determined. All seemed now to hang on the vagaries of a
stubborn wasting disease.

The irony that all that the Scots had endured and overcome at Longshanks's hand might now be lost to a wasting illness was not missed by Tayg. He did not think there was another leader who could unite the varied peoples of Scotland. The loss of Sir William Wallace had been a terrible blow to their fight to rid themselves of England's grasp but the Bruce had stepped in and raised Sir William's banner of freedom with admirable strength and passion.

Now, though, 'twas rumored that the king would not last the night. Gillies had been sent hither and yon in search of a cure. Healers had come from as far away as the Kilmartin glen in the far west. But hope blew away on the sharp winter wind.

Tayg stirred the fire and glanced across its feeble flames at his companions in this endeavor: red-haired Duncan MacCulloch, his best friend and cousin; auld Gair of MacTavish, whom he'd met when first he joined the Bruce's band; quiet young Tearlach Munro, another cousin; and Tayg's older brother, Robbie the Braw, revered by all who knew him. Only the king was a better leader of men as far as Tayg was concerned.

But even Robbie wore the expression so common among their company: fatigue edged by despair. Indeed, each of his companions wore it as they sat hunched near the fire. All were good men who had lost someone or something to this constant battle against both the English and their own countrymen. Each had his own reason for being here, not the least of which was an abiding belief that King Robert was the last hope for Scotland's future. 'Twas a heavy mantle indeed for such a young monarch.

The Scottish earls had not been quick to rally to the cause. The Munros' own neighbor and ally, the Earl of Ross, was none too pleased that the sons of Munro were following the king, for Ross was on the side of whoever won this fight for Scotland and he had not yet firmly laid his sword at anyone's feet. Yet Tayg's brother Robbie had decided to support the Bruce and their father had agreed.

Tayg had had no particular opinion about this fracas when Robbie had dragged him into battle. He had thought 'twould be a grand adventure and that he would watch Robbie's back, protecting his own selfish interests in the future.

But it had turned out to be much more than that.

He had come to admire the men he fought beside and even more the man who led them, the man who lay dying within the timbered walls atop the hill. 'Twas a bitter fate to sit and wait for death.

Just two days past, the Earl of Buchan had attacked a scouting party and butchered the lot of them, leaving them for the carrion crows and magpies to pick at. The gossips claimed that the Bruce had attempted to rise from his deathbed to lead a counterattack, but the king had not been seen.

A sudden cry of surprise went up throughout the camp. Tayg and his companions rose as one, peering into the dimness. Out of the dusk loomed a knight in full battle gear upon a silver-gray charger. As the knight drew closer his surcoat revealed the rampant lion of Scotland, blood-red against a glowing golden background.

A chorus of cheers erupted even as Tayg solved the puzzle for himself.

"The king!"

"The king lives!"

Cheers rose around him as the camp of nearly seven hundred surrounded the man they had all thought lost to Scotland.

The king raised his hand and a hush fell over the army. "'Tis I!" His voice wavered slightly but then steadied.

Shouts surrounded him, louder this time, filling the air with excitement and hope. Tayg felt the weight upon his heart lift.

The king signaled for silence again. "We have grave work this night and I would not leave you to accomplish such alone." His voice was now strong and carried easily over the heads of the hushed crowd.

Tayg worked his way nearer to the man who was not so very much older than Robbie. He was near enough to see a lingering pallor to the king's skin and the dark hollows of his shrunken cheeks, but his posture was erect, his voice strong, and there was a glint in his eyes that bespoke an inner fire that had not been dampened by illness. 'Twas a miracle!

"We must repay Buchan for the slaughter of our men two days past. I will not let those noble warriors of Scotland go unavenged. We march within the hour!"

Yet another cheer ripped through the throng and Tayg added his own voice to it.

The king turned back to the fortress, leaving the army to break camp and prepare for battle. Orders were shouted and everyone scrambled to pack up their meager belongings and get back to the business of war.

Tayg fought his way through the crowd back to the hissing fire. Duncan joined him, along with their other companions, each lost in his own thoughts after the momentous arrival of the Bruce within the camp. Tayg watched as a cluster of women passed close by and one, a familiar plump lass with a long amber-colored braid, and held back from the others and sidled nearer to him.

"So ye'll be off then, Tayg?" she asked.

Tayg gave her a grin. "Will I be missed, Siusan?" She was one of the women who followed the army, keeping them fed and their clothes relatively clean. Tayg flirted shamelessly with all the women, enjoying their attentions nearly as much as he enjoyed watching them move about their work, hips swaying, hands in graceful motion.

"Aye, ye'll be missed. Though 'twill be blessedly less squabbling amongst the lasses with yer pretty puss busy in battle." She gave him a smacking kiss then sobered. "Be ye careful now."

"As careful as one can be in battle, sweetling." He winked at her. "Never you worry, I shall return to cause more squabbling soon."

Siusan looked at him and for a moment he thought she was going to cry. Tayg took her work-roughened hand and kissed it as gallantly as he would the queen's. "Be you careful, too, lass." The girl nodded then hurried away to catch up with the other women.

Duncan shook his head in wonder as he packed his belongings. "Even a call to battle by the Bruce himself does not stop your wooing of the lasses!"

"And why should it?" Tayg said, shoving a wooden cup into his pack. "She is scared, just like the rest of them. Where's the harm in lifting her worries a bit and reminding her that there are better things for men and women to do than tramp off to war?"

"And no one lifts a lass's fears so well as Tayg," young Tearlach said as he spread out the remains of the fire then kicked dirt-crusted snow onto the fading embers, snuffing them out with a pathetic hiss.

Tayg suppressed a shudder. The king had come so close to the fire's fate.

"'Tis a wonder he is up and about," Duncan said, his voice low, his thoughts clearly following Tayg's. "'Twas already passing amongst the men that he was dead, yet there he sat upon his horse as if he had just come from a council of war."

"'Tis curious." Robbie stared at the dying embers. "One of the healers must have found a way to defeat the king's private enemy, whatever 'twas."

"A witch," Gair said. "Norval of Dummaglas saw her. Auburn hair, tall. She hails from Kilmartin, so Norval says."

Tayg shrugged. "Perhaps 'tis only the attentions of a

bonny lass that revived him. 'Tis often I've seen braw
Duncan here revive himself when his Mairi tends his
hurts." He glanced at Duncan and grinned, glad to break
the somber mood. His friend's pale freckled face grew
red, starting at his neck and rapidly rising to meet his hair,
which was very nearly the same color, though with a faint
cast of blond.

"Do not let the whelp embarrass you, Duncan," Robbie
said, sliding his battle ax into his belt. "You ken well how
he fairs with the lasses."

Laughter circled the fire.

"Aye. It has ever been so with this one." Duncan
grinned at Tayg this time but there was something serious
tucked away in that familiar expression. "Woo them. Bed
them. Leave them with their heads spinning so 'twill be
months before they'll even look at another lad. That's our
Tayg. He has never been able to choose but one lass."

"And why should I when there are so many who are
willing to share my company"—he winked at quiet Tearlach, the youngest of the bunch—"and my bed?"

"Why indeed?" Gair agreed. "'Tis a bit jealous of the
lad's way of charming the lasses, I am. Though I would
not want my daughters in his company . . . nor my wife,"
he added with alarm in his voice though the grin was still
in place on his battle-scarred face.

"I have never charmed a man's wife, nor his sweet-
heart." At Duncan's snort, Tayg turned to him. "Not once
I knew."

"He tells the truth there, though I did have to knock
him on his arse to get his attention," Duncan said. "'Twas
lucky for me you had only just turned your interest—and
your charm—towards my Mairi. She was not yet under
your spell."

"Ah, smart lass, that Mairi," Gair said.

Tearlach laughed and the others grinned at the sound

that would have been unthinkable in the camp of cold and dispirited men just minutes before.

Robbie yanked the drawstring on his pack closed with a little more viciousness than was strictly necessary. "You are welcome to try to woo my timid little betrothed, brother," he said.

The sudden silence was all the greater for being surrounded by the noisy bustle of the army preparing to leave.

"Nay," Tayg said with an exaggerated shudder. "She is too plain for my tastes, and too old."

Robbie laughed, though 'twas a bit forced. "Aye, she is both, for me as well." He shrugged.

Tayg covered his surprise at his brother's unusual candor by turning his attention to checking his weapons: claymore on his back, dagger at his waist, *sgian dhu,* a small knife, hidden in a special sheath under his armpit. He knew the lass was not of Robbie's choosing but never had he said as much.

His brother was a better man than he, Tayg mused as he swung his pack onto his shoulder, picked up his targe—a round wooden shield—and moved with the others to form up in the rather loose way of Highlanders.

The army moved out, jogging up the road toward the waiting army of Buchan. War had taught Tayg that life was short and hard and one should take pleasure when and how one could, for there was not an abundance of it in this time and place. Yet Robbie would shackle himself to a woman he could find no pleasure in.

"Why did you not refuse her?" he asked at last.

Robbie was silent for so long Tayg began to think he had not heard the question. "I could not," he finally said. "You ken well that this is a political alliance to assuage the worries of the Earl of Ross."

Tayg nodded.

"To refuse the lass would have alarmed Ross; 'twould

have harmed the clan and that I would not do. 'Tis enough that I have placed the clan in this position by following the Bruce. 'Twas only right that I do what I must to safeguard those who remained at home."

"But you are not the only one fighting here."

"Nay, but someday I will be chief and the clan must know that I will do what is necessary for the good of the clan."

Tayg thanked the heavens that he was the second-born. Robbie could have the life of chief of Clan Munro. Tayg, as his brother's champion, would serve the clan, too, but he would have more freedom when it came to picking a wife and to living his life.

Several horses cantered by, the Bruce on his silver-gray charger in the lead, moving rapidly toward the front of the column of men. Pride filled Tayg's chest and an unyielding determination wrapped thickly about him.

Before Robbie could wed, before either of them could get on with the life he chose, this battle must be won. Tayg knew too well how many young men had died at the hands of the English and their Scottish supporters. He knew more would die in the coming fight as well, but he no longer believed he had any choice—not in this. He would fight for King Robert. He would fight beside his brother for Scotland.

And after the battle was won, God willing, he would see Robbie lead their clan into a peaceful future.

chapter 1

Early December, 1308, Highlands

Tayg pulled his shaggy Highland pony to a halt and gazed down over Culrain, the glen of his childhood. He had delayed this return for nearly a year while he served with the Bruce, but he could no longer deny his fate.

Robbie was dead. Tayg did not wish to be chief, but he knew there was no other choice, for Robbie had made Tayg promise to fulfill his unfinished duty to the clan.

Now the time had come to face destiny and he would do it as Robbie would have. He sat up straighter, arranged his cloak and settled his mouth into the serious expression Robbie always wore.

He nudged the pony forward.

It carried him along a snow-edged trail that led into the heart of the village. As he passed the outermost cottages with no notice from the inhabitants, he was unaccountably relieved to escape the usual clamor when someone returned after a long absence.

But 'twas not to be. A dog barked. A child ran round the corner of another cottage and slid to a stop.

"Robbie?" the lad said and Tayg looked behind him, half expecting to find his brother there. "Nay. Tayg! Da, 'tis Tayg!" he shouted running to the cottage door and flinging it open. "'Tis Tayg!" he yelled again.

Doors flew open and the lane was quickly flanked by Tayg's kin, old and young alike, lining the way and shouting his name as if he were a great war hero—as they would have greeted Robbie.

Tayg waited for the silence to descend, but it didn't. There were shouts and laughter and a lightness to the people's faces he had not seen when last he was here, nearly a year ago when he had brought Robbie's body home to be buried.

He stopped the pony in front of the largest structure in the village, the hallhouse. The three-storied stone building commanded the foot of the lane and was surrounded on three sides by a loop in the river, making it more defensible than any other place in the village. It served both as his parents' home and as the central storage and social building for the clan. His mother, Sorcha Munro, stood at the top of the long narrow stair rising to the only entrance. Her thin face looked older than he remembered, but her thick, braided hair was still a deep shade of sable, and there was a crackle in her eyes that told him she could still make sure her husband and her remaining son did as she wished them to.

Tayg offered her a smile and was pleased to see it returned. She had been overcome with grief when they had buried Robbie and he had not thought to see a smile on her face ever again. He turned his smile into the cocky grin that had melted her anger when he was a youngling and prone to trouble. Her smile broadened and she shook her head as she started down the stair.

His father, Angus Dubh, chief of Munro, stood at the bottom of the stair, his night-black hair beginning to show strands of silver at his temples and in his heavy beard, though the great bear of a man looked as strong and sturdy as ever he had.

Tayg dismounted and handed the reins to a young lad standing nearby with his mouth agape as if Tayg were a monster with horns instead of a warrior returned from war. Tayg winked at him and a blush rushed over the lad's cheeks. Tayg turned to his parents.

"Da. Mum." He didn't know what to do next but his mum, as always, did. She moved forward and enfolded him in a fierce embrace. His father joined them and Tayg felt much of the tension he had carried with him these many months drain away.

It was good to be home.

A *few hours later, after much conversation with his mother* over the well-being of his many cousins who also served with the Bruce and a good hot soak in a real tub, Tayg adjusted the pleats of a brand new plaid his mum had brought him. The weaver had experimented with new dyes and patterns and this was the best of what she had produced, saved for just this occasion.

Tayg admired the crimson crossed with the brightest green he had yet seen in a plaid and a watery blue with just the smallest line of brilliant yellow crossing through it all. 'Twas not a plaid he would wear when hunting, nor fighting, for 'twas bright of hue and would easily be seen but 'twas an excellent change from the browns and greys he had worn so much of late. The colors seemed to lift his spirits and he began to look forward to the evening spent amongst his friends and family.

Mum had said a bard was with them for the winter, a happy but unusual arrangement as bards tended to winter-over in the larger castles where there was more coin to be earned. This one was apparently wooing a lass in the village and had visited the clan often in recent months.

Tayg reached for his claymore, then remembered where he was. A sword would not be a necessary addition to his festive attire this evening. He did slide his dagger into its sheath and checked that his *sgian dhu* was in its place. Some things would not be left behind no matter where he was.

Satisfied that he was ready to face the clan, he left his chamber on the topmost floor of the hallhouse and descended the twisting narrow stair to the middle floor which was given over almost entirely to a hall. Tonight it was filled with trestle tables groaning with food and people enough to make the large chamber feel crowded but somehow cozy. A fire roared on the hearth at one side of the room and at the far end was a dais where a long table had been placed. Four chairs had been arranged near the center of the table facing those gathered in the hall.

Tayg could see his mother and father already seated there. Beside his mum was an empty chair and next to that sat Duncan MacCulloch, his cousin and best friend since they were wee lads. Duncan had left the fighting when he had been badly injured at Balnevie some seven months before. Tayg was glad to see that his friend appeared fully recovered and, from the way he was cutting into his food, there had been no lasting effect upon his sword arm. Relief poured through him though he had not been aware of holding more than a passing concern over Duncan. Duncan would be his champion when Tayg became chief and he was counting on his friend's level head to help him fill Robbie's considerable brogues.

He made his way quickly to the table on the dais, nodded at his father, kissed his mother on the cheek and took his place beside her. Duncan clapped him on the back and managed to grin while still chewing.

"You look well," Tayg said as he helped himself to a platter heaped with thick slices of roasted beef. "Where is Mairi?"

Duncan grinned. "She is not feeling well."

Tayg looked at his friend, puzzled by the grin.

"She is with child," his mother said, passing him a tureen of turnips and leeks.

Tayg looked back at Duncan and couldn't miss the pride in the other man's face. "Congratulations! So you're to be a da. How soon?"

"Another two months, though the midwife says it could be a bit more. Mairi is uncomfortable, but happy."

Duncan filled a tankard with the dark ale Tayg had missed so much in his travels and Tayg raised it.

"May you have a strong and healthy bairn," he said, then took a long slow draught.

For a time there was silence as they ate and Tayg mulled over the ramifications of Duncan's impending fatherhood. He had not worried much when Duncan had announced that he and Mairi would be wed. That event had changed Tayg's life little. Duncan had happily followed Tayg and Robbie off to war even though it meant leaving Mairi behind. But he had not rejoined them after his injury healed and now Tayg knew why. Duncan had responsibilities that now went far beyond a pretty wife.

It seemed he and Duncan both had responsibilities they had not held a year previous.

After Tayg had devoured a second helping of everything, he refilled his tankard and looked about the hall. The bard had left his dinner and sat before the fire, quietly playing on his harp, stroking the strings with his long-fingered hands as a man tenderly strokes a woman's cheek. 'Twas no wonder lasses tended to flock about

bards, giggling and vying for their attentions, when the
bards all but seduced them with their playing and singing.

He shook his head at the thought then turned his attention back to Duncan. For the next candlemark they traded
tales of all the men they'd fought beside, even planning a
foray to visit auld Gair who lived but a day's ride from
Culrain. As the conversation wound down, they sat com-
panionably drinking their ale, each lost in memories of
earlier days. Slowly Tayg realized that his name was
being sung. 'Twas a song he had never heard before, a
song that repeated his name again and again. He sat forward, concentrating on the lean bard and the words he
sang with such fervor.

> *Braw Tayg of Culrain slashed his way through the*
>   *line*
> *But two hundred* sassenach *more did he find.*
> *So he took Buchan's men with naught but his blade*
> *'Till none save he stood on that cold winter's day.*

"That is utter nonsense," Tayg said, looking to Duncan
for agreement. "'Twas nothing like that when we faced
Buchan at Balnevie."

"True," Duncan said, "but nevertheless 'tis a most popular song." He nodded in the direction of the bard. Tayg's
quick glance startled more than one lass out of making
moon eyes at him. The lads were less circumspect, openly
grinning at him. A granny even held his gaze for a moment, then nodded her head as if she had taken his measure and come to some conclusion.

There were groups of women, three here, five there,
who bent their heads together in hushed conversation,
then they would giggle and each of them steal a look at
him, then more giggling and more whispered talk.

"There will be trouble in this hall, mark my words,"
Duncan said.

"What kind of trouble?" Tayg asked.

"The kind only you can create, my braw lad," his mother replied from his other side. She had sat in silence, observing for a long time. "The lasses—and their mums—are plotting over you already."

Tayg laughed. "That has never caused trouble—well, never much trouble—in the past."

"Do not laugh, my darling boy. There is nary a lass within a day's ride of Culrain who has not swooned over the stories of 'brave Tayg' in battle, 'charming Tayg' in the hall. Your time in service to the king has honed you like a fine sword. You are more handsome than even your brother was, bless his soul. You are returned from war a valiant warrior of the king, and you shall be chief after your father. Nay, 'tis nary a lass within *two* days' ride of Culrain who has not dreamed that you would return and fall at her feet, begging her to wed you."

He listened absently to the bard, watching the lasses and wondering if one of them would someday make him wish to marry. They seemed so . . . alike. He hadn't been gone so long that he didn't know every one of them, had since they were all wee lasses. There were pretty ones and plain ones, some were thin and others more plump. Some had auburn hair and others blond, but none of them stood apart from the others. None of them were truly different from the other lasses. Most were pleasant, and in that regard would be fair as a wife, but none of them stirred him. Well, some of them stirred him, but only in a physical way. None of them captured his mind and heart the way Mairi had Duncan's or even the way his mother captured Da's. Still, perhaps one of the lasses listening raptly to the bard sing about . . .

Tayg listened more carefully. Surely it wasn't another song about him. He rested his head in his hand. This had to stop. The songs were absurd, elevating a simple warrior to the level of a hero.

The bard finished the song with a flourish on his harp and applause erupted from the crowd. Several of the lasses tittered, then cast him knowing glances over their shoulders. Lasses were always fluttering around him like beautiful moths drawn to a flickering flame.

"'Twould appear I am to enjoy myself," he said, more to himself than to his companions.

"That you must not do," Sorcha said, catching his full attention with her serious tone. "'Tis time we spoke of your future."

He had made peace with his future, yet a chill ran down his spine at her words. The grimace that passed over his father's face served to strengthen his unease.

He pushed his chair back and propped his feet upon the table, affecting an unconcerned pose. "Wish me well, Duncan. 'Tis my future we discuss."

Duncan smiled. "Perhaps you shall like your future. It seems to me that you are ready for it." He raised his cup to Tayg and drained the contents. "For me, I'm off to see to Mairi's comfort."

"Give her my greetings," Tayg said, then turned his full attention to his parents. He didn't see any sense in putting this off any longer than his year of fighting already had. "My future?"

Angus rose from his seat and paced the length of the dais. Sorcha watched him, but she would not meet Tayg's eyes. His parents' unusual behavior made the skin on his scalp prickle, not unlike the way it did just before the enemy surged into battle. He glanced from one parent to the other, waiting for one of them to speak.

At last Angus sighed and propped a hip on the table so that Tayg was trapped between his parents. A lively tune at odds with the serious looks on Angus and Sorcha's faces flowed from the bard.

"You ken you are to be chief, aye?"

"Aye."

"You have proved your mettle this year past. I believe you will serve the clan well."

Tayg forced himself to maintain his relaxed pose, watching and waiting as he had done so often in war. "I shall do my best. I promised Robbie 'twould be so."

Angus actually smiled. "I do not doubt it. Robbie would not allow his responsibilities to go unanswered. He was always very serious in that way."

"Aye, he was."

"As we would ask you to be," Sorcha said.

The prickling spread from his scalp down his back and he found himself braced for battle.

"Sorcha, I do not think 'tis the time now to speak of such things."

"Wheesht, Angus, 'tis past time for the lad to wed."

"Wed?" Tayg's feet thumped to the floor and he reached for his tankard. The growing gleam in his mother's blue eyes worried him and he realized 'twas too late to escape before she sprang whatever plan she had on him.

"If we are to avoid much turmoil within these walls we must see you wed immediately. 'Twill be a long and dismal winter if the lasses are at odds over you, especially with their mums pushing them all to it."

"I do not wish to wed."

"Few men do until confronted with it," Sorcha said. "There are plenty of willing lasses here in Culrain. You shall wed before the month is out and all will be well."

"Nay, 'twill not be well! Nay," he said again, stalling for time while his mind searched for just the right argument to stay his mother's plan. "I need a year at the very least, perhaps two."

Angus laughed quietly. "I would give you more than that lad, but I'm afraid your mother does have a point."

Tayg held out his tankard which Angus quickly refilled. He let his head drop back against the chair and he stared up at the smoke-darkened ceiling. He was only just home, only now coming to terms with his new role in the clan, yet already Mum was pushing him further.

He knew he would be judged by his reaction but he could not take this task upon himself. 'Twas enough to step into Robbie's shoes and lead the clan. 'Twas his duty and he would fulfill it. "I do not wish to marry . . . yet," he said, still staring at the ceiling where he would not have to see the stubborn gleam he knew to be in his mother's eyes.

"But—" Sorcha placed her hand upon his arm.

He held up a hand to stop her words.

"If I am to take Robbie's place," he said, finally facing her, "then you must trust me to do what I deem best. Marrying hastily will do naught but bring strife to these good folk, and to me. Tell everyone—especially that bard—that I will choose a wife when I am ready to. If there is trouble I will do my best to defuse it. And tell him to stop singing those damn songs."

"See Sorcha, did I not say so?" Angus said, grinning as if Tayg had felled the biggest stag in the wood.

"Aye, you did but 'twill not be enough."

"I will not be forced to wed one of these lasses. Were it not me, 'twould be someone else they bickered over. Besides," he said, looking over the young women enjoying the bard's entertainment, "I have known them all long enough to know there is none amongst them whom I wish to wed."

"Then we will arrange another—"

"Nay. I will find my own wife."

Sorcha looked at him, her gaze level and unwavering. "You are to be chief. It is your duty to do what is best for the clan. As long as you are here and not wed you will cause trouble amongst the women. 'Twill be good for no one."

Tayg sighed and prayed for strength against his

mother's strong will. "Then I shall leave. I shall return to the king's service—"

"Wait, lad," Angus said. "As it happens, I have a task needs doing that will serve to delay"—he looked pointedly at Sorcha—"what your mother fears will happen. 'Twill also give you the opportunity to meet other lasses who may . . . appeal to you." He motioned Tayg to follow him into his private chamber.

"Angus." Sorcha's voice was low and her displeasure with his interference was clear.

"The lad is right, my love. He should not be forced to wed so hastily. I did not like that it was necessary for Robbie to wed a lass he did not fancy. The lad here is wise enough to see the folly in such a plan. We will buy Tayg and you some time." He leaned over and kissed his wife on the cheek. "Go. Spread the word that Tayg is leaving immediately on the king's business. Make sure that bard understands that if he wants to continue to enjoy the company of the Munro lass he fancies he will cooperate—and he'll stop singing those songs."

"Or telling those tales," Tayg added.

Sorcha looked first at her husband and then at her son. She rose and hugged Tayg. "I do not want to see you unhappy. There is enough of that in this life, but we must consider the clan—"

"Go now, love," Angus said and Tayg was surprised to hear the softness in his father's voice.

The two men watched her walk to the bard and draw him away from the circle of listeners, then Angus wrapped an arm around Tayg's shoulder and led him into the chief's private chamber. Tayg had always thought of this chamber as the bear's den, a dark little space where Da and Robbie would seclude themselves for hours, shutting out all others while they discussed who knew what. The small chamber was almost too warm after the drafty hall so Tayg left the door open, allowing the heat to mingle with the cooler air as the room's somber mood mingled with the bard's lilting music.

His father stood at a battered wooden table that took up the center of the room. He tapped a parchment, pinned to the table with bricks of peat, with a thick finger.

"I received this just a day past. The Earl of Ross, that daft bastard, could have had the bard tell me what he wished instead of sending this drivel"—he banged the table with his fist—"but he does so love to show off his writing."

"You ken he has someone write it for him, do you not?" Tayg asked.

"Aye, but he never hesitates to boast of the fact that he sends his messages in a written hand. Some fool notion of making sure his words are not mangled by the messenger. Fah. As if a bard would mangle any words. 'Tis a daft idea. Writing only leaves the message where others may find it. If 'tis truly important, it should never be set to parchment!"

Tayg just nodded as he scanned the jagged writing. He could read, but it wasn't a skill he used often, and like any skill, it grew rusty with disuse. After a few moments, though, he had recovered the knack of it and began reading aloud:

"Angus Dubh of Munro, my greetings." He ran his finger along the parchment as he deciphered the rest of the words there:

> "*Be it known to you that Lord Robert, the illustrious king of Scotland, shall grace Dingwall Castle and its inhabitants with his most gracious presence on the third day before Hogmanay to witness the marriage of his sister, Lady Maude, to my son and heir, Hugh O'Beolan.*
>
> "*He commands each of his loyal chiefs to attend him there so that he may know them and receive*

their fealty. Our king is particularly anxious to re-
ceive such from the MacDonells of Dun Donell.
   "'Tis your duty to see this message delivered to
the MacDonell chief, and to each chief your servant
may find between Culrain and Dun Donell."

It was signed with the earl's mark and an ornate seal of
red wax with a sprig of juniper pressed into it.

Tayg considered what he'd read for a moment, scanning the words once more to get the sense of them. He
glanced up at his father, who wore a deep scowl.

"Why would he not send his own man to the Mac-
Donells?" Tayg asked.

"The better question is why did he bother to put such a
task to parchment?" his father said, pacing in a circle
about Tayg and the table.

"To make sure his words were not mistaken?"

"Nay, 'tis a simple message with little to complicate its
delivery. There is more here, but I do not see it yet."

"'Tis nothing more here, Da."

"Ah, lad, there is," he growled. "Just as a voice can
imply the true or false intent of the spoken word, so
parchment and quill can tell you more than is strictly written."

Tayg leaned against the table and waited for his father
to explain.

"You have been with the king. What do you know of
this?" Angus gestured at the missive.

Surprise coursed through Tayg. His father was asking
his opinion? Very well, a test. "'Tis an uneasy alliance,"
he began, "between the king and the Earl of Ross, despite
the impending marriage of the earl's son to the king's sister. 'Tis no secret there is little trust between Ross and the
king as of yet."

"Aye," his father said, stroking his black and silver
beard, "So Ross needs to offer proof to the king that he is

a loyal servant, and what better way than to have as many folk as possible attest to such after seeing or hearing of this document."

Tayg nodded and followed the line of reasoning. "He wants this conspicuous display taken to each chief, so that they too may attest to his loyalty when they greet the king at Dingwall."

Angus nodded and paced.

"But why have one of our kin carry it?" Tayg mused.

"Ah, 'tis simple, that one. The earl would not wish to send one of his own kinsmen into that stronghold. There is no love lost between the Earl of Ross and the Mac-Donells."

"So we, as loyal allies of the earl's, but who have no argument with the MacDonells, are selected to trek into the bens at the start of winter."

"You see?" Angus said, grinning as if Tayg had surprised him. "There was more to the missive than the words written upon the parchment. Perhaps your time with the king has honed your mind as well as your sword arm."

Tayg tried to ignore the reference to his previous lack of interest in the politics swirling around the clan. Serving in the king's cause for more than a year taught a man many things besides the art of battle.

"'Twill not be an easy journey," Tayg said. "And Hogmanay is less than a month away."

"Aye, 'twill likely take a fortnight or more to complete the task, and then only if the snows hold off." Angus pulled a rolled parchment from a shelf below the table, spread it over the missive and began studying what appeared to be a map.

Tayg considered the task. A fortnight journeying through the Highlands. Dun Donell would not be an easy trip even in high summer when the days were long and the weather gentle. This would be a fortnight, all told, in the cold, traveling from village to village, castle to castle all alone. A fortnight might give him the time he needed to figure out how to avoid his mother's solution to the problem with the lasses or, if he must wed, at least he would have this time to choose from other lasses he might meet along his journey. His father's plan became clear.

"So I shall take this missive to the MacDonells," he said, "thereby serving the king, the Earl of Ross and escaping the clutches of both Mum and the other scheming women." He tried to suppress the smile that fought to spread itself over his face. "And perhaps I shall find a lass I might wish to wed—one who is not enamored of the bard's version of Tayg of Culrain." He glanced at the map.

Perhaps 'twas better in more ways than these for him to leave the comforts of his home for a while longer. Perhaps this bard would be gone by the time Tayg returned from his travels or at least his songs would have ceased. Or he would have moved on to another village where he would tell the same stories and sing the same songs and spread this drivel even farther into the Highlands . . . if others had not done so already.

He was daft if he thought escaping Culrain would solve this problem. The bards had no doubt spread these songs and tales across the Highlands. Such things were meant to lift the spirits, and songs of bravery in war were always the first to spread. No wonder his mother claimed the lasses were scheming to marry him. With drivel like that to contemplate, the lasses would be lying in wait for him, especially if word got out that he was journeying into the bens. Ballocks! 'Twould be an escape from his mum's scheme but no reprieve from marriage-minded lasses.

Applause drifted through the door and he heard the bard's clear tenor voice beg the crowd's pardon while he took a wee break.

There was the life. A bard traveled freely, unencumbered by responsibilities. He had the attentions of the lasses but not the burden of their aspirations. He had all the good of life and very little of the bad. If only . . .

Of course! A simple bard could do what Tayg of Culrain could not. A bard could deliver the Earl of Ross's missive, make light with the lasses and enjoy the hospitality of anyone he encountered on his journey. The only responsibilities he would have would be to entertain his hosts with songs and stories and the latest gossip. True, Tayg didn't sing all that well, but he told stories as well as any trained *seanachaidh* and he used to play the frame drum a bit when he was a lad. He knew gossip aplenty from spending months in the king's army. How difficult could it be to pretend to be a bard—at least once he left the country where his face was known?

"I shall leave at first light." Tayg quickly rolled up the Earl of Ross's parchment.

Angus actually chuckled. "Wise lad. I'll do what I can to dissuade your mum from finding you a lass herself. In truth I think she sees trouble where it is not or perhaps she simply pines for your bairns. See that you do not return too soon or we may see you wed too quickly yet."

Tayg had packing to do, and a drum to find, for he would be quit of these walls before sunrise. He gave a nod to his father and left the bear's den, happy in his prospects, at least for the present.

chapter 2

"Leave my chamber now!" *Catriona MacLeod glared* at her eldest brother, Broc, and pointed a finger at the door.

He was aptly named, closely resembling the badger both in appearance and in temperament. Tall with a sharp face, midnight hair and small eyes, he was quick to pick a fight and ruthless in defending his right to order about his many younger siblings. Catriona, the youngest, knew well how to deal with his brand of arrogance.

He stepped toward her. "I am not finished instructing you in—"

"It seems to me that the last time you 'instructed' me your porridge was burned every morning for a month, your bed collapsed beneath you and—"

"Enough!" he bellowed. Catriona enjoyed the crimson cast to his skin.

"I am a woman grown and will run this castle as I see

fit. If you do not like it, leave. 'Twould improve the smell greatly."

He stepped closer until they were nearly nose to nose and she could see the hardness in his dark eyes.

"You will not run this castle with your demands and threats much longer, Triona," Broc said. "Soon I will become chief, then my wife will see to its running and finally I will have some peace, a decent meal and no more of your cutting tongue."

"Are you not forgetting something?" she said, moving away from him but not being so stupid as to take her eyes off him.

"I never forget—"

"You have no wife. Pity no one will marry a mighty lout like you."

"Unlike you, dear sister." He surged forward and grabbed her arm, squeezing hard. Silently she cursed herself for not evading his grasp, but she would not give him the satisfaction of knowing he hurt her. "You will be married sooner than you imagine."

Catriona's skin crawled at the quiet threat in his loathsome voice.

"What do you mean?" she asked, despising the glint that danced in his eyes as a genuine smile spread across his face.

Nothing good ever came of Broc's good humor.

"You will find out soon enough." He released her and turned to leave. Catriona heard him snicker. "You will get your due."

"Tell me what you know or I'll see that what remains of your precious hair falls out by month's end." Catriona knew each of her five brothers' weaknesses and Broc's was his hair. Long admired by the lasses for its glossy ebon waves, now, at only eight and twenty, it was thinning rapidly.

Broc grimaced but turned back to face her. "Your betrothed"—the smile on his face turned to a sneer—"is to arrive a sennight hence. Three days more and you shall be married. We shall be rid of you."

Stunned, Catriona stared at him. "Who?" She hated that the word came out in a whisper.

"'Tis a good question, that," Broc said. "There is only one clan in all the Highlands who is so desperate for an alliance as to accept Triona the Shrew as a bride."

"Who?" she asked once more, her voice firmer now as she glowered at Broc. He was dangerously close to smiling again. *"Who!"*

The smile crashed across his face and she wanted to smash a fist into it but she had never been successful against her brothers that way and she needed to know her destiny. With a huge effort she held her fists at her sides, digging her fingernails into her palms.

"Who am I to wed, Broc?" her voice dripped with the contempt she felt for this brother, but she knew he would not recognize it for what it was; he was too dense, too concerned with his torment of her to see it.

"Should be Da who tells you—"

"'Twould be a pity if you lost the rest of your hair. 'Tis the only thing the lasses like about you."

He blanched.

She cocked an eyebrow at him in perfect imitation of his favorite expression when he had her in a corner.

"Very well, I shall tell you," he growled, "but you will do naught to make my hair fall out."

Catriona nodded. She had had no hand in his loss so far so 'twas an easy promise to make.

"'Tis a MacDonell lad who has agreed to take you." His voice was nonchalant, as if he spoke of the weather, but the malice was back in his eyes.

Catriona felt the blood drain from her cheeks and she was suddenly cold to her bones. "Nay, 'tis not . . ."

At Broc's huge grin and quick nod her knees went

weak but she knew better than to allow him to see how
horribly his news struck her. She pushed past him, almost
daring him to grab her so she could react as she had as a
child, all fists and feet, flailing away at his tenderest spot.
But 'twas a long time since she could get away with such
behavior. Frustration shook her and she raced for her father's chamber as Broc chased her down the corridor.

"Father!" she yelled as she neared the chief's chambers.

Ignoring the closed door, she shoved it open and strode
straight for the slight, gray man sitting behind a table,
squinting at a parchment filled with tiny marks.

"Broc must cease baiting me or I will not be held responsible if he can no longer father an heir."

Without looking up Neill MacLeod answered her.
"Wheesht, Triona, I am figuring."

Catriona huffed, but stood her ground. 'Twas not unusual to be ignored by her father.

"Broc says I'm to be married off to that dog-faced son-
of-a-MacDonell."

Her father continued to ignore her as he silently
mouthed the numbers he was laboriously adding up.

"Father!"

Still he mouthed the numbers.

It was ever so with him, attending to the minutiae of in-
ventories, the petty squabbles of the clan. Never did he
give her the same level of attention. In desperation, she
picked up the ink well he was absently reaching toward
with his quill and held it out of his reach.

"Triona! Damn it girl! Now I've forgotten the number I
need to write down."

"Seven hundred thirty-one." She held the ink for him to
dip his quill into, then waited while he slowly wrote the
number. When he was done writing and before he could
start adding more numbers she said, "Broc says you will
marry me to Dogface MacDonell."

Broc chuckled behind her. "His name is Duff Mac-Donell, and he is their chief. 'Tis a good match for you, Triona."

She swung round to face him only to find three more brothers ranged behind him. Callum, Gowan and Jamie tended to travel in a pack. They were stair-stepped in height, hair ranging from a rusty brown to nearly as black as Broc's, and their expressions were always that of placid sheep, which was how Catriona tended to think of them. Now they were a step behind Broc, as usual. Only Ailig, the youngest son and her occasional ally against the others, was not present. This, too, was no surprise as his way of dealing with their eldest sibling was mostly to avoid him.

"I was not speaking to you," she said, glaring at Broc with contempt. She went around the table, the better able to command her father's attention.

"You ken I will not marry him. I'll not bend to the likes of Dogface MacDonell!"

"Nor anyone, it would seem, daughter."

"Bending serves no purpose. You bend to no one. My brothers do not. Why should I?"

"There is bending and there is choosing. You have done neither. You do not bend to my will, yet neither do you choose a husband. What am I to do with such a willful child?"

"I am not willful." She chose to ignore the raised eyebrows of every man in the room. "I simply will not be sacrificed."

"We are not sacrificing you."

"Nay," Broc said under his breath, but still loud enough for her to hear, "we are gladly giving you away." One of the sheep snorted.

Triona gripped the inkwell tightly, fighting the urge to hurl it at Broc's smug face. Instead she slammed it down on the table, then belatedly remembered the stopper wasn't in it. Ink fountained up and she reached out and caught most of it in her cupped hands before it could do more than splatter the parchment full of numbers.

"Triona!" Her father whisked the parchment out of danger. Her brothers chuckled. She glared at them as ink dripped from between her clenched fingers, splattering on the now empty table top.

"What's so funny?" Her brother Ailig, youngest but for her, entered the chamber, pushing past the sheep. He took one step into the room and seemed to immediately grasp what had happened. He grabbed a rag from a table near the door and set it where Catriona could let the rest of the ink run into it.

"Nice catch." He smiled at her but the smile stopped short of his eyes and his voice sounded weary.

This was her favorite brother, indeed the only one she liked, fair-haired and unlike the others as much in manner as in appearance.

"Who's done what to whom this time?" Ailig looked first at Catriona, then at Broc and the other brothers still ranged behind him.

"You have not told Ailig?" She directed this to her father. "Were you afraid he would tell me?"

"Nay. Broc has spoken out of turn," Neill said, sending a stern look at his eldest. "We were to announce the betrothal at the evening meal."

Shock coursed through her for the second time this morning.

"You were not going to tell me until you announced this before the entire clan?" She wiped her hands on her gown leaving long black streaks of ink on the amber fabric. Neill studied the parchment he held safely in his hands.

"I will not marry him," she said as much to herself as to anyone else in the chamber. She turned to her father, her gown gripped in her ink-stained fists. "If you make me,

I'll . . . I'll . . . I'll stab him in his sleep. Then you'll have trouble on your hands!"

"Triona—" her father reached out but she evaded him and fled the room. Broc's self-satisfied chuckle followed her down the empty corridor.

.

C atriona *stormed through the bailey to the main gate,* scattering children and chickens ahead of her. As she left the castle's confines, the magnificent vista of Loch Assynt opened up before her in all its early winter glory. The snow-clad peaks of Quinag rising on the opposite shore were reflected in the loch's mirrored surface. As she neared the rocky beach, she slowed her steps. Ice clung to the verge and spread thickly upon those rocks that poked up from the dark watery depths.

A breeze, gentle for December but still cold, tugged at her ruined gown. She wrapped her arms around herself, wishing she had stopped long enough to retrieve her cloak before venturing outside. Winter was upon them and she realized the timing of this ill-fated attempt to marry her off could not have been better planned. Soon the snows would reach down the slopes of the bens and into the glens. Everyone in the Highlands would hunker down for the winter. They would wait out the long dark months until the coming of gentler weather when the thaw would begin. Only then would anyone venture far from their own safe homes.

She gazed up at Quinag. The crystal blue sky set against the white peak created a stark, glittering contrast. She loved this view, this peaceful spot, where she need not be on her guard against her brothers' constant enmity.

Surely this marriage was Broc's plan. He was the one who most wished to rid himself of her and what better way to accomplish that than to marry her off just as winter was about to cut them off from the wider world? She'd have no hope of returning home for months. Not that she would have any reason to return, other than to make Broc's life a living hell. 'Twas not a bad idea, that, except clearly she was not wanted here by anyone. Anger warred with hurt and a painful sense that she'd been abandoned amidst this horde of men. Not for the first time she wished she had a sister, a mother, even an aunt nearby. She needed an ally.

She picked up a round, white-flecked rock and let the frost on it melt against her anger-heated skin. Damn them all, brothers, father, everyone, she thought as she aimed at one of the icy rocks far out in the loch. She let her stone fly, hitting her target hard enough to shatter the ice covering.

"Is it safe to join you or are you likely to pelt me next?"

She turned and glared at Ailig. His sandy hair fell in scraggly waves about his serious face and his eyes were such a pale shade of blue they sometimes looked silver, as they did now. He wore a faded blue plaid over bare legs, though he had donned his low leather boots in deference to the cold.

This youngest brother, just two years older than her own nineteen years, was the bravest of them all. Though Broc delighted in causing her anger, Ailig was the only one who ever dared approach her when she was already angry.

"Are you?" he asked.

"What? Oh, going to pelt you?" She shook her head and turned back to the loch. "You are safe enough, though there are plenty of rocks to hand should I have need."

"Warning taken. I thought you might need this." He draped a cloak over her shoulders.

Ailig's calm voice contrasted with Broc's condescending tone as sharply as the sky contrasted with the mountain peak. She wanted to throw herself into his arms and let him comfort her as he used to do when they were children, telling her stories of his stays in Edinburgh to take her mind from the badgering of her elder brothers. But she had long ago sworn not to show her weakness to any of them again, not even to Ailig. She pulled her cloak tightly about her and turned her attention back to the loch.

"The snow is farther down the mountain this morning," he said. " 'Twon't be long before it fills the glen."

" 'Tis why this is happening now, is it not? Winter is upon us, but not quite?"

Ailig nodded. "No doubt." He rested his arm across her shoulders and pulled her close. "I would not have kept such news from you had I known."

Catriona shrugged, unable to speak lest she give in to that softness she kept buried deep inside her, safe from hurt. Broc's blusterings and taunts never threatened her control like this brother's gentle caring did. She had not cried since her twelfth summer yet Ailig's simple gesture brought tears that clogged her throat. But she would not allow them to fall. She leaned her head on his shoulder, accepting the comfort she would not ask for.

"What will you do?" he asked after a moment.

Anger swamped her again. Catriona took a deep breath and stepped out of Ailig's embrace. She drew the cold air into her lungs and wrapped her anger back around her like a heavy cloak.

"I will not marry Dogface MacDonell. There is no advantage there for me, nor for the clan. Indeed, the only advantage is to Broc, who will rid himself of the thistle in his shoe, and to the MacDonells who will gain the advantage of our strength and reputation."

"Aye, I see it the same."

"Then why is Father allowing this?"

Ailig shrugged, then tossed a few stones into the water. After a moment he turned to her. "I think Father tires of Broc's complaints and the constant rows between you. You refused to choose a husband for yourself—"

"None were—"

"I know, but you have given him little choice. He must marry you to anyone he can convince to take you before it becomes Broc's responsibility at midsummer."

Catriona winced. "So I am to be punished for speaking my mind. Do you truly believe this should be my fate?"

"Nay, I do not. I have spoken with Father and the rest of them time and again, but you know they do not listen to me any more than they listen to you."

She turned her back to him, unwilling to let him see how the truth of his words hurt her. Truly they were both invisible as far as Father and the other brothers were concerned. Well, *she* wasn't completely invisible, but only because she poked and prodded everyone by speaking the truths no one wanted to hear. Ailig *was* invisible, though. He was quiet and thoughtful and disinclined to brawl with the other four. 'Twas an unfortunate thing neither being seen nor acknowledged, making one bitter and angry, though Ailig seemed to tolerate it better than she.

When she had control of her voice again she faced him once more. "What was your counsel that they did not heed?"

She could tell he was considering his words carefully, probably seeking the kindest way to say something he knew would anger her, for even Ailig was not immune from the slice of her tongue now and again.

"Speak, brother."

"Very well. I suggested they seek an abbey that would take you, else find you a husband from a far distant clan who would not know of your . . . reputation."

"So you would hie me off to strangers, too."

"Aye, but for your *own* good, not Broc's. You might be happy in a place where you could start anew, a place where they might come to value you beyond your connections to this clan. A place where you could begin fresh."

"I do not need to begin fresh. This is my home and I'll not forsake it for Broc's pleasure."

Ailig shook his head. "Nay, but you will forsake it for your own pride."

"Nay!"

"Aye, lass. You fight so hard against Broc you see naught but that which causes him the most grief. For once think what may be best for you. Is it staying here and being forced to marry Dogface? If you refuse to change your path, you will marry him and neither you nor the clan will benefit. If you choose for yourself what you will do, then what does it matter if it suits Broc's plan as well?"

"Whatever are you blethering about?"

"I am simply asking you to look beyond baiting our brother and think. How can you turn this to your advantage? If you cannot, then you will be wed to Dogface. The banns will be called a week hence and three days after Broc will have won—and you will have lost all that you might have wished for in this life."

Ailig moved closer again, taking her shoulders in his hands, forcing her to look at him. "My sister, your sharp tongue is like spark to tinder for most who know you. Do not underestimate Duff MacDonell. He's not one to take a tongue lashing from anyone and he will not bother with the petty tricks of brothers. I fear for more than your happiness with that one."

"Do not worry. I'll not marry him—nor any Mac-Donell. Ailig, you remember . . ."

"Aye, but Triona, you've brought this upon yourself, refusing those few lads who dared ask for your hand in marriage. Da is desperate, and Broc pushes him to remove you from Assynt."

"But there are others I could wed. We have allies who have sons. One of them will surely—"

"Do you really think Da would risk an alliance by sending you into a friendly clan's midst?" He shook her, then released her shoulders and paced away from her. "Even you do not know what you will say next. If you would only stop and think before you speak, then there might be a chance for you to be happy."

"I do think."

"Aye, but not until after the trouble is done and there is naught to do to fix it. Your heart is good, Triona. But your heart is not strong enough to overcome your mouth. Nay, Da cannot chance that mouth on a friend."

Catriona found herself speechless. Ailig spoke the truth about many things. Why should she think he spoke less than the truth about her?

He stepped forward, embraced her, then placed a gentle kiss upon her forehead. "Think, Catriona. Think. The MacDonells will be upon us in a sennight and you must decide what you will do before then. Your future depends upon it and you do not have much time."

"Broc has seen well to that." She looked up into her brother's pale blue eyes. "'Twould be better for everyone were you the eldest brother."

Ailig gave her a sad smile. "But I am not. 'Twould take nothing less than a king's command to see me leading this or any other clan."

Catriona's heart lurched. Of course. "Then get one."

"What?"

"Get the king's command. You are well known to the Bruce's brothers, are you not? You told me yourself how you spent time in their company in Edinburgh."

"Those were but tales. I spent time in the places—"

"If you were to go to King Robert and explain that you are the only brother fit to lead—"

"I will not." The hard edge to his voice, so unfamiliar, stopped her, forced her to really look at him. "I will not go to the king with such talk. My duty is to the MacLeods, to

Assynt. Where is your duty, Catriona? What is best for the clan in this?"

Startled by the coldness in his voice, the sharp glitter in his eyes, she could only stare as he turned and strode back to the castle.

C atriona stood by the loch for a long time after Ailig left, trying to think, trying not to panic, trying to understand what her brother had counseled her to do, and why he refused the obvious solution to both their problems. Ailig was forever saying that which you expected, but also saying that which didn't reveal itself until later. Where she met the challenge of her other brothers and her indifferent sire head-on with temper and verbal barbs, Ailig kept himself apart from the fray, nudging them all in the direction he deemed best with a word here, a subtle expression there, and sometimes by his silence. But he was not silent this time. Nor was he subtle.

Her life was over and the clan would surely come to harm if she did not find some way to change her father's mind. She wished for neither and she had precious little time to avert disaster. She'd not see the MacDonells drag the MacLeods into the muck that was Clan Donells' lot in life. 'Twas surely a misplaced loyalty on her part but she could not do less than what was best for her clan. She was daughter to the chief and despite her trials with her brothers she had a duty—it had ever been her duty—to safeguard the clansfolk, even, as was the usual case, when it meant protecting them from Broc, their future chief.

Daft idiots.

But what was she to do? She needed a plan.

She could find another husband and have the banns read before Dogface's arrival. She shook her head. Even if there was a man she could imagine being married to, none of the lads she knew would have anything to do with her. There were no lads within a day's ride of Assynt who would ever consider marrying her.

And none she could stomach being married to, even for the good of the clan.

An abbey then, and the religious life. Poverty, chastity and obedience. She shuddered. She was not suited to such an existence and well she knew it. Poverty she could survive, but she wished for children of her own someday—a little one who would love her for herself alone—and obedience? 'Twas not one of her strengths. And if she could not obey? At least with Broc she knew what to expect for retribution and had her own successful ways of dealing with it. Retribution in God's house would be another thing altogether and she had no wish to test it. No, the restricted life of a nun would not suit her at all, never mind that 'twould leave Broc with no one to check his lunacy. Nay, she was needed here as long as Broc or the sheep were in charge.

Then what? Marriage or the abbey were a woman's only choices unless you were that rare herb-witch who lived alone in the deep wood. She turned and faced the gray hulk of Castle Assynt. For all the annoyances of her family the thought of living forever alone, truly alone, not just lonely, made her quake. She did not wish to live without the company of people—even the MacDonells would be better than that . . . perhaps. But the clan . . .

Catriona could not move as her thoughts twisted round and round on themselves, writhing and tangling like a basket full of snakes—and just as vile.

There was no escape. She could see no way out that was not horrid to consider. Marriage to Dogface or life in the abbey. She had no one to turn to for help, no one to even give her a moment's pity. The only thing that she could do was to be so awful, so horrible, so completely unwilling as to make Dogface change his mind about marrying her. But the thought of facing him made her tremble, and that weakness made her furious. She clasped her hands to still them. Nay, she would not face him.

Anger boiled through her veins, heating her until she was pacing the shore in long fast strides, searching for something to throw, something she could hurt the rest of them with as much as thrusting her into Dogface Mac-Donell's arms would hurt her. She could not give herself to him. She would not.

She would die before she would leave Assynt with Dogface—or he would. There must be some way . . .

Sudden realization filled her with hope and dread. She had no choices left. She must not be in Assynt when Dogface arrived. She couldn't be. If she removed herself, temporarily, from her home she could thwart Broc and Dogface. A memory shimmered in her mind from a time long past. She had wished for a sister or a mother, but she had none of these. She did however have one aunt, her mother's sister who lived in a village near the sea. She had traveled there once when she was little, before her mother died. 'Twas not far to the sea and they were kin. If Catriona asked for her aunt's hospitality, she could not refuse. She'd leave in the morn and would arrive before nightfall. No one would think that she would go there.

Satisfied that she had found at least a temporary solution, she drank in the view once more. She would leave, for her own purposes, as Ailig had counseled, and all would be well.

After all, if she stayed she would have no choice but to stab Dogface in his sleep.

Tayg Munro sat on a wobbly three-legged stool in the Great Hall of Dun Donell Castle, his back comfortably near the fire, his shallow drum resting on his thigh. He smiled at the small crowd gathering about him.

It had taken him three hard days to get to Dun Donell.

The weather had remained clear, though cold, else it
would have taken him days longer. He'd stayed in a village of MacKensies the first night. It had been uncomfortable since he was well-known there and was greeted as a
hero. He had behaved as Robbie would have. Indeed he'd
been grateful for the necessity as many lasses, some too
young even to wed, had plied him with drink and a few
had offered more than wine or ale. None of these lasses
knew aught but that he was the Tayg of the songs and
tales the bards and *seanachean* were spreading about; that
he was to be chief of Munro, and he had a bonny face.
'Twas *nothing* they knew of him.

He had taken his leave gratefully and traveled hard
until he came upon another village where he had passed
yet another uncomfortable night, though for different reasons. He had enjoyed his newfound anonymity, though his
first foray as a bard had not gone well. He had taken his
leave before sunup. From there he had traveled hard directly to Dun Donell, wishing to get this task done so he
could get on with enjoying a more leisurely trek through
the Highlands. He had arrived well past the early setting
of the sun and he planned to stay but one night as well,
not wishing to chance discovery of his true identity.

But for now he must make a better show of being a
bard. It wasn't as easy to impersonate one as he had
thought 'twould be. People had expectations and he certainly hadn't lived up to them at the last village. Thank
goodness his natural charm had enabled him to bluff his
way through the evening. This time he had a better idea of
what needed doing.

First he would sing an old ballad, something melancholy and familiar to those gathering about him. Then
he'd tell a story or two. He could tell stories all night
long. 'Twas the singing and the playing that vexed him.
After the stories, he'd sing another, slightly livelier, tune
then move into the news and gossip. If he gauged it right,

a few songs would be all he needed to get him through the evening—and none of them would be about Tayg of Culrain.

Well then, to begin. He took a long swig of ale to bolster his courage and began the rhythmic beating of the drum. When he thought he'd got the beat going well enough to add the complication of a tune he began to hum the melody. Perhaps he could get the growing crowd to sing with him so his voice would not have to carry all on its own. He hummed a bit louder, but no one joined in.

When he decided there was no putting it off any longer, he launched into the sad song, only to realize he was beating the drum too quickly. Stumbling over the words as he adjusted the tempo, he noticed a few surprised looks on the faces around him. A child giggled, and he felt his cheeks heat. What had he been thinking when he decided to do this?

He stumbled over the words again and lost the beat. Pulling his thoughts back to the song, he drew it to an early close, took another long pull of the ale and went with his strength.

"As you can see, I'm not much of a singer." Scattered laughter met him and he tried not to mind. "But I am an excellent storyteller, one to rival the king's own." He flashed his smile at a lass sitting close and was rewarded with a dimpled grin.

"What story will you tell?" she asked.

"Ah, what sort of story would you like?" he asked the crowd, searching the faces there for any possibilities.

"One with monsters and gore!" yelled a lad with a dirty face and a tangled mop of blond hair.

"Ah, you wish to hear of the English then, and Longshanks, their dearly departed king?"

A loud chorus of boos and hisses had him grinning.

"A story of war and victory!" someone yelled.

"A love story!" yelled a lass from the other side of the circle.

"Ah, I have just the thing," Tayg said, anxious to avoid any songs that might refer to him. "And 'tis true, too. Have you heard the tale of the mad chief and the fair healer? Nay? Well then, gather round, and I'll tell you about the evil doings way down to Kilmartin."

Tayg launched into a story he had heard shortly after the miraculous recovery of King Robert last winter, though he did his best to embellish the love story with as much intrigue and horror as he could. When he ended, the crowd applauded and begged for more, so he told a story of a man who had come from the mists of time to claim his own true love. This tale was full of sword fights and miracles, and he had the crowd firmly under his spell right up to the very end when the villain was sent off into a blast of fire. This time the crowd erupted into cheers and Tayg felt very pleased with himself. Maybe this wasn't so hard after all.

"Tell us another, bard."

"Aye, soon. For now though, I am hungry and the smell coming from those platters is most appealing!"

The crowd looked around, apparently surprised to find the food had been brought into the hall without them noticing. Everyone agreed with him and scrambled to their seats. Tayg placed the drum carefully on the floor next to his stool, then sauntered over to a table, finding a place where he could view the entire hall while he ate.

He settled himself in between two pretty lasses, one blond, one auburn-haired. Both giggled when he grinned at them. As he reached for a platter of small pies a hush fell over the crowded hall.

Tayg looked up in time to see the chief settle himself at the head table at the far end of the hall. Duff MacDonell was a large, ugly man. His skin was pocked and his lank, brown hair hung in his nearly colorless eyes. His nose was so long it seemed to push his mouth down his jutting chin.

His personality matched his looks.

Tayg had delivered the earl's message to the chief as soon as he had arrived. Duff had seemed oddly glad to receive the summons to greet the king, not at all the reaction Tayg had expected.

Duff MacDonell was a well-known firebrand with delusions of greatness. He was a bully and his clan was ill-liked because of it. Something was not right here. Maybe 'twas the odd gleam in his eye as Tayg had recited the message to him. Maybe 'twas the way the young chief had commanded him to wait for a message to deliver to Assynt without asking even if he was bound there.

Maybe he just did not like the man.

Tayg shook off the odd feeling and turned his attention back to the food in front of him. After a minute, the hum of quiet conversation once more filled the space.

"You know he's going to bring that shrew here to live amongst us, do you not?" his dinner companion on his right said.

"A shrew?" Tayg admired the blond lass and considered his chances for a tumble with her later.

"Aye, he's to marry the Shrew of Assynt, then he'll bring her here to Dun Donell. She is said to be as ugly as Duff and twice as mean."

"Why would he wed such a lass? 'Tis not for love, is it?"

"Oh, nay," said the auburn-haired lass on his left. "Our Duff has a plan. The shrew has five braw brothers and her father is kin to the MacLeods of Lewes, who control much of the islands and the coast. Duff seeks to ally us with them."

Tayg chewed a tender chunk of venison for a moment before he realized exactly what the implication of the alliance meant.

"So your chief, he has no hope for King Robert's cause?" Perhaps the king was more right than he knew to command the MacDonell to appear in Dingwall and swear fealty to the crown. Or was it already too late?

The auburn lass shrugged. "I know not and I care not what alliances come of the wedding. 'Tis the women of the clan who will have to live most with the shrew. 'Tis the women of the clan who will have to teach her to mind her manners if she wishes not to be taken to the sea and left on a rock to drown."

Tayg chuckled. "I do not envy the woman her time here."

"I do not envy her wedding Duff, either," she said. "Netta there," she nodded at his blond dinner companion, "hoped to wed him, but as for me"—she looped her arm around Tayg's and leaned close enough so he could feel her soft breast pressed against him—"I prefer a more bonny countenance upon a man." She smiled broadly at him and batted her eyelashes.

Tayg grinned at her, then glanced at blond Netta. A well developed tear spilled off her lashes and trailed prettily down her cheek. He'd long ago learned that many lasses could cry when they thought 'twould benefit them. He was wise to her game but would play along. Perhaps he could learn more about his host, whom the king clearly had reason to distrust. He wiped away that tear then leaned close.

Nuzzling her ear, he murmured, "'Tis clear the lout does not deserve you."

Her eyes widened and the smile was back. He grinned at her and waggled his eyebrows, drawing a soft laugh from her.

"Will you tell us another story?" the other lass asked, drawing his attention back to her.

"I will, just as soon as I finish this delicious venison pie." He signaled for his ale mug to be refilled, then quickly ate his meal. He might not wish to wed, but he could hope to have his bed warmed by one of these fair lasses this night, and if he learned aught of use to the king from her, then 'twould be doubly worth his time. Perhaps his trip to Dun Donell might not need to be so hastily concluded after all.

When Tayg was done eating, he returned to his stool by the fire. His dinner companions followed quickly behind him, claiming seats where no one would obstruct his view of their charms. He warmed his hands, smiled at the two lasses, then took up his drum again. Quietly he played and sang a few easy songs he had known since he was a wee lad. The noise of the people still eating covered up his mistakes, and lent him a feeling of fading into the background that made him relax a bit.

Slowly, more people filtered back to sit about him, listening while they talked quietly with their neighbors. He winked at Netta and the other lass, then glanced about the circle at the other friendly faces there. As he relaxed more, he found it easier to weave the melody through the beat of the drum without tripping one over the other. As he ended the song, he reached for his mug. He took a long drink, watching over the rim as his host moved through the crowd toward him.

He did not wish to speak with the man again, though 'twas impossible to avoid, he supposed.

Tayg lowered his mug, resettled his drum on his thigh and prepared to start another song. But he did not get the chance.

"Come with me," Duff said, grabbing his elbow and nearly tumbling the drum to the floor.

Tayg shook off the man's grip and slowly leaned the instrument against the stool once more. He turned to his audience and bowed low as he had seen many a bard do. "I shall return to amuse you shortly," he said with a pointed look at the chief.

The man snorted and led the way out of the crowd to a deserted table in a darkened corner of the hall.

"Take this to Assynt," he said, shoving a folded piece of parchment at him.

Tayg took it, turning it over to peer at the other side but there was no seal to indicate the author of the document, only a thick unmarked blob of grey wax.

"Do you wish to tell me what it says so that I may repeat it at Assynt?"

"Nay. 'Tis . . . private; a note to my betrothed. See that her brother, Broc, receives it. He will see 'tis read to her."

Tayg raised an eyebrow.

"See it done," Duff said. "If you leave here by first light and ride hard, you can reach Assynt by sundown."

"I thought I might bide here a day or two." He watched the chief's face and realized this was a man who brooked no argument from anyone. You did what he demanded or you paid the consequences. He had served with men like this and had little use for his type.

"You leave in the morn."

"But I have discovered . . . reasons . . . to stay longer," Tayg said, adding a cocky grin. Truly were it not for his bonny dinner partners, he would not care to stay beyond a single night but he could not keep from goading Duff. He did not care to be ordered about by this man.

"You will leave in the morn. You will not be welcome here beyond the morning meal."

Tayg looked again at the parchment in his hand. From what the lasses had said, he did not think this was a love note. His mind worked quickly. This man did not know he could read. He was trusting a missive to him to deliver to the brother of his intended. If Tayg found the wax seal loosened and just happened to read the contents . . .

"As you will," he said, tucking the note in the small leather sack hanging from his belt. He walked away quickly, not wishing to give the MacDonell time to dismiss him.

What was so important about this other clan and their shrew? Were they all gathering against King Robert? As soon as he was clear of this wretched clan's lands he would read the note and then he just might have to deliver it. After all, what better way to find out what the two clans were up to, and if they threatened the king and Scotland, than for a bard to sit amongst the folk and trade a tale or two?

chapter 3

Catriona led the blue-black horse that belonged to her middle brother, Gowan, through the bailey. She would have taken her mare, but the horse was pregnant and could not travel as far nor as fast as Catriona needed to this day. She had brought little with her, a change of clothes and enough food for a single day. More would have raised suspicions and that she could not do.

Her plan depended on her behaving in a routine way, so she had broken her fast and tended to her daily duties. Broc had, as usual, sought her out to make her miserable, taunting her with her impending doom which had resulted, in part because it suited her purposes, in one of their usual rows. Now she was leaving to ride off her temper, or so everyone would assume. She had borrowed Gowan's horse for three days now, riding out for several hours after seeing to the business of the castle, returning a bit later each day. No one would expect her today until well after the midday meal. By then she would be nearly to her aunt's village by the sea. Once there Catriona would secure her help in hiding her until the hated Dog-face MacDonell gave up and returned to his home. That would give her the winter to convince her father that marrying her to the vile man would accomplish nothing good.

Outside the gate she mounted the horse and headed toward the loch. There she would turn away from her destination. As soon as she was out of sight of the castle, she would circle back and take the correct trail. She hoped her deception would throw off anyone who came searching for her.

The loch stretched before her and Quinag rose on the far side, but today the sky was steel grey, and the mountain's peak lay hidden in a heavy mantle of clouds. She stopped for a moment, as she always did, and admired this peaceful spot, but she could not tarry long. She would return to her home soon. For now though, she must continue as if 'twas any other day. She turned the horse and rode quickly away from Assynt.

When she rounded an outcropping that hid the castle from view, she kicked the horse into a gallop and raced down the trail, away from her home, away from her family that made her miserable and away from a marriage she refused to even consider. She leaned low over the powerful horse's neck and let him fly. The cold wind pulled at her cloak but the exhilaration of being free overrode any discomfort. When they came to the deer trail she had found yesterday, she guided the horse to it and circled quickly behind the castle and back to the trail that this time would lead to her destination. In no time, she would smell the salt-tang of the sea air. Soon she would be at her aunt's. Her father, Broc and the sheep would not know where she had gone. They would be left to explain to Dogface why he had traveled all this way when there would never be a bride for him at Assynt.

Catriona took satisfaction from the difficult position she had left her family in. She urged the horse faster, twining her hands in his mane, letting the wind pull her hair from its braid, enjoying the cold bite of the rushing air on her cheeks for a long time until at last the horse began to slow of his own accord. Only when he came to a stop did she realize her stomach was grumbling with hunger. She looked up, trying to determine the hour, but the grey sky had lowered until it appeared to hang just above her head, blotting out the sun. The bens were swathed in dusky light, only their rocky feet visible beneath the clouds. The wind, which she had thought was due to the horse's swift pace, pulled at her cloak, swirling it about her as if trying to wrench it away.

How far had she ridden? She could see nothing familiar and snow was beginning to swirl on the wind. Surely she should have reached the sea by now. She looked about, certain that the crash of waves upon the rocky shore was near. Perhaps the clouds dampened the sound? But the smell . . . she sniffed. She remembered the smell of the sea from her single visit to her mother's people, but the sharp clear scent of salt and spray wasn't on the wind. Snow was.

Panic gripped her for a moment until she forced herself to breathe deeply and think clearly. Had she gone the wrong way? She had a terrible sense of direction, 'twas true, but she had planned everything. If she had not let herself revel in her escape she might have watched more carefully. Perhaps she had simply made a wrong turning . . . but no, the loch was still beside her so that was impossible. She had only to travel to the end of the loch, then continue on the same well-worn trail to the sea.

The horse cropped at the sparse mosses that grew along the trail. She pulled at the reins, trying to yank his head away from the browse. He shook her off and continued eating. She dared not get caught out in a snowstorm. She must find shelter, soon. Winter was upon her. She took another deep breath and tried to stay calm, never her strongest skill.

She could turn back the way she had come, return to Assynt, but she would not. She would have to continue on, find shelter and quickly. Once she was safely out of the oncoming storm she would figure out where she had erred and find her way to the sea. But that would come later. For now, she needed shelter, and from the looks of the rapidly lowering sky she had better find it soon.

She pulled on the horse's reins again, and once more he snorted and tossed his head. She prodded him with her heels. Still he did not budge.

Snow stung her face and her temper snapped. "You addlepated horse!" She kicked him hard, pulling on the reins at the same time. The horse reacted, but not as she wished.

Catriona flew through the frigid air and landed hard on her back, knocking the breath from her and momentarily causing the world to darken. When she could breathe, she gingerly got to her feet, thankful the wretched horse had thrown her into the hillocks of moss and dead heather instead of onto the rocky section of the trail they had just passed through.

She glared up at the recalcitrant animal and grabbed for the trailing reins. The horse danced backwards, just out of reach. She stepped forward. He sidled to the left. She lunged. He pivoted and raced away, quickly disappearing over a rise.

Catriona stood there, in the middle of the trail, gaping at the empty landscape. The horse had abandoned her.

"Aaaahg!" She allowed all of her frustration and anger loose in that one screech, then proceeded to call the horse every name she had ever heard her brothers use, plus a few they had not the wit to think of.

" 'Tis quite the genteel language you speak."

Catriona screamed and whirled, finding herself face-to-face with yet another horse.

"How dare you sneak up on me like that!" she said, stepping back to look up at the rider.

The smirk that curved the man's full lips and sparkled in his eyes was quickly replaced by a look of amused appreciation that Catriona had never seen in a man's eyes before.

"Are you in need of help?" he asked, raising his eyebrows and smiling.

The man was beautiful. He sat at perfect ease in the saddle. His shoulders were broad, his hair a rich brown and his mouth . . . something about his mouth made her breath hitch and her mind fill with fluff. She tried to speak but couldn't seem to find any words.

"Are you hurt, lass?" Concern replaced the smile on his face.

Catriona looked away, trying to order her muddled thoughts sufficiently to reply with something other than an inarticulate gurgle.

"I'll not harm you," he said.

She looked back in his direction but chose to focus on the horse's ears instead of the man's intriguing face. "My horse has run off." She was surprised at the breathless sound to her voice, which served to fluster her further.

The appreciation slipped from his face to be replaced with a concern. "Are you harmed? May I see you home, then? If you are alone it cannot be far."

"Nay, I . . ." What to say? She would not return home, for that would be humiliating and her fate would be sealed. And she knew Broc would never give her a second chance to escape.

"We must reach shelter. I am bound for Assynt Castle."

Catriona shook her head, her mind racing. He was going to Assynt! She could not go there, yet she had no horse, no shelter nor food, nor even a plaid to wrap herself in against the cold. She had little hope of surviving the oncoming night without this man's help.

He reached down, extending his square hand. "Step up on that rock and grab hold. I'll swing you up. Let's get you to Assynt and in return for my good deed, you can see that they provide me with a warm meal and a place by the fire for the night."

She clasped his hand, momentarily distracted by his sure voice and the way his callused skin felt against hers, warm and rough and strong. Slowly, as he waited for her to climb up behind him his words sank in.

"I will not go home," she said. She forced herself to look up into surprised eyes that matched the color of his hair.

"There's a storm breaking over our heads and you would not take shelter?"

"Nay." She worried her bottom lip with her teeth. "I will not go to Assynt."

"The storm is upon us and I fear we have but little choice."

She tried to free her hand from his warm grasp but he held it tightly. "I said I'll not go to Assynt."

"You must. There is nowhere else close enough. Dun Donell is a hard day's ride from here."

"I'll not go there, either. I am bound for the sea and my aunt's village."

"The sea? The sea is behind you, lass."

"Nay, 'tis just beyond the loch," she said but her voice wasn't as strong as she wished, for snow was catching in his eyebrows and on his lashes and she couldn't seem to focus on aught but his face.

"Aye, that end of it," he said pointing behind her. "I do not know what you run from, but it cannot be worse than a winter storm at night."

"Little you know."

"I know enough to recognize a stubborn lass when I meet one. If you ride with me you can gaze upon my countenance as long as you wish," he said with a cocky grin.

"Why would I wish to do that?" Catriona jerked her gaze from his face to the middle of his broad chest, though that wasn't any less distracting. She tried again to remove her hand from his, but still he held on. She shook herself from her odd distraction. He would not let her go. He meant to return her to Assynt. Panic pushed its way once more into her thoughts. She pulled harder and he suddenly released her. She stumbled back, nearly falling over a rock. She caught herself then leveled her stoniest glare at him.

"Be on your way. I shall see to my own well-being."

T̲ayg *missed the feel of the beautiful stubborn lass's* cold hand in his but he feared he would hurt her if he did not release his grip.

Irritation sawed through him. He had no time for stubborn lost lasses. The storm was upon them, they needed to find shelter and after reading the message Duff Mac-Donell had given him for Assynt, he was sure there was a plot afoot, only he couldn't tell exactly what it was. He had to get to Assynt. 'Twas his duty to the king and this lass was getting in his way.

He'd tried charm. He'd tried reason, and judging from the thickening snow and gusty wind he had little time left for arguing, but he could not, in good conscience, leave the lass to freeze—no matter what else needed doing. He must find shelter for them immediately. He had little reason to believe she could care for herself. She was here in the midst of the wilderness, alone and unprepared, and he would not have her death upon his conscience. He had enough to worry about without that.

Tayg sighed and pasted his best grin-and-bear-it smile on his face. "I will not harm you, lass." The glare in her eyes said she did not believe him. "Nor will I take you to Assynt for it seems 'tis too late for that now." He looked about him in the gloom, then back at her. Her shoulders had slumped and she was chewing on her lip again. Just watching her straight, white teeth catch her lip made his mouth go dry. He forced his mind back to the trouble they were in and thrust out his hand once more.

"Come, lass. I will not allow you to stay here." He watched as the ebony haired beauty raised her chin so that she appeared to look down her nose at him despite the fact that he sat a horse and she stood at his feet. Her shoulders once more squared and he could swear she readied herself for battle. What had he said to get her on her guard again? He had no time for this.

"We must . . ." He moved the horse towards her. "Find . . ." He swiftly reached down and scooped her about the waist, swinging her up and over his lap in one sharp jerk. "Shelter." She was lying facedown with her stomach across his knees. After a split second of silent surprise, she started to scream and kick and flail. Tayg kicked the horse to a trot, thus silencing her as the horse's movement stole her breath.

"Just what I need," he muttered to himself, "daft lassies bent on killing themselves and me."

"I'm not . . . bent . . . on killing . . . anyone . . . yet!" Her voice was muffled and breathless in a far different way than it had been moments before.

Daft git. Silly beautiful woman. Tayg shook his head. She *was* bonny. Ebony hair, pale perfect skin, eyes so blue he could not name their shade. And her mouth was lush and dewy. But then he remembered her words when first he saw her and the stubborn tilt of her chin. She was not your usual sort of lass.

• • •

The animal's warmth under Catriona, and the man's warmth around her, were a welcome relief from the battering wind's frigid fingers, though her awkward, infuriating position across his lap had her fuming. The familiar feelings of anger and frustration were an odd sort of comfort against the panic that had blossomed within her when he had said he would return her to Assynt. For now, he could not. As soon as she found an opportunity, she would disappear.

She tried to hold on to her breath as the horse jostled her. Slowly she realized they were heading uphill, but she did not remember any hills along the loch shore.

"Where are you taking me?" she shouted over the wind and the jingling of the horse's tack.

He said nothing, but she felt him nudge the horse faster. Catriona tried to hold her head so that it neither banged against the man's leg nor bounced about in the air. She finally found a way to rest her forehead against his calf that was not too uncomfortable. She still was short of breath, but if she did not fight the horse's gait she found she could breathe.

Eventually she became more aware of the man whose lap she lay in. His legs were hard and thick with muscle. His stomach was flat, but also hard, as her shoulder could attest to. She was sure she would find a lean waist and she remembered his broad shoulders. The man fairly radiated the strength of a warrior. She relaxed a bit more, comforted in spite of herself. She should have feared him . . . nay, she should be angry with him, and she was, but there was something about him that almost soothed her.

He was right. She was daft.

Just as she was finally getting properly warm the horse stopped and the man slid her down to her feet, nearly oversetting her as he dismounted. Catriona sucked in deep lungfuls of the frigid Highland air and felt the awful tingling of blood rushing back to her feet.

"Wait here!" he shouted, though she could barely hear him over the raging wind and blowing snow. He pointed at a dark cleft faintly visible in the rock wall ahead. "I will make sure 'tis empty!" He handed her the reins and left her beside the animal. She fumed at his command, but she was light-headed from her upside-down ride and her feet felt like lead, so she stood, angry still, but she knew she had nowhere else to go at this moment. She watched as he disappeared into the cave, then moments later reappeared and beckoned her forward. Catriona pulled on the reins and forced her feet to move.

The man said something, but she was too busy trying to maintain her balance to listen. He grabbed the reins from her as she passed into the cave. Stopping just inside, she shook the heavy wet snow from her cloak, then moved deeper into their sanctuary.

It was a cozy space, though not large. Perhaps the man could build a fire near the entrance. She could dry her clothes—if only she had something else to wear while she did—but Gowan's horse had run away with all she had brought with her. The man pushed her aside as he led the horse out of the weather and into their shelter.

"There is barely room for us in here. Is there not another cave for the horse?" she asked.

"There may well be, but horses create a blessedly large amount of heat. We'll need his help to stay passably warm this night." He led the large brown animal to the back of the cave and secured his reins to the ground with a large rock.

Catriona couldn't help but notice that the horse's coat and the man's hair were the same color, like prized chestnuts, glossy brown, almost black.

"I'll find something to burn for a fire."

His rich voice drew her gaze to his mouth and a funny twisting, warm feeling swept over her.

"You find my fire kit. 'Tis in my saddlebags," he said,

his impatient tone, so much like Broc's, effectively ending the interesting feeling. She glowered at him as he stomped out of the cave and back into the arms of the now raging storm.

The numbness of her toes and fingers finally convinced her to do as he said despite the tone he took. She pulled the bags from the horse's back, dropped them to the floor and poked through his things finding extra clothing, a sack with a small drum, travel food, and a small leather bag containing two pieces of flint, a quantity of shaved bark and dried heather blossoms. The knife she carried at her waist would provide the iron needed to raise a spark with the flint.

She grabbed the fire kit and the food, then shoved the other things back in the saddlebags. She set the items beside her, pulled her cloak close and sat, her back against the wall, waiting for him to return.

She waited a long time. Her feet no longer tingled from the blood rushing into them but rather from the cold. She tucked them up under her in an attempt to keep warm. It was a long enough time that her thoughts began to flit around her situation.

She needed a new plan. This man wanted to return her to Assynt and that would not do. If he was correct and she had traveled in the wrong direction, she would have to go past Assynt to get to her aunt's village and that also would not do. If she continued the way she had been traveling, she would eventually end up at Dun Donell, and that was another thing she would not do.

All she could do for now was to sit here, in a cave, somewhere in the wild Highlands with a storm raging outside, waiting for a strange man to return. She didn't know whether to pray the stranger returned soon, or didn't return at all. A simple trip had been complicated by her own lousy sense of direction and the icy blast of a sudden winter storm. What had she gotten herself into?

Just as the last of the light was about to fail, her rescuer stumbled back through the opening, his arms full of snow-feathered branches and heather twigs.

Catriona rose, relief flooding her. Yet she dared not let him see how scared she had been while he was gone, nor how grateful she was for his return. To show her weakness would be to invite torment.

"I thought you had gotten lost," she said.

"I have an excellent sense of direction." He glanced at her as he dropped the wood near the entrance.

"I found this," she said, ignoring his jibe. She grabbed the fire kit, dropped it in his hand, then quickly pulled her arm back into the relative warmth of her cloak.

Catriona watched him as he stood near the opening, shaking the snow off. He shoved his fingers through his snow-dampened hair, drawing her attention once more to its subtle waves and rich color. She admired his simple grace as he prepared a fire pit near the entrance, then set about building a fire, always moving with confidence and a hint of a swagger, as if he expected her to be watching him. It took some time, but eventually he managed to ignite the tinder, then the damp kindling and finally a small fire flickered to life. Immediately Catriona moved to it.

"That is not nearly enough wood to keep us warm through the night," she said as he carefully added another piece to the small blaze.

"'Tis, but if you wish, you are welcome to collect more."

"I have no desire to go out in that blow." She rubbed her hands together, and held them to the fire until she realized they were trembling. She pulled them back and clasped them together where the telltale sign of her weakness wouldn't give her away. "Besides, 'tis your fault we are in this mess. You should gather the wood."

He stopped feeding the fire and looked up at her, his face cast in shadows. "How is this my fault?" he asked.

There was a dangerous edge to his voice that she had not heard before.

"If you had not argued with me, we could have found a real shelter, maybe a cottage or a shieling. Shielings are always left with either peat or wood for travelers' fires."

He shook his head and returned to his task. "You are right, there."

"I am?" The words popped out before Catriona realized she had voiced them. "Of course I am."

He chuckled. "Aye, of course you are, though 'twouldn't be a shieling nor a cottage. We would be warm within Assynt Castle, food in our bellies and a blazing fire at our feet. You would be home."

Catriona hunkered down, not wishing to sit on the cold stone floor, but needing to be close enough to the fire to see his face. What did he know of her?

"Why do you want to go to Assynt?" she asked.

"I have a message to deliver there, and I am quite fond of food and shelter." He bent low and blew at the bottom of the fire, causing it to leap a bit higher and burn a bit brighter for a moment.

"Why are you traveling at this season?" She settled on a cushion of her skirt and cloak. Her legs were tired from her own travels this day.

"I told you, a message."

"Hmph. Anyone may carry messages. You have a drum. Are you a bard?" The look that passed over his face was fleeting, but she thought it was embarrassment.

"Aye, a bard, and a messenger, and, apparently, the rescuer of young women too confused to know east from west."

Catriona flushed but would not let him distract her from her questions. "Who is your message for?"

He shook his head and continued working on the fire. "'Tis for Duff MacDonell's betrothed. Catriona is her name. You probably know her. From the tales I've heard she is an ugly, shrew of a . . ." Catriona flinched as if he had struck her. He looked at her face. "Nay, you could not be . . ."

"I am not ugly," she said around the tightness in her throat. She had heard the description often enough to wonder at its truth, but she never let on how much she loathed it. Catriona held out her hand. "Your message is delivered. You've no need to continue on to Assynt, now."

The man shot to his feet and he started to pace the confines of the cave. "You cannot be she. You are not ugly."

"Nay, I am not ugly." She squared her shoulders, lifted her chin and leveled her most terrorizing glare at him. "I am Catriona, daughter of Neill, chief of Clan Leod of Assynt. Tell me the message and your duty will be done."

"You have forgotten an important piece of your identity," he said, his voice as icy as the wind blowing outside the cave.

"And that is?"

"You are betrothed to Duff MacDonell."

"I will *never* wed that dog-faced son-of-a—" Catriona clenched her teeth, unable to think of a suitably contemptuous name for the man. "I deserve much better."

"Do you, now? How much better?"

"Better than you," she said, though she did not see how any man could be better to gaze upon than this arrogant example.

"If you had been listening to silly romantic tales like every other lass in the Highlands, you would know there are no better than me."

She laughed, a silvery shimmering sound. "I listen to the tales of Sir William Wallace, of King Robert the Bruce and of the brave warriors who fight for Scotland's freedom."

"Like Tayg of Culrain?"

"Aye, like brave Tayg of Culrain."

Catriona watched first pride, then anger flood his eyes.
He stood and without another word left the cave.

W hat had possessed him to ask such a thing? Tayg
      stomped through the growing dark, not daring to
go far from the frail light of the fire in the cave mouth. He
was cold, but not from the weather. That lass, that beautiful lass with the well-honed mouth, was the shrew of Assynt, soon-to-be betrothed of Duff MacDonell. If she was
found here, with him, alone 'twould be exceedingly easy
for her family to insist he marry her. After all, he was a
much better catch for their shrew than that upstart Mac-
Donell with daft dreams of greatness. What a cruel joke
that would be, to let him escape his mother's machina-
tions only to fall into the lap of someone even Mum
would not think to saddle him with.

He would not wed that woman, that shrew. He did not
care how beautifully her midnight blue eyes flashed in the
firelight, or how her silky black hair begged a man to
thread his fingers through it. He was supposed to be on a
mission in the king's service, not lusting after a difficult,
daft lass who could ruin his life if she discovered his true
identity.

So what was he to do? What could he do? He would
have to return to the shelter of the cave soon for the snow
was flying thick and wet and sideways. He was hungry.
He was tired. He was cold. And he feared that the lass
within would destroy his life, simply by her presence.

Tayg took a deep, cold breath and tried to calm his jumbled thoughts into some kind of order. There was nothing
to do for the moment, except make sure they survived the
night. When daylight came, no matter the weather, he
would take her near to Assynt and leave her there to return or not as she deemed fit. He would have returned her
to relative safety and would not have her fate further im-

pinging on his conscience. If he never set foot in Assynt
they would never know who her rescuer was. *She* did not
even know who he was, though he had nearly given himself away. He would have to be more careful, play his part
as bard as if his life depended upon it. He was afraid it
did.

He also would learn no more for the king, but perhaps
he had learned enough. He had delivered the missive, and
had the other from Duff, though it made little sense. He
had done as he had been instructed to. Perhaps he had
done enough.

So, he had a plan. Pass the night as best they could taking care to keep his distance. Return her to her family on
the morrow, then slip away unseen. That would solve all
his troubles where this lass was concerned. By midmorn
he would be back on his way, peacefully alone, free to
find the king with what little news he had garnered from
Duff.

Uneasy with his plan but unable to see an alternative
solution to his sudden troubles, he returned to the cave,
ready to do what he must to survive the night in the company of the beautiful shrew.

T hey shared a meal of dried beef and drier oat cakes
in relative quiet. Tayg saw no reason to reveal his
plan for the morrow to the lass, thereby destroying the
tentative truce they had achieved. He was nearly certain
she had been lost when he came upon her, so in the morn
he would agree to take her wherever she wished. He
doubted she would know where he was really taking her
until they arrived, at which point he would deposit her on
her own two feet, point her toward her home and ride
quickly out of sight.

"Why do you scowl so?" Catriona asked.

"Am I?"

"You look like a fat barn cat, contemplating an interloper. Or is it simply that you care not for the repast?" She examined a piece of meat in the firelight and shook her head. "I do not find much satisfaction in eating leather."

"'Tis beef and you should be happy with it. 'Tis more than you would have had were it not for me."

She notched her chin up, but did not look at him, nor did she admit he spoke the truth.

"I would have my message," she said after a moment. "Tell me what it says."

"You are full of pleasantries." He fumbled in the pouch at his waist and drew forth the crumpled piece of parchment the MacDonell chief had given him. "I do not know what it says," he said, handing it to her. "The MacDonell said I should deliver it to your brother, Broc, and that he would read it to you."

"That lout can no more read than I," she said, breaking the blob of wax that had sealed it. "Ailig, he has been to Edinburgh and was trained in the arts of reading and writing and figuring. Broc has no time for such things."

Tayg watched as she puzzled over the writing.

"I do not know why Dogface would send me a message, unless 'twas to threaten me. Do you think 'tis a threat?"

Tayg reached for the parchment and tilted it so the firelight fell upon the spiky writing.

"I shall arrive three days early. The wedding must take place immediately. The spider watcher awaits Seona's greeting and we will not disappoint. I expect you to ride as soon as the bedding is finished."

An eerie crawling sensation prickled his skin. He looked up to see Catriona's eyes wide with astonishment and her mouth gaping open.

"You can read!"

Blast and damnation. No bard of his supposed rank would have such a skill. "A little. I was to be . . . I was to be . . . a monk," he finished, almost on a question, waving the parchment in front of him to draw her attention back to it and away from his mistake. This bard business was going to be harder than he thought.

She glanced at the missive and Tayg saw the astonishment burn away and anger replace it. "I shall never wed that man and I certainly shall not bed him! He is so daft he even confuses my name and Broc's broadsword."

The venom in her voice had Tayg thankful it was not him she spoke of. "Your brother named his sword?" He tried to hand the parchment back to her but she leaned away from him, as if it were a severed head he held.

"I do not want anything of that beast Dogface, not even his words. Burn it. Use it for kindling. I do not care, just never speak those words again!" She wrapped her cloak tightly about her and lay down near the fire with her back to him.

Tayg watched her for a moment, then turned his attention back to the message that had upset her so. 'Twas clear from the writing the lad was no romantic with soft words and false love to woo a wife with, especially if he could not even remember the name of his betrothed. From the sound of it, the man wanted as much to do with the lass as she with him. 'Twas not unheard of in the Highlands for such a marriage to occur, but usually when there was this much rancor between the bride and groom, the family called it off and found another, more acceptable, match.

He read the words again, trying to figure out what it was about them that nagged at him so. The MacDonell

wished to rush the wedding . . . perhaps he feared his
bride would run away. Tayg smiled at that thought. He did
not wish to disappoint the—he looked back at the paper.
Spider watcher. 'Twas an odd thing to call someone, unless—

Tayg read the message yet again, this time remembering the message he had delivered to the MacDonell and
the unexpected glint of pleasure in his eyes at being commanded to appear before the king. The king . . . He'd
heard a tale that told of the king and how he had watched
a spider in a cave and drawn courage from the determined
creature. So the MacDonell wished to take Catriona . . .
nay, he did not say Catriona, he had used the name of
Broc's sword. . . .

A cold sweat broke out on Tayg's brow as the true intent of the message slammed into him. This message had
been intended for Broc, not Catriona, and it outlined the
alliance between the clans—and the first task that would
test it, taking up swords against the king! Tayg was sure
of it.

The MacDonells and the MacLeods rode to meet the
king and 'twas not to give fealty. The two clans rode
against King Robert and Tayg held the evidence in
his hand. What to do? He could not ride against the
MacDonell by himself and Catriona's clan would
not help him. Indeed, if spending a night alone with her
wasn't enough to anger them, riding against their ally
would.

That left warning the king. He must ride to warn the
king himself. He had the evidence. The task fell to him
alone.

He regarded the lass across the fire. Perhaps not alone.
He had the evidence, and he had a hostage, who had provided the needed clue to understand the message and who
might yet reveal more information that would be of use to
the king. He folded the missive and tucked it in his pouch.

So much for leisurely adventures or even not so leisurely spying through the Highlands. He must make for the king as swiftly as possible, which would then put him back in the path of Mum's scheme too soon. Tayg wanted to punch something. All his plans were ruined by a conniving dog-faced chief. He could save his king, or he could save his freedom, but he could not do both, and worse yet, he would have to take the shrew with him.

Truly, there was no mercy.

chapter 4

𝒞❧

C atriona *turned over and faced the fire. Her back was* a little less than frozen. She could not say as much for her front. The fire flickered in the dark cave, casting just enough light to show the man sleeping on his back, his well-formed trews-clad legs sticking out of the plaid which served as both bed and blanket. The scowl was gone from his face, leaving in its place an almost graceful peace that softened his mouth and relaxed the furrows from his brow. He looked perfectly comfortable there on the hard cave floor across the meager fire from her, yet she was freezing and the ground was hard and lumpy. Her heavy winter cloak did little to cushion her from it. She dug a rock from beneath her hip and decided to give up on sleep. Sitting up, she arranged her clothing to maximize any warmth it might afford.

What she really wanted was a plaid to wrap herself in as he did, or at least a pair of Ailig's cast-off trews to keep away the drafts that slipped up her skirts. But those were back in Assynt and she was here with this stranger, his horse and—wait. There had been a pair of trews in the saddlebags! Surely the bard would not wish her to remain cold.

She rose quietly and moved to the back of the cave where the bags had been left. Slowly she lifted a flap and dug her hand into the first bag. Food. She moved to the next. Oats for the horse. The third was the one. She pulled out a pair of woolen trews. They were big, but they would do. She tugged off her boots, slid her legs into the garment, then put her boots back on her cold feet before standing and pulling the woolen leggings up. It took her some time to unfasten her belt, arrange the loose waist of the trews under her gown, then fasten the belt again over her gown to hold the trews up. They didn't solve the problem of cold completely, but they helped. She moved back to her spot by the fire.

Settling back as near to the fire as she dared, she gazed at the flames, then found her attention pulled to the sleeping form of her companion. He turned toward her suddenly, startling her, but he quickly settled back into his deep sleep, one well-muscled arm tucked beneath his head. She remembered how strong his arms were, how his warm hand had enveloped hers and how muscular his thighs had been as she lay across them on the ride to this cave. He really was a braw man, though in sleep he looked younger, less concerned than when he had been awake, as if he shed his cares in his dreams. But what cares could a bard have beyond learning the latest news and singing for his keep?

She had cares, and not small ones, cares she must attend to.

Leaving had at least kept her out of Dogface's hands, and from the sound of the message the bard had read her—she still marveled that he could read—she had left none too soon.

But what was she to do now? If she continued with her

original plan she would have to travel past Assynt to get
to her aunt's village by the sea. She had no wish to go
anywhere near her home until she was sure Dogface had
departed and would not be returning. That meant her
aunt's was no longer her destination. Then where could
she go?

Not Assynt, nor Dun Donell, nor the sea village, nor an
abbey. She shuddered. The list of where she would not go
was growing longer by the moment.

A new thought had her shuddering . . . 'twas not unheard of for a bride to be married by proxy. Nay, Broc
would not do that to her . . . would he? She must not
panic. She was smarter than Broc, so there must be a way
around this problem. Perhaps he had not thought of a
proxy wedding . . . but he would, eventually. Someone
would mention it, probably Dogface, though she still did
not understand why he wished to wed her. But 'twas just
the kind of thing he would suggest, for he was too like
Broc in that he did not brook with others thwarting his
wishes. She would not be safe from the vile man unless he
could not wed her.

An idea formed, faint at first but as she mulled it over it
became clearer, stronger. She must wed another before
Dogface or Broc could find her and seal her fate. Even if
they did marry her to Dogface by proxy 'twould not hold
up if she had previously consummated a union with another to whom she had freely given her vows.

She must marry. She must marry soon.

She watched the sleeping man across from her. He was
very pleasant to look at but, nay, he would not make for
the sort of husband she needed. She must find someone
with enough strength and power to stand up to Dogface,
and to Broc, for 'twould come to that, she was sure. She
needed a hero like those in the songs the bards sang . . . a
hero like Tayg of Culrain.

She considered that for a moment. As far as she knew

he was unwed and a second son. He was loyal to the king, for he had fought by King Robert's side for many months. He was faithful, strong, brave. All the things she needed in a husband, for herself and for the clan. But would he take her to wife?

She would bring a powerful alliance as her tocher, along with wealth. He was said to be the very opposite of Dogface and Broc. Perhaps if she could not convince Tayg of Culrain himself she could convince the king to pledge them for 'twould be to his benefit to seal an alliance between his loyal man and one of the far Highland clans.

The king. She had told Ailig to seek the king's support to make him the next chief of Clan Leod, yet he had declined, most forcefully, to do so. But that did not mean that she could not petition the king. Ailig had asked her what her duty was. Was it not to see to the well-being of the clan? Marrying Dogface would not speak to the well-being of the clan. Broc stepping into her father's place as chief would not speak to the well-being of the clan.

But if she were to secure a strong alliance to one such as Tayg of Culrain and if she were to secure the king's command that Ailig should be chief of Clan Leod of Assynt after his father, then *that* would speak to the well-being of the clan.

Of course her tongue might not endear her to the king . . . or to her intended husband. Anger rose in her that she would have to hide her true self, but Ailig's words of counsel came back to her. With a little effort to curb her tongue she would serve her own purposes, securing a future she could contemplate without revulsion. After all, marrying a hero would be very different from marrying a rogue. She smiled to herself. She had a plan. She would away to the king in the morning with, or without, the bard.

•   •   •

Tayg awoke slowly and stared at the opening of the cave. The snow had let up while he slept and the sky was just beginning to turn a deep predawn grey. He glanced across the fire at the sleeping lass who had managed to destroy his adventure merely by standing on a trail in front of him. He risked a forced marriage to the bonny but irritating lass. He risked his life if the Mac-Donell realized what Tayg had learned. He risked his future happiness by returning from his adventure before his father could thwart his mother's plan to lock him in marriage by month's end.

He stood and settled his plaid about him while he glared at the lass. How was it possible that a chance meeting with someone on a deserted Highland track could change so much? He stomped over to the saddlebags. The Shrew of Assynt. Hell and damnation. Not only was he obliged to quit his journey and hurry to the king's side to warn him of the conspiring of the MacDonells and the MacLeods, but he must take the shrew with him.

He dug out the sack of oats he had brought for his horse and fed the shaggy animal. Damn and hellfire! He could not be caught alone with the shrew. He would be doomed and his mother would not care one way or the other. Nay, it could not happen. And her brothers? What would they do if he and Catriona were found together? Kill him or force him to wed her. Somehow he couldn't see the difference in those fates. And the damage was done, as far as her family would be concerned. They had spent a night, however chastely, together, alone, in a cave in the wilds.

What to do? 'Twas clear that they must get to the king as soon as possible. 'Twas also clear that no one must know they were together until they reached the king. If all else failed, he would depend upon the lass to refuse to be trapped into wedding him. But how? His glance fell upon the drum sack laying by the saddlebags. Of course, a bard would not serve her purposes; a lass like her needed security and alliances.

He would have to trust that she would not deign to have a bard . . . but just in case, he would make sure she did not want him. Aye, that was the way of it.

Pleased with his plan he moved to her side to wake her. She was truly beautiful in her sleep. Her face was soft, her skin creamy in the pale dawn light. Her hair was like liquid night and her lips . . . he shook himself. Nay, she was the Shrew of Assynt and if he did not watch himself, she could ruin the rest of his life, not just the next sennight.

He nudged her with his toe. "Wake up. 'Tis time we left this cave."

Her eyes opened slowly and just as slowly she turned her head to look at him. Dreams still veiled her eyes and he could see her confusion.

"Wake up. 'Tis time to travel."

Her vision cleared and her eyebrows drew down, a look of irritation replacing the soft sleepy one. Suddenly he realized there was one sure way to make her keep her distance from him.

"Rise. We head to Assynt. I will return you to your family and let them deal with your disloyalty." Tayg was pleased with the harsh edge to his voice. 'Twas a perfect imitation of his brother and it earned him an even deeper scowl from the lass.

"I told you last night, I shall not return to Assynt."

"And I have decided 'tis not worth the risk being found in your company."

"Risk? What is your risk? No one knows I am with you nor do they have any reason to believe I would be. My brothers do not even know of you."

"Aye, they do not, but the MacDonell, he bade me deliver his missive."

"Which you have done."

In theory he had, but he knew the missive had not gone

to its true recipient. He did not wish to bring her thoughts back to the strange damning message, though, so he changed the subject.

"You will be tracked."

"Not in the new snow. What is the true reason you do not want to do as I wish?"

He watched her, judging what would anger her the most. "I have three." He held up his index finger. "I do not wish to travel with a shrew." Her face darkened like a winter storm about to break and he hurried on, raising a second finger. "I do not wish to anger the MacDonell." He held up a third finger and waggled them at her. "And you will slow me down from my task." He quickly turned to the saddle-bags and began searching for something to break his fast.

"Is that all?" she asked, her voice sharp.

"That is enough," he said keeping his back to her, though he was inordinately curious to see her expression.

"I can do nothing about being the Shrew of Assynt so that does not merit discussion. I do not give a rat's arse if Dogface MacDonell is angry or not, and as for slowing you down, if we both ride the horse 'twill not happen."

Tayg glanced over his shoulder at her. She was standing, her feet planted and her fists clenched as if she prepared to battle him physically if necessary. Good. Just a little more.

"The horse cannot carry both of us for long, and neither of us in this deep snow. You will slow me down, and I must reach the king as soon as possible."

A light shone in her eyes and Tayg had the distinct feeling of falling into a deep pit from which he might never extricate himself.

"I thought you were bound for Assynt, yet suddenly you are bound for the king? What business have you with the king?"

'Twas a good question and he didn't know how to answer it without giving away what he knew. Her loyalty to her clan, despite his jibe, just might override her hatred of the MacDonell if she knew why they rode for the king.

"Well, bard? Are you on some errand for him? Are you a spy, perhaps? Do you come to the Highlands to report on the doings of our clans?"

He had to be careful now. "I am . . ." he cast about for a plausible story, after all, he was an excellent storyteller, so this should be simple . . . "I am on a mission for the king."

"And that would be?"

"I search for brides." 'Twas easier to stick close to the truth than to weave a completely false tale.

"But the king is wed already."

"Aye, but he, he . . . he wants the Highlands settled in their support for him, so he seeks brides for several of his allies' sons."

"And these sons would be . . . ?"

He did not like lying to the lass, nor did he care for the glint of curiosity in her eyes, but he had little choice. Tayg rummaged through the saddlebag and pulled out a wedge of cheese hoping to distract her from her questions with the offering of food to break her fast. He carved off a chunk and tossed it to her, surprised when she caught it deftly, though almost absently. He then took one for himself and put it away.

"Do you not know for whom you seek brides?" she asked.

"I am not at liberty to speak of the king's plans." He moved back by the fireside and sat, watching her, judging this to be the moment to lock her into his plan.

"So you see, lass, you cannot come with me. I will return you to—"

"Nay, you will not. There are no eligible lasses at Assynt save for me, so you need not waste your time traveling there. You need to return to the king quickly, so you say. You have your mission to complete, and I find that it serves my purposes as well."

"What?" Tayg felt control of the situation slipping away from him.

"I have need to rid myself of any possibility of marriage to Dogface. I am not fit to live the life of the convent, therefore I must marry. I think Tayg of Culrain would suit well, for me, for my clan and for the king's purposes. I would hurry to the king to seek his support in this before Dogface and Broc find me." Her face lit in a wide grin and Tayg had to look away else become completely entranced in her azure eyes that glowed with sudden glee.

"I will help you find eligible brides," she continued, "and you will help me when we meet the king. Yes, 'twill serve both our purposes well."

Sweat popped out on Tayg's brow despite the cold of the cave. She wished to marry him? Impossible. He thought he had left marriage plots behind when he left Culrain and his mum. She had been wrong, his mum. His fame was spread well past a two-day ride and now he faced a conundrum.

He needed the lass as hostage for the king. He no more wanted to see her wed to Duff MacDonell than she did for 'twould bode ill for the king and for any possible peace in the Highlands, if not for all of Scotland, for to force the king to defend his realm from the north and the south would divide his army beyond use and all of Scotland would suffer for it. How was it that one irritating lass could be a pivot point for a kingdom's future? How was it that that irritating lass saw him as the answer to her troubles?

He considered her for a moment. 'Twas true the king would see merit in an alliance between Tayg and this lass. 'Twas true a marriage between them would bind her clan to his against the MacDonells. 'Twas true, but Tayg had no wish to marry such a lass as this one. If he was to marry, he would wish for a sweet wife. Life was hard enough without shackling oneself to a shrew. And yet he needed to take her to the king.

An idea formed. He would find her a husband before they reached the king. There had to be other clans between here and Dingwall with lads loyal to the king. 'Twould only require convincing them to marry the lass . . . a task that might prove to be impossible.

He looked at her where she sat, watching him, waiting for his answer. A bonny smile played over her full lips and twinkled in her midnight blue eyes while her clever hands worked a complicated braid with her ebon hair. If he could convince her to hold her tongue 'twould be no hardship to sway a lad toward such a beautiful lass. But could she hold her tongue?

He would have to find out now.

"What's in it for me?" he said.

She seemed startled by his sudden question.

"I am a bard on the king's business. What advantage does it serve me to help you in your quest?"

"I will not . . ."

She blushed and his mind rapidly followed the direction her thoughts had clearly taken. His blood rushed and he damned himself for the unwanted reaction to the image of what she suggested.

"I do not want you in my bed," he said quickly. In fact he wanted her as far away from his bed as possible, no matter what his body's reaction was to her, for to bed the wench would play into her plan to marry him.

"I do not have any coin, but that I can get for you, after, or if you prefer I will find you a place where you may winter over. You may decide as you wish." She rose and brushed dirt from her skirts. "But let us go now, bard. We have a long way to travel to meet the king." She was lifting saddlebags and settling them on the horse.

Tayg smiled at her back. "What if we chance upon a village, or someone who may know you? How will you explain traveling, alone, with a bard?"

Catriona turned from the horse.

"I am not known east of Loch Assynt, at least not by anything but reputation. No one will recognize me. You yourself said I was not ugly, though 'tis what the gossip-mongers say about me. Besides, I can disguise myself somehow . . . maybe as your sister? That would work." She kilted up her skirts, tucking them into her belt and exposing a familiar pair of trews beneath. "See, I can dress the part of a traveling wench. No one will suspect."

Tayg worked hard not to grin. She was smart this one. A disguise would help but he needed to see if she could take the part one crucial step further.

"Once you open your mouth everyone will know you are the Shrew of Assynt. Word of your whereabouts will quickly get to your"—he chose the next word carefully—"betrothed."

She narrowed her eyes and pressed her lips together. She stared at him, fire snapping in her gaze, but did not say anything. Perfect. She was perfect.

"Right. So you can act the part of an indignant sister, I dare say you've much experience with that."

She nodded her head. "You are taking me with you to the king, bard. Perhaps he will wed me to Tayg of Culrain, or we may find me a husband along the way while you search for brides—as long as we do so quickly. I will not let Dogface find me." She gave him a smug smile and turned back to loading the horse.

Tayg rolled his eyes. So she would be his sister, but he would not chance a village until he was sure she could hold to her part. For now, though, they must get away from the shores of Loch Assynt before her family found them.

He walked to her side and rummaged in one of the bags. He pulled out an old length of red and black plaid and handed it to her.

"Wrap that about your head to keep you warmer." He pulled his extra pair of mittens from another bag. "Do not let your fingers freeze."

He finished arranging the bags on the horse and grabbed the reins. As he led the beast to the cave entrance Tayg glanced at Catriona. "You can keep the trews," he said.

"I intend to," she replied, following him out of their shelter and into the brightening dawn.

The snow was deep and they had been slogging through it for hours. Tayg didn't even look behind him, not wanting to care how tired the exasperating lass was. If he didn't look, he didn't have to know. To her credit, she had not asked for his help, though he was sure she had slipped several times given the surprised *whuff* sound he heard from her periodically. It took all his self-control not to help her, not to put her on the horse and see to her comfort. 'Twas a test, he reminded himself for the hundredth time. He needed to see if she could mind her tongue, could truly play her part, even in adversity, for their safety—and his future—depended on keeping their true identities secret.

"Whuff!"

He winced, sure that her bottom was getting good and sore, but he had a part to play, too, and charming Tayg was not it.

"Bard."

Tayg continued on, pulling the horse through a deep drift of heavy wet snow.

"Bard!"

He stopped and slowly turned. He looked at her sitting splayed in the snow, a scowl upon her wind-reddened face. He cocked an eyebrow at her but said nothing.

"I am hungry," she said. "I have needs to tend to," she added, looking away.

"Then tend to them."

"Will you wait?"

His own stomach grumbled and he realized it had been

a long time since they had broken their fast. He nodded
and dropped the horse's reins to the ground.

Catriona struggled to her feet, headed off the trail and
behind a large boulder. After a few moments she returned.
Tayg handed her an oat cake and some dried venison. He
took his cup, scooped it full of snow and handed it to her.

"What am I to do with this?" she asked.

"Hold it in your lap while you eat so your body will
heat it. By the time you are done eating you will have
water to drink."

She actually smiled as she pulled the cup beneath her
cloak. She shivered. "'Tis a wee bit cold."

Tayg chuckled. He ate slowly to give the lass a chance
to rest. He had been hard on her, pushing the pace through
the deep snow so relentlessly that he was tired himself.
He watched her as she stared up at the clouds. Fatigue
showed in the shadows under her eyes, but she had not
complained. 'Twas wholly unexpected, that. He would
have thought she'd demand he let her ride, or stop often to
let her rest, or at the very least he expected she would find
cause to complain about his company, the weather, the
trail or any number of other things.

Yet she had not.

She looked at him suddenly and caught him staring.
"Do you know where we will stay this night?"

"Nay."

"Is there a village nearby?"

"Nay."

"Can you say aught besides *nay*?"

Tayg fought the smile that threatened him. "Nay."

"Irritating man," she said, though there wasn't quite the
sharp edge to the words there had been earlier.

"Nay." This time he did smile and she answered with a
silvery giggle.

"You are not nearly so adept at annoying me as my
brothers are."

"Is that a complaint or a compliment?"

She considered for a moment, then shrugged. "I suppose it is a compliment." She drew the cup from beneath her cloak and smiled as she peered inside it. "I would not wish anyone to aspire to the likes of my brothers, especially Broc, the eldest." She drank down the water and he admired the pale slender column of her throat. She handed him the now empty cup.

"You do not get along with Broc?"

She gave a most unladylike snort. "I do not."

"I wonder why that could be?" He cast her a sideways glance.

She stood, her hands braced upon her hips and a look of consternation on her face. "Because he is a loud, nettlesome oaf of a man. He has not the brains to mind his own business, much less the clan's. Because he thinks that a woman could not possibly have an intelligent thing to say. Because he delights in humiliating . . ."—she stopped and took a deep breath—"everyone."

" 'Tis glad I am that I asked."

"Are you ready to proceed? I would prefer to sleep in a bed this night. I've no liking for sleeping in snow."

Tayg rose and gave her a mocking half bow. The shrew had disappeared for a few moments and he had glimpsed a softer woman underneath, but the shrew was not long subdued and he found himself grateful for the reminder.

They trudged along, following the downward path of a burn, iced over except for the trickle of water left in the very center of the stream bed. Tayg turned his thoughts to his immediate problem—could he trust her to hold her tongue? It had not taken much effort to set her temper off just now.

A familiar earthy-sweet odor insinuated itself into his musings. He stopped so quickly the horse's nose nearly rested on his shoulder.

"What is it?" Catriona demanded.

Tayg smelled the air, crisp from the new snow, but tinged with the distinct scent of burning peat. There was just the slightest breeze to mark the direction of the smoke's origin.

Catriona pushed her way past the horse through the knee-deep snow. "Well, bard? Why are we stopped?"

"We need to get off the trail for a while," he said, quickly calculating what direction they needed to go to avoid whatever dwelling lay before them. He wasn't ready to test their ruse on living, thinking people just yet.

"Why? No one follows us."

"You do not know that. Do you wish to give the Mac-Donell a clear path to track you?"

Catriona looked back at the deep furrow in the snow where they had passed. "But no matter where we go we will leave a trail. Would it not be better to stick to this clear road where others may also pass and cover our tracks with their own?"

The lass was smarter than he had expected.

"We cannot chance meeting . . . anyone," he said at last.

Her delicate eyebrows drew down in a look of puzzlement. "I thought we agreed I would act as your sister, and since you are behaving as irrationally as my brothers, I find that will be an easy task."

"Aye, so easy you will not remember to mind your tongue."

"I will remember."

"Even if you do, how can you guarantee that there is no one who will recognize you?"

"I told you, I have never traveled this way."

"Aye, but that does not mean that whomever we chance to meet has not traveled to Assynt."

Tayg knew a moment of victory, but it was short-lived.

"Very well, then we must disguise me by more than simply calling me your sister."

Tayg groaned. The lass would not give up. But they could not take the chance. "A bard's sister will have to perform for her keep."

"Nay, 'tis you who will have to perform for our keep. I can simply ask hospitality—and offer my brother's fine skill as a bard."

This time it was Tayg who snorted.

"You have your mission, too," she continued. "How will you report to the king on brides if you do not venture into the villages to meet them? 'Twould not hurt for me to meet any eligible husbands, either."

She had him. If he intended to keep her with him without force, he needed her to believe his story, but he could not bear the thought of being caught with her before they reached the Bruce. He looked at her carefully, assessing those features that would most make her recognizable.

Quickly he took inventory: glossy black hair that fell, even braided, to her waist. Eyes the blue of the midsummer night sky when the sun barely set and the colors of the world were dark and intense. Skin pale and perfect. And her mouth, soft and inviting.

His body tightened and he fought the pleasure derived from merely looking at her. His imagination leaped, unwanted, to contemplating what it would be like to touch her.

He was doomed. He must do something. And he had to do it quickly.

"We'll see what we find," he said, sending a silent prayer that wherever the smoke came from it would not be upon their path. For now, he needed to get away from her before his body and his imagination ganged up on him and he did something he would forever regret. "If we find someone, we shall have to make you plain before they see us." He turned away from her surprised look and continued on the road they had been traveling.

chapter 5

Pungent peat smoke greeted Catriona long before the village came into view. Fatigue unlike any she had known dragged at her feet, making it harder and harder to lift them. Thank goodness the bard and his horse were breaking the trail for her or she would have given up miles ago.

He stopped ahead of her and waited. If she didn't know better, she'd think that was concern on his face, but he was nearly as hateful to her as Broc, so that was impossible. He would not care if she were sinking into hellfire with a rock tied about her neck. But that wasn't fair. If she was truthful with herself she must admit that he had been kind to her in a gruff sort of way. He had even made her laugh. She did not want to like the man, but she had to admit, at least to herself, that he was not so bad as most.

She caught up with him and was puzzled by the odd look in his eyes, almost as if he had never seen her before.

"We need to hide your hair before we enter the village, and smudge up your skin," he said to her.

She merely nodded, wondering if she'd be able to force her feet to move again now that she had stopped. She looked up at him and saw the unmistakable mark of concern in the lines of his face and the slant of his eyebrows.

"You need not worry, bard," she said. "I will not say anything to give myself away."

He stared at her a moment, as if she were some odd bit of flotsam he'd found, then turned to rummage in a saddlebag. He pulled a length of stained linen from it and handed it to her.

"What am I to do with this?"

"You need to fashion a wimple, if you can, or at least a veil. The more of your hair and face that are obscured, the less chance you will draw attention to yourself. We will both regret it if you are recognized."

Of course. She pushed the hood of her cloak back and loosened the plaid scrap she had looped about her neck. Pulling her heavy braid out from beneath her cloak, she coiled it around her head and tried to hold it in place with one hand while she wrapped the cloth about it with the other.

Just when she got the cloth in place, the braid slithered out of her grasp. She started over, and once more, just as she was about to get the linen in place, the braid escaped her.

"Here, let me hold your hair," the bard said, his voice strangely husky.

He stepped behind her and took her braid from her hand, wrapping it inexpertly, but gently about her head. Catriona shivered at the pleasing warmth of his fingers against her scalp as she finally managed to wrap the cloth securely and tie it in place at the back of her head. When she was done she turned to face him.

"'Tis no wimple but 'twill serve the purpose," he said,

reaching out and tucking a stray tendril under the material.

His fingers were remarkably gentle against her wind-chapped cheek and a curious warm chill ran through her where he touched her. He stared at her for a moment as if frozen to the spot.

"Bard?" She touched his arm and he jerked, as if burned by her, then quickly bent and dug into the snow at his feet without a word. When he reached the rocky ground underneath he dug until he had a small handful of dirt. He added a bit of snow to it making a muddy mixture, then he rubbed his hands together letting most of the dirt drop back to the ground. He reached toward her face again and Catriona pulled back.

"I'll not hurt you, lass, but we must distract from your beauti—from your pale skin." Gently he ran his thumbs over her cheeks in what felt more like a caress than anything else. He ran a finger along her nose, as if memorizing the line of it. Slowly he drew his palm over her chin. His eyes followed the path his hands took and Catriona was mesmerized by the strange sensation of his soft touch spreading the cold, gritty dirt. She found it hard to breathe and he seemed to be having the same trouble. Her skin felt heated and she did not know what to do with her hands. He finished by brushing away much of his handiwork with the backs of his fingers, once more lingering over his task.

At last he stepped back. She licked her lips nervously and watched him swallow, his eyes fixed upon her mouth. For a moment they stood there, silent, watching.

"I think that will do," he finally said, that husky note once more in his voice. He bent to the snow again and cleaned his hands. When he faced her he wore his usual slightly perturbed look.

"You understand what you must do?" he asked. "How you must behave?"

"I do, bard," she said in a breathless voice. She cleared her throat and pushed the disturbing sensation of his hands on her face from her mind. "I am well versed in the behavior of a sister towards an older brother." That was better. "'Twill not be difficult."

He nodded but didn't look convinced. In fact, he looked a bit like a man heading to the gallows.

"I can do this," she said, laying a hand on his arm. "Do not worry."

He backed away a step, breaking her touch, then picked up the reins and moved on toward the smell of peat smoke.

"Bard, wait!" she called.

He stopped and looked back at her as she caught up to him.

"Do you not think a sister would know her brother's name?"

"Tayg," he said, and she saw him wince as if he had not meant to tell her.

Surprised, she asked, "Like brave Tayg of Culrain?"

He turned and began walking again. "'Tis a common name among Clan Munro."

"Then you are of that clan?" She loped along behind him, trying to catch up with his long strides despite her fatigue. "Is that why you were angry last night? Are you rivals, perhaps?"

"Save your breath, lass," he said. "The sun is nearly set. If we are to chance this I would reach our destination before full dark."

Catriona followed him, trying out his name in her mind. Tayg. It summoned to mind images of a man in battle, the king's banner flying over his head, sword drawn, a battle cry upon his lips. But this Tayg was a bard, not a warrior. She tried to adjust the image to one of a bard, seated in a hall, but she could not. Now there was a face on the warrior, and it belonged to this Tayg. She shook her head at the nonsense. 'Twas an uncommon name, to be sure, yet it connected him to his clan. 'Twas a good name—for a bard or a warrior.

"H*elloo!" Tayg called as they entered the village* just as the last light was about to fade from the sky. Heads poked out of cottage doors but no one spoke to them. "'Tis a bard I am, in search of a warm meal and a place to sleep out of the cold for me and my sister," he said loudly.

"Welcome, bard," a booming voice called from a larger building set at the far end of the small village.

Tayg and Catriona walked past a dozen small stone cottages thatched with heather. The earthy smell of burning peat hung low over the settlement. The blanket of new snow was broken in dirty trails leading from each dwelling to the main path on which they now trod through the center of the village. 'Twas not so different from every other Highland village Tayg had ever seen, including his own.

When they reached the foot of the trail, a barrel-chested man greeted them from the doorway of a house that was easily twice as big as the others they had passed.

"I am Farlan, Chief of the Mackenzies of Fionn. I welcome you to our village."

"I am—" Tayg hesitated. He did not wish to give their true names. "I am Duncan and this is my sister Mairi."

"We have been long without the merriment of a bard, good man. If you will entertain us, we will be happy to provide a warm meal and a place by the fire for the night."

Tayg grinned. "Aye, that would be a fine trade, Farlan."

"What brings you wandering in such weather, and with your sister?"

"Ah, well now, there's a complicated tale," he said,

stalling. What was wrong with him? 'Twas stupid not to
have thought of these questions before. The lass had his
mind running in circles instead of attending to their survival. "I am escorting my sister to her new family. She is
to wed." 'Twas not so far from the truth.

"And this groom could not come to claim her?"

"Nay." Tayg glanced at her and shook his head slightly.
He should have devised a plausible story with her before
they entered the village so they would not betray one another, but he had not been able to think of aught except to
hide her loveliness. And then the wide-eyed look of wonder on her face at his touch had nearly undone him. He
had come so close to tasting her . . .

Farlan cleared his throat.

Tayg shook his head and tried to rid himself of the distracting memory and focus on the tale he must weave to
keep them safe. He hated it, but he had to trust her to go
along with the tale he was concocting.

"Her betrothed had an accident hunting and has broken
his leg. 'Tis impossible for him to travel now, yet they are
anxious to begin their married bliss."

He slanted a leering grin at Catriona who, to her credit,
did not respond to his jibe with anything except a narrow-
ing of her eyes and a pursing of her lovely lips. 'Twas
silly to bait her, and yet he found he could not help himself.

"She is nearly an old woman and does not wish to give
the lad a chance to change his mind."

The chief guffawed. "If she is old, then I am young, but
then time is different when you are in love." He chucked
Catriona under the chin and Tayg prayed she would not
bite the man. To his relief she did not.

"'Tis not every day a perfect match presents itself," she
said, her head dipped demurely, though her glare was
aimed firmly at Tayg. "Should you not explain your other
purpose to our host, my brother?"

Tayg started, then realized she could not be speaking of the plot against the king. "What other purpose?"

"The bride search, of course." She looked at Farlan. "You'll have to forgive him. The cold has addled his brain."

"'Twill do that, aye, but what's this of a bride search?"

Catriona stepped closer to Farlan and looped her arm around his as if taking him into a great confidence. Tayg wondered what she was up to.

"Have you not heard that the king seeks to marry off his loyal followers' sons?" she said.

Farlan shook his head. "That news did not reach us."

"My brother has been sent to spy out the bonnyst lasses in the Highlands to present to the king as prospective brides."

Tayg scowled at her but she just flashed a cheeky grin at him.

"Surely you have some bonny lasses here," she continued.

"We do. We do, indeed," he said, his eyes lighting with delight. "My own daughter would make a grand match for any lad."

"Do you have any sons?"

Farlan blinked at her.

"Oh, not for me. I have heard that a clan near to the sea has a bonny daughter ready to wed. I merely thought . . ."

"'Tis a fine thought, lass, but my sons are all long wed. Did the king bid you find eligible sons to go with those brides?"

"Nay, I simply wish all lasses could be as blessed as I to be wed to a brave, braw lad."

She batted her eyes at the chief and Tayg struggled not to burst out laughing at her performance. She was far better at this than he would have thought.

Farlan chuckled. "Well, 'tis only a daughter I have left to settle, lass. But come, you are both cold, no doubt. Let us continue this conversation inside. Give your horse to Ian here." He shoved a lad who had been lurking nearby toward them. "He will see 'tis well tended."

"Our thanks," Tayg said, pleased to change the subject. "If we can warm ourselves and sup, I would be happy to entertain your kinsmen this night."

Farlan ushered them into the building, followed by most of the villagers, it seemed. He ordered several people off to gather food and drink, then led Tayg and Catriona to a table near a roaring fire at the end of the hall. A platter of mutton and one of roasted onions and turnips were quickly placed before them, along with a pitcher of ale. Trenchers were laid out with a horn spoon set upon them and wooden cups set next to the pitcher.

The hot food was delicious and they ate quickly. Tayg was pleased to see the color return to Catriona's smudged cheeks. The lass could rest here while he tried to be a bard again. He would follow the course he had followed at Dun Donell, depending more upon his storytelling ability and less upon his dubious talent as a musician.

Farlan joined them, a ginger-haired lass at his elbow. "Good bard, this is my daughter, Sweet Dolag."

Tayg looked up at a lovely lass of perhaps ten and seven. Her copper hair framed a heart-shaped face with a riot of curls, but her eyes were cast down so that he could not tell their color. She was bonny, but not as bonny as Catriona. Tayg held his breath a moment, appalled at the thought. He must remember his purpose for traveling with Catriona and not let her beauty distract him. He needed to remember that she was a shrew and a hostage. Determined to redirect his troublesome thoughts, he rose and gave a nod of his head, like a small bow.

"'Tis pleased I am to make your acquaintance."

The lass colored prettily. She sat beside her sire on the bench directly across from Tayg and Catriona, who set her spoon and knife aside and watched the father and daughter.

"What news have you?" Farlan asked.

Tayg chewed for a moment, then said, "'Tis not much news this time of year. The MacDonells are well." Catriona muttered something but he could not make it out. "Though the Beatons raid their livestock. The MacLeods of Assynt are as ever"—he glanced at Catriona—"arguing amongst themselves."

He winced as Catriona ground her heel on his toes under the table while smiling across the table at their host. Tayg jerked his foot from beneath hers, quickly moving all of his toes out of her reach.

"What news have you?" Catriona asked Farlan.

"Ah, there is little to tell. The snows have been deep in our glen though 'tis but December. 'Twill be a long cold winter I fear."

Tayg nodded. "There was little snow to the south when I traveled there a sennight past but here 'twould appear winter has settled in long since."

There was a silence and Tayg tried to ignore the palpable expectations rolling off of Farlan.

The man grinned at Tayg and patted his daughter's arm. "My Sweet Dolag will make a fine wife. She is kind, and sweet, and demure. She is well-trained in the running of a hall or a castle. She cooks and sews and is good with the wee ones."

Tayg squirmed at the man's listing of his daughter's qualifications. 'Twas like listening to a man speak of his favorite hunting hound. He was suddenly struck with the realization that he really should use this opportunity, and his anonymity, to see if he could find a lass he could be happily wedded to. If he did not find one before he reached the king, his mother would do the choosing for him. A shiver ran down his spine. That would never do. And what better way to audition a wife than this?

"Does she have a sense of humor?" Tayg asked, a grin on his face to disguise his serious question. Whoever he ended up bound to had best be able to laugh at his jokes.

Farlan frowned. "What use is that in a wife?"

Tayg laughed as if he'd been funny on purpose. "Aye, just so." Did the lass never speak for herself? "And what of you, Sweet Dolag? What do you wish for from a husband?"

At last she glanced up at him. "Wish for?"

Tayg nodded at her and she glanced at her father, as if asking him for her own opinion.

"I . . . I do not know. I suppose I wish for a husband who will care for me and our bairns, provide enough to eat, a home. What else should I wish for?" she asked, a very serious look upon her face.

"Do you not wish for love?" he asked.

"Of course. Doesn't every lass? But 'tis seldom found." This was certainly true in Tayg's experience. "I do not expect it. If I am lucky, I will grow to love whomever I marry."

"'Tis a sad way to approach marriage," Tayg said. He had heard enough from this lass. She was sweet, no doubt, and biddable, but he could not see himself spending a long winter's night with her. Nay, she was too shy and sober for his liking, despite the apparent promise of her ginger curls.

He drained his ale cup and reached for the sack containing his drum. "I think 'tis time to make merry," he said. He pulled out the drum and ran his hands over the stretched skin, warming it slowly as he had seen bards do many times. He searched his memory for other things he had seen bards do, other than flirting with the lasses. Of that he had no need for practice.

Pulling an empty bench near the fire, he settled himself so his feet could be warmed while he played. As before, the crowd gathered around him, some pulling benches close, others standing, and the children all perched at his feet. He began with the same slow ballad he had played at Dun Donell, only this time he managed to get the beat right. He started in on the words, careful to keep the beat of the drum even and the tone of his voice melancholy.

When he was finished the crowd applauded and he asked what kind of story they would like to hear. While he told the tale of the Mad Chief again, he noticed Catriona moved to the edge of the circle and stood across from him, watching him like a cat about to pounce on a fat mouse.

The applause sounded again at the end of the story and he reached for his cup, slurping down the contents.

"Sing us another song, bard," someone yelled from the edge of the crowd.

"Aye, sing us a love song, something sweet and romantic."

He looked over the rim of his mug into the deep-blue eyes of the speaker, Catriona.

"I have another tale to tell—"

"But brother, we want a song. A lovely song. You know 'The Maiden's Choice.' Sing it for us."

Tayg glared at Catriona.

"Ah, lasses," she said, raising her voice, "my brother needs a bit of enticement. 'Twould seem a full belly has him in a melancholy mood, and a man's no good to anyone in a mood like that, now is he?" She had the audacity to wink at him while the lasses giggled and the men guffawed.

"I do not need your help in that arena, my dear sister," he said, raising his voice to be heard above the laughter.

"Nay, 'tis not *my* help you'll be needing, mayhap . . ." she threaded her way into the circle and made her way around it. "Mayhap you need a bit of inspiration? You should sing a song to a lass . . . this lass," she said, pulling

Dolag into the middle of the circle. "She may rouse you to better than you have sung so far."

Tayg scowled at Catriona but managed to smile a split second later when Dolag glanced shyly at him.

"Ah, Dolag," he said, deciding to play along with Catriona and best her at her own game.

"'Tis *Sweet* Dolag," Farlan said from across the circle.

Tayg nodded. If he did this right he could please Farlan and pay Catriona back for putting him in this difficult position. She would regret both grinding his toes and meddling with his performance. He narrowed his eyes and concentrated on Dolag, Sweet Dolag, he reminded himself.

"Ah, Sweet Dolag of Fionn." He flashed her his cheekiest grin and winked at her, making sure Catriona also saw that wink. He watched as Dolag's cheeks flushed pink just from that little bit of flirting. Here was a lass unused to the attentions of a man. She would be easy to flatter. He began a simple beat upon his drum.

"Sweet Dolag of Fionn, a sweet thing she is. Her hair is like fire, her face like a p—" he stumbled over the beat as he tried not to say the first rhyme he thought of: pig.

The crowd howled, but Farlan did not look happy and Dolag's lower lip trembled.

"My apologies," Tayg said quickly. "I do not usually make up songs so hastily," he added. "Let me try again, for such a pretty lass deserves a pretty song."

Farlan's head bobbed in agreement, and the pink deepened on Dolag's cheeks.

"Let me help you, brother," Catriona said as she stood by Dolag's side.

"Nay, you have helped enough."

Again the crowd laughed loudly.

Tayg started the beat upon his drum again. "Fair Dolag of Fionn, fine of face and of form. She shines like a flower on a bonny Spring morn."

"Och, that's better, lad," Farlan shouted.

"She is never a shrew, a hen or a brat. She never dissents." He looked at Catriona so he could be sure she understood his point. "Never talks back."

Tayg let the beat flow for a moment, while he thought of something else to sing.

"Fair Dolag of Fionn, has grace like a cat. She sings like an angel—"

The crowd hooted and Dolag ducked her head, staring at her feet. "'Tis clear he has not heard her sing, then!" someone shouted from the crowd.

Tayg smiled, "And—"

"Is blind as a bat!" another voice shouted from the other side of the circle.

Tayg tried not to smile. "You are unfair to lovely Dolag," he called out, hoping to win a smile from the embarrassed lass. But she just hunched her shoulders and stood there. "She is fair and fine and bonny and true," he sang. "Unlike my own sister who is ever a shrew!" he finished with a flourish.

Raucous applause greeted his effort with back slaps from those near him, and hearty guffaws from all gathered around. Tayg glanced at the two women standing before him. One look at Dolag told him she had had enough of his attentions. One look at Catriona told him his jibes had hit home. Where Dolag was crimson and ducked her head as if to hide, Catriona stood, her fists on her shapely hips, her chin set and her skin flushed with anger.

"I have a fine idea," he said, still beating the drum, but looking Catriona straight in the eyes. "I'll sing a song we all know. You can all join in and give Sweet Dolag," he gave the lass his best "you're-a-rare-lass" look, "a respite from your ribbing."

This did win him a small, shy smile, which he answered with another grin and a wink. Once more the lass turned crimson. She was demure, to be sure, but too much. She was so meek he feared her own bairns would mistreat her. Tayg could not see himself wed to someone who would take such teasing not only to heart, but would not stand up for herself.

He sighed and launched into a well-known, slightly bawdy, song which, to his relief, the crowd eagerly joined in on. Catriona glared at him as she forced her way through the circle of Mackenzies and stormed from the hall.

C atriona stomped out of the crowded hall and into the cold night air. Clouds scudded across a pale sliver of moon as if in a hurry to be on their way. Which is what she should do. Be on her way. She paced along a well-worn path through the snow. That arrogant, irritating, exasperating bard! He had poked at her pride, prodded her temper, all the time knowing that if she had not held onto her tongue they would both be in deeper trouble than they cared to even contemplate. And then he had called her that most hated word: shrew.

Only the thought of forever being bound to that ruffian had given her the strength to keep silent. How dare he call her those things in front of these people! He was as bad as her brothers. As stupid as her father. As insufferable as . . . as . . . she couldn't think of anything as insufferable as His Bardship. If he *was* a bard, for he sang like a dying toad.

Catriona pulled her cloak close about her. She had reached the far end of the village so she turned and paced back toward the hall.

She was heartily sick of having the shrew moniker pinned to her. And 'twas somehow worse coming from him than from Broc, from whom she expected nothing better. She would have to get him back. Poke and prod him to the point of embarrassment in front of strangers . . . well, she had done a wee bit of that already. But he deserved more. So much more. 'Twas too bad she needed his help, else she'd leave him here to wink and grin like a fool at sweet silly Dolag who had not the wits to strike back when she was so mistreated. She'd best find some backbone for no one would wish to wed such a pathetic creature.

Of course Broc said no one but Dogface would marry her, but at least it wasn't because she was pathetic. Better to speak your mind loudly than to have no mind to speak of.

She turned to pace back to the far end of the village. She had not been able to strike back at Tayg's words as she wished lest she confirm the not-so-subtle hint he gave of her identity. But she would have her revenge.

There were the easy ways, of course. Dumping a bucket of water on him while he slept was always effective, though his clothing would be wet and they would be delayed from their trip. No, not that then.

If the snow was not so thick upon the ground she could gather dead, prickly thistles and place them in his bedding. She had gotten Calum several times with that one when she was little, but he had finally gotten wise and begun to check his bed *before* he climbed into it. Apparently there were certain parts of a man's body that did not take kindly to the prickly thistle. She smiled as she remembered the look of pained surprise mixed with grudging respect she had seen on Calum's face.

But the snow was too thick and the moonlight too pale to go gathering thistles. She could not sabotage Tayg's food, for she ate it, too. Dung in his shoes, snow in his bags? Nay, all would delay them and she would not allow Dogface, nor her family, to catch up to her until she had secured her future and the clan's with the king. There must be something . . .

As she turned to retrace her steps toward the hall, she

saw the door open and Tayg step out of the dimly-lit interior into the night. She slowed her steps, watching carefully as he moved toward her.

"Are you not cold?" he called to her.

"I am too angry to feel the cold," she said, though that odd warm chill washed over her with his words.

He had the audacity to chuckle. "You drew that upon yourself."

"By asking that you do your job?"

They met halfway between the hall and the end of the village, facing each other on the path. "By putting Sweet Dolag before the crowd like that. 'Twas not a kind thing to do."

Shame flashed through her, surprising her with its sharp twisting in her gut. 'Twas not a feeling she was overly familiar with, nor one she liked, and it angered her that he should make her feel it. "I have seen bards do such many times," she said, her voice purposely sharp.

"Perhaps, but I do not know of any bard who would pick such a timid lass to put before a crowd."

The disappointment in his voice grated on her, raising her irritation with him even further. "But did you not need to see her strengths and weaknesses so that you may inform the king of her qualities? Did you not need to see that she is unsuitable for him?"

"Him?" He looked down at her as if she were a recalcitrant wean. "Do you think she is a rival in your plans for poor Tayg of Culrain? 'Twas not necessary to embarrass her in order to find out her true character, Catriona of Assynt." His tone cut her, shaming her again. "She did that just fine on her own while we ate. It did not need your pointing out her faults for all to witness. I have no doubt that all here know of her frailties and of her strengths."

"Strengths? She has no strengths. She is all aflutter over a little teasing. She is without sufficient backbone to even stand up for herself—"

"Then perhaps you should have done it for her."

"Me? I do not owe her anything!"

He shook his head and said quietly, "Aye, you do not owe anything to anyone, do you? You are the most selfish person I have ever met."

"I . . . why should . . ." She glared at him. He did not know her, did not understand her. How dare he judge her so harshly. "'Tis not true. I care only for my clan."

He shook his head and gave a half-laugh. "Nay, you care only for yourself and your troubles. You do not have half the dignity of that timid little sparrow inside." With that he turned and strode back toward the hall.

Catriona couldn't believe what he had said. Selfish? And how much dignity could Dolag have when she allowed her own clan to tease her so with nary a retort? Determined to strike back at him, determined to make him feel the same gut-twisting she endured at his words, she launched herself after him, grabbing him by the arm and forcing him to face her.

"I don't know where you get the nerve to speak to me this way. 'Twould only take a word from me and you would be stuck with me for the rest of your life!"

"Aye, lass, and you would be stuck with me," he said, his voice low, his warm breath washing over her face. "Can you say which is a worse fate?"

Catriona's heart was beating fast and she felt strangely light-headed, almost as if she stood outside herself watching these strangers argue as they stepped nearer and nearer to each other. She struggled to hold fast to her anger for another deeper, darker emotion was threatening to sweep over her. She swallowed. "'Tis easy. I would never spend my life with you." She struggled to think of the one thing that would drive him away from her. "I must wed a better man than you," she hissed.

He didn't even have the good manners to flinch. Instead he cocked his head and pursed his full lips as if she were a puzzling child. "So you say. How do you know another man is any better than I?" His voice was quiet now, yet there was something dangerous about it.

"Anyone would be better than you."

"Even Dogface MacDonell?"

She tried to say aye, but she could not utter that large a lie, even to make her point.

"So there is at least one man I am better than. You have a fine sense of gratitude toward someone who saved you from freezing to death, found you a hot meal to warm your belly and a place by the fire to rest your head this night." He grabbed her by the shoulders, looked her in the eye, then lowered his gaze to her mouth. Catriona's breath hitched at the intensity, the concentration, in his cinnamon eyes.

"We are lucky they are not making us sleep in the snow after that performance in there," he said, as if to himself.

"'Twas you who called her a p—"

Before she could finish the word, something snapped in his eyes and Tayg leaned in and covered her lips with his own.

Catriona gasped but was immediately mesmerized by the sensations his touch sent racing through her. He took advantage of her hesitation and pressed his lips to hers again, softly yet firmly. Catriona felt a thrill run through her, that same warm chill she had experienced when he had helped her hide her hair. Intrigued, she let him continue the kiss. Standing perfectly still she let her eyes drift shut so she could better concentrate on the surprising sensations that were coursing through her. His lips were warm, gentle as they played over hers. She rested her hands on his arms and stepped a bit closer, giving in to her instincts.

•　•　•

Tayg *pulled back and looked into her midnight eyes.* How could such sharp words come from such a sweet mouth? His gaze moved from her surprised eyes to her full lips and, God help him, he kissed her again.

This time, however, she leaned into him. He moved his hands to her face and tilted her head to get better access to that surprising sweetness. He plundered, kissing and nibbling, letting his pent-up frustration guide his actions instead of his head. He needed more, wanted . . .

Tayg coaxed open her mouth, then taught her the delights of the deeper, more intimate kiss. He pulled her against him, crushing her soft breasts into his chest. A small moan escaped her and he smiled against her lips.

"See, lass," he said, nibbling first on the corners of her mouth, then moving to that tender spot below her ear, "there are better tasks for a tongue than slicing away at a man's pride."

Catriona went from warm and pliable to cold and stiff in a heartbeat. She shoved him hard and he stumbled backwards. Tayg wished he was the one who had held his tongue this time.

"If you ever try such a thing again," she said, poking him in the chest with one sharp finger and glaring up at him, her eyes narrowed and her temper clear, "I'll slice more than your pride." She shoved him again then swept past him and into the hall.

Tayg stood there, trying to figure out what had just happened. What was he thinking, kissing her? Was he daft? He no more wanted that woman than he wanted Dolag. Then he laughed at himself, for certain parts of him were quite certain he did want her.

He took a deep breath and tried to calm his blood. She was the oddest mix of prickly pride and soft, sensuous woman when she allowed herself to be. The memory of her molding herself to him, that small sweet moan escaping her dewy lips. Och! If he continued like this, he'd have to sit himself down in the snow before he could return to the hall.

He looked up at the sky, the stars filling the heavens now that the clouds were nearly gone. Good, perhaps tomorrow would be a good day for traveling. If only he could leave Catriona here—but that was impossible. He was just going to have to find some way to stop this unwanted attraction he felt before he ceased thinking altogether and did something really stupid.

Tayg rolled over and stared into the dying fire. Each time he had drifted off to sleep he'd dreamed of the kisses he had shared with Cat. Waking each time with a start when the lass he kissed turned from a bonny young woman into a wild cat-a-mountain who flayed his skin with its claws. 'Twas an image he should hold close for she was as dangerous to him as any of the hungry cats that roamed the Highlands.

He glanced over at the sleeping subject of his troubled night. She slept, oblivious to the problems swirling all around her. He sat up, adjusted his plaid and belted it tightly about him. If he could keep the terror of his dream in his mind he felt sure he would not be tempted to kiss those amazingly sweet, soft lips . . . no, he must not let his mind wander to that again. She was as feral and dangerous as any cat and he would not forget it again.

He rose from his pallet and slipped away from the sleeping Cat. Outside the air was cold and misted with a heavy fog, the pale grey light of winter's late dawn barely piercing the billowy stuff. He looked about for a privy but could not see far in the fog. He shrugged and headed for the nearby wood. A privy was not a necessity.

He trudged between the hall and a cottage and into the wood. Just as he was about to slip back out of the cover of the forest, he heard voices and the muffled sound of horses in the snow cover. His scalp tingled, a feeling of danger long experience had taught him to heed. He circled behind the cottage and crept along the far side until he reached the front that faced the trail he and Cat had arrived on last night.

The fog was still thick, and the voices were muffled. He waited.

"Good day to you!" a deep voice yelled as if from beneath a thick blanket. "Are you not up and about yet?"

There was something oddly familiar in the voice—not the voice itself, but rather the cadence or perhaps the demanding inflection as if the speaker expected . . .

Tayg froze.

"Aye, we are out and about this morn." Farlan's voice drifted to him from somewhere in the direction of the newcomers. "What would *you* be wanting in Fionn?" His voice did not hold the welcome he had shown Tayg and Cat the night before. Today he sounded wary of the newcomers.

"We search for a lass, a shrew-mouthed lass you should not wish upon your worst enemy. She is here and we come to relieve you of the burden of her company."

The tingling in Tayg's scalp spread down his backbone. He knew without a doubt that the newcomer was none other than Cat's brother.

Broc MacLeod had found them.

chapter 6

Tayg crept closer, keeping to the deeper shadows in the vague fog-shrouded dawn. No doubt Broc had tracked them through the snow. It took precious little skill to follow a sole rut in the fresh snow. But what did the man know? Tayg moved closer to the front of the cottage and peered carefully around the corner.

The thick fog made details hazy, but 'twas clear that Farlan stood facing the newcomer . . . newcomers, Tayg corrected, for there were at least three horses. The fog parted unexpectedly and Tayg swallowed an oath. He pulled back behind the corner of the cottage, but could still hear the conversation.

"And why would you be chasing a lass through this weather? Has she stolen your manhood, perhaps?" Farlan's voice had an odd edge to it.

"'Tis none of your concern, auld man. I am Broc MacLeod of Assynt—"

"I ken well who you are, lad, so do not take that tone

with me or I'll drop your wee arse over yon cliff. Trouble
licks your heels like a loyal dog and 'tis a rare man in the
Highlands that does not ken it."

There was a moment of silence and Tayg could imagine
the bluster that was going on between the two Highlanders.

"We have followed her trail through the snow. It led us
here. We will have the lass back."

"We have no—how did you describe her?—*shrew-
mouthed* lasses here. The lasses of Fionn are sweet-
tempered as clearly your lass is not."

"She is not mine."

"Then why do you track her?"

There was more silence, then Broc cleared his throat.
"She is my sister, betrothed to our ally. I have sworn to
bring her back for her wedding. Where is she?"

"I told you. There is no lass here by that description."

"Then who made the trail to this shite-hole?" Broc was
clearly losing any patience he might have started with.

"The bard did," a small voice piped up.

"Alasdair!" Farlan's voice was stern, reminding Tayg of
his own father's voice when Tayg had raised his ire. "Get
you back to your mother's skirts and leave this to your el-
ders."

He winced in sympathy with the lad. Though he could
not see him, he was certain there was a slump to his
shoulders and an anger simmering at his sharp dismissal.

"There is a bard here?" another voice asked, masculine,
but not as deep as Broc's.

"I see not what a bard has to do with your run-away
lass."

"There was some sign that two people traveled the trail
we followed," a third voice said. "Was there a woman
with this bard?"

There was a long silence and Tayg chanced another
look. The fog had closed up around the band of men again

but he could still make out the form of Farlan standing there, his thick arms crossed over his barrel chest. His shoulder-length brown hair was wild about his head and though the fog sought to hide him from Tayg's view, 'twas clear Farlan glared at the men in front of him.

At last he said, "Aye, there is a woman with him; his own sister."

"How do you ken she is his sister?"

"'Tis easy enough to tell. He introduced her. He baited her. She baited him—but she had no shrew-mouth. The bard bested her easily enough, as any older brother should. Aye, they are brother and sister, no doubt to my mind."

Broc snorted, sending the fog swirling about him. "Triona has plenty of experience being bested by an older brother. 'Twould be an easy part for her to play. I shall see this lass for myself," he said. "Come lads. If Farlan will not show us where to look we shall have to find her ourselves."

Tayg was certain Farlan would not allow a search, but he took no chances. He sprinted around the backside of the cottage and dashed to the hall.

Cat was the link between Dogface MacDonell and the brothers MacLeod. As long as Tayg controlled her fate there was a chance the plot against the king would fail. He could not see either clan trusting the other without such a link between them. Even if he did not make it to the king in time to warn him, keeping Cat from marriage to the MacDonell chief might be enough to fray the tempers of the conspirators and stop them.

He laughed to himself. 'Twas feeble reasoning, but he would not look at other, more personal reasons, for keeping her with him.

Tayg slipped through the doorway and made his way down the hall to where Cat still slept near the fire. He nudged her with a hand on her shoulder. "Wake up," Tayg whispered as she tried to shrug off his hand. "Your brother is here."

Catriona's eyes popped open. "What?"

"Broc. He is here, asking for you, and others with him."

She sat up, her eyes wide, with fear skittering through them. "I will not go with him!"

"Wheesht! I ken that. Come," Tayg said, as he gathered his own belongings. "We must away, quickly and quietly."

"But why . . ."

"Do not ask questions. Unless you wish me to reconsider my plan and leave you here to face him alone?"

"I shall ask any question I deem—"

"Ask later. Leave now. Broc will be here any moment."

She glared at him, but quickly stood and pulled her cloak about her, rolled her blankets and tucked them under her arm. "I am ready."

Tayg was surprised that she gave in so quickly. Broc must be formidable indeed.

"There is only the one door which faces the village, but there is a thick fog to cover our passing. Be very quiet, for sound is unpredictable in such weather."

He grabbed her hand and she followed him without another word. Tayg told himself he held her hand only to make sure she did not get lost in the fog, or so that he could quiet her with a squeeze if necessary. But he also knew that the grudging trust she showed increased the warmth of her touch and pleased him to no end.

They left the warm confines of the hall and moved quickly along the edge of the building to the horse byre. Tayg was grateful so many feet had packed down the path between the buildings so their footsteps would not show. They slipped inside and Tayg had his horse saddled and their goods loaded in no time. He led the animal out of the stable, vaulted into the saddle and held his hand out to Cat.

"Get on," he whispered.

She hesitated when angry voices wafted through the fog as if ghosts argued. Whether Farlan delayed Broc and his men for the purpose of letting them escape or simply because he did not like the man mattered not at all to Tayg. Once all was settled with the king, Tayg would have to send his thanks to Farlan. But still Cat stood, transfixed by the voices. Nothing would be settled if the lass would not climb up.

"Do you wish to be taken back to Dogface trussed up like a gutted deer?"

She gasped and whipped her head around to look him in the eye. Fear made her eyes bleak and Tayg found himself wishing to reassure her. Before he could say anything she took his hand and scrambled up behind the saddle. As quietly as he could, Tayg guided the horse out of the village.

C atriona looked back over her shoulder, afraid they would be spotted at any moment and Tayg's harsh words would become a reality. Thankfully the fog remained, obscuring all but the faintest dark outline of the hall.

"Enough! Where is she?" It was Broc's voice. Thank all the saints that the bard had discovered Broc before Broc had discovered . . . The fog parted for a moment. Catriona shrank against Tayg's sturdy back but could not look away.

'Twas not just Broc who had come after her, but all her brothers! She could not take her eyes from them, but they thankfully had their backs to her. She blinked, willing the fog to cover their escape once more. Suddenly Ailig, her youngest brother, glanced over his shoulder. He seemed to look directly at her, but then he turned away again just as the fog finally obeyed her heartfelt command. She listened for Ailig's voice, for the sound of pursuers. But there was none.

They made the cover of the forest and Tayg continued into its dark depths. Catriona noticed that little snow had made it to the ground through the thick pines and the close-growing, leafless birches. Their tracks would not be so easily followed here.

Tayg nudged the horse to a swifter gait and they rode in silence save for the pounding of the horse's hoofs. When they were well away from the village, he allowed the horse to slow and finally to stop.

Catriona needed to walk, needed to rid herself of the nervous energy that had accompanied her sudden awakening and their swift departure.

"Let me down," she said.

Tayg let her slide down, then followed her. "So you heard him?" he asked.

"Aye, though 'twas more than just Broc."

Tayg's eyebrows rose and Catriona nodded.

"'Twas all of them." She did not tell of Ailig's glance. Obviously he had not noticed them so there was no reason to disturb the bard with the news.

"They know you are with me," Tayg said.

"How?"

"I heard them talking to Farlan. They know I arrived with a lass, though Farlan assured them you were my true sister. Broc did not believe him, thus the argument."

"So, they suspect but they do not know for sure." She paced the trail they had been following. "We must find a place to hide. They are not likely to give up just because we have eluded discovery this time."

"They will have a bit of scouting to do, for there were few clear tracks to follow in the village and now we lead them on a merry chase." He grinned at her. "We will continue this way for a while, then circle round to our true path."

Catriona looked about her. "What?"

"This way," he said, pointing in the direction they had been traveling, "lies north. Our path to the king lies south along the river."

Catriona's eyebrows drew down over her eyes. "Why are you doing this?"

Tayg pulled a carrot from a bag and fed it to the horse. "He is tired." He grabbed the reins in one hand and her hand in the other and led them down the track.

"Why, bard?"

He continued, practically dragging her along. Catriona trotted to keep up.

"Tayg?" she said, hoping his given name would tease him into speech.

He looked at her. "You wished to see the king. Perhaps I am daft, but I will see you to him." He cocked a grin at her and broke into a run before Catriona could press him further.

Eventually Tayg turned aside onto a deer trail and Catriona dropped back to follow him and the horse. She was tired and desperately needed to rest her aching feet.

She followed Tayg and the horse as they descended into a deep ravine along a faint trail. She was grateful Tayg had helped her this morning, though she still did not understand why he had done it. It seemed the perfect opportunity for him to rid himself of her.

She thought back to when he had awakened her. Why hadn't he just left her there? He'd made it clear he did not wish to travel with her. He'd made it clear she was not a welcome partner. So why had he helped her when 'twas clearly to his benefit to leave her there to face her wretched brothers alone? It made no sense.

"We'll stop below for a rest and a bit of food," Tayg said over his shoulder to her.

Her stomach growled and she realized she was hungry and thirsty. They had not eaten, had not stopped, had barely spoken since they had escaped from the village. He'd stopped her questions, bullied her out of the village and told her she could ask questions later. Well it was later now, and she would have some answers. She would know what he was up to, for he was surely up to something.

She glowered at the broad back before her. His glossy brown hair shown in the filtered sunlight. His plaid flapped back and forth, sweeping his well-formed trews-covered legs in time with his step. But the horse was between them.

She sped up, protecting her face from low branches as she slipped past the horse and made her way to Tayg's side.

"Why did you help me?" she demanded. "You wanted to take me back to my brothers from the start. Why didn't you leave me to them now?"

He said nothing, staring straight ahead.

"Bard!" She smacked his arm with her fist to get his attention. "Why would you do such a daft thing?"

He glanced at her, but she could read nothing in his expression. He shrugged and lengthened his stride. Catriona had to jog to keep up with him or chance being overrun by the horse. The trail pitched suddenly downward and she stepped quickly to the side, letting the horse block her from the object of her rising ire. She followed more slowly, picking her way down the icy slope carefully. She would have an answer. She had too much experience with brothers and their schemes not to recognize the signs. She also had plenty of experience getting her answers from them. Tayg would be no different. 'Twould only require persistence.

A burn came into view and Tayg bounded the last few feet to its edge, dropping the reins as he went. He knelt by the edge of the water and dipped his face to it. Sitting back on his heels he turned and glanced at her, his eyes dark and serious.

"Come and drink."

But Catriona was unable to move. All her anger and frustration drained from her as she watched the glistening droplets that clung to his lips. Every sensation that had coursed through her last night when he kissed her careened through her again, stealing her breath and making her feel uncomfortably warm despite the chill in the December air.

"Cat? Are you not thirsty?"

She nodded and forced her feet to move, though she did not trust her voice. The urgency to get away this morning had pushed the memory from her mind—and her body—which now remembered it vividly! Never before had she felt the liquid heat that had coursed through her. Never before had she had the kind of disturbing, though not distressing, dreams she had experienced last night.

Part of her wanted to experience that wonderful, dazed feeling again, but a sterner part of her said it would be dangerous. Too dangerous to allow that kind of feeling out. Never before had she been so willing to give up control of herself and just be. 'Twould not be prudent to allow herself to fall into that situation again. 'Twas pure folly, but it had been unlike any folly she had ever known before.

She knelt beside him at the burn and slaked her thirst, but she did not allow herself to look at him.

H ours later Tayg glanced up at the darkening sky. They needed to find a place to pass the night. They had left the caves behind and the forest offered little in the way of true shelter from the elements. At least the sky was mostly clear. If it didn't snow they would be fine under the open sky. If it did, well, they would manage that if they had to.

A bit of cover would be in order, however, just in case they didn't throw the brothers off as much as he hoped.

Tayg spied a copse of young pine trees, ringed by evergreen shrubbery with long, densely covered branches. He veered off the trail towards it.

"Where are you going?" Catriona asked.

He looked back at her. She stood in the trail, fists on her hips, her mouth drawn down into a most unbecoming frown. She was angry that he would not answer her questions, but he did not know how to answer them. The truth could not be told, even the part he was sure of. He did not wish to get tangled up in lies, so the only thing to do was to avoid answering. Of course the look on her face back at the burn had stopped not only her questions but very nearly his heart. He could have sworn the look was desire, bare and bold. Perhaps it had been, for it reminded him of the look on her face when he had foolishly kissed her the night before. Yet she had quickly mastered that softness.

"We will stop for the night here," he said, then turned back to the copse.

"Where?" she shouted after him.

Tayg kept going, leaving the horse at the edge and pushing his way into the dense bushes. Once beneath the canopy of spreading branches he discovered exactly what he had hoped was there—a thick cushion of pine straw in a small cleared space. 'Twas a spot the deer most likely used, and while it was not exactly a roof over their heads, it was big enough for the three of them. It would provide cover from the trail and would keep most snow off of them if the weather changed.

"Bard?" Her voice came from outside the copse and carried a slight wobble as if she were afraid. "Bard? Tayg?"

He smiled to himself. Yes, they had cover from the trail. Apparently she couldn't see him even from a few feet away.

"Tayg!" A note of panic had invaded her voice.

He stepped forward and stuck his hand through the prickly, aromatic foliage.

"Oh!"

She was close. He crooked his finger, beckoning her within. He drew his hand back and parted the branches just enough so he could peer out at her.

" 'Tis cozy in here, and sheltered from the trail. We dare not make a fire, in case . . ."

"Aye, in case Broc and the sheep were not fooled by your wee trick."

He winced at her tone, more than at the words. "Would you have preferred I left you there to wait for your brothers to find you?" He grabbed the horse's reins and forced him to pass through the bushes. The branches snapped back into place and Tayg was rewarded with her exaggerated huff.

He led the horse to one side and looped the reins over a branch. He lifted the bags from the saddle and dropped them in the middle of the circle, wincing when the drum boomed as the other bags fell on top of it.

" 'Tis a fine bard you'll make if you do not have an instrument to play."

He glanced back to find her standing inside the shelter with her arms crossed. She had one raven-colored eyebrow raised.

"I am tired. 'Twas a slip. I'm sure the drum is fine." Just to prove his disguise he rearranged the bags and slipped the drum free. He ran his hands over the tautly stretched skin as if he knew what he was looking for. There were no obvious holes in it. He could only hope there was not some less obvious problem. Shrugging, he tucked it back into its protective bag.

Catriona still stood, arms crossed, combat in her face. He rose.

"What plagues you, lass?" he asked as he freed the horse from its saddle.

"Me? I have no troubles, other than that I am traveling with a daft man who will not explain himself."

"I do not have to explain myself to you."

Catriona stalked over to him and stuck a finger in his chest, her eyes blazing. "Aye, you do. Why did you not take advantage of the situation and rid yourself of me?"

The air crackled between them as they stared at each other, she waiting for his answer, he trying to figure out what answer to give. He saw temper flare in her eyes, and a tiny tremble at the edge of her mouth that betrayed her fear. But fear of what? The lass did not seem to fear much of anything. Him, least of all. He reached forward and ran the backs of his fingers over her soft cheek. The temper faded and something deeper rose in her gaze.

"I think it was because of this," he said, dipping his mouth quickly to hers.

Sparks flew through him and he recognized the truth of his words. Despite her sharp tongue, her kiss was liquid fire, burning through his veins, sweeping reason from his mind.

Cat swayed almost imperceptibly towards him, then quickly seemed to remember herself. She stepped back, her hand to her lips, her eyes wide.

"Do not ever do that again," she said, though he saw her chin tremble, and knew well the fire that burned in her eyes, for it burned just as brightly in his belly. She might not want his kisses, but she burned just as much as he did from them.

He grinned at her and gave a little bow. "As you command, my high-and-mighty lady."

"I am not, nor will I ever be, lady to a bard. Neither will I play your harlot while we travel to the king."

"You are no harlot, only a difficult, ungrateful woman. Tayg the Bard will not touch you again, of that you can be sure." As long as he could control his impulses. What had come over him? He did not wish to entangle himself any further with this woman, yet here he had succumbed again to the siren call of her lips. Thank goodness she had regained control of her senses before he had done something truly daft. He gave himself a shake and returned his attention to the horse.

"Make yourself useful," he said, sounding like Robbie when facing a battle. 'Twas the only way to hide his rising frustration from the disturbing lass. "Find some water for us, then we'll sup. 'Twill be dark very soon." When he realized that he had not heard her stir, he glanced over his shoulder. She stood there, back straight, nose in the air and fury in her eyes.

"What?" he asked.

"I do not take orders like some serving wench."

He rose and faced her, his own temper rising to match his frustration. "Indeed, you do not." He took a deep breath and tried to remember she was a lass, not a soldier from the army. "I beg your forgiveness. I have been too long in the company of soldiers." Surprise shown in her eyes and he realized he had slipped in his persona again. "'Tis where I learned the battle songs," he said. To distract her from his words, he flashed his never-fail grin at her and bowed low. "I will make beds for us. Will you fetch some water?"

He leaned down and hooked the strap of his water skin with his fingers, swinging it to her in one smooth motion. She snatched it from the air without ever taking her eyes from his.

"I do not know what you are up to bard, but do not think you can fool me with your words."

"If you would rather make our camp I shall be happy to fetch the water." He waited for her to decide.

After what seemed hours she finally let out a growl and a muttered oath, then turned and ducked under the shelter-

ing branches of their hideaway. Tayg turned back to his
work, still grinning. She was as prickly as a gorse bush,
but there was something underneath that difficult exterior
that was in need of a bit of tending. Every once in a
while—like when he kissed her—her softer side would reveal itself. Still, she reminded him of the cat-a-mountain
in his dream: soft fur, sharp bite. 'Twas one good thing
about kissing Cat; she could not offer biting comments
when her mouth was so engaged.

He realized suddenly that he no longer thought of her
or called her by her given name. Nay, she was Cat to him,
and the name fit her well, claws and all. Tayg smiled
again and returned to his work.

They passed an uneventful evening, with episodes of
silence followed by moments of glaring, followed by
Cat's studied disinterest. When they finally lay down on
their separate pallets, Tayg watched her rigid back, limned
by the faint moonlight, until, after a long while, she relaxed and her breathing became slow and even. He was
going to have to do something about his growing attraction to her, and soon. It made no sense that he should be
attracted to her. She was trouble and he had enough of
that in his life.

He flopped over on his other side so he could not see
the gentle slope of Catriona's hip in the wan moonlight.
Nay, he would not allow himself to succumb to the temp-
tation of her lips again. No matter what else happened, he
knew this was not a woman he wished to wed, and kissing
would lead to other, more intimate acts. Then, when she
found out his true identity, she could use that shared intimacy to solve her problem. She had heard the songs and
tales. According to his mum, every lass who had ever
heard them wanted him for a husband. She was no differ-

ent. She was trouble, and he had to get her to the king. Quickly.

He flopped back the other way, but squeezed his eyes shut so he would not see her ebon hair. Behind his lids her image floated, soft, beckoning him. Tayg groaned and struggled to remember his duty.

chapter 7

Tayg awoke with a start. For a moment he didn't know where he was, then slowly he focused on the snow-flecked greenery over his head and the warm, softly snoring woman nestled in his arms. He rubbed his cheek against her hair and inhaled the scent of sleepy Cat . . .

Cat? In his arms!

Catriona slept, her softly rounded bottom nestled into his lap, her stomach slowly rising and falling under his hand. He jerked his hand away and rolled away from her onto his back.

Holy Mother of God. What had he done? What had *they* done? The predawn sky seemed to stare at him through the dark circle of foliage as if watching him.

Quickly he pieced the night together: they had kissed, eaten a cold meal, he had suffered her glares and ill-temper, then they had gone to sleep, on their own pallets of bracken and blankets. He had done nothing. They had gone to sleep separately. He raised his head and looked around. She had moved from her place, near but separate from him, to his side.

Tayg raised up on his elbows and looked over at the perfect profile of her pale face. The traveling was hard on her, showing in the bruised-looking shadows under her eyes. Her hair, which had escaped its ugly covering and its tight braid, lay about her like an ebony pool. He turned towards her and lifted a heavy, silky lock, letting it slide through his fingers.

She was beautiful. Sleep softened her features from their usual belligerent form to one of vulnerable innocence. 'Twas an odd thing to consider but the truth of it struck him hard in the belly. An unfamiliar urge to protect her warmed and alarmed him.

She stirred and opened her eyes.

Tayg rose as casually as he could manage, though the blanket that tangled about his feet made it difficult. "Good morn," he said.

"Good—" Catriona sat up, the same glare glittering in her eyes that had been there the previous evening. "What do you think you were doing?"

"I was sleeping. And you?" He pointedly looked to where she had started the night, well away from where she had ended it.

"What are you saying?"

"I'm saying naught. But 'twould appear that you were cold in the night and sought a wee bit of shared warmth." Tayg was irritated at her attitude. She spluttered, but simply rose and left their cozy thicket, crashing through the woods beyond.

His skin itched when he remembered the feel of her soft curves nestled up against him. 'Twasn't the first time a lass had climbed into his bed in the night. Though usually the outcome was more pleasurable than this morning's. Hastily he released the twisted and tangled plaid from the belt that held it about him. He spread the plaid on the ground and began to regather the pleats, distracting himself by folding the heavy material just so. When it was pleated to his satisfaction he slid his wide leather belt under the garment, laid down atop the plaid and buckled it about him again. Lastly he rose, adjusted the pleating about his hips and drew the loose ends up to fasten them at his shoulder with the large silver brooch that had belonged to his brother. That done, his mind quickly returned to the lass crashing about outside their shelter.

Irritation that she should be so offended at the idea of snuggling up with him surged through him. Most lasses were quite happy to receive his attention, but this one . . . she was soft and greedy when he kissed her, but then she would pull the mantel of her temper over her and prove her right to the shrew moniker. And yet, despite her sharp tongue, he could not wrench his mind away from the feel of her in his arms, the woad blue of her eyes when they went liquid with desire, for he had seen desire written on her face as clearly as he saw disdain there.

What was he to do about this growing attraction between them? It would not do to allow it to continue. She did not want him—except if she knew his true identity—and he most certainly did not want her. She was bonny, but her mouth was as prickly as a thistle . . . well, her words were prickly, her mouth, he remembered, was soft and sweet and—

He had to do something and he had to do it quickly. Maybe she would fall down a ravine and drown in a burn. Nay, it would solve his immediate problem but he'd never be able to live with himself if he let that happen. Not to mention he wouldn't have a hostage for the king.

The king. He must keep his duty sharply in his mind. Aye, if they traveled hard they would arrive at Dingwall Castle in time to warn the king and they would be too exhausted to indulge this passing unwanted attraction. And if he kept her angry, then her words would also serve to keep him focused on her faults instead of on her attributes. His mind drifted to her many soft attributes.

Cat's crashing drew closer, jarring Tayg back to his problem. He looked up through the thick evergreen branches and noticed that it was nearly full light. They had wasted precious time cuddled up like two bear cubs. His mind veered to other, more interesting ways they could have warmed themselves. He struggled to remember the king, the plot, the snow—anything but her.

He could not allow such thoughts where Catriona the Shrew was concerned. Kisses had been dangerous enough. But now that he had the feel of her, he was in even greater peril. Giving her any hint of her growing power over him would only land him in more trouble. Something had to be done. It had to be done now.

He gathered up their blankets, shoving them into a leather sack. He grabbed the water skin and drank the last of it, swishing it around to relieve the sour taste in his mouth. Finally he pulled the last of the oat cakes and what was left of the dried venison out of the nearly empty food sack and set it out for their morning meal. When he returned from a brief trip into the wood he found the object of his tangled thoughts quietly breaking her fast.

"We need to fill the water skin again," he said.

She nodded, but did not look at him.

"We must away now. Precious daylight is being wasted and we must hurry your cause to the king's side.

This time she did look at him. "Aye."

Tayg paced the small space, uncomfortably aware of her. "Your brothers, 'twill not be long before they find our trail again."

"You led them astray. We have need to hurry, but we are safe from them."

He stared at her. "Do not play the stupid wench with me. They followed you as far as Fionn. They suspect that you are with me. How long do you think it will take them to realize we did not continue in our first direction? How long before they find us, alone, together?"

"We will have to stay ahead of them, then." She shrugged and finished her oat cake with dainty little nibbles that nearly distracted Tayg from his purpose.

He pushed his fingers through his tangled hair, forcing his mind away from her pale, perfect skin and back to the need to escape her company while his duty to the king held him in this purgatory. "They are on horses. Do you truly think we will outpace them when we must share but one?"

She looked at him, chewing her venison, but said nothing.

Confounding, irritating, beautiful, irritating, he reminded himself, woman. He was going to have to be blunt to get a reaction from her, and he desperately needed a reaction from her.

"What about this morn?" Ah, that made her blush and avert her eyes, but still she did not rise to his baiting. "Do you plan to sleep with me each night? For if you do, we best change our story. 'Twould not be seemly for a brother and a sister of our advanced ages to sleep together so."

"'Twill not happen again," she said.

He watched as she pressed her lips together until they became a thin line. Her back was straight and she had raised her chin just a fraction of an inch. She was nearly there. 'Twould take only another nudge or two and the shrew would appear, insuring his safety—at least his safety from his own daft impulses.

He stepped close to her, his legs nearly touching her knees. He reached down and lifted her chin so she had to look up at him while he leered down at her, doing his best to discomfit her, to draw forth the shrew. He desperately needed to see that difficult lass and not the warm woman who had slept in his arms.

"Ah, but can you guarantee that, lass?" He wanted to

see her as tumbled topsy-turvy by this situation as he was, wanted her to react as he knew she would, saving him from his own folly. "For I cannot guarantee that I can be such a gentleman should you linger in my bed again."

"I did not—" She burst to her feet, her eyes narrowed, her food forgotten. Nearly nose to nose with him she stared into his eyes. "I would never linger in the bed of a lowborn bard who cannot even sing a proper ballad, nor play a simple drum. I would never sully myself with such as you!" Her hands were fisted at her hips and her voice rose with each word, sharper, shriller.

Tayg refrained from grinning at her for he desperately did not wish to spoil her mood. This was exactly what he wanted: the shrew in all her glory. He stepped back, needing the distance more than he needed to maintain his antagonistic posture, and bowed low.

"I would not ask you to sully your precious reputation with such as I—what little reputation you still have." He waited a heartbeat to let his jab sink in, then rose from his bow and cocked an eyebrow at her, daring her, begging her, to sally forth with another diatribe against him.

"My reputation is—"

"In shambles," he finished for her. "We have been seen traveling together and at least your brothers suspect the truth. What husband will the king be able to give you when that is known?"

She took a deep breath and for a moment he thought he saw fear in her eyes, though it was quickly replaced with the familiar hard determination.

"My brothers only suspect. They know nothing for sure. As brother and sister we are perfectly proper traveling together. Once I explain my plight to the king, all will be well and no one need ever know we traveled together."

"You would have the world work as you will it, though it seldom goes with your or anyone else's plans."

She glared up at him. "I decide my fate, no one else."

"Very well. Then decide your fate for this day. The sun is well up and we have wasted precious daylight. We should be away."

She watched him for a moment, then scooped up the water skins and once more disappeared through the green walls of the copse.

Tayg watched her go. He had successfully roused the shrew, bringing a sparkle to her eyes and a flush to her cheeks.

Unfortunately, it had not had the desired effect upon him.

*C*atriona led the way back to the trail, her thoughts swirling like storm clouds surging on the wind. The man had deliberately baited her. She was sure of it, for hadn't her brothers, especially Broc, done so all her life? But why? He had provoked her before but never had she felt he had done so on purpose. He had pushed her to keep up, questioned her about things she'd rather not speak of, teased her, but not with the purpose of raising her temper, though he frequently had. This was different, and she wanted to know what he was up to. One thing she knew about men, when they were up to something it was best to find out what they planned so you could defend yourself.

They reached the trail they had traveled the previous day, their tracks all too clear in the undisturbed snow. She struck out in the same direction they had been traveling, secretly pleased that she had known which way to go without his help. She struggled along a few strides, breaking the path through the knee-high crusted-over snow when Tayg strode past and took over the lead once more.

It was ever so in her life, always trailing along behind some male. At least her brothers had a legitimate claim to going first as they were all older than she, if you could call that a claim. But Tayg, he had no reason to treat her like she was some ridiculous wean, unable even to find her way along a clear trail. And he had the audacity to suggest she had slept—not with, maybe against—him on purpose, indeed, that she had "lingered" in his bed. As if she would do such a daft thing. Of course it had been awfully cozy, snuggled up against . . . no, 'twas a daft thing to do and 'twould not happen again.

She was set to find a suitable husband, Tayg of Culrain or another if the king so wished. Someone who would keep the clan from Dogface's grip despite her brothers' plans. But all that would be for naught, as Tayg had so sweetly pointed out, if she was ever found in such a position with the bard.

The bard. Hmph. If he was a bard, she was the Maid of Norway. Never had a bard treated an instrument with such disregard as this one did. She watched the drum bag bang against another sack at the horse's side. Last night he had dropped things upon it. Nay, he was no bard.

She remembered his performance in the village hall at Fionn. He was a fine storyteller, but he knew less than she did about singing or playing. And that pitiful song he had made up about poor Sweet Dolag.

"You know you cannot sing a note," she said, tired of arguing only with herself.

He glanced back at her. "I suppose you could do better?"

"A squealing piglet could do better."

"Ah, I'm less than some wee swine now?"

"Aye. That you are."

"What have I done that's got your tongue wagging again?" She could swear she heard a smile in his voice. He was definitely up to something.

She ran to catch up with him, grabbing his sleeve and stopping him. "What have you done? You forced me to act your sister—"

"I did not force."

"Then you embarrassed me, calling me names in front of the entire village of Fionn." Her voice rose with each point.

"And you had naught to do with that situation?" he asked, his eyebrows raised and his mouth drawn into a line, though the corners seemed to tremble slightly, as if he struggled to keep them under control. "You take no responsibility when 'twas you that pulled the lass before the crowd and left me no choice but to sing to her?"

"I take responsibility when it is mine to take. You had no need to include me in your ridiculous excuse for a song. That debacle was entirely your fault." She stabbed him in the chest with her finger to emphasize her point. "You are just like all the other men in my life—"

"Do not lump me in your life. I am but a reluctant victim of your scheming."

"Aye, a reluctant something, but not a bard."

"Ah, we're back to that, are we?"

"We're back to that. What are you really? You cannot sing better than any average Highlander. You cannot play even half as well as you sing. So what are you? A spy for the king, come to the Highlands to see if we are behaving ourselves? A convict escaped from Edinburgh's gaol? Maybe some earl's son off on a lark before winter sets in good?"

Tayg's face went as white as the snow that surrounded them, but she was not sure which of her possible explanations had hit home.

"Any of those would be better than what you really are," he said, his voice tightly controlled. "A spoiled wee lass, too hardheaded to see her own folly."

"I am a grown woman, bard. And the only folly I see is in continuing to travel with you." Catriona swung away from him and headed down the trail.

Tayg's laughter followed her. Whirling around she shouted, "Why do you laugh at me?"

"Because you are heading back to your home." At her blank stare, he added, "You are going the wrong way if you wish to get to the king in Dingwall!"

Catriona looked about her and was horrified to see that she was indeed retracing their steps. Her face heated and Tayg laughed again as he turned to continue in the correct direction.

"You would not have made it past Loch Assynt without me," he said.

The words hit her in the stomach as surely as if he had thrown a punch. Too angry to speak, she reached for the only weapon she had . . . snow.

Scooping a large handful into her makeshift mittens, she packed it quickly, as her brother Ailig had taught her. Aiming, she let the snowball fly. It landed with a faint "thud" and a splat right in the middle of Tayg's back. The impact made him stagger a little, then he turned, a look of fury on his face. But Catriona had another missile ready and she let it fly, this time splashing over his chest. At least she had learned something of use from her bullying brothers.

Fury was quickly replaced with determination on Tayg's face. When he stooped to scoop up his own snow, Catriona darted behind a tree, grabbed more snow and prepared her next volley. She peered around the tree just in time to be splattered with flying snow as Tayg's barrage hit the trunk just beside her. He darted behind a tree and she used the opportunity to change trees herself. When he looked out, she let hers fly, hitting him square in the face.

"Ah! I'll get you!" Tayg raced towards her, one hand scrubbing snow from his face, the other arm cocked to let his snowball fly.

Catriona quickly rearmed herself, then raced away from him through the forest. This time, though, Tayg's aim was true and she stumbled forward as his icy ball slammed

into her back. She turned and threw hers, missing him as
he stepped behind yet another tree. Catriona took off
again, darting from tree to tree until she thought she was
far enough away to stop and form several hard-packed
balls. She grabbed the edges of her cloak and formed a
pocket to hold her arsenal, which she quickly loaded into
it. She peeked out from the tree to see where Tayg had got
to when she felt a light tapping on her shoulder.

Whipping around she came face-to-face with him. He
promptly dropped his snowball on her head. Snow slid
down her face and under her collar.

"Why you—" But before she could think of a good
name to call him he was racing away again.

She chased him, throwing ball after ball, hitting him
with some, missing with others, which elicited wild
laughter from the demented man. Her last one landed
against his backside. He stopped to face her, trying to look
indignant, but the grin on his face, combined with bits of
snow, pine straw and odd bits of bracken, made him look
rather silly. Catriona covered her mouth, trying to stifle a
giggle.

When he started at a run towards her again she waited
just until he thought he had her, then sidestepped out of
his way. He skidded to a halt, his back to her. She couldn't
help herself, she leaped onto his back, knocking him face
first into the snow.

"Get off me!" His voice was muffled by the snow.

"Not until you admit I've won."

"I'll teach you—" Tayg flipped over, grabbing her and
pinning her beneath him in one fluid demonstration of his
strength. "Now what are you going to do?"

Catriona's hand was flung out to the side. She quickly
grabbed as much snow as she could. "This!" she said,
bringing her arm up and smashing the snow against his
bare neck.

Tayg's grin froze and he tried to get her hand away

from his exposed skin. She took advantage of his distraction and managed to flip him over onto his back in a move she'd learned from watching her brothers wrestle. He quickly took back command of the situation and before either of them realized what they had done they were sliding down the steep side of a gully.

They slid to a stop at the bottom, just shy of a small burn, their arms and legs all tangled together.

"Are you hurt?" Tayg asked, his voice full of concern.

Catriona considered a moment. "Other than a bit of snow in places I'd rather not have it, I'm fine. You?"

Tayg burst out laughing. "Aye, I'm fine, too. Who taught you—" His question was cut off by Catriona's renewed assault. This time he had an ear full of the cold stuff. Quickly, he flipped on top of her again, pinning her beneath him. He grabbed her wrists, rendering her his captive.

Catriona breathed hard, trying to catch her breath which suddenly seemed to have escaped her. Each time she pulled in the crisp wintery air, her breasts rose, brushing against his hard chest. Her nipples puckered and a strange pressure began low in her belly. His chestnut eyes mesmerized her, and she had the sudden understanding that he was breathless, too.

A yearning sang in her head, though she wasn't sure exactly what it was she yearned for . . . perhaps his kiss? Aye, that was it. She wished his soft lips upon hers again. She wished him to run his hands through her hair, caress her skin, ease this ache deep within her. She raised her head from the snow, as he lowered his. Catriona closed her eyes and waited.

She felt the change in Tayg's body first, a sudden tenseness, followed by complete and utter stillness. She opened her eyes to see him peering up at the top of the ravine, his attention no longer on her. Disappointment surged through her, chased by frustration, but before she could say anything he had his hand over her mouth.

"Shh. Rider," he whispered.

Catriona nodded slightly so he knew she understood. Who was up there? It could not be her brothers, could it? Suddenly she realized that their horse was up there in the wood somewhere, abandoned during their battle. Would the rider notice it and the snowy trail that must lead over the ravine's edge? They were surely discovered.

She heard the rider draw near but the horse did not slow. They remained as they were for several minutes, making sure the horse and rider were truly gone.

Tayg took his hand off her mouth, then seemed to realize he was still lying atop her. Quickly he rose, the intimate moment lost to stark reality. Tayg offered his hand to help her up and they spent a few minutes brushing off the snow and bracken they had collected in their slide down to the burn side.

"I will fetch the horse," Tayg said. "Wait here. Stay out of sight as best you can. Perchance I can see who rides above."

Unwilling to trust her voice lest her frustration show, she nodded, then turned her back to him while he climbed up the slope.

She stared down at the ice-edged burn. What had just happened? They had been laughing, racing through the snow, having fun. Catriona tried to remember the last time she had had fun. It must have been when she and Ailig were children. She remembered climbing trees with him, running wild over the heath and swimming in the frigid waters of Loch Assynt. It seemed as if that must have been another person, not her. Just as she could not connect herself with the lighthearted, laughing lass who had pelted Tayg with snowballs.

She tried to bring back the feelings of exhilaration she had experienced just before they tumbled down the slope, but lost herself in those darker, more earthy sensations that had enveloped her as they lay at the bottom of the slope. Had he wished to kiss her, too? She had thought so, but then the rider came, breaking the spell their play in the snowy forest had woven about them, reminding them of what they risked if they were found in each other's company. Especially if they had been found entangled as they were.

Her cheeks heated as she tried to hold the memory of that moment, his weight upon her. His eyes seeing only her. His lips, full and fascinating.

Nay, 'twas folly. Aye, Tayg the bard was a handsome man, with more than his share of charm when he chose to use it. But he was a bard. He could not further her goal to protect her clan from the stupidity of Broc and the sheep.

She shivered, realizing for the first time that she knew naught of the man she planned to wed. Was Tayg of Culrain handsome? The songs said so. Was he kind? Intelligent? Charming? Would he have a slightly crooked smile? Full lips . . .

This would not do. She must get her mind off Tayg the bard and fill it with what was necessary to win a husband. Aye. That she must do, and the bard must help her. She would keep them both from further folly. She would keep the conversation trained on her goal and she would enlist the bard's help, prying from him any knowledge he had about his kinsman, preparing herself so that she might present the most appealing version of herself to the king and her future groom when the time came.

Aye, that was her plan. There could be no more play, and no more anger, for that was what got her in trouble over and over with this man. She would be reasonable, and he would help her reach her goal.

Whether he wanted to or not.

chapter 8

*B*y the time Tayg had returned from collecting their horse and trailing the rider far enough to determine that it wasn't Catriona's brothers but rather a lone traveler, the lass was shivering from her snow-dampened clothes.

They walked briskly and much more quietly than they had at the start of the day, quickly warming up as they crossed the narrow burn then turned to follow it to where it finally met the River Cassley. Little passed between them, and Tayg wondered if that playful side he had glimpsed was allowed out often. From Cat's reaction he guessed that even she had been surprised by it. Pleasantly surprised, if her pliant body and upturned lips had been any indication of her mood.

He grinned to himself. She was as complicated as a well played chess game, showing herself in feints and glimpses, then retreating back to the shelter of her shrewishness. Of course, she hadn't retreated that far back this afternoon. Nay, she had been positively quiet, compliant.

He suspected she was doing a bit of thinking about their situation—which was becoming more dangerous by the day. Not only were her brothers searching for them, but Tayg was finding it increasingly difficult to stay away from her. Even when she'd cut him with the sharpness of her tongue this morning, his blood had pumped and his heart had raced as no other lass had ever made happen. Maybe it was simply that he never knew what she was going to say—or do—next.

He smiled as he remembered the cat-a-mountain that had leaped upon his back, knocking him face first into the snow. Oh, he'd have to get her back for that one . . . though that would be inviting more moments that he dared not allow. Perhaps he would have to let it pass. Perhaps.

They trudged on, little passing between them except for the occasional look when Tayg glanced back to make sure she still followed. She seemed as lost in thought as he and he did not know whether that should frighten him or please him.

They paused briefly to eat the last of the food. If they did not find a village in which to bide the night Tayg was going to have to do some hunting, which would mean delaying their journey. There was precious little daylight for traveling this time of year as it was. He did not want to squander it chasing hares through the snow. The sooner they got to the king, the better it would be for both of them—and for King Robert.

The afternoon wore on. The river wound in and out of sight as the trail swung first around the edge of a slope, crowding the riverbank, then away to become a smoother path through the trees. As they neared the river after one of these forays into the wood a huge flock of snowy white whooper swans swooped over them, their wings whistling in the crisp air as they glided in to settle in one of the slower flowing parts of the river. Green-headed mallards and sharp-billed goosanders gathered in rafts on the water and Tayg found his mouth watering at the thought of fresh, roasted duck, or savory swan instead of the dried provisions he'd eaten too often of late.

They needed to find another village, or at least a cottage where they could resupply. He knew Duchally, a village with a proper castle, lay somewhere ahead of them, but whether it was a mile or ten, he could not tell.

He glanced back at Cat, who plodded along in the trail he and the horse made. At least in that way he was able to make the journey a little easier for her, though earlier his attempt to break the trail had triggered their snowball fight. He grinned just as the wind hit him hard in the teeth.

The sky was no longer bright and sunny but Tayg had been so distracted by his thoughts of a hot meal and of his companion's deadly aim with a snowball he had not noticed the change until now, when it was almost too late.

'Twas a dangerous thing to travel in the Highlands at any time of the year and not pay close attention to the weather. It could change from balmy and brilliant to vicious and deadly in a trice, no matter the season. Tayg looked up where the peaks of the mountains had been visible not long before. A gauzy grey haze shrouded their crowns and crept down their sides, obscuring the outline of the peaks even as he watched. The pewter sky was lowering rapidly, the clouds growing darker, flatter. Dangerous.

"We've got to find shelter!" Tayg yelled to Cat over the rising wind.

C atriona clutched her hood under her chin to keep it from blowing off in the sudden icy blast. "Shall we look for a cave?"

"Nay! This storm looks bad. We need food and fuel if

we do not want to freeze. We need to find Duchally and beg their hospitality."

She nodded though she did not wish to have to dissemble before another crowd of strangers. On the other hand, being alone with Tayg was not something she wished for either. Well, if she were honest with herself, some deep, unfamiliar part of her wished for exactly that. That part wished to see how far his charm would go, and what he was hiding behind it. But such a way led to disaster. Folly. A crowded castle would be better and if it meant playing the part of his sister again, then so be it. She had played the part of sister her entire life. A few more nights would not change anything.

And they needed to get out of this weather.

Just that fast the storm was upon them. The wind picked up snow from the ground in frigid gusts, blowing it around them in shifting waves of icy-white misery, now in their faces, now down their backs, now lifting their cloaks and pulling as if to yank them away.

Catriona hunched over, leaning into the gusts until she almost walked into the horse's backside. Tayg had stopped and, for a moment, she thought they must be lost.

"Are you all right?" Tayg asked as he appeared in the swirling ground snow which now was joined with painful pellets from the sky.

Cat nodded, unwilling to uncover her face from the plaid she had wrapped about her neck and looped over her mouth and nose. Her fingers and toes were so cold they hurt, but that was better than not being able to feel them at all.

Tayg looped something over her hand and she realized it was a rope.

"Hold onto that. I've tied it to the horse's saddle. I do not want you wandering lost in the whiteness, lass," he said. His voice was so soft, and so full of concern that she didn't have the heart to complain about the reference to her lack of directional sense. She gripped the rope hard, glad that he had looped it over her wrist, too, in case her hands did go numb.

"I thought I smelled smoke a moment ago, though with the wind 'tis impossible to tell what direction it might have come from. I hope 'tis Duchally and we can escape this blast soon."

She nodded again. Tayg looked at her for a moment, then returned to lead the horse.

Catriona's world quickly became defined by the faint outline of the horse's dark rump, the painful tingling in her fingers and toes, and the unrelenting whiteness of the stinging snow. Her cloak and the plaid protecting her face quickly gathered a heavy layer of snow. If they didn't find shelter soon . . . her mind sidled away from the thought. Tayg would find them shelter. He had taken care of her so far. All would be well . . . it had to be.

Just when she thought she could go no farther, she felt a tug on the rope about her wrist and had to almost run to keep up with the horse and his unseen guide. Her leather boots squeaked in the granular snow. Her feet were numb and she slipped repeatedly, barely managing to stay upright. When the horse slowed again a few minutes later she huddled at its side, letting it block some of the wind. She squinted into the whiteness.

A castle seemed to rise from the swirling snow, a grey giant looming over the river. Catriona had never been so glad to see stone walls before. Tayg glanced back at her and she nodded at him. They covered the distance to the gates at a trot, the promise of a fire and shelter from the maddening wind lending them a surge of energy—enough to make it to the gate which was, blessedly, open.

Guards stopped them long enough to determine their business. They seemed well pleased that a bard had come along with this first serious blast of winter. A lad of nine or ten led them to the stable where another lad took the horse, promising to give him a good rubdown and a bucket of oats. Tayg and Catriona grabbed their belongings and followed the first lad back out into the weather long enough to cross the deserted bailey and up a stair. Just before they stepped out of the cold they stopped and shook as much snow from their clothing as possible, then entered the chief's chamber.

The chief was seated at a table, his back to a roaring fire. His greying hair was pulled back in braids at his temples, revealing a face of middle years, and he was wrapped in a plaid so old it had no particular color. Tayg and Catriona waited at the back of the room, puddles of melted snow spreading about their feet, while he conversed with a trio of white-haired men.

Catriona shifted from one foot to the other, trying to overcome the pins and needles that heralded the return of feeling. Her hands and face were starting to thaw, too. She peeled off her mittens and stuffed them under her arm while she tried to chafe some warmth into her hands. The chief swiftly completed his business with the men, then nodded at the two of them to come forward.

"Good day," Tayg said, his voice bouncy and cheerful.

"Good day to you, sir," the chief replied, looking from one to the other of them. "What takes you traveling in such foul weather?"

Tayg told him the same story he had told Farlan of Fionn, that Catriona was being taken to her husband. She had to admit that he was an excellent storyteller, remembering the details of her supposed betrothed's hunting accident, his broken leg, her desire to rush to his side and Tayg's selflessness in escorting his sister though the winter was upon them. In fact, she realized, he told it better this time, embellishing it with bits of humor and playing up her love for her beloved Rory. Rory? She'd best remember the name.

"We beg your hospitality," Tayg was saying. "In exchange, we will entertain you well. Cat sings like an angel." Catriona glanced at him, startled since he had never heard her sing. He winked at her, then turned his cocky grin back to the chief. "I tell a grand story." Cat snorted but covered by pretending to cough. "Together," he continued, "we will more than earn a night's rest and a meal or two."

The chief looked at them. "You do not look like brother and sister."

Catriona bit her lip to hold back the retort that leaped to her lips. Tayg glanced at her as if to remind her to hold her tongue.

"We have different mothers," came his quick reply. "I look like our father, but Cat here favors her mother."

"Ah," the chief said. "'Tis often so, is it not? Well then, I offer you the hospitality of my castle. Cat?" He looked to her for confirmation of the odd byname.

Catriona nodded.

"You may stay with my daughter. 'Twill be a cold night and her small chamber will be warmer than the hall. I cannot give you a chamber of your own for we are suddenly overrun with guests this day. I have never seen so many traveling so late in the season."

"Other travelers?" Tayg asked. His voice was light but Catriona recognized the tension that wrapped about him suddenly.

"Aye, a tinker, my neighbor's wife and her cousin, another traveler from the west. We do not have over many chambers for guests."

"We thank you for your hospitality, sir," Tayg said with a little flourishing bow. He nudged Catriona.

"Oh, aye, we thank you most humbly," she said, adding a small curtsy to compliment Tayg's bow.

The chief smiled. "I fear you will be earning your keep well with this storm. You may find yourself amongst us for the winter."

"Nay!" they said together.

The chief looked at them, his eyebrows raised.

"We will be on our way as soon as possible," Catriona said, glancing at Tayg. "My Rory needs me," she added with what she hoped was a wistful smile.

"Aye, and he will wait until you can arrive safely and unfrozen, lass."

Catriona started to reply, but Tayg cut her off. "We are grateful for your hospitality however long we must impose upon it."

The chief agreed and called over the lad who had brought them to him. "Kester, show the lass here to Isobel's chamber and show the bard to the Great Hall. I expect you are both wishing for a hot meal and a warm fire?"

They nodded.

"A meal will be served shortly. If you will join me in the hall, you can begin to earn your keep by telling me of your journey."

"We thank you," Tayg said. He took Catriona's arm and they followed the lad out the door.

They stopped in the Great Hall and Tayg was introduced to the few folks gathered there. Catriona knew that a crowd would soon form asking for news and songs, but she was too tired to care. She hadn't slept well the night before, then their fight through the snow and wind this day had sapped her energy. What she really wanted was a bath warm enough to chase the cold from her bones, some clean clothes and a soft bed.

As she turned to follow Kester out of the hall, Tayg grabbed her arm lightly, pulling her near him.

"Tread lightly with your tongue, my Cat. We do not want these kind folk to regret their hospitality."

"I will say—"

"What you must. I know," he said, his mouth drawn into an un-Tayg-like frown. "Just try to say what you must with a light step. Do not draw attention to yourself that way, for 'tis how your brothers describe you first. Remember that you are not Catriona the Shrew here, but Cat, a lass traveling with her brother to meet her beloved. I know you can do this." He held her glance for a moment. "Make me proud," he whispered.

With those strange words, he released her and lightly pushed her toward the waiting lad. She rubbed a sudden aching pain in the middle of her chest with the heel of her hand and wondered how she could have indigestion when it had been so long since she'd eaten. She rolled Tayg's words around in her mind and rubbed the pain again. She glanced back over her shoulder at the bard just before Kester led her out of the hall. Tayg had already been drawn into conversation with one of the castle folk.

The lad led her through several cold, dark passageways and at last to a chamber. He was just opening the door for her when a girlish voice shouted, "Hold!"

Kester grinned and turned in the direction the command had come from. "Now you'll meet our Isobel," he said to Catriona. "She's the finest lass in all the Highlands." He turned a grinning face to her, then realized what he'd said. He had the grace to blush crimson just as the lass came to the top of the stair and hurried down the hallway towards them.

Catriona felt her stomach drop as the blond beauty smiled at her.

"I understand you're to share my chamber," she said, her brown eyes twinkling with delight. "'Twill be wonderful to have someone to talk to!"

Catriona tried not to groan. Talk was the last thing she wanted just now, but a whisper of Tayg's voice floated through her mind, reminding her to step lightly, to make him proud. And oddly she wished to.

Isobel took her hand and pulled her into the cozy chamber. A wood fire crackled in the fireplace and beautiful tapestries covered the walls. A huge bed with a deep mattress nearly filled the room. It was hung with lush curtains of blue and saffron. Catriona eyed the bed with a desire so strong it was all she could do to keep from flinging herself onto it.

She turned as the door closed, shutting her in the chamber with Isobel. She heard Tayg's odd words again, "Make me proud." No one had ever asked such a thing of her. She was unsure how to go about doing as he asked until she remembered his advice to "tread lightly." He wished her to mind her tongue; to be Cat rather than Triona.

Her first instinct was to say something nasty to Isobel just to show Tayg that he could not tell her what to do, but then she looked at the happy young woman before her and did not have the energy to pour icy water on her enthusiasm for no reason other than to irritate Tayg.

"You look very tired . . . um, I'm sorry, I do not know your name," Isobel said.

"Cat," she said quickly, realizing that Tayg's odd name for her rolled off her tongue easily.

Isobel quirked an eyebrow at the name but said nothing. So that was what it was like to tread lightly. The girl's restrained reaction reminded her of her father's favorite admonition to her. "If you can't say something nice, keep yer gob shut."

"Would it be possible for a bath to be brought—"

"'Tis on its way already," Isobel cut her off. "Let me take your things. If you like, I can have your clothes cleaned for you."

"Yes . . . I mean, no. I shall have to wear these again." At the girl's puzzled look she added, "We . . . we . . . lost my sack of clothing in the storm." She hoped the lie was convincing.

"Well these are beyond wearing," Isobel said. She
cocked her head and studied Cat for a moment. "I think
we are of a size." She turned to a trunk at the foot of her
bed and rummaged through the contents for a moment,
then drew forth a beautiful gown the deep blue of woad-
dyed cloth. It was cut simply, but the color was so intense
it made Catriona want to stroke it.

"'Tis the most beautiful gown I have ever seen," she
said.

"I would be pleased to lend it to you while yours is
being cleaned."

Catriona took a step forward, her hand outstretched to
caress the finely woven wool. She could well imagine
herself in such a gown, all eyes upon her as she entered
the Great Hall. The color would compliment her deep
blue eyes and pale skin. She would leave her hair uncov-
ered. Tayg would see her as she should be . . .

She jerked her hand back, as if burned by the fabric.
"No, I cannot wear such a magnificent gown."

Disappointment trembled on Isobel's lips and in her
eyes and Catriona realized how sharp her words had been.

Tread lightly.

Make me proud.

'Twas in her own best interest to do as he asked. She
certainly wasn't going to watch her tongue for his sake.
She smiled at the girl before her.

"You should wear this gown tonight. Your father said
there were many guests seeking shelter from the storm
within these walls. You should be the one to shine in such
a gown when hosting so many."

The girl's disappointment diminished and Catriona realized she really was trying to be kind. Well, if treading
lightly meant letting this lass be kind, she could find a
way to do so without drawing such attention to herself.

"Do you have another? Perhaps something a bit
plainer? I do not wish to draw all eyes to myself as that

grand gown shall do." There, the truth stated quietly and Isobel was smiling again, though not as broadly as before.

"Aye, I have another, but I've never met a lass as beautiful as you who did not want to draw a young man's attention to herself."

Isobel's casual compliment shocked Catriona. She turned to the fire and warmed her hands for a moment as she tried to make her voice work again.

"I did not mean to embarrass you," Isobel said quietly.

Cat glanced over her shoulder and smiled at the girl.

"I have no desire to draw such attention to myself." At least not right now, she added to herself.

A knock on the door interrupted the conversation, much to Catriona's relief.

Isobel opened the door. Two lads hauled in a fair-sized wooden tub while four lasses followed with kettles of hot water. After several more trips, they had the tub filled with delightfully steaming water. In the meantime, Isobel had pulled out a block of precious castile soap, a length of linen toweling, a comb and a much less attention-drawing grey-green gown. When Catriona tried to ease the tangles from her hair, her chilled fingers would not cooperate. The other young woman gently took the comb from her and began the task herself. All the while, Isobel kept up a one-sided conversation, telling Catriona all the castle gossip, about her herb garden and the storm which Auld Anne's creaky knees always predicted.

As Catriona settled herself into the tub she hoped Isobel would leave her alone for a while, but the lass just perched upon the end of her bed and continued to prattle away. Heat soaked slowly into Catriona, chasing away the last bits of frosty cold that had lodged in her bones. She nodded occasionally, or grunted, more to keep the lass company than because she felt it necessary to participate in the conversation.

There was a pause in Isobel's monologue when Catriona ducked under the water to wet her hair. As she lathered it, there was silence. She ducked under again to rinse the soap and when she sat up once more Isobel had moved to the side of the tub.

"If you like I'll pour some clean water over your hair."

Catriona smiled, feeling more relaxed than she had in days. She nodded and leaned her head back while the warm water sluiced over her.

"Tell me about your traveling companion. He is not your husband, is he?"

The question caught her off guard. "Nay, he is my brother."

"And he is a bard?"

Catriona nodded, sinking deeper into the tub until her chin touched the water though her knees were raised into the frigid air.

"Why do you travel with him?"

The girl had too many questions and Catriona too few answers. "Tayg takes me to my betrothed," she said, keeping to Tayg's story.

"Tayg? That is your brother's name? I have only heard that name once before."

Damn. Had Tayg given his name? Nay, she did not think so. The chief had referred to him only as bard. She would have to warn him that she had slipped and used his true name. "'Tis a common name in Clan Munro," she said.

"Aye, 'tis where the other who bears that name is from. Tayg of Culrain, son of the Chief of Munro." Isobel got a dreamy lost look on her face that made Catriona uncomfortable.

"So you have met the warrior Tayg?" Catriona asked, prepared to pepper her with questions if the answer was yes.

"Nay."

Catriona felt a moment's disappointment but was too content in her bath to dwell on it.

"But I have heard he is seeking a wife," Isobel continued. "Or at least his mother seeks a wife for him. I have heard he does not wish to wed. I have also heard he is a charming, braw man."

'Twas more than Catriona had heard from the songs and tales of the man. "Yet he has taken no wife," Catriona said before she could stop herself.

"He has not. Some say he wishes a love match, others say he is tired from war and would simply wait a bit before tying the knot with a lass. Whoever marries him, 'twill be a good match. He will be chief of a great clan, close kin to the Earl of Ross, and thus to the king himself. For me," Isobel continued, "I do not wish for one who will be so much in the center of events, though he *is* said to be well favored, charming and, well . . ."

Catriona glanced over and realized the lass was blushing.

"What?"

"Well, I have heard—"

Catriona was getting tired of those three little words.

"I have heard that he does not leave a lass . . . unsatisfied."

"Unsatisfied?" What was she talking about?

"Aye." Isobel leaned close, whispering in Catriona's ear. "In the ways of men and women."

At Catriona's puzzled shake of her head Isobel added, "When he couples with a woman . . . in the bed!" Isobel covered her mouth with her hand as if she couldn't believe she had said the words aloud.

All Catriona could think to say was a sort of stunned, "Oh."

"Who are you bound to marry?" Isobel asked quietly.

Catriona thought quickly. What name had Tayg given? She needed to get it right. Rory. But he had not said what clan. She thought of Tayg's way of storytelling. What

would he say? He'd use as much truth as possible and he
had named the man . . .

"Rory of Clan Munro." Catriona busied herself lather-
ing her arms. "Do you know him?" she asked around the
huge lump in her throat. If she was ever to be exposed for
a liar 'twould be now.

"I have heard his name, but know nothing more of
him."

Relief surged through her.

"He lives in Culrain, too, does he not? Is that where
you are bound?"

Catriona made a noncommittal sound.

"I hear the king will be there soon," Isobel said.

This got her attention and she sat up a bit. "The king
will be in Culrain? I thought he was for Dingwall."

"Aye, he is, for his sister's wedding, but first he tours
the lands of those who have sworn fealty to him. 'Tis said
he is bound for Culrain by week's end. Perhaps you shall
see him. I should like to meet King Robert someday. . . ."

Catriona glanced at the girl. Isobel sat upon the end of
the bed, her feet on the trunk, her arms wrapped about her
legs and her chin resting on her bent knees. Her eyes held
a wistful look, as if she gazed at something far distant that
she longed for.

"Are you betrothed?" Catriona asked, surprised that she
truly was curious about this girl. Normally she cared not
what others did or thought.

Isobel's attention snapped back from whatever far away
scene she imagined, and she focused again on Cat, who
leaned back in the still-warm water to let the heat soak
into her.

"Am I what?"

"Betrothed."

"Nay."

Catriona considered the lass. Blond hair, long and silky
with just enough wave to make it seem constantly shifting

in the flickering firelight. Her eyes were warm and friendly and seemed huge in her perfectly oval face. She was beautiful, charming in a talkative sort of way and clearly of marriageable age. She would be a good match for a more serious-minded man, a man who needed a bit of a push to enjoy himself. Isobel needed someone to temper her chatter but who would appreciate her sweetness.

"Surely you do not have much competition for the attentions of the young men."

Isobel shrugged. "There are none here that I would have, and though I have met many potential husbands—for it seems that all who travel this region pass through Duchally—I have not yet met one I wished to marry."

Catriona leaned her head back and stared at the planked ceiling. "I'd wager Ailig would appeal to you," she said.

"Ailig? Who is he?"

"My—" Catriona sat straight up in the tub. What had made her speak of Ailig? What would Tayg do now? He would keep close to the truth. "My cousin. He is from Assynt, though I have never been there," she added quickly. She had neatly directed the conversation away from her supposed husband-to-be and now was in danger again. Details, believable details, that's what Tayg used to distract from the truth.

"He is the youngest son of the MacLeod, and, I have heard," she said, using Isobel's words to draw her in, "the only brother with any brains. He is fair, like you. You would have lovely bairns."

"Is he not brother to the Shrew of Assynt?" Isobel asked, handing the toweling to Catriona as she stepped from the cooling water of the tub. "I do not think I would wish to marry into such a clan."

Catriona felt her temper rise, but she remembered Tayg's words and struggled to hold her tongue. She briskly dried herself and casually asked, "Have you ever met the . . ." Catriona could not bring herself to say shrew. "Have you ever met the lass?"

"Nay, but her reputation flies upon the wind. She is your cousin, too. Have you not heard of it?"

Catriona shook her head and wished she could figure out how to stop this conversation without causing suspicion.

Isobel settled herself back on the foot of the bed. "I have heard she is a shrew with a tongue as sharp as a well-honed dagger. She can flay the skin from a warrior with nothing but her words. It is also said that her clan runs scared before her. She is sharp-faced, and her body is shriveled to match her soul. 'Twould not suit me to go from my own family to living in the company of such as that."

Catriona had gone stone-still at this news, her face hidden behind the linen she now used to dry her hair.

"'Tis funny we should speak of her," Isobel continued. "I was just talking with a traveler who said the shrew had been sold to the MacDonells, though I imagine if they weren't so hard put they would have turned down the tocher, no matter how grand it was. But then the MacLeods of Assynt have plenty of wealth to be able to marry off such a daughter as that shrew. Perhaps I should meet this cousin of yours after all . . ."

Catriona felt the heat rise in her cheeks and quickly turned her back to the girl while she finished drying herself.

"Sit there by the fire and I'll comb your hair for you again," Isobel said.

Catriona wrapped the linen about her and did as the girl bade her, not wanting to face her until she could be sure this unfamiliar embarrassment was under control. Was this how she was seen by everyone? By Tayg? Shriveled up, sold to anyone who would take her?

Isobel's gentle ministrations, combined with Catriona's fatigue, slowly lulled her into a near trance.

"There," Isobel said, "your hair is smoothed. Sit here before the fire while I take your clothes down to the kitchen. I shall set someone to washing them, then we'll get you dressed, and if you'll let me, I shall arrange your hair for you."

"Why are you being so nice to me?" Catriona asked suddenly, then slapped her hand over her mouth as Isobel had earlier.

Isobel laughed and Catriona couldn't help but smile back at her.

"You are our guest, silly. Besides, there are blessed few lasses my age here. I have no one to gossip with, no sisters nor even any close cousins. You have not told me once to cease my prattling as my father loves to do. We shall be fast friends."

Catriona nodded, as amazed by Isobel's answer as by the realization that by following Tayg's request she had earned a friend, perhaps the first in her entire life. "We shall be fast friends," she said and felt a grin spread upon her face.

As long as Isobel didn't find out who she truly was.

chapter 9

Tayg had positioned himself so he could see the entry into the Great Hall. He had been waiting a long time and still Catriona had not appeared. The longer they were apart, the more he feared her temper and sharp tongue would reveal her identity. Her safety—and his—depended on their ruse. Which meant they were in danger of discovery, for the woman had no clue how to mind her tongue, or how to blend in with those around her.

Indeed, blending in was not something he could ever imagine Cat doing. The deep blue of her eyes against her pale, creamy skin and the inky curtain of hair all served to draw the eye to the lass. The stubborn set of her chin and the glint of determination so often found in those azure eyes held one's gaze.

He smiled to himself at the image. She was never predictable . . . well, except when he sought to goad her temper, but even that, he realized, was becoming less predictable. She was, after only a few days in his company, becoming more adept at controlling her temper and her tongue. She was entertaining, keeping him forever on his toes, challenging him as no lass ever had. She was nothing like the lasses his mother would have him choose from.

Nay, he'd not like one of those lasses who fawned over him because of the tales and ballads. Which was why 'twas important for him to find a lass for himself, and soon, for eventually his mother would win and he would marry. And of course it would come much sooner than he had hoped. As soon as he had delivered Cat and the damning missive to King Robert, his mother would have him in her snare again. 'Twould be far better to always travel with Cat, forever on guard for a prickly barb slung his way, or a soft kiss to be stolen, than to suffer a lass his mother chose.

Sweet Saint Jude! What was he thinking? His duty was to his clan, never mind that to be forever saddled with that cat-a-mountain would be worse than being wed to dull Dolag of Fionn . . . or the supposedly bonny daughter of Duchally's chief.

He looked about him, searching for both Cat and the daughter. He should at least meet the other lass . . . just in case. He watched as people began streaming into the hall interspersed with gangly lads carrying trays laden with food.

"Where is she?" he muttered under his breath, not sure which lass he most wanted to see first.

"Who?" came a quick quiet reply near his left ear.

He whipped his head around to look at the woman next to him. "Cat?"

"Do you like my disguise?" she asked, winking at him.

She stepped back just far enough for him to take in the plain grey-green gown and the veil and wimple that covered her hair, neck and much of her beautiful face.

"'Tis very . . . fetching . . . for an auld woman."

She frowned at him, but then a smile peeked through.

"Then I have done well. Isobel wanted me to leave my hair down with just a ribbon woven through it, but I thought 'twould draw too much attention." Her expression turned more uncertain. "I did well, did I not?"

"Aye, lass. You did very well. I did not even see you enter the hall, though I was looking for you."

The smile was there again and he had to take a deep breath to slow his heartbeat. He had to stop this foolishness. "How many people did you insult while you were away?"

That did it, extinguishing the spark of pride he had seen in her eyes and replacing it with the more familiar temper.

"I insulted no one, bard. I was a model of well-tempered behavior. Indeed, I have made a . . . friend."

Shock and jealousy coursed through him in equal parts. "Who?" he asked before he could remind himself he did not care.

"Isobel," she said lightly, though the spark of anger still flashed in her eyes. "The chief's daughter."

"Ah, good then," Tayg said, affecting an air of interest he did not feel. "You shall introduce me to your friend. I should like to make her acquaintance, see if she will suit the king's need for wives for his loyal followers, or perhaps for me," he added before he could stop himself.

"You will not like her," she said, her teeth gritted together now. "Isobel is a sweet lass, but talkative, a gossip even. Her favorite three words are 'I have heard.' You would not want to spend time with such a talkative one as she, though the king might find her suitable."

Tayg was watching her with amusement now. "And how is it that you know what I admire in a lass?"

"I . . . I . . ." She glared at him and changed the subject. "She says my betrothed, Rory of Munro, is known to her. I was able to avoid her questions, but do you not think 'twould be wise to tell me something of the man so I may answer next time? I was able to keep her chattering about castle gossip, and news of the king—"

"The king?"

"Aye. He is touring the Earl of Ross's allies before he attends his sister's wedding at Dingwall Castle. Perhaps we can meet up with him sooner than we thought?"

Tayg was impressed in spite of himself. She had listened to him. He took her hand and raised it to his lips.

"You have done well, Cat," Tayg said, looking her in the eye. "I am proud of you." The shock on her face was priceless and Tayg grinned. "Has no one ever told you that before?"

"Nay. Never. Are you sure?"

This time Tayg laughed out loud. "Aye, I am sure. You have done very well to make a friend and disguise yourself so. You should be proud of yourself."

The perplexed tilt of her eyebrows had him reaching out to smooth her brow when a melodious voice stopped him.

"Will you not introduce me to your brother?"

Tayg whipped around. Before him stood a woman near to Cat's age with a perfectly formed face, waves of golden hair and sparkling brown eyes. Here was a woman a man could fall for. He glanced back at Cat whose expression had gone carefully neutral.

"Are you not going to introduce us, sister?"

"Aye," she said, moving around him to stand next to the golden lass. "This is Isobel, daughter of Hamish, chief of the Beatons of Duchally. Isobel, this is Tayg the Bard."

Isobel batted long lashes at him and smiled. Her teeth were not perfect, but teeth seldom were. Tayg smiled back at her, then glanced at Cat who sent him a smile framed with dewy lips, straight white teeth and laced with sarcasm that only he would recognize. The urge to lean forward and kiss her grabbed him and he fought against it. He did not need to encourage this attraction he felt, and it would not do to kiss one's sister as he wished to kiss Cat. He flashed Cat a quick grin then, desperate to separate himself from this woman he was coming to admire as much for her spirit as for her bonny form.

"'Twould be an honor to escort you to your table," he said to Isobel with a small bow and a cheeky grin. Isobel smiled at him and took his offered arm. Quickly he led her to the table at the head of the hall, leaving Cat standing there watching them go.

C*atriona watched the two weave their way through* the crowded hall, heard the low rumble of Tayg's voice as his mouth dipped near Isobel's ear and her answering tinkle of laughter at whatever remark he had made.

She quickly moved to the last table in the hall, in the darkest corner, but took a seat where she could see the table on the dais where Tayg had obviously been invited to sit next to the vivacious Isobel. Her stomach felt hollow and her chest ached. One moment she had felt like singing to the rafters, basking in the glow of Tayg's unfamiliar praise, the next she wished the stone floor would open up and drop her into the depths of the earth as he turned his charm upon Isobel. Her first thought was to pitch a goblet at the lass's retreating backside but the memory of the hour they had spent becoming friends stopped her. If this was what it felt like to have a friend— wanting to strike out but unwilling to hurt her—she wanted nothing to do with it.

She picked at the food on her trencher and drank her watered wine sparingly. After a while Tayg rose from his seat, gave a small bow to Isobel and the chief, and sauntered back toward her. He stopped at a table midway down the hall and picked up his drum sack which she had not noticed there. He looked about, his eyes quickly honing in on her in her dark corner. He quirked an eyebrow, as if to ask what she thought she was doing, hiding in the shadows, then shrugged and pulled a stool into the aisle that ran between the long rows of tables.

Catriona found her appetite had picked up a bit as he'd moved away from the main table. She turned her attention to finishing the fine meal before her and poured herself another goblet of wine from the ewer that stood nearby.

She listened as Tayg sang a simple ballad, one so old everyone knew it well enough to sing along. He was good at that, getting the others to cover his mistakes, even sing the songs for him. He could tell a tale better than any *seanachaidh* she'd ever heard, but music was not his strength. How had he ever thought to become a bard?

A funny question formed in her head: how *had* he come to be a bard? He was poorly trained, if trained at all. He knew only the bare rudiments of drumming. His voice, so rich and animated when he told his stories, was rather thin and unsure when he sang.

Catriona pushed her trencher away, nearly toppling her empty goblet. She tried to think back to when they were at Fionn. His performance tonight was better than that one had been, but only a little.

She rose from her seat and moved toward the crowd. She watched as Tayg sang a line, then listened as the weans belted out the answering line. He laughed, rich and deep and full of simple joy.

He was enjoying himself.

She circled around the gathering, watching Tayg's face until she was behind him. She focused on the faces, young and old, surrounding him. Smiling, friendly, open faces. How did he do that, put people at ease with a quick joke, a simple tune played haltingly on his drum, a pat on a shoulder, a grin you couldn't help but answer with one of your own?

He paused in his drumming and looked over his shoulder at her, catching her eye. She quickly looked away, too caught up in her musings to answer the challenge she saw there.

The unruly song was followed by stories, different from the ones she'd heard before, and all the more entertaining for their novelty. This was the point where she had goaded him into the song for Dolag, but she would not do such tonight. Nay, he could do as he wished and she would sit and listen, wait, for what she wasn't sure, but there was something to wait for.

Loud laughter met the end of his second story. He beat the drum again and started whistling a familiar tune, but not one the Beaton clan knew. They could not as it was the tune he had made up for Dolag. Catriona glared at the back of his head just as he changed the tune to a popular love ballad.

Isobel beamed at Tayg, who smiled as broadly as he could and still sing. He glanced at Catriona, but she refused to acknowledge him. She continued slowly circling the people, watching the faces, though mostly she watched first Isobel, then Tayg, then Isobel again. Their attention was entirely on each other. What did he think he was doing? Isobel was no lass to spend her virtue on such as he. If he dared so much as to kiss her friend, Catriona would rip his eyes out . . . or maybe just his tongue.

But that thought was a mistake, for thoughts of his tongue reminded her of the kisses they had shared, and the one they almost shared lying at the bottom of the ravine, near the snowy burn. She remembered the snow-ball fight and the way he had grinned at her, laughed with her. Something in her gut twisted. He was a fickle beast. But then again, he was just like all the other men in her life.

But he wasn't really like all the other men in her life. He wasn't using her to his own end, in fact it was just the opposite, she was using him to her own end. To take her to the king, to keep her from her family's plans for her future. She did not deserve the fate they would have her accept. Which was exactly why she must make her own.

She stopped her circling at a point directly across from the bard and slid onto the end of a bench. The man next to her smiled, drawing her attention to him. Something seemed familiar about his long misshapen nose and the hooded appearance of his dark eyes. She could not place him, but then, clans intermarried so often, perhaps he was a cousin of someone she knew, and thus shared a passing resemblance that tickled her memory but had no true memory to attach itself to. Catriona did not return the smile but rather turned her attention back to Tayg. He had launched into another one of his stories and the group was captured in his spell.

"He tells a good yarn, that one does."

Startled from her reverie, she looked up into the face of the man seated next to her. Lank, oily hair hung in his face, partially hiding his sallow, pockmarked skin. His thin lips were compressed into nothing more than a line across his face as he waited for her to respond. She nodded, not wishing for any company that would require her to watch her words and her manner. But the man was not as perceptive as Tayg would have been. Instead of seeing her desire to be alone with her thoughts, he continued.

"He passed through my castle less than a sennight ago. Though he did not have the poise he carries now," he said quietly, as if to himself.

"No one has more poise than that one," Catriona said.

"Aye, though his seems to have grown quickly since he was at Dun Donell."

"Dun Don—" Catriona locked eyes with the stranger sitting next to her and fear skittered over her skin. She ducked her face, praying the wimple would cast a deep shadow over it. "He has traveled far, then," she said, keeping her voice as light as she could.

"Aye, and 'tis not easy traveling this time of year." He'd turned his attention back to Tayg. "Most bards are seeking their winter's refuge by now, but this one . . ."

"So you have traveled from MacDonell lands, too?" Catriona ventured to ask, fearing the answer almost as much as the not knowing.

"By way of Assynt." He glanced back at her. "I was to meet my bride there, but she has disappeared." He studied her profile a moment, then seemed to dismiss her, turning his attention back to the gathering. "I sent a message with yon bard for my bride, but it never arrived. I would know why he did not finish what he set out to do." The man's voice was a deep and angry rumble.

Sweat dampened Catriona's skin, but she could not make herself move. Her gorge rose, and she placed a hand on her stomach, willing it to behave. Her mind raced but she could not fix it on any thought save that of escape. Yet she dared not leave in any way that would draw the attention of the man sitting beside her.

For though she had not seen him in six or seven years there was no doubt that man was Dogface MacDonell.

Tayg *knew something was wrong just by looking at* Cat. The way she held her head, her face cast downward, deep in shadow, wasn't right. Catriona usually thrust her chin out as if daring anyone to thwart her. Now, though, she sat with her shoulders hunched, and that damned veil and wimple covering her perfect skin and ebony hair.

He caught the beat on his drum quickly just as his distraction threatened the rhythm. He began a bawdy song, a bit too bawdy for so early a gathering, but the folk joined in with glee, singing loudly and banging their tankards and goblets on the trestle tables, drowning out his less than rich voice.

Tayg would be glad when this bit of mummery was over. It was one thing to skulk around letting folk believe he was a bard when—he winced at his own poor ability to carry the tune—it was so clear he was not. It was something else to maintain the facade with Cat, who was finally beginning to listen to him, soften toward him.

He glanced back at Cat, but she had disappeared from her place at the edge of the circle. He looked about, sure she would be moving closer, ready to take a jab at his singing, or put him on the spot again to compose a song about some poor unsuspecting lass. Of course, if 'twas a song about Isobel . . . his eyes flitted over the crowd until they came to rest on the beautiful, flaxen-haired lass.

Wherever Cat had got to, she could not cause too much trouble with most of the castle folk gathered about him. Perhaps he should take the opportunity and see what he could learn of the chief's daughter, beyond her penchant for gossip. After all, so far on this misbegotten journey Isobel seemed the most likely candidate if he wished to choose his own bride.

Aye, he would take this opportunity to speak with the lass while Cat-of-the-sharp-tongue was not about. He needed to see if she would make a suitable wife for him. There was plenty of time later to find out what ailed Cat. He drew the bawdy song to a close and smiled at Isobel.

"I would sing a song for Isobel, fairest daughter of your clan," he said to the gathering.

"Aye, that she is," Kester, the lad who had shown him around earlier, agreed.

"Tell me about her, then, so that I may choose a fitting song." He inclined his head in the lass's direction and graced her with his cockiest grin. She returned the grin, then scooted forward a bit on her bench to look at Kester.

The lad's face had gone rather pale when he realized that Tayg was serious, and he had to clear his throat several times before he was able to speak.

"Uh, well, she is bonny."

"Aye, that she is," Tayg agreed as he watched the boy's pale face turn a faint pink.

"And her hair is like silk."

"And how would you know that, lad?" came a booming voice from across the crowd.

Kester seemed to take courage from the teasing tone. He straightened his shoulders. "Anyone can see 'tis true," he said, beaming now. "And her skin, 'tis white as new snow."

"Ah, I can see that for a certainty," Tayg said, winking at the grinning Isobel. "But what of her disposition? Is she shy and coy? Is she sharp of tongue? Does she mind her da?"

"You ask a lot of questions, bard," a new voice said quite near to him.

"'Tis necessary if I am to sing her a song in praise of her virtues." Tayg turned to find the man staring at him— Duff MacDonell—and he wasn't happy to see Tayg from the stony look in his eyes.

"I have heard you sing before, bard. Any lass with an ounce of pride would not wish for you to sing her praises."

A hush fell over the gathering.

"My singing troubles you?"

"Aye. You sang at my hall not so long ago, though in truth you have improved since then."

"What about my song?" Isobel broke through the tension before Tayg could think what story to tell the Mac-Donell about the undelivered missive. Slowly he turned his attention back to Isobel and grinned.

"You shall have it," he said, eyeing the MacDonell as he moved around the circle to sit on the bench Cat had vacated. Of course. Cat had noticed Dogface and had left before he realized who she was. At least now he understood why Cat was nowhere in sight. She would be collecting her belongings and getting ready to leave the castle. He cast a glance up at the high windows but it was too dark to tell if the snow still fell. Would she wait for him or strike out on her own? She'd be daft to leave without food, without someone to watch over her.

Without him.

"Bard?"

Tayg's attention was quickly pulled back to the moment and he shoved the sick feeling in the pit of his stomach away. He had to finish up this farce first, escape Dogface, then find Catriona and see what she planned.

"I think I have it," he said, as if he had been deep in thought over which song to sing. In truth, he only knew a few well enough to play so the decision was quick. He launched into a well known song about a beautiful lass and her ardent lover as Dogface glowered at him.

Tayg *excused himself, promising to return soon. He* tucked his drum into its carry sack and laid it next to his belongings which sat in a corner of the hall. He dared not take his things with him as Dogface watched him carefully. He worked his way toward the end of the hall leading to the privies. He did not think Dogface would follow him there, especially if he thought Tayg was returning immediately.

But he wasn't, of course.

He had to find Catriona. He needed to know what she was up to. He couldn't chance her falling into Dogface's hands. Her future, and the king's, depended upon it. He didn't want to think about the order of his concerns at the moment.

He exited the dark confines of the castle into the snowy, deserted bailey. The storm had increased and the snow whipped about him as it was driven by the wind from the night-dark sky. Tayg shivered. He should have taken the

long way, through the castle corridors instead of cutting
across the open bailey. But he didn't want to waste the
time.

They were going to have to leave now, without his
bags, for he could not risk returning to the hall. He had
been safe from Dogface's questions so far, but soon all
would seek their beds and he would be left to explain why
he was traveling with the man's intended and taking her
and Dogface's missive to the king.

'Twould be simpler if he could just abandon her here.
That would distract Dogface long enough for Tayg to get
away. The king would still be warned of the plot against
him. Whether or not he had Cat as a hostage wouldn't
matter that much.

But he couldn't abandon her. There was something
about her that pulled at him. Despite her prickly behavior,
there were moments when he spied the woman underneath. She used her temper like a suit of armor, but every
once in a while . . . he remembered lying atop her after
their tumble down the snowy hill that morning, her mouth
moist and inviting, her twilight-blue eyes twinkling and
her pale skin flushed.

He shook himself and pulled his plaid about him.
'Twould not do to dwell on such things. The king would
decide her fate and he was sure 'twould include marriage
to someone who could control the wayward MacLeod
clan. He was destined to lead his own small clan, 'twas
his duty, and hers. They would see their duty done.

Tayg started toward the tower where Kester had es-
corted Cat earlier. Just as he reached the middle of the
bailey a commotion at the gate made him stop. Five riders
erupted from the gatehouse clad so heavily in snow-
blanketed skins and woolens they looked like little more
than great hulking lumps upon their mounts.

"You there!" one of the lumps shouted at him.

He looked the snowy furs over. Something about these

men made him wary. He stood his ground and answered, "Aye?"

"Will you give us leave to bide here until the storm passes?"

The voice was almost familiar.

"'Tis not my place to grant such leave. I am but a traveling bard and a guest, myself." Tayg moved around them, keeping his distance, and a veil of snow between them. "'Tis a bad night to be traveling."

"Aye. Where is the chief?"

"I do not know, but his daughter is there," he said, pointing at the Great Hall.

The largest lump dismounted, shaking snow from his mantle. "Are there many guests here this evening?" The hulk moved closer to Tayg.

"Aye."

"Is there a lass amongst them, dark haired and evil-tempered?"

The hair on Tayg's neck rose and all his senses sharpened. "Nay, none that I have seen."

"Indeed."

The way the man said "indeed" reminded him of Cat's more caustic moments. No doubt these men were her brothers. It wasn't bad enough Dogface had found him, but now these great louts had, too.

He watched as the hulk came nearer, circling Tayg as if sizing him up. The size of the man and the beady black eyes barely visible in the gloom made Tayg think 'twas probably Broc, based on Cat's description, though 'twas possible another brother took the lead. Tayg tried to breathe evenly, keeping his stance ready but nonchalant. He must tread very carefully here and pray Cat didn't choose this moment to make her whereabouts known. Of course she knew Dogface was in the Great Hall so she might just do the right thing and stay hidden until he could sort this out.

"Well, then," Tayg said, flashing a false grin at the circling man, "I'll find my bed then. The chief's daughter is in the hall." He pointed the direction. "Isobel is her name and she's a bonny lass who will no doubt welcome you to Duchally properly."

He turned back the way he had been headed when the party entered the bailey. A sharp grunt from the hulk had him turning and reaching for his dirk but the man crashed into him before he could pull it free of its scabbard. He hit the ground hard. The air whooshed out of his lungs. A fist crashed into his face. The man leaned over him, lifting him by his tunic front until they were nose to nose. Now Tayg could see the temper in the beady eyes.

"Whose bed will you find, Bard?"

Tayg said nothing.

"Do you not know who we are?" the huge man asked.

"Nay," Tayg lied, holding fast to his feigned ignorance. "But I do not think the chief will take kindly to you attacking a guest to whom he has offered his hospitality."

Tayg glanced around him at three other large men arranged about his head. He thought there had been five. Snow seeped into his clothes dragging his thoughts away from counting hulks. The largest man still loomed over him. He would do well to talk his way out of this mess. Despite his battle training, he was out-fisted and out-weighed by any two of them.

"You are the bastard that stole our sister away. Where is she, bard?" Now Tayg was certain this man was Broc MacLeod, Cat's eldest brother, and he drove home his question with another fist to Tayg's face. The other brothers were silent, though the fury could be plainly felt in the tension surrounding him.

"What say you?" Broc pulled him roughly to his feet, and Tayg began to look for an escape.

"I do not know the lass you speak of, and if she is evil-tempered, why would anyone take her anyway?" He quickly noted that the fifth brother was there, though standing back from the others as if he only watched. "Is she a great heiress?" he continued. "An astonishing beauty? Well versed in bedding a man?"

The last earned him the angry outcry of the four brothers surrounding him. He realized the depth of his mistake when they began pummeling him with meaty fists. Tayg was no stranger to a good fight and he landed a few well-aimed punches, bloodying at least one nose, splitting a lip on another, doubling one of them over with a vicious kick to the groin.

But he was badly outnumbered.

With a mighty backhand, Broc sent him spinning into the snow. Tayg pushed to his hands and knees. Blood dripped from his nose and lip, staining the snow. Before he could rise a roughly-shod foot landed squarely in his ribs, sending him sideways into more snow. Another kick landed just where the first one had. Pain knifed through his side and he curled to protect his ribs from further abuse. Someone reached down and dragged him to his feet again, shoving him roughly against a stone wall.

Tayg gasped for breath as he watched the man's arm slowly pull back, the fist clenched tightly, then speed toward his face. Just in time Tayg rolled to his right, feeling the wind of that punch just as he heard the dull crunch of fist against stone wall. A howl went up.

Tayg used the confusion of the howling man and the cover of thick snow and darkness to limp as fast as he could towards the nearest doorway. He was jerked to a stop by a hand in his hair. Another brother appeared in front of him and proceeded to rain punches to Tayg's stomach and ribs. Tayg tried to defend himself, but there were too many of them. When the one punching him stepped back, the hair-grabber let go, dropping Tayg into a groaning heap at his feet.

"Now perhaps you'd like to tell us where Triona is," Broc said, his voice low and menacing.

Tayg's head hurt as he tried to decide if she was worth dying for. If the brothers took her back to Assynt, who would be harmed? Anyone within striking distance of Cat's dark temper. And the king, he reminded himself. He tried to push himself to his knees, buying himself time. The king and Cat would be the worse for it.

His stomach clenched at the idea of Broc trussing Cat up to haul her home. His gorge rose at the idea of Dogface kissing her, bedding her . . . breaking her fiery spirit. Damn! Cat didn't deserve that fate.

Tayg shoved himself to his feet, his fist swinging upward into Broc's chin so hard the man was knocked off his feet and onto his arse. He turned and punched another in the gut and managed to land another fist to one of their noses but there were too many. Quickly they had him pinned to the cold ground again, Broc kneeling atop him with his knee on his chest so Tayg could barely breathe.

"Where is she?" Broc demanded again.

If keeping Cat's whereabouts a secret—not so hard to do, since he didn't know where she was at this moment— kept her from Dogface and these rogues, he would keep his silence or better.

"Do you mean that shrew who was at Fionn," he gasped, "dark hair and a tongue like a well-honed claymore?" He sneered and hoped his face showed as much disdain as Broc's did.

"She left Fionn with you," one of the brothers said. Tayg didn't take his eyes off Broc though. It was clear who was in charge of this rabble.

"She did not. She disappeared during the evening. I left alone at dawn. 'Twas a braw lad she wandered off with."

A kick to his side knocked the breath from him and made his vision go black for a moment.

"Truth, you bloody bastard. No one would go off with Triona."

Tayg grunted his agreement.

"Where is our sister?" This from a brother who had said nothing so far. His voice was quieter, firmer than the others, and somehow more dangerous.

"What passes here?" a hesitant feminine voice called from the top of the steps leading from the Great Hall.

For a moment Tayg thought all was lost, but then realized it was Isobel, not Cat, who called to them. He allowed himself a moment of relief as the men hesitated. One of them landed one last kick to his ribs before they all turned to face Isobel, blocking Tayg from her sight.

"What are . . ." She approached them slowly, peering around them when she got close enough. "Bard? Bard!" She barged around the men and knelt beside him.

"I'm fine, lass," he said, slowly rising to his feet. "These lads mistook me for someone else." He rubbed away the blood trickling from his nose with the back of his hand and tried to stay steady on his feet. He glared at Broc, daring him to sully his sister's virtue by revealing the truth.

"You should find them a warm place in the hall," Tayg said to Isobel. "I'm sure they will be grateful for a hot meal and plenty of ale." He turned, needing to get away before he said something that would get them all in trouble.

"I shall send your sister to tend you," Isobel called after him as she herded the brothers away from him.

He could well imagine the reaction of the brothers MacLeod to that remark. He raised a hand in a wave, but limped as fast as he could towards the far tower.

'Twas not the most heroic exit, but at least he was still walking.

For now.

chapter 10

Catriona paced the small confines of Isobel's chamber. The fire did little to warm her, though sweat made her clothes stick to her. How had Dogface found her? Was it just coincidence or was he after her? It didn't matter. She would never marry the man. She must get away from here now and find the king. Immediately. But Tayg was still in the hall, entertaining her nemesis. Didn't he know who Dogface was? Hadn't Tayg seen him sitting right there in their midst? Nay, he was too busy flirting with Isobel.

She glared at the two leather sacks she had packed. Somehow she had to get Tayg out of the hall and they had to escape before Dogface realized who the wimple-clad woman he had spoken to was. But Tayg-the-flirt wouldn't come looking for her even if she had left precipitously. He was having too much fun. What did it matter if the man who could ruin her clan and her life sat across from him. He wouldn't leave until he was ready. So she would have to convince him he was ready, but she couldn't risk going back in there.

Face-to-face with Dogface once was too much. She wrapped her arms about her, trying to stop the trembling that had started in the pit of her stomach and was quickly spiraling out until her hands shook and her teeth chattered. That had been too close. She wouldn't give Dogface another opportunity to figure out who she was.

If only there was someone she could send. Someone who would help her . . .

Isobel.

Isobel would help her. She had said they were friends. But Isobel was probably still in the hall herself, so that wouldn't help. Catriona bit her lip to keep herself from wailing out loud. There was no one else to help her.

There was no one else to help her.

If the bard wished to stay there a minute longer he could face Dogface all he wanted. He deserved as much. If she had to continue on alone, she would do just that. She didn't need him. She could do perfectly well on her own.

She would leave now while Dogface was sitting addle-brained in the hall with Tayg and Isobel. No one would discover she was missing until morning.

If anyone would miss her at all.

The bard certainly wouldn't. She should have known the kisses they had shared hadn't meant anything. It was abundantly clear where his interest lay. If he could convince Dogface that he knew nothing of her, he would be safe. Even if Dogface did discover the truth, Tayg would tell him 'twas all her doing. She was daft, and difficult, and no one he'd ever willingly travel with. He'd be extraordinarily happy to rid himself of her company, just like everyone else always was.

And Dogface would believe him. What choice would he have since Tayg clearly spoke the truth?

Very well. She'd go alone. Tayg could take care of himself. He didn't need her and she didn't need him. She didn't need anyone.

Catriona wiped her hand impatiently across her cheek where one fat tear had escaped. Tears were useless. It wasn't like she'd never been betrayed before. She would live. She had little choice.

Catriona yanked on her confining wimple to cover more of her chin, donned her heavy cloak, grabbed her travel sacks and slipped out of the chamber.

The passageways were empty save for the eerie flickering of torchlight scattered here and there along the way. Everyone must still be gathered round Tayg, listening to his stories, surely not his songs. She tried not to think about the grin he'd have on his face, the waver in his voice when he got to a tricky part of a song, or how, when he told a story, his words could wind around her like a lover's embrace, warming her, transporting her away from herself.

She swiped another errant tear from her cheek and called Tayg every evil word she had ever heard her brothers utter. Somehow, it didn't help.

She made her way down the tightly turning stair, not bothering to silence her muttering.

"Where are you off to?"

Catriona froze then squinted into the darkness at the bottom of the stair.

"Were you leaving without me?" Tayg's voice, laced with teasing, but something sharper, too, washed over her.

Relief surged through her. He hadn't abandoned her. Hadn't betrayed her . . . or had he? She tried to press the relief back until she was sure why he was here.

"Why aren't you entertaining? 'Tis early yet for a bard to leave his hosts." Catriona let all of her anger and fear loose in those few words. She moved slowly toward the bottom of the steps, keeping out of his reach, but trying to get a clearer look at his shadowed face. If she could see his eyes, she could tell his intent. She was sure of it.

"It seems you are sought after," he said.

"And yet you dallied?"

Tayg leaned against the door, his face deeper in the shadows cast by the flickering light of the torch. "I was detained."

Catriona flinched at the anger in his voice.

"You'd do well not to return to the hall," he said.

"I've no intention—Tayg!" She watched as Tayg slowly slid down the door. Catriona dropped her bags and rushed to him, dropping to her knees next to him. "What happened?" she whispered, trying to control the shaking that was starting in her voice and rapidly spreading once more to the rest of her body.

Catriona reached out and smoothed his hair away from his face. She gasped at the damage she found. "Did Dog-face do this?"

"Nay, not your betrothed."

"He's not—"

"Your brothers did this."

She sat hard on the stone floor. "My brothers?" she whispered.

"It seems there are many who seek your company."

"But none who want me." Damn. Why did she say that? She did not want to sound so pitiful. "They have found us, all of them."

"They have not. They have only found me. They do not know you are here, at least not yet. Unless Dogface recognized you."

"I do not think so." She lightly touched his cheek where the clear outline of a set of knuckles showed. "Why?"

"Why did they do this?" he said, wincing when she once more reached towards his battered face. "They suspect you are traveling with me. For some reason they did not believe me when I said I did not know you." Half a grin peeked out of his bloodied lips.

"How dare they!" Catriona got to her feet and hauled Tayg to his. "You wait here. I'll teach them to hurt my bard." Her statement quivered in the air between them. "You would think they'd know me well enough to see this is my fault," she said, hoping he'd not noticed her rash words.

Tayg held her shoulders and forced her to look into his brown eyes. "Nay, lass. You do not want to go after them. Dogface is out there as well. Even with your formidable temper, they have the advantage over us in numbers."

Panic welled in her. Dogface and her brothers, all here. The walls closed in on her and she couldn't breathe, couldn't think. But she could. She must. Tayg was hurt and they were trapped unless they left immediately. Catriona looked back at the packed sacks she had carried down with her. She had all she needed, but she couldn't leave Tayg here to take more abuse from her brothers, nor from Dogface.

"Can you walk?" she asked.

"If I must."

"Let us go now, while we can."

"There's a storm on out there, Cat. I don't know how far I can walk."

"I'll not go without you," Catriona said, her voice sharp.

Tayg tried to smile, but winced when his lip began to bleed again.

Catriona gathered her sacks. "Where is your drum?"

"In the hall with my belongings. I had to leave everything there as I could not appear to be leaving."

"We'll have to leave it then. We dare not go back to the hall to fetch it. Perhaps I can find another cloak for you."

Catriona pressed her side to his and hooked an arm

around him. He hissed as her hand brushed his tender ribs, but she said nothing. Her mouth was set in a grim line.

"If you're determined to go out in that storm, you'd best leave me here, lass."

"I said I'll not leave you. Broc will kill you the next chance he gets, and you're in no shape to defend yourself. I'll not have your death on my conscience," she said, striving for a teasing tone.

She pushed away from the door, pulling him with her. A floorboard creaked over their heads, sending panic spiraling through her. Desperate to protect him should Dogface or her brothers come looking for him again, she rapidly searched her mind for options. They could not chance being seen by whoever walked overhead, yet they could not leave until she had at least the rudiments of travel clothing for Tayg.

She spied a small door under the stair. That would do. Whether 'twas a storage room or a stair leading downwards mattered not. Catriona dragged Tayg to it, awkwardly pushing it open while balancing him against her. She shouldn't have noticed the warmth of his body pressed up against hers. She shouldn't have noticed how she just fit under his arm, nor how her skin tingled where his heat mingled with her own, easing the irritating trembling that still plagued her.

She shouldn't have, but she did.

He stifled a groan when he had to bend slightly to pass through the door, bringing her attention away from her own sensations and back to his injuries. Catriona looked around the dark, cramped, storage room, unable to see far past the doorway. With difficulty, she dropped her sacks, unfastened her cloak, then lowered Tayg onto it.

"We've got to bind your ribs, tend to your face and find you a cloak," she said, more to herself than to him. Remembering the linen toweling she had used for her bath, she bade him be silent until she returned. Moving quickly but quietly, she raced up the twisting stairs, ducking into the shadows twice as men tramped through the corridor toward the far tower where the soldiers were housed.

When at last she made it to Isobel's chamber she paused and looked to each end of the torch-lit hall. No one. She shoved open the heavy oaken door only to have it hit something and stop abruptly. A thick groan came from within the chamber followed by the sound of something heavy hitting the floor.

Catriona pushed the door open far enough to peek around it and into the chamber. Crumpled in a heap on the other side of the door was Dogface. Fear twisted in her gut until she realized he was unconscious. She must have knocked him cold with the door, but what was he doing in Isobel's chamber in the first place? She pushed the door a bit harder. Despite Dogface's crumpled form, she needed items from the chamber and she had no time to search elsewhere.

She squeezed into the chamber, avoiding Dogface as much as possible. What if he woke to find her there? Terror gripped her but she forced herself to move. Quickly she grabbed the linen toweling, now dry from the fire. She could rip it into long strips for binding Tayg's ribs. She lifted the blanket from the bed, then snatched a candle from the unlit candle stand, squeezed back out the door and swiftly returned to the stairs. Just as she reached the bottom step the outer door opened. Cat froze, sure she would now face her brothers. What would happen to Tayg if they took her?

A golden head looked around the door and Cat released her breath. Isobel looked concerned as she pushed the door closed behind her.

"Cat!"

"Wheesht!" Catriona moved quickly to her side, a finger to her lips lest they draw attention to themselves.

"Did you see the bard?" Isobel whispered. "These

awful men attacked him, but he seemed so sure they had mistaken him for someone else . . . I took them to the hall."

Catriona stood mute. Isobel didn't know. Somehow she had not figured out they were Catriona's brothers, that they were after her, nor did she seem to know that Dogface also sought her. She really was still safe as long as she and Tayg could get out of here before her brothers or Dogface found her—or found him again.

Impulsively, Cat decided to trust Isobel, not with the whole secret . . . but with a part of it.

"I do not know who those louts search for, but there *is* another in your hall I wish never to see again."

Isobel's eyes lit up with curiosity. "There is?"

"Aye. Come. Help me tend Tayg's hurts and perhaps you can help us before that one realizes he knows me or the others pummel Tayg again."

Isobel nodded immediately. Catriona lit the taper from a nearby smokey torch and led the girl into the storage room.

The three made hasty plans while Catriona bound Tayg's ribs. Soon Isobel left them to await her return to their cramped space below the stair. Tayg dozed off and on but Catriona kept her vigil, alert to even the smallest sound lest they be discovered. Deep into the night Isobel finally returned with Tayg's cloak and news that Dogface had stumbled back into the hall shortly after she had returned, a great lump upon his head and a scowl upon his face, but he had said naught to anyone about what had happened.

All the visitors were now snoring in the Great Hall. Tayg's horse and his belongings awaited them by the postern gate. It took both Catriona and Isobel to get Tayg on his feet and out to the horse. It was only with his clearly painful help that they were able to push him up into the saddle. Isobel opened the gate which thankfully swung free without so much as a scrape or a squeal of hinges. Catriona gave the lass a quick fierce hug.

"I will see you again," she said.

"I would like to dance at your wedding," Isobel said with a sly cutting of her eyes to Tayg.

"It's not . . ."

"Wheesht. Go now. The storm is strengthening and you need to get to shelter quickly. Remember, stay close to the river, then follow the first burn uphill. The traveler's hut is not far, but 'twill be far enough for tonight. The storm will cover your tracks and I will keep your absence hidden as long as I may."

"I do not know how to thank you." Catriona gave her another hug.

"'Tisn't necessary. We are friends. I do not like having my friend's . . . brother . . . attacked in my own home." Isobel handed her a screened lantern, the flickering candle just visible through the cracks in the shield. "Do not show the light until you are well away from the castle. Follow the line of trees to the river, then go left, downstream. Now go!"

Isobel put the horse's reins in Catriona's hand and pushed her through the gate. As soon as the horse followed her through she heard the muffled sound of the door closing and the bolt being thrown. There was no turning back.

She turned into the wind and followed the snow-covered trail down to the riverside mumbling Isobel's final instructions all the way.

C atriona trudged through the increasingly deep snow. If it weren't for the occasional snorts of the horse behind her, and the times she had to stop and force the beast to follow her through deep drifts, she would have felt completely alone in the snow-filled darkness. Tayg was silent. He had been hurt badly and she wasn't even sure he was conscious. Every so often she would stop and reach up to make sure he was still slumped in the saddle. She did so now, eliciting a moan when she missed his leg and touched his side.

"Tayg?" she nudged his leg. "Tayg, you must awaken." She held the lantern Isobel had given her high to cast its weak circle of light on his battered face.

Slowly, he opened his eyes. "Are we there?" he asked, though he did not sit up.

"Nay. I have not found it, though we have not reached the burn yet . . . at least, I don't think we have."

Tayg closed his eyes again, abandoning Catriona once more.

She sighed and turned back in the direction she thought they should journey in, back into the face of the wind-driven snow. The river ran somewhere to her right and sooner or later they would encounter the burn. Isobel had said not to cross it, but to travel up it, looking for a giant boulder that sat at the foot of a huge, ancient pine tree, not far from where the burn met the river. She said if you looked just so at the tree's limbs they pointed up the embankment directly to a traveler's hut. Unfortunately, in the middle of the long winter night, with the wind blowing the heavy snow into her face, Catriona didn't think she'd see the burn until she fell into it, never mind the tree.

But she had to keep going. If they stopped they would freeze. Tayg might anyway, though the horse should help to warm him a little. Catriona shook her shoulders, loosening the snow that clung to her cloak. They needed shelter, and a fire, and something warm to drink soon. She wiggled her toes, grateful that she could still feel them.

They moved slowly forward, Catriona breaking the trail, the horse moving behind her, balking occasionally.

Tayg's continued silence scared her more than anything. He was completely dependant on her to see them safely to the traveler's hut. She bit her lip, ducked her head down to keep the driving snow out of her face, and forced her feet to move. She would not let him die. Her breath hitched. She owed Tayg too much. He was her bard. She'd see him to safety, then tend his hurts. How could she do anything less?

Her foot slipped and she heard the crunch of brittle ice, then felt the sharp slice of cold water seeping into her boot. The burn. She backed up, shaking the water from her foot. Her mind flitted around the knowledge that she was in serious trouble if her boot turned to ice or her skin froze. She lifted her lantern and tried to make out shapes in the darkness.

The snow was swirling about her causing moments where all she could see in the feeble light was a heavy curtain of white shifting and dancing against the night's black blanket. She bent, lowering the lantern through the whiteness until she could make out the edge of the burn.

Uphill.

The single word formed in her thick brain like a beacon in the night.

Uphill.

She turned and picked her way up the steep, slippery slope. Each step squeaked in the icy snow and she realized that she could no longer feel the foot that had gotten wet. Wind whistled down the hill sending biting snow into her face, then shifted suddenly and gusted from behind as if it quarreled with itself over whether it should be coming or going.

A vicious gust caught her by surprise, shoving her to her knees and knocking the lantern from her hand. She watched as it rolled into the whiteness and disappeared.

"Nay!"

"Cat?" Tayg's voice came from the complete blackness

around her. He was depending on her. She had to get him to safety.

She struggled upright and trudged back to the horse. Cat leaned for a moment against Tayg's leg, needing the reassuring warmth of him to know she wasn't all alone in this. She rested her head against him and fought the tears of frustration, anger and fear that threatened to overwhelm her.

"You can do this, lass," Tayg's voice drifted down to her, quiet and weak enough to scare her. "I know you can do this, Cat."

"The lantern is lost," she said, hating the sound of defeat in her voice. "I do not know how I can find the shelter in the darkness."

"You can. Clear your mind. Concentrate on Isobel's words. She's our friend. She would not lead us astray."

Tayg's confidence warmed her. The memory of her first friend gave her resolve. She would do this. She must. Tayg was depending on her. And she would not let Isobel blame herself for sending them out into the storm. She reached up to place her hand gently on Tayg's back. He lay still upon the horse's neck again but she could feel him breathing, shallow and quick. He had not left her.

Near.

The word was another beacon in her muddled thoughts. Isobel had said the shelter was near where the burn met the river. They must be near the shelter.

She moved forward, glad she had remembered Tayg's trick of looping the reins around her wrist so she did not have to worry about frozen fingers losing their grip. She tugged and got the horse moving again. Almost immediately she stumbled over the lantern. She reached down and retrieved it. The precious flame was gone, but the lantern was sound and the candle only half burned. Once they found the hut she could kindle a new flame.

The horse snorted and she tugged on the reins, forcing

the unhappy animal to follow her up the steep slope. Three steps, four . . . All she could see was deepest black. All she could feel was the bite of snow driven into her raw skin by the never-ending wind. Another step and another. 'Twas all she could think of until suddenly she realized the wind had all but stopped, as if she had stepped out of a fast stream and into a pool where the current eddied and paused.

Cat reached forward, her hands outstretched and took another step. Nothing. Another step. Nothing. Another and her mittened hands bashed into something hard that stood directly in her path. She felt around until she was sure this was a wall made by man. Relief surged through her. She'd done it! She'd found the shelter. She turned to Tayg, grinning, but he just groaned. She had to get him out of this storm. She had to get herself out of it, too. As quickly as her frozen mind could work she began to feel to her left and her right, searching for a door.

She led the horse along the edge of the shelter, searching for the door on the first wall and around the corner to the second. Finally she found it on the far side of the small hut. She took the reins from her wrist and looped them around the latch then pushed open the door.

"Tayg, we made it!" she said as she moved inside and looked around. Water sloshed in her boot and she realized that they were not safe yet. It was as cold inside the hut as it was out, though at least the wind was stopped. She needed to get Tayg off the horse and into shelter. The horse would have to come in, too, both to keep it safe and to help warm the space. She needed a fire. She needed to get her wet clothes off. Tayg's too.

She stepped outside and moved to the side of the horse, untying the tether that had helped hold Tayg in the saddle.

"You must awaken," she said, shaking him. When he didn't respond, anxiety poured through her. "Tayg! Awaken!" She winced at the note of panic in her voice, but there was no help for it. Her mind was slow and she knew they were still in grave danger. She was tired, cold, hungry and scared. He damn well better not have died on her just when she had rescued him.

Gently she poked him in the ribs. "Tayg!" she said in her nastiest voice, hoping to rouse him, "I cannot carry you so you'd best wake or I'll leave you here in the snow. At least then I wouldn't have to listen to your pitiful singing anymore."

Slowly, Tayg opened his eyes and pushed himself up until he was sitting, though he swayed enough so Cat grabbed his arm.

"You need not take that tone with me, lass," he said, a hint of a smile in his voice, though the groan that followed told her how much pain he was in.

He all but fell into her arms as he tried to lower himself from the saddle.

"I'll take whatever tone I must, bard." She wrapped one arm around his waist and grasped his arm where it draped over her shoulders with her free hand. "Come on, then. My feet are freezing and I've still got to start a fire."

Tayg grunted and moved slowly with her. She stopped them just before they entered the hut and took care to shake as much snow as possible from their cloaks then led him into the cavelike shelter.

She propped him against the wall at the back of the space and headed for the door again. "Where are you going?" Tayg asked, his voice pain-sharpened.

She sighed. "I've got to get the horse in here."

Catriona settled the horse on the opposite side of the hut from where she had left Tayg then pulled the door firmly closed behind her, shutting out the wind and swirling snow, and enclosing them in complete and utter darkness. She tried to think what to do next but she was so cold and so tired she could barely stand.

Heat.

Yes, that was always the first thing Tayg did when they made camp. His first priority was always a fire. Isobel had said the hut was stocked with wood, as most such huts were. There was only the task of finding it in the dark, building a fire in the as yet undiscovered fire pit, then the small problem of actually getting it to burn.

Catriona began searching along the walls and quickly stumbled into the woodpile, which was neatly stacked right next to a pile of dried heather and other tinder. She gathered up the makings of a small fire and turned to what she hoped was the middle of the chamber. She stubbed her toe on the ring of stones that defined the fire pit and quickly laid the fire. She groped for the horse who blessedly made enough noise with his shifting and occasional snorts that he was easy to find. She felt her way through the bags that Isobel had managed to remove from the Great Hall until she found the fire kit.

She knelt by the ring of stones and laid the fire starter kit in her lap so she could peel off her sodden woolen mittens. She had to take a moment to warm her fingers with her breath before she could pull her *sgian dhu* from its sheath at her waist, grasp the flint and bring the two together. Another moment and she had sparks, but it took longer than she wished before she finally had a tiny flickering flame lick to life in the bits of heather. Finally the delicious smell of burning wood rose into the frozen air.

She sat for a long time, feeding the fire, tending it carefully until she had a roaring blaze going. Only when she was sure the fire would not go out did she move to Tayg's side and begin to remove his wet clothing.

chapter 11

Tayg woke slowly, aware of a pleasant warmth along his back and the weight of several blankets over him. When he could finally get his eyes to focus it was on the glowing embers of a fire. He didn't remember building a fire. Truth was, he didn't remember much. His stomach growled, his ribs and jaw hurt, and his bladder complained.

He tried to rise, only to realize the warmth along his back was connected to the viselike grip about his middle. Cat was snuggled up to him, keeping him warm though he could feel her shivering. Carefully he pried her arm from his waist and gingerly rolled to face her. She shifted closer to him until her head rested against his chest. He wrapped his arm around her and started rubbing her back to warm her while he considered his surroundings and struggled to remember how he had come to be here.

Gradually bits and pieces of the night and their flight from Duchally Castle came back to him. He remembered

the beating the MacLeod brothers had given him. He remembered the look of concern when Cat found him, followed by righteous indignation when she discovered who
his attackers were. But then his memory went fuzzy.

Flashes of Cat and Isobel huddled together, then cold
and pain as every step the horse took jarred his tender
ribs. Nothing more . . . except a vague memory of gentle
hands removing his sodden plaid and apparently his
trews.

He glanced over his shoulder toward the glowing fire.
His clothes were draped from pegs on the wall. The horse
was contentedly sleeping, his head drooping and one hind
leg cocked in repose.

Catriona had managed to get them here. She had very
likely saved his life. He smoothed a strand of hair away
from her face and was rewarded with a contented sigh. He
marveled at what she had accomplished.

Catriona MacLeod was a bundle of contradictions. One
moment he wanted to throttle her, the next to kiss her.
One moment she was scolding him and the next she was
carefully binding his ribs or trying to warm him in his
sleep. She was not the shrew she appeared to be and she
certainly wasn't the shriveled crone the gossips gave her
to be.

Nay. She was a bonny lass, with a sharp tongue, true,
but a sharp mind as well. And he was proud of her. Less
than a sennight ago he had rescued a lost lass from a
snowstorm. This night—if 'twas the same night—she had
rescued him with the help of a new friend. It was almost
as if she had never been given the opportunity to be herself. She was more than anyone had guessed. More than
she knew herself.

He kissed her forehead lightly, inhaling the sleep-warm
scent of her, then lightly stroked her silky hair. In the dim
light from the fire he couldn't see more than the paleness
of her skin and the dark fringe of eyelashes against it. She

was truly a bonny lass, a sweet lass in her own tart way, a staunch friend in the face of trouble. He remembered the sound of her laughter and the sweet taste of her lips. She was brave and determined and, he realized with a start, loyal. He felt a warmth spread through him that had nothing to do with their shared body heat.

She did not deserve to be married off to that ugly, traitorous, horse's arse of a MacDonell who clearly did not want her for herself. She did not deserve to be hunted down by her brothers, who clearly did not understand how strongly she hated—or was it feared?—Dogface. Either way, how could they hunt her and force her into wedding him?

Separately Dogface and the brothers would have been formidable foes. Now they would no doubt join forces and he and Cat would have to be even more careful not to be discovered.

He remembered the missive he had intercepted. Dogface suspected Tayg had the damning parchment, but he didn't know Tayg could read it, had read it. And the longer it stayed that way the better. So many problems and they all seemed to be drawing together—her brothers, Dogface MacDonell, the missive threatening the king. Even his own mother's plot to marry him off seemed to be tied into this mess since that's what forced him into this position in the first place—and what kept him from revealing his true self to Catriona.

Cat sighed, drawing his attention away from the downward spiral of his thoughts. She was tired and cold, and he was injured thanks to her brothers. No matter what happened they were in this together now. They would discuss what to do when she awakened and they were both clearheaded.

He carefully rose, pulling a blanket about him. He placed a log on the fire and fanned it to a blaze, then retrieved his dry clothes from his bags.

• • •

Catriona sat across the fire from the sleeping Tayg. At some point in the night he must have moved because she had awoken to the pleasantly disturbing feeling of being surrounded by him, or nearly so. He had been scooped against her back, his arm tucked around her waist, holding her tight against him though she clearly remembered pressing up against his back last night, desperate to warm him. And he had not been clothed when she went to sleep. She vividly remembered struggling to get him out of his wet things while averting her eyes from his battered body. He had dressed himself sometime during the night.

Now she sat across the fire and stared at his bruised face in the flickering light. It was light out, though the snow still raged on the wind. Dogface, Broc and the rest of the sheep would be after them soon. The smell of the fire would draw them to this hut. Their sanctuary would quickly become a prison and she feared that Broc would finish what he'd started with Tayg.

Anger slithered up her spine and settled its teeth around her heart. Why didn't Broc give up? And why was Dogface so determined to marry her? Surely he loathed her at least as much as she loathed him. She would not make a good wife to him, so why?

She leaned forward and stirred the stew she had made from the supplies Isobel had provided. A smile warmed her face as she thought about the golden-haired lass. She was a true friend and Cat still could not quite understand how that had come to be. Oh, she knew she had followed Tayg's advice—though she would be sure not to tell him that or she'd forever have to listen to him gloat. A lump formed in her throat. At the moment she would like to hear a bit of gloating from him.

He was so still, his face so battered. She wanted to awaken him, just so she'd know he was going to be well, but she let him sleep. There was little else she could do for him at the moment. Keep him warm. Feed him when he awoke. And wait.

But not too long.

If there had been room in the confines of the hut, Catriona would have paced. But there wasn't, so she satisfied the need to move by braiding and re-braiding her hair. Isobel had said she would send the brothers and Dogface off in the wrong direction but Catriona knew that would not last long. Broc was an excellent hunter and he would know quickly which way Tayg had gone—and which way he hadn't—though the storm would slow him down. She had no doubt that soon, Broc would find their trail, despite the snow and wind. She and Tayg would be trapped.

Then what would happen? She'd protect Tayg as long as she could. Ailig sometimes could be prevailed upon to take her side against the other brothers. Perhaps that would work. But not likely. From Isobel's description of the fight, Catriona was sure Ailig had done nothing to stop it. Nay, Broc would see Tayg punished—a bard daring to travel with his sister.

And she would be dragged back to Assynt and forced to marry Dogface.

She would die first.

"You look cold, lass."

Catriona startled then frowned. Tayg's voice was scratchy, but strong.

"'Tis winter in the Highlands. Of course I am cold." She dropped her braid and stirred the pot again. "Are you hungry?"

Tayg sat up slowly, as if testing his body. "Aye. You cooked?"

Catriona glared at him. "I cooked."

Tayg frowned at her. "I see you're feeling back to your old self."

She ladled the stew into a wooden bowl and handed it and a horn spoon to him.

"We must leave here as soon as we can travel," he said.

She nodded and watched him eat the stew.

"We cannot stay here. Your brothers and Dogface will track us down."

She nodded again. "But you can't travel yet. We must wait here—rest—another day." She worried her lower lip with her teeth.

He regarded her for a moment as if she held some secret he could read in her eyes. "Do not be afraid, lass."

She glanced at his strong hands with the battered knuckles holding his bowl, then up to his bruised face.

"'Tis not me I am afraid for." Her voiced was strained despite her efforts to sound annoyed.

A slow smile spread over Tayg's full lips and an answering heat spread in Catriona's chest.

"You fear for me?" he asked, his voice low and husky.

"I . . . I . . ." Catriona busied herself with another bowl of the stew. She lifted the spoon to her mouth, then lowered it and glared at the grinning bard. "I wish to get to the king as soon as possible and I need your help to do that. I do not fear for you," she said quickly, then turned her undivided attention to the food in her bowl.

His soft chuckle irritated her. Damn the man. She was afraid for him, but she'd not say so. The gloating would be bad enough over what she had already admitted to.

After a few moments of silence, save for the horse's soft snorts, Tayg put his bowl down. "Why do your brothers wish you to marry Dogface?"

Caught off guard by the concern in his voice, she glanced up and was shaken to find the same concern shining from his eyes.

"I do not know," she whispered. "I do not know why Dogface would want me, either."

She dropped her gaze to her bowl for she was unused to

such concern from anyone and did not understand why it made her want to curl up in his lap and cry.

"I will never marry him."

"I do not blame you. Indeed, I would not let you. He is an ugly brute and a horse's arse besides."

"You would not let me?"

He took a deep breath. "Isobel is not your only friend. I could not in good conscience let you marry one such as he." Tayg put his bowl down. "Besides, he was not looking for you at Duchally."

She didn't know which of his statements disturbed her more—that he would not let her marry Dogface—a nervous thrill ran over her skin; that he was her friend; or that Dogface was not looking for her. That one was easier to think about; she'd think about the others, and what they meant, later.

"He was looking for me," she said. "He was there, sitting next to me in the Great Hall, and later in Isobel's chamber." Her voice rose slightly and she tried to hide the shrill edge that had crept into it.

Tayg moved stiffly to her side of the fire, lowering himself to face her, his legs folded between them. "He . . ." He closed his eyes and shook his head. "'Tis not you he is after, lass."

"He thinks I am to be his bride. Who else would he be after?"

"Me."

Catriona's breath hitched. "What do you mean?"

"He is after me. I have something he wants."

"Well, if you wish to think of it that way, I'll not stop you, but it comes down to the same thing. He wants me."

Tayg smiled, picked up her hand and held it between his own. "Nay, you misunderstand. You forget the missive. I have his message that was to be delivered to Broc though he said 'twas for you. 'Tis not something either of them would wish to fall into the wrong hands. And mine are definitely the wrong hands," he said raising her hand to his lips and gently kissing her knuckles.

Catriona was mesmerized by the soft feather-light kiss. He lowered their hands, but he did not release hers. What had they been talking about? Oh yes, the missive.

"But you read it to me," she said, her voice more breathless than she liked.

"Aye, but there is more there than the words say, Cat. Clearly you know nothing about the intent of the letter. That is all to the good. If you know nothing about the intent, then you cannot be held responsible for it."

"But I do know about the missive. Leaving Dogface's intent to my imagination will surely not be wise."

He shook his head.

"Is it important enough that if something should happen to you another should be able to deliver it into safe hands?"

"Nothing will happen to me, lass." He rubbed a thumb over her palm and Catriona found the sensation both fascinating and comforting. "Just be assured that Duff— Dogface—does not know you were in that castle. He is after me."

Catriona yanked her hand away from his caresses and quickly folded her arms, hiding her hands from him.

"Then why was he in Isobel's chamber?"

"Perhaps he saw me heading to that tower and was searching all the rooms—hers is amongst the first he would come to."

"Perhaps, but it does not matter which of us he searches for. If he finds you he will also find me and we'll both be in bigger trouble for it."

Tayg placed his large callused hand against her cheek. Catriona struggled not to lean into it, not to relish the comfort she gained from his skin against hers, not to sink into the sensual haze he called forth in her with just a glance or a touch. She struggled to maintain her glare.

He smiled, his eyes twinkling, and before she realized what he was up to, he had hooked his hand behind her neck and pulled her toward him, halting her forward motion with his kiss. Surprise kept her from reacting and before she could even think, she was engulfed in that delicious heat that she had experienced twice before.

His kiss was soft and demanding at the same time and she found herself answering every challenge of his lips, his tongue, his hands in her hair. He groaned and pulled her closer still, deepening the kiss.

Her heart seemed to stop, then start again double-pace. She closed her eyes and surrendered to the amazing sensation of being the sharp focus of all his attention. She wrapped her arms around him and felt him lift her into his lap, all the while kissing her as if he never intended to stop.

And she did not wish to stop.

Their plaid blankets slipped down around their waists, but the heat between them warded off the cold. She slid her fingers into his hair, slanting her head a bit to enjoy the feel of his lips on hers even more. A haze seemed to fall over her mind, as if she had drunk too much whiskey, yet her senses were acutely aware of every place he touched her, every change in the pressure of his hands upon her, every shuddering breath he took. He pulled her closer until there was nothing separating them but the thin barrier of their clothes and kissed her again.

She was aware of the pressure, gathering deep within her, centering itself between her legs and in her breasts where they pressed against his chest. She was aware of the answering pressure of his arousal. He shifted his hips against her, holding her close, his lips leaving trails of heat as he kissed her neck and the hollow at the base of her throat. She heard herself moan, but could not stop it.

He caressed her bottom, ran his hands over her back and into her hair. The heat of him warmed her and height-

ened the pressure until she couldn't think clearly. Vaguely
she was aware of him tugging at her shift, then clearly she
felt the heat of his hands directly on her skin, her breasts.
It was exquisite. She tugged at the laces of his tunic, but
when he lowered his mouth to her nipple, increasing the
pressure unbearably, she could do nothing but lean into
him, urging him to . . . she wasn't sure what, but she
wanted more.

His hand moved lower, gently pressing her legs apart.
She could do nothing—wanted to do nothing—but com-
ply as his mouth covered hers once more and she lost herself in his kiss. Then she felt the warmth and the weight of
his hand in that place where all the pressure centered.
That wanting place.

Her mind went blank. She could think of nothing, only
feel the heat of him cradled against her, the urgency of his
mouth on hers. She never wanted this moment to end,
never wanted these heady new sensations to cease. And
yet she strove toward some new height until suddenly she
was there, in a moment where all ceased to exist except
the exquisite sensations coursing through her. Abruptly
the pressure broke, splintering and spiraling out through
her.

*Tayg wrapped his arms around her, holding her tight as
her breathing slowed.* His own breathing was ragged,
his own need held tightly in check. What had he done?
Despite his spontaneous nature, he had never been so
driven by the hunger for a woman that he did not think
through what he did. Never had the need to find that passion, to ignite it, made him forget where he was and who.
And yet, though he had held onto just enough sanity not
to roll her onto her back and take her hard and fast, he
could not keep himself from touching her, driving her, sat-
isfying her.

Teaching her what she had to look forward to in his bed.

His breath hitched. Was that what he wanted? Did he really want her in his bed?

Cat nuzzled his neck, her body draped against him in her languor. Absently, he ran a hand along her back and she tucked her hips against his. He went still as a craving for her raced through him, stronger than before. Her passion, her abandon, had challenged what little control he had left.

Aye. He wanted her in his bed. More than he had wanted any woman before. But did he want the rest? Marriage, bairns, Catriona the Shrew? He did not wish to marry, but he must. Was this the woman he could spend his life with? Wanting to bury himself in her wasn't enough. Could he live with her day in and day out, or would she drive him mad? How could anyone know? How could he?

Besides, she would want a husband to bide with her at Assynt and help her control her brothers. Tayg shuddered. He couldn't see subjecting himself to that rabble again—especially on a daily basis—nor could he understand why she would want to. For once his responsibilities at Culrain, to his clan, stood as an advantage. He would never be allowed to shuck his mantle of responsibility to go live amongst another clan.

He stroked her chilled cheek and an odd melancholy drifted over him.

"Cat, do you think you could release my tunic, love?"

"Hmm?" She sat up enough for him to see her face, satisfaction evident in her faint smile, and the dazed expression in her eyes. She moved to kiss him, then stopped. The dazed expression cleared and confusion replaced it. Catriona stared at him then glanced down at her hands, fisted in his tunic. She abruptly released her grip.

"What have we done?"

"Nothing irreversible, lass," he said, carefully pulling her shift up to cover her beautiful full breasts before he reached for them again. He pushed her back gently until she slid off his lap. He glimpsed dark curls between her legs glistening with the result of his lapse in judgment and struggled to remember why he could not finish what he'd started. She caught the direction of his gaze and quickly covered herself, drawing her knees up again and wrapping herself in one of the blankets.

"What did you do to me?"

Tayg took a deep breath and caught the musky scent of her satisfaction. "'Tis more what you do to me, lass." He shook his head at his own traitorous words.

"I did nothing to you!"

"We'd best get some sleep—"

"I'll not sleep with you!"

"Nay, I know. I did not mean—"

Cat rose and moved to her pallet, gathering it up from its place next to his and moving it to the opposite side of the fire.

"You will not touch me again. You will not kiss me. I cannot give myself to such as you."

"Such as me?" Anger rose in his gut, though he knew he should not take her words to heart.

"You are a bard, and not a very good one at that. You have no power to help me keep my brothers from—"

"What makes you think any man will stand up to your brothers for you?"

The look of panic on her face didn't match the cutting edge of her tone or the agitated way she was arranging her pallet.

He had scared her.

He had scared himself.

●   ●   ●

Tayg *lay for a long time, staring into the darkness, lis-* tening to the keening wind, struggling to ignore the black humor that had descended on him when Cat had pulled away and made it plain what she wanted . . . or rather what she didn't want . . . or who.

And yet her body told him otherwise. He knew she reacted as strongly as he did when they touched. When he kissed her, she had leaned into him, pulled him closer, been just as stunned by the intensity of each kiss as he was.

He turned onto his side—it was a bit less tender now than when he had awakened—and faced the fire and the shadowy lass who slept on the other side of it. He missed the feel of her curled up against him. He wanted . . . more.

But he shouldn't. He couldn't. He dared not entangle himself in such a way with a lass like Catriona MacLeod. 'Twas dangerous enough that they traveled together. If they were found together no one would believe her virtue was unsullied. He would be forced to wed her—assuming her brothers did not kill him first. 'Twas a daft notion, marrying the Shrew of Assynt. Marrying Cat.

He turned his back to the fire and stared into the darkness for a long time, reminding himself of all the reasons he did not wish to marry. He tried to think of reasons Cat would not make a good wife, but he kept remembering the feel of her lips on his and her hands fisted in his tunic. Quickly he forced his thoughts back to why he didn't want a wife but his reasons seemed feeble even to him. It was a long time before sleep finally took him.

The next day passed slowly. *Tayg tried to venture out* to gather wood but a few minutes in the battering wind and he returned to the relative warmth of the hut worn out and weak with only a few measly branches to show for his effort.

Catriona had fussed over him, making him lie down again, covering him with all the blankets and stirring up a stew that tempted his belly despite the meager ingredients she had available. He didn't think he was really that badly off but he was enjoying her attentions too much to do anything to make her stop. He spent the day watching her as she moved about their makeshift home, caring for and cleaning up after the horse; mending first her clothes and then his; cooking; tidying. She even beat the dirt from his plaid and his cloak.

What she didn't do was talk to him. She wouldn't look him in the eye, and she was careful not to let him touch her, except to check the bindings on his battered ribs.

After a while Tayg rose once more from his pallet but there was nothing for him to do but try to pace in the tiny cottage. There was nothing to do but sleep, eat . . . his gaze lingered over the oddly still Cat sitting by the fire. A strange prickling sensation seemed to take turns running down Tayg's spine and wriggling in his belly. Nay, there was naught to do but sleep, he told himself firmly. 'Twasn't right, this situation. 'Twasn't natural for him to have to fight his desires like this. And yet he must.

In desperation he grabbed the sack that held his drum. She didn't think he was a bard. Well, he could act the part now. A bard would entertain when faced with a long cold confinement. He could entertain her when he dared not do anything else.

Tayg fit the beater into his hand, positioned the drum on his leg and began tapping out a simple rhythm. Catriona rose and moved to her pallet. She lay down on it, pulling a blanket around her but watching him.

Tayg sang to himself at first, listening to the combination of his voice and that of the drum. He learned to beat it in different areas for a slightly different quality of sound, moving his hand over the face of the drum as he'd seen others do.

He tried a second song and then a third. He thought Catriona had drifted off to sleep when he was surprised to hear her lovely voice joining with his, weaving around the melody in a haunting descant.

"You are better at this than I," he said when the song ended. She gave him a wan smile and he started into another song, more lively this time, happy for a Scottish tune. Again she joined in, picking up the melody, adding trills and flourishes that he had never heard before.

"You are quite the bard yourself, sweet Cat."

The startled look in her eyes told him he had said something he shouldn't. He quickly started playing the drum again, humming the first thing that came to him.

"Are you trying to anger me now?" she asked.

He shook his head but continued humming the oddly familiar tune. He couldn't quite find the words yet, but he knew they would come in a moment. They must.

"Once again you do not recognize what you are humming, do you?" Cat said.

"Aye . . ." but he didn't, not quite.

"Sweet Dolag of Fionn, a sweet thing she is," Catriona sang to him.

"Her hair is like fire, her face like a pig," he finished with a grin. "Ah, yes, now I remember it. I think I will leave out that last bit when I sing it for the king."

"Why would you sing that drivel for him?" Her voice was sharp.

"You do not like my song?"

"'Tis no song, that. 'Tis worthy of a drunken fool, no more."

"Ah, but if you were to sing along as you were a moment ago, 'twould elevate it above a mere tavern song. How else am I to tell the king of the lovely lasses I have met?"

Catriona sat up and laughed. "What makes you think any of these lassies wish for the king to give them to his warriors? I suspect even the famed Tayg of Culrain is like any other man anxious to take up the reigns of power: cocky, arrogant, unaware of the needs and feelings of those around him. Why would a woman wish to be given to any of them?"

Tayg winced inwardly at her description of him and felt a moment of kinship with her. To be described in such a way to one's face, as he had done to her, was not an elevating experience.

"That is not Tayg of Culrain you describe," he said, making sure his wry grin was in place, "well, except perhaps the cocky part, but then he has reason to be." After all he was pulling off this bit of mummery, wasn't he?

"If he is cocky, he is all the other. In my experience they come all of one."

"And your experience of men is so vast?"

She glared at him. "Vast enough. I have lived in a household full to the rafters of men my whole life. I think I understand them as well as any woman may."

"'Tis sure you do." He beat a slow rhythm on the drum, then looked back at her across the crackling fire. "You would judge all men against your brothers."

"They provide plenty of experience for me. Each is different, each a blight on society in his own way."

"All of them?"

"Sometimes Ailig is fine—on his own—but when the others are around, he does not stand up to them. He does not speak his mind."

"As you do."

"Aye. As I do."

"And you hold Ailig in contempt because he does not behave as you do?"

"Nay. I do not hold him in contempt, though that is an apt description of my feelings for the rest of my brothers. With Ailig I feel . . . pity."

Tayg's hand stilled on the drum. "Pity? Why that?"

Catriona pulled at the edge of the plaid she had wrapped about her and shrugged. "It isn't as if he lets the others tell him what to do, he just does nothing to stop them. Ailig is quiet and keeps to himself more than the three sheep do. He doesn't seem to care."

"About what?"

"About his pride, about the thoughts of others. He is willing to be ridiculed, derided, mocked without calling the offender out, without defending himself in any way. He has this funny little almost-smile he gives as if he finds it all slightly amusing. Just once—"

"You'd like him to stand up to them."

"Aye. Just once."

"Why?"

She looked at him, a puzzled expression on her face. "So they will stop, of course."

"Ah, and that has worked so well for you."

Did she not see that Broc still played her as well as the finest harpist in the land played his instrument? It seemed that Ailig had discovered the secret to coping with her family. Too bad the hard-headed Catriona couldn't let go of her pride long enough to see what was really happening.

"Once I was made a fool of because I was too enamored of my brothers to think for myself. I will never put myself in such a situation again."

Something in her tone told Tayg they were not speaking of the same thing. The lost look on her face tore at Tayg and he sensed he was finally seeing the true woman beneath the shrewish exterior she held up to the world. That tough, prickly persona protected the softer side of the lass which he glimpsed too rarely. He stayed quiet, not wanting to break her mood. He was intrigued by the hurt lass in front of him. Never would he have guessed that such lay hidden beneath the surface.

"If I tell you something, will you promise never to

make a song of it?" Now she did look directly at him, apparently gauging his sincerity before she decided to continue.

It was an easy promise to make so he readily agreed, his curiosity piqued by her change in manner and her sudden willingness to reveal something of herself. She seemed convinced of his promise and she looked away again, absently braiding her hair.

"When I was but ten and two we were constantly struggling with the MacDonells. They would steal our cows. We'd steal them back, plus a few of theirs for good measure. Jamie and Ailig would go along, but Broc, Calum and Gowan were the instigators of much of the mayhem that took place. One time their prank went wrong and a cottage was burned. I do not think anyone was hurt, but the MacDonells did not take it well. One thing led to another and before long my da and the chief of the MacDonells exchanged messages calling for a halt to the nonsense of the young men before it escalated beyond the stopping place."

"Why would they care?"

"We had long been neighbors, friends even."

Tayg nodded, understanding instantly the way of these things. "What happened?"

"When the two chiefs demanded their sons cease the raiding and the fighting my da left it to Broc, as the eldest, to make amends with the MacDonell lads."

Tayg shifted, sensing that what came next was the real heart of her story.

"I did not know any of this at the time, you understand. I was but a lassie, just showing signs of . . . of womanhood." She ducked her head.

"And a fine woman you've grown into." Tayg couldn't stop the whispered words and they earned him a shy smile. Another conundrum. Shyness from Catriona? "Go on," he encouraged.

"Broc told me he had an important job for me. I did not understand him yet. He was my eldest brother and I idolized him. He was quite used to telling me to do things and having me jump to his command, as I did this time.

"He sent me with a message for the MacDonells. He had it written on a piece of parchment. I wondered at the time why he had done that, and how, for Broc can neither read nor write, but as I said, I idolized him and did as he bade me, thinking to make him proud of me.

"I rode a pony out to the place I was told to meet the MacDonells and I awaited them. When they arrived 'twas only a few lads Broc's age. I did not know them but their leader was Dogface. He was ugly even then."

Every nerve in Tayg's body tingled but he sat, still and silent, letting her continue if she would.

"I was nervous," she said, twisting her braid in her hands. "I had never acted the messenger for my brothers before. I handed the message to the first one who approached and he handed it back to Dogface. It took a while for them to figure out the words, but finally they did."

"What did it say?"

"It bade them hand over their weapons to me and all would be forgiven."

"What!?"

"Aye, 'twas the same reaction the MacDonell lads had. They laughed, then said 'twas fitting that the witless MacLeods would send a lass to do a man's job."

"They did not—"

She looked up at him, her eyes big and full of old hurts. "They tried. They grabbed me, stripping my clothing from me until I wore naught but my undershift. But I managed to club one in the head with a rock and kicked the other . . . Dogface . . . in the groin. He could not move, so in pain was he, but he bade the rest throw me in a nearby bog to rot. They said . . . insulting things about me and about my family while I struggled to escape the muck. They took my pony and left me there."

"Your brothers did not follow you out there?"

"Nay. You see I was supposed to be a humiliating messenger for the MacDonells to receive, the task not deserving of the time of a man."

"Instead the MacDonells humiliated the messenger."

She nodded.

"What happened when you returned home?"

"'Twas late that night when I shouted at the gate to be admitted. My brothers, all but Ailig who was away in Edinburgh, were summoned and when they saw me . . ." She shook her head. "They were not kind. I caught the ague because of that night spent in cold muddy clothes. If it were not for my nursemaid I probably would have died. I have never trusted my brothers since."

Tayg did not know what to say. The story explained much about Cat's relationship with her family and everything about her hatred of Dogface. Neill of Assynt was daft to allow his sons to treat her so. How could the man allow a betrothal between them . . . unless he did not know of the event.

"They were the fools, Cat," he said softly, wanting to comfort her, to thank her for sharing this with him for he was certain she had shared it with no one before him. But he didn't know how. If she were another lass he'd take her in his arms and comfort her, but she had forbade that and he knew his own control was tenuous at best where she was concerned.

"We shall have to leave here tomorrow," he said at last, not knowing what else to say. "This storm has raged long enough and we dare tarry no longer."

Catriona nodded, but did not look at him. Her eyes were trained on the fire between them.

Tayg turned his attention back to his drumming.

After a little while she turned her back to him and the

fire, pulling the plaid tightly about her, accentuating the curves of her waist and buttocks. Tayg tried to concentrate on his drumming, keeping it light when he wanted to fling the thing across the room and gather her into his arms. Pride was important to Cat, and loyalty. 'Twas why she was so prickly—her pride had been stolen and her loyalty betrayed by those closest to her. He doubted she had let anyone close enough since to hurt her more—except for him. She had let him in, close, though she had not wanted to. And he would not betray that hard-won trust. He would not see her hurt again.

Perhaps now he could avoid the little traps Broc and the others had set in her personality. She had a pride as large as his, but he now knew it to be a fragile thing.

C atriona lay still, *trying to ignore the quiet tapping of* Tayg's playing. He was improving, which made her think again that he was no bard, else he would have been a better player to begin with. It did not matter, though. 'Twas not a problem she need bother herself with. As long as he got her to the king she cared not what he was.

And to that end she must reconsider her plan. Trying to be nice to him had resulted in an increase in the intimacy growing between them. The flare of passion that had ignited between them when they argued was nothing compared to the far more disturbing events this quiet mood between them had led to. What had come over her?

She knew better than to trust a male like that, to give up control for the intoxicating feelings he roused in her. She could only hope that there was no opportunity for him to use her behavior, or her tale of woe, against her. Why she had told him she wasn't sure, though the sense of shared pain at her brothers' hands had perhaps lulled her into confiding in him. Broc repeated the tale regularly, still. It seemed to be his favorite memory of her childhood days and only by severe measures had she convinced him on occasion to keep his gob shut.

But Tayg was different, or maybe 'twas only that he made her feel different, precious, cherished. Nay, 'twas only his way of muddling her mind. She would have to watch him carefully. There was no reason to believe he would be any different from her brothers, whether it was to use his knowledge against her, or to let others use it, did not matter. Nothing but grief would come from her behavior here in this travelers' hut.

But she was having trouble convincing herself of that.

This man, this Tayg the Bard, was having a bad effect upon her, unsettling her with his drugging kisses and his cocky smile, then berating her for mistreating Dolag, then trying to help her escape discovery by her brothers. Just when she thought she knew what he would do next, he surprised her by doing something completely unexpected, as he had last night. The memory of the intoxicating feelings washed through her, making her itchy to experience them again. But she wouldn't. Ever.

She wasn't going to fall for his particular brand of manipulating her. He was keeping her off balance with his unpredictability and she wasn't going to let him win. She would just have to keep her guard up all the time, as if he were one of her brothers or Dogface.

Aye. That was what she'd have to do. Protect herself before his soft lips and sweet kisses prompted her to more foolishness—no matter how wonderful those moments had been.

The only question was: how?

chapter 12

E arly the next morning, before the sun had done more than lighten the sky from black to a heavy gray, Catriona and Tayg set out from the hut and ventured into the waning storm. They shared the horse despite the heavy snow, leaving Catriona free to peer into the gloom about her. The storm had left behind bent trees, broken branches and a deep blanket of white that seemed to glow in the early morning twilight. Those trees that remained standing tall appeared to wear beautiful white gowns with long trailing hems where the wind had driven the snow into high drifts against their towering trunks. Catriona smiled and turned her face up to the gentle snow that now floated lazily down to add a lacy edging to the trees' dresses.

The horse slipped and slid down the hill back to the trail, clearly as anxious to escape the confines of their temporary home as she and Tayg had been. Riding double had not been Catriona's choice, but the snow was so deep that Tayg had convinced her 'twas necessary if she did not wish to start the day cold and wet. She tried to keep herself away from his back, tried not to let her thighs touch his, tried not to notice the way his warmth beckoned to her. When the animal stopped abruptly and shifted its weight, Catriona would have slid from her precarious spot behind the saddle if Tayg hadn't reached back and caught her.

"You'd best hang on to me if you don't want to land in the snow," he said.

The grin on his face told Cat that he knew exactly why she didn't want to do that. Touching him was dangerous. When she touched him her mind went blank of everything except his heat, his smell and the tantalizing tingling that his fingers left wherever he touched her.

He raised an eyebrow at her. "Does something vex you?"

Cat glared at him and wrapped her arms loosely about his waist.

"You'll have to hold on a wee bit tighter than that if you do not wish to continue your fall."

She huffed out her breath and tightened her grip. She did her best to ignore the way his back fit just perfectly to her front, inviting her to rest her cheek against him, the way her thighs hugged tight behind his, the way her legs spread, cradling his backside against her growing heat. Her mind tried to spiral down to that place where all thought vanished and feelings reigned supreme but she struggled to keep her wits about her.

"Do you think Dogface and my brothers were traveling together?" she asked, trying to distract herself from the sensuous fog that threatened to overtake her.

"They did not arrive together . . . nay, I think Dogface was looking for me and your brothers, quite obviously, were looking for you. I expect there was some surprise when they discovered they had been led a merry chase to the same place."

Catriona considered that for a moment. "Did Dogface

ask for his missive back? Did he ask you why you hadn't delivered it to Broc?"

"He did not have the chance, but I do not think he cared over much whether I still had it or no. I think he planned much the same for me as your brothers delivered."

"Then there is more to this chase than a simple undelivered missive."

"Perhaps it is because I have taken you away from him."

"You have not taken me anywhere." Good. An argument would suit her fine.

He looked back over his shoulder, a question in his eyes.

"You have not. I made you bring me with you. 'Tis different."

"If you say so," he said, turning away again.

"Besides, you said he did not ken I was with you."

"Ah, so I did."

"Then why is he after you when he kens nothing about me being here?"

A clump of snow fell from a nearby tree, spooking the horse enough to make him dance sideways. Cat was forced to tighten her grip about Tayg's waist. When he had the horse under control again she resumed the conversation.

"You did not answer my question," she said.

"I did not."

"Was there a lass at Dun Donell? Did you take another lass from Dogface?"

Tayg laughed. "I thought I did not take you."

"You ken what I mean."

"Aye, but you are the only woman between us, whether he knows you are or not."

"Then what?"

"Why do you wish to know?"

"Why do you wish to keep me from knowing?"

Tayg was silent for a moment. "'Tis for your own safety."

"Ignorance will not keep me safe if he catches up with

us. He will assume I know whatever it is you have against him."

"Leave it be, Cat."

"I do not wish to leave it be. I wish to know what it is you hold between you that Dogface would follow you through the wintery Highlands for." She thought for a moment. "Not a woman; then wealth, or knowledge, perhaps? Nay, Dogface is too stupid to have knowledge of any sort, useful or otherwise."

"You underestimate him. He may be ugly and all you do not wish for in a husband, but he is not stupid. If he was he would be less dangerous."

"Ha, then it is knowledge you have."

Tayg shook his head and urged the horse through a deep drift. "You do not know what you are talking about, Cat. Leave it be."

Catriona smiled to herself and snuggled closer to Tayg's back. "I must be getting close."

"Aye," Tayg said, a strangely tight sound to his voice as he shifted in the saddle. "What do you wish for in a husband?"

"You are changing the subject."

"Aye, but still I should like to know."

"Other than that he not be Dogface MacDonell?"

"Other than that."

Catriona closed her eyes and tried to imagine the perfect husband. "He would be kind. Thoughtful. He would not vex me constantly as every other man I've ever known has done."

Tayg snorted. "What would he look like?"

"He would be tall, but not so much taller than I am. He would have dark hair and twinkling eyes and a mouth with dimples on either side. He would laugh a lot, and make me laugh."

"Is that all he would do?"

Catriona's breath caught in her throat at the quiet question that seemed to roll over her skin like hot water, leaving an almost painful awareness behind. "What do you mean?" she asked.

"What about bairns? What about cherishing you? Do you not want that, too?"

"Aye, a perfect husband would give me bairns, too."

"And the other?"

Catriona felt her cheeks heat and the spiral tighten. "And the other, but that will not be."

"You do not think you can find such a man?"

"I never will. Not one who will wed with me."

"How can you be so sure?"

"Because such a man does not exist. 'Tis but a silly dream."

"Then why do you wish to marry at all?"

Catriona was quiet for a while. Why indeed? To keep from marrying Dogface certainly. To keep her clan safe from an alliance with the MacDonells. But 'twould do little to keep Broc from doing something else equally as stupid. If she could convince the king that Ailig was the best man to lead the clan, then she would have accomplished something good for the clan.

Perhaps there was also a desire to prove to her brothers that she could guide her own life, that she could do better than the lot of them? But how was it guiding her own life to pick a man for a husband without ever knowing his character, his substance? How would any man solve the problems she had with her brothers?

In a moment of blinding clarity she realized nothing she could do would solve her problem with her brothers, and her chances of convincing the king to set the last son before the first was ludicrous.

Perhaps what she really needed to find was someone who would help her balance out her brothers' unreasoned behavior, someone they would listen to and respect enough to allow him to have a say in the running of the clan. Someone who would listen to her, too. Someone who would make her feel cherished and wanted, who would make her blood sing as Tayg—

Nay, her brothers would never accept the counsel of a lowly traveling bard who could not even sing well. They would ridicule her for her selfishness in choosing such a man for a husband, bringing nothing of value to the clan and ruining the alliance Broc deemed so important with the MacDonells.

She took a deep breath to still the rushing of her heart. She must continue on to the king and perhaps she could entreat him to find her someone her brothers would count as worthy, who might also be acceptable to her as a counselor. It did not matter whether he would suit her, fulfill her dream or not. She must not think of herself. The clan was important, her own desires . . .

"Well?" Tayg asked.

"What?"

"Why do you wish to marry?"

"I have told you before. Why do you think my answer will be different now?" she snapped, angry that he had forced her thoughts in this direction.

Tayg shook his head and sighed as if he truly had expected another answer from her.

But there could be no other answer.

The snow finally ceased while they ate a midday meal. Tayg handed Cat the usual oatcake and dried venison then pulled a stoppered bottle out of the bottom of the bag.

"What's this?" He held the bottle up for Cat to see.

She shrugged. "Why would I know? 'Twas in your pack. Perhaps 'tis another of your secrets."

Tayg's eyebrows lowered over his dark eyes as if he was studying something small and ugly. Cat clamped her teeth together to keep from sticking her tongue out at him.

She'd been angry since the end of their conversation hours earlier. How dare he get her thinking about what she couldn't have, would never have. A perfect husband. Hah! Life was too complicated for such a thing to exist.

Tayg pulled the leather stopper out and sniffed. A huge grin spread over his face, making his eyes twinkle amidst the fading bruises and bracketing his tantalizing mouth with deep dimples just before he leaned his head back and took a swig.

"Ah. Aqua vitae," he said, then took another pull from the bottle.

Cat could only stare at him, all her words about a perfect husband crashing around her like a stormy sea. She had described Tayg. Described each of the things about him she had come to admire both physically and for his character. Except for the vexing part. But she had described the perfect husband.

Cat gasped.

"'Tis only whiskey, Cat, nothing to be gasping over."

He passed her the bottle. She took it, being careful not to touch his fingers. She lifted it to her mouth only to realize that the heavy glass was warm from his lips. She drank, then nearly choked as fire poured down her throat and burst to life in her gut. Painful coughing burst from her. Tayg moved to sit beside her, lifting the bottle from her hand and handing her a water skin.

"Drink this," he said, brushing a stray hair away from her lips.

She managed to sooth her throat with the cool water, then jabbed her elbow in his ribs.

"Oof!"

"Do not touch me again."

"'Tis a good thing you do not have Broc's fists."

Catriona froze. His ribs! She'd been so vexed with him she'd forgotten all about his ribs. "Are you well enough to be traveling like this?" She didn't regret the sharp edge to her voice. She *was* still angry with him.

"I am well enough, and we have no choice. I think the ribs are not broken, just battered. The binding helps, though your elbow does not."

" 'Tis a shame we cannot bind your mouth, too."

He shook his head. "Do you know you retreat into the shrew whenever you are afraid or threatened?"

"I do not."

"Aye, sweet Cat, you do, though you should be neither with me. Are you afraid of me?"

Cat stared at him, at the face that had become so familiar to her that she could describe him with her eyes closed . . .

But 'twas not him she was afraid of, 'twas herself and the way she reacted when he was near. She rose to her feet and moved to the far side of the clearing they had found.

"I am afraid of nothing, bard. Surely you know at least that much about me by now." She turned away from him and the disappointment she saw in his eyes, surprised at how much that disappointment was mirrored in her own heart. 'Twas not his fault her heart was misbehaving. But she'd not act on its promptings. For once she would use her head. She must. Her future—and that of her clan—depended upon it.

They had struck a tentative peace since resuming their journey along the snowy trail next to the ever-widening river. He didn't antagonize her. She didn't snap at him. In fact, she had relaxed enough to fall asleep, her cheek resting against his back, her arms slack about his waist. He could almost imagine she liked him. She liked him well enough to worry over his well-being. She liked him well enough to melt into him like a fine beeswax candle beneath a flame when he kissed her.

He took a deep breath and tried to calm the surge in his body that happened whenever he thought about those kisses, her lips and the way her body warmed under his hands.

He took another deep breath. He would have to tell her the truth about who he really was and soon. Yet there seemed so many reasons not to reveal the truth, at least not now. She was content to travel with her bard. She was relaxed, easy, and only when she was afraid of something did she retreat back into the shrew. The closer they became, the softer she became.

Dangerously soft.

Of course, once he revealed himself and his true purpose in bringing her to the king, all that would change. She would hate him. He could hear her calling him a liar, hear the hurt in her voice, see the hurt in her eyes. He didn't want to cause that hurt, but he couldn't keep the truth from her forever, just a day or two more. Soon they would be nearing Munro land where he would be known. But not yet. The quiet was healing. The trust inherent in her relaxed form was wonderful. And he was not ready to lose that.

A deer crashed out of the woods on his right, spooking the horse. He grabbed Cat's arms just as she tightened her grip, pressing against his tender ribs just a little too hard.

"'Tis all right, lass. Just a red deer."

"Too bad we cannot stop and hunt him. I would like some fresh venison," she said, her voice sleepy and warm. Tayg found himself wishing to hear her like that more often.

Almost immediately another deer crashed out of the forest, nearly running into the horse this time, scaring it into a sliding sidestep on the icy trail. Tayg struggled to calm the horse and the deer disappeared down the trail the way he and Cat had come. Just as suddenly a horse carrying a great lump of a man crashed out of the woods where the deer had emerged from and nearly collided with them, pushing them dangerously close to the steep bank of the river.

"My apologies," the man said as he struggled to control his snow-white horse.

"You nearly sent us into the river!" Cat's voice was filled with alarm. Tayg moved their horse away from the edge of the trail.

"Aye, mistress, I should be more careful. I was chasing a deer."

"It went that way," Tayg said, pointing a thumb over his shoulder, "but 'tis long gone by now."

The man nodded. "I should not have allowed myself the pleasure of chasing him, but it has been a long time since I hunted." He smiled at them. "I am Friar John of Auskaird Abbey. Where are you bound, friends?"

"To Dingwall," Catriona said. Her voice was calmer now, though Tayg found it hard to breathe with the grip she had about his middle.

"Ah," the friar said, "I'm bound near there. Have you heard of the new abbey the Earl of Ross's sister has founded?"

Tayg nodded. Catriona shook her head.

"Ah, 'tis a modest place, yet. The abbess has only a small number of followers, though 'twill grow quickly I am sure. I am bound there to help organize their accounts and of course to attend the wedding of the king's sister and the earl's son." His grin was so wide in his round face that it seemed to stretch from one ear to the other.

"You should travel with us, then," Catriona said.

Tayg twisted in the saddle to look at her, his stomach suddenly knotted. Did she want them discovered? She lifted an eyebrow as if daring him to contradict her, then made a point of separating herself from him. So that was it. She wanted to use this friar to protect herself from acting on the feelings that were becoming more and more evident, more and more difficult to ignore.

"That would be delightful," said the friar, as he made his horse move beside them on the path. "But you have not told me how you are called. I cannot travel with complete strangers," he added with a smile.

"I am called Cat, and this is Tayg."

The friar cast a startled glance at Tayg.

"I am a bard," Tayg said quickly, before the friar could ask a question he really did not want to answer just now.

The friar looked at him a moment, then turned his attention to Cat. "'Tis pleased I am to make your acquaintance, Cat and Tayg the bard."

Tayg saw a glint in the friar's eye that made him nervous. He did not recognize the man, but that did not mean the friar did not recognize him. He would have to find out what the man knew, but not while Cat was within hearing distance.

They headed down the trail, the horses side-by-side here where the trail was relatively wide.

"Why are you traveling this time of year?" the friar asked after a few minutes.

"To be wed," Cat said, her voice held a strange smugness to it that picked at Tayg's temper.

"You are not wed? Why are you waiting for Dingwall? You should not be traveling alone together when you are not wed."

"We are not—" Cat started but Tayg cut her off.

"The wedding will be with the blessing of the chief and, if we are lucky, the king, which is why we are bound for Dingwall."

The friar's heavy black eyebrows drew together, forming a deep V over his eyes. "But your chief is . . . Angus Dubh of Culrain?"

Tayg tried to suppress a flinch. Did this man know him, then?

"And you had to fetch your bride?" the friar continued. "Why did her family not bring her to you?"

"The bride has no family," Cat said quickly, before Tayg could cut her off again.

Tayg pinched her arm where it was looped around his waist.

"Ow!"

"Oh, I'm sorry, love. Did I pinch you? She is such a tender thing," he said, with what he hoped was an innocent smile.

The friar just nodded. "I had thought to pass the night with my cousin's family. You shall come with me and we shall travel to Culrain together. I hear the king shall be there before he travels to Dingwall for the wedding. You may receive what blessings you like and I shall serve as suitable escort for you."

"Nay," Tayg and Cat said in unison.

"Your offer is kind, but we have been delayed already. We need to travel as fast as is possible," Tayg said. "We have come this far alone, another day or two will make no difference."

"I cannot agree, young bard. 'Tis not right for the two of you to continue on so, without the vows and God's blessing. You must allow me to escort you or—"

"Oh, we have said vows, friar," Cat said.

Tayg and the friar both twisted in their saddles to look at her. Tayg tried to signal her with his scowl to be quiet but she just grinned and wrapped her arms tightly about him, pressing her breasts into his back and temporarily blanking his mind.

"How is this, lass?" asked the friar, his bushy black eyebrows moved lower over his nose.

"You are right. 'Twould not be seemly for a maid to travel unescorted with her betrothed, so we said our vows in front of witnesses this very morning, before we left on this journey. We travel to Culrain"—she looked at Tayg for confirmation but he just rolled his eyes—"for the chief's blessing and, of course, a celebration."

The friar grinned. "Then this is your wedding night?"

Tayg felt Cat go stiff against his back, but she did not

pull away. The distracting pressure of her breasts pressed up against him, even through his thick cloak, made it hard to concentrate on the quagmire she was creating for them to slog their way through.

"My cousin's is not far. We shall have a wedding dinner there and you shall have a bed for your wedding night instead of some hard-won place in the snow." The friar nudged his horse to a faster pace and pulled ahead, leading the way.

Tayg glanced over his shoulder and glowered at Cat. "Our wedding night?" he said, pitching his voice low and easing all the innuendo he could into the words.

She scowled back at him. "Do not get any ideas, bard. 'Tis no wedding night. 'Tis but a warm place to rest, then we can be on our way again. I am cold and hungry and you are not yet healed."

"You did not have to lie to the man."

She had the grace to blush. " 'Twas out of my mouth before I could stop it."

"Well say no more then, lass. We shall have to tread very lightly and take care not to give ourselves away."

Tayg turned back and stared over the horse's head. Wedding night. How was he supposed to keep his hands off the lass when their hosts expected them to be anxious newlyweds? He could barely keep his hands from her when he did not have such opportunities as were about to present themselves. He took a deep breath and began to go over his list of reasons why he should not want Cat . . . only he couldn't remember any.

For now, they were stuck with the friar, at least as far as his cousin's cottage. If he thought hard enough, and kept his mind away from the image "wedding night" conjured in his head, perhaps he could find a reason why they could not stay the night in a comfortable, warm cottage, in a real bed . . . together.

He tried to banish the image of Cat, sprawled across his

own large feather bed, her silk-soft ebony hair spread around her and her pale skin glowing in candlelight.

He groaned. Perhaps they would just slip away in the night. After all, they had done so before. They were getting quite good at slipping away unnoticed.

If they didn't, he wasn't sure how either of them would sleep this night.

D*eep snow slowed their progress so it was near dark* when they approached the cousin's cottage. The familiar aroma of peat smoke lay gently about the squat structure. In spite of the dangers inherent in spending more time with the friar, who seemed to know more of Tayg than he had said, Tayg was grateful for the promise of a warm meal and a place by the fire for the night. Catriona shivered against his back and he knew she too would be grateful for the cousin's hospitality. Still, the cousin's family could know Tayg and there was the problem of the friar believing this to be their wedding night. The first he could do nothing about, at least not at the moment, but the second he could. He had decided they would sleep by the fire where surely they would be surrounded by the family and the friar and thus could not give into the increasingly hard-to-ignore attraction that blossomed between them.

The horses stopped in the cottage's dooryard, drawing Tayg's attention back to the moment at hand.

"We will wait here while you greet your cousin and his family and tell him of his additional guests," Tayg said. He gripped Cat's arm when she made to dismount. She glared at him, but stilled at his look. She was cold, as was he, but he needed a moment alone with Cat to get her agreement for his plan.

Friar John rounded his own horse and looked up at Tayg, a determined look upon his pudgy face. "Nonsense, lad. Get you and your lady off that horse and come in from the cold. Gair and Lina will not mind the extra company."

Tayg jerked at the name. It could not be. 'Twas a common enough name, Gair, and surely they were not so close to Culrain that this could be . . .

The Friar reached up to help Cat and Tayg had no choice but to allow her to swing down. He followed quickly, dread twisting in his gut, his senses fully roused as if for battle.

Cat touched his arm and he was surprised by the concern in her eyes. "Tayg, what is it?"

"Mind your tongue, Cat," Tayg whispered to her. He was rewarded with a glare.

"I do not need to be reminded, bard." She twisted the word so that it was more akin to an epithet than a title.

Had she noted the friar's reaction to his name? Did she doubt him, too? Nay, she was simply nervous and cold and thus she retreated into her prickly self.

"We must act as newlyweds," he said, waggling his eyebrows at her in an attempt make her smile.

"I realize that," she said, her voice sharp and abrupt.

"You say that as if 'twould be a horrible fate," he said, tucking her hand into his as they followed the friar. "Would it be so horrible?"

Cat started to reply but stopped, a shocked look in her eyes.

"Come, come, my children. 'Tis bitter cold and I smell something delicious within." The friar banged once on the door with his fist then swung it open with a bellowed, "Hellooo the house!"

Tayg and Cat were left standing by the door looking into a room filled with people. A large, round woman in a simple gown of rusty-red stood by the hearth stirring up something in a huge blackened cauldron. A linen veil covered her head but a long ginger braid, liberally laced with steely grey, snaked down her back.

"Och, John!" she called, a huge smile on her face. She brandished her ladle in an odd salute. "Come ye in and be welcome!"

Children were everywhere, some laughing, some fighting, some setting dishes on the end of a rustic table near the fire, but all stopped and rushed the friar as he entered with squeals of glee, giggles of delight and hugs.

A man descended a ladder at the back of the cozy room, his feet visible first, then the rest of him followed out of the loft. Tayg's fears gripped him. He was caught.

Auld Gair, who had fought with Tayg and Robbie for the Bruce, jumped off the last rung of the ladder and turned to the newcomers.

"John," Gair said, "we'd thought you lost in the storm!" He strode across the room and caught the friar up in a huge hug.

Tayg squared his shoulders and prepared himself. Any moment now, Gair would notice him and expose him for who he truly was. He could not lie to Gair; indeed, the man would help him get to the king, but Catriona would not understand. She would see only that he had lied to her, betrayed her, used her, for she would understand, once the missive's true meaning was revealed, why he took her to the king. She was too smart not to. And he desperately didn't want to hurt her. He needed time to explain everything to her. But he would not have the time.

Gair and Friar John slapped each other on the back and traded fond insults for several minutes while Tayg felt sweat run down his back as he waited for the inevitable. Cat stood silently next to him, unaware of how much she would hate him in another moment or two. He squeezed her hand. She startled, then gave him a tentative smile, but he did not have time to wonder why.

"Let me introduce my young friends." The friar's booming voice jerked his attention away from Cat and back to the problem at hand.

"Ah, they are a bonny pair," Lina said. "We shall be very happy to host them on this, their wedding night."

A grin spread on Gair's face and Tayg couldn't help but return it.

"Wait a moment, I know this whelp." Auld Gair pushed past his cousin and grabbed Tayg by the shoulders. "I thought you were still with the Bruce, but here you are with this lovely lass. Your wife, I hear." He smiled at Cat. "Ho, ho! His wife." Gair did a little hop and rubbed his hands together. "I wonder who won the wager, me lad. 'Twas said you'd never be able to choose but one lass, and yet you have chosen very well indeed. She is a pretty thing and no doubt took a bit of wooing from you."

He clapped Tayg on the back but Tayg could think of nothing to say.

"What?" Gair said to his wife who was standing, her hands, one still gripping the ladle, fisted on her ample hips and a look of extreme irritation on her face.

"You and the lad can trade stories later. For now they are cold and wet and there are horses to see to. Come lass, what was your name?"

"Cat," Tayg said. "Her name is Cat. Perhaps you could find her a warm spot near the fire while Gair and I take care of the horses?" He had to get the man aside quickly. He had not given him away yet, and Tayg thanked the heavens for this small reprieve, but 'twould not take long for Cat or the curious friar to start asking questions about how the two knew each other. If he could manage it, he would have Gair be silent on the answers, at least until he could explain it all to Cat.

chapter 13

O ne of the children led Cat to a stool near the fire while Lina returned to stirring her cauldron, turning a spit with several roasting birds on it as she passed.

The heat was so intense after the biting cold of their day's journey that it almost hurt to breathe and Catriona could feel the cold sink deeper into her bones as if it sought to hide from the warmth.

Cat settled herself on the stool and someone pressed a mug of ale into her hand. Lina and the children seemed to be content to let her sit silently while they continued with the meal preparations and Cat found herself glad, for she had much to consider from the last short while, Tayg's quiet question being foremost in her mind.

"Would it be so horrible?" he had asked. She thought over the day's journey spent mostly riding behind Tayg, the horse's movements rocking her against the man's broad back. The occasional misstep causing her to tighten her grip about his lean waist. The cold enticing her to snuggle up against him taking what warmth she could. She had struggled all day to keep from remembering the way he had made her body hum and the world go away that night in the traveler's hut.

Would it be such a terrible fate to be married to Tayg the Bard instead of some unknown? Aye, it would. Forever traveling. No home of her own. How would they manage children? That thought brought her back to the memories of his kisses and caresses, the way he made her burn for his touches. She had an idea that certain parts of being wed to the bard would be quite pleasant . . . but that was impossible.

She must wed someone who would live at Assynt, someone who Broc would at least allow to counsel him. It was different from what she had set out to do, and yet, essentially it was the same. She must complete her task. A part of her shuddered at the word "task." Marriage should not be a task, it should be a blessing, a wonder, a bond. But she could not indulge in such soft dreams. She had set out to save her clan from the rash behavior of her brothers and marrying the bard would never do that.

She needed to know how she was going to stay away from him this night.

Physical distance with a fire between them was all that had prevented her from throwing herself in his arms while they were at the hut. There must be a way to keep him away tonight, too.

His quiet question slipped back into her thoughts. Would it be such a horrible fate to marry Tayg the Bard? For her clan, aye, but for herself . . .

"From the smile on your lips I'm guessing you are contemplating your wedding night, eh, lass?" Lina said. "Never you worry, there's a fine bed above in the loft where many of these weans were conceived." She winked. "'Tis a lucky bed, that."

Catriona felt her skin heat and her immediate problem

returned to her thoughts. Their hosts thought them newlyweds, though the man, Gair, appeared to know Tayg and
did not expect to see him with a wife. She thought back to
the brief introductions. The man had known Tayg though
Tayg had been tense at the meeting and unusually silent.
He squeezed her hand 'til it hurt, yet she had the distinct
feeling 'twas not to keep her silent. And he had hustled
the fellow out to the stable quickly.

The fog in her mind caused by the sudden change from
cold to heat cleared.

What did the man know about Tayg that made the bard
so nervous? For that matter, he had been nervous when
they met the friar, too. She looked about and found the
man in question sitting upon the floor with a wee lass settled in his lap and a lad not much older than the lass leaning over his shoulder. The three were deep in conversation
broken now and again by wild giggling from the weans.

Tayg had used his trade, declaring himself a bard
quickly when the man seemed to recognize his name.
Surely his pride in his profession did not reach so far.
Nay, there was something these two men, the friar and his
cousin, knew of Tayg, and no doubt the bard was securing
the silence of Gair, who knew him from his time with the
Bruce, which raised still other questions . . . but she had
no time for that now. She would know what these men
knew of her companion, for to be kept in ignorance was
dangerous, and now was her time to discover it. She rose
and placed her cup on the hearth.

"I will go and help Tayg," she said the name loud
enough for the friar to hear, but he did not react.

"Och, lass, I know you are newly married, but he will
return soon."

At first Cat didn't understand what Lina meant.

"Ye'll have plenty of time with him—let him and my
husband trade their stories alone for a few moments.
There will be less of them we have to listen to later that

way." But the grin on her face belied the tone of her voice and Cat realized the woman thought she missed her new husband. Very well, 'twould serve her purposes to act the love-sick wench and 'twas obviously expected. She cast her gaze down and tried to give a nervous giggle.

"I do not like him long from my side," she said to Lina. "I know 'tis silly, but 'tis the truth."

"Aye lass. The stable is around the back of the cottage. Just follow the walls around and tell Gair I need him to fetch more peats."

Catriona clutched her cloak to her and quickly left the cheery warmth for the dark cold of the night.

Tayg and Gair trudged out into the cold and gathered the horses. Two nearly grown lads helped carry in the travel bags but Gair managed to send them back in the cottage quickly. He grabbed the friar's horse by the reins and led the way around the side of the cottage to the byre attached to the back wall. Inside was quiet and smelled of warm animals and clean straw. They worked in silence for a few moments, taking the tack off the horses and rubbing the tired animals down.

"Well, lad, ye dinna seem too pleased to see Auld Gair."

Tayg looked up at the older man and realized he was not so old as he remembered. Gair was just past his prime, but not yet old and feeble. And the glint in his eye told Tayg that the man was still plenty sharp in the mind.

"'Tis very pleased I am to see you, Gair. 'Tis only that . . ."

"'Tis only that you thought to keep yer bonny wife a secret a bit longer, eh? I have heard the tale from Duncan that yer mum wishes ye wed and that ye went searching for a lass on yer own. 'Twould appear yer

search went well." Gair leered at Tayg and he found
himself blushing.

"Aye, she is—"

"Ye need not worry about this night, lad. I ken ye've a
fine way with the lasses but I'll say naught more about it.
'Tis yer wedding night and there is no sense in starting off
yer married life with tales of other lasses. I have not lived
with Lina all these years and not learned a wee bit about
what a woman wants to hear, and what she doesn't."

"Yes, but—"

"'Tis proud of you I am, Tayg. Stepping into Robbie's
place, taking up his responsibilities when 'twas clear you
had no desire to. In the time ye fought for the Bruce I
watched ye grow from a wee whelp along for a grand adventure with yer brother to a man who could lead men
into battle and out again. I only hope ye have chosen a
lass who is worthy of ye and all that ye will be in the future."

Tayg swallowed an odd lump in his throat, overwhelmed at the unexpected praise. He wanted to tell him
'twas not all true but the man's pleasure was too strong.
And if he were honest with himself he wished it to be the
truth too much. But the truth was dangerous.

Truth would force Catriona to marry him, though she
would not be happy about it. If they could find some way
to make her feel her clan was in safe hands, then maybe
she would accept her fate. But she might never come to
trust him again.

And he didn't want to lose that trust, though it was inevitable. Eventually she must find out who he really was,
and what his errand to the king was for. If Broc was im-
plicated, would she be satisfied with another brother in his
place, leading the clan? Would another brother be any better?

A sudden understanding and resolve formed within
him. Gair was right, he was no longer Robbie's shadow,

following him about and doing his bidding. He was his own man, capable and proven in battle. He desired Cat and she desired him, though she fought herself over it. She had said she wished to marry him, though she did not know it was he she spoke of. He would make it the truth. He would wed the lass, thus solving his problem and hers. Her clan would be allied to his and through that connection they would be allied to the king. Even if they did not declare themselves for the king they would not be bound to the MacDonells; Broc would surely be ousted as the next chief, and perhaps he could arrange some sort of advisor for her other brothers so such things would not happen in the future.

But first, he must ensure that she learned all this from him, not from Gair, nor from the friar, for he now knew why the friar seemed to know him. Gair was one for tales around a fire at night. The *seanachaidh* were not the only ones to spread tales.

"Gair, I need your help," he said at last.

"I will see you have privacy this night."

"Nay. Aye. But that is not what I wish to ask you."

Gair shot Tayg a curious glance over the horses' backs.

"The lass does not know who I am. She thinks me a simple bard and I would not have her find out the truth from anyone but me."

Gair stood perfectly still, his eyebrows drawn down. "She does not know who you are?"

"Nay. I did not wish to wed a lass who thought only to marry a man of heroic tales." Gair nodded. "I have traveled as a bard on the king's business, and for that reason, too, I would keep my true identity hidden a while longer."

"The king's business?"

"Aye, and here again your help is needed."

Tayg quickly filled Gair in on the plot against the king, though he said nothing about Cat's part in it. Some things did not need to be revealed.

• • •

Gair finished with the friar's horse just as Cat entered the stable. "I see ye could not stay away from Tayg here any longer." He grinned at Cat and she, much to Tayg's surprise, grinned back at him.

"'Tis true," she said, moving to Tayg's side and placing a hand lightly on his arm. "I did not wish to be parted from my new husband even for such a brief time."

Tayg started to laugh but stopped abruptly when she stood on his foot just hard enough to remind him of the pain she could cause. She was up to something. The thought made the hairs stand up on his neck.

Gair moved toward the doorway. "I'll leave you two alone for a moment." He winked at them. "I'm sure Lina needs something."

"She does," Cat said. "Peats. She bade me have you bring more peats."

"You see, Tayg, it does not take long before you and she will know the other so well as Lina and I do. Do not tarry long in the cold, lad." With another cheeky grin he left the byre.

"What are you planning?" Cat asked from right beside him.

"The only plan I have is to have a warm meal and share a warm bed with my new wife," he said.

"There will be no sharing of a bed."

"Nay? And yet these fine folk believe we are newly wed, thanks to you."

"I told you, 'twas not done on purpose."

"And yet it is done and we must act the part else someone may suspect that we do not tell the truth. Would you have them learn who you really are and that you travel with a bard unattended?"

Panic flitted across her face, then the familiar determination took over. Her chin notched up slightly.

"We will leave now," she said, moving to where he had only minutes before placed the saddle.

"Nay," he grabbed her arm and spun her around to face him. "We will not leave."

She was mere inches from him, her hands on her hips. "If we stay, we chance being found out. 'Tis clear Gair knows you, and the friar, too. 'Tis equally clear you are not the type they ever expected to take a wife. They will become suspicious if we do not act the part convincingly enough. We will not fool them."

"You cannot act the part?" he asked, knowing he could all too convincingly.

"I can, but I do not think 'tis a good idea."

She was right. He was having a hard enough time not touching her, not kissing her, not . . . right now. But something in him pushed. He needed to know if she wanted him as intensely as he wanted her.

"We must act the part, lass. The horse is tired, as are you. We have no food, no hope for as comfortable or as warm a shelter for the night, and I confess I am quite sore still from your brothers' attentions to my ribs. We must stay and we must play the part you have laid out for us."

She chewed on her bottom lip for a moment. "What must I do?"

A lazy smile stole across his face. "You bade me not to touch you, not to kiss you again. I fear I shall have to ask your leave to do so, for 'twill be expected."

He watched as the meaning behind his words sank in. She squared her shoulders, pushed her chin up another notch and nodded. "Very well, you may do those things, but"—she pointed a finger at him—"only as is necessary to convince our hosts."

"And can you act the newlywed lass in love with her husband?" he asked, pitching his voice low but lacing it with just enough sarcasm to anger her.

"I can. I can be the perfect wife."

Tayg snorted. She had no idea what she was suggesting, what it would mean to act like lovers. The image of the two of them tangled together in his bed crashed through his mind. Frustration boiled up in him. He took a step closer to her, wanting her to feel all the pent-up desire and need he felt, wanting her to struggle as hard with it as he did.

She stood her ground as he knew she would. Slowly he moved closer still until his mouth was next to her ear and her breath, shallow and quick now, warmed his cheek.

"*Can* you act the perfect wife?" he whispered, his lips almost brushing the shell of her ear. "Can you let me touch you?" He ran a hand up her arm then trailed his fingertips across her chest and down the valley between her breasts.

"Can you touch me, pretend to be anxious to be alone with me?"

She leaned her head away from him as he feathered kisses down her gently arched neck.

"Can you share a bed with me and not wish me to bring you pleasure?" he said, staring now into her hooded eyes as he brushed the backs of his fingers over the slope of her breasts.

Her eyes went dark and hot and her breath came faster as he lifted the weight of her breasts in his hands, flicking his thumbs over the erect nipples that pushed against the fabric of her gown.

She kissed him then, fast and hard, her fingers threaded through his hair, her lips hungry on his. He groaned and reached to pull her against him just as she stepped backwards into the dark.

"I can," she said, her voice quiet and sure but her body, the need in her kiss, gave her away, and Tayg knew she wanted him.

God help him.

He had no doubt they could act the part of lovers now. The question was, could they bear the heat between them? Would they be able to deny the inferno when they were alone again? Would they survive its ashes when they parted?

Tayg shook his head and turned to finish caring for the horse, ignoring the singing in his blood and the pounding of his heart.

C atriona heard more than saw Tayg tending to the horse. The stable was completely dark now, the last glow of the sun gone from the snow outside the door. She stood perfectly still, unwilling to move until she got her jumbled emotions and traitorous body under control. Her heart felt ready to burst and she could not catch her breath. Need so strong it hurt pulsed through her until she could barely think, could only feel. Never had she experienced such desire. The man made her skin so sensitive that every touch, every breath, every look burned over her, through her. With a word he fanned the smoldering ember in the pit of her belly into a roaring fire that threatened to burn away all that she knew, all that she thought she wanted, all that she was.

"Mistress? Master Bard?" a lad, a young man really, called from just outside the stable as if he hesitated to enter. "Mum says yer supper is ready and ye should come and warm yerselves by the fire."

Tayg turned towards the voice. "I am nearly done with the horse. We shall be there in a moment."

Catriona was amazed at how calm his voice sounded, how sure, how Tayg, as if nothing unusual had happened. And perhaps it hadn't, at least for him.

He had been testing her, she realized. He had been trying to see if she could manage her emotions enough to play the part of loving wife and not get swept up in it.

Anger fanned the flames to a bright new color. How dare he play with her feelings that way, with her body? But now she knew what he was up to. She could play his game as deftly as he did. She would prove to him that she could act the perfect wife *and* keep herself, her emotions, her desires, under control. 'Twould be up to him to meet the challenge.

She took a deep breath and left the stable. She needed a moment to compose herself, set her own plan, then she would show him who was in control.

Catriona sat at one end of a bench at the family's table. Tayg sat to her left, too close, and Friar John filled the seat at the head of the table on her right, his back to the warming fire. The family, Gair, Lina, and their five children who ranged in age from six or seven to nearly grown, sat around the rest of the well-worn table. A large wooden bowl at the near end held a thick savory stew filled with chunks of succulent beef and vegetables. A long tray sat at the far end of the table, laden with perfectly roasted pigeons. Ale filled cups and each person at the table had a wooden trencher and a horn spoon. Two tallow candles fixed in simple holders sat amidst the food and illuminated the feast. Catriona was impressed with the quantity of food and the tableware. But part of her tensed. Family meals had never been an easy part of life in Assynt.

A stack of bowls sat beside Lina, who ladled the stew into them and passed them down the table. The four lads all seemed to reach at once for the pigeons. Lina cuffed the oldest one on the back of his head between passing bowls.

"Mind yer manners, Niall," she said. "We have guests this night and they shall choose first." Lina smiled at Catriona. "Would ye be liking a pigeon?"

"Thank you, I would, but I would not take it from your weans," Catriona said. She was aware of Tayg's startled look, but she ignored it. She would surprise him in more ways than one this night.

"My weans get plenty to eat," Lina said as she motioned for the tray to be passed to her.

"'Tis plain they do," the friar said, spearing a pigeon with his knife as Lina held the tray in front of him. "Niall there has grown near a foot since last I saw him, and 'twas only a year past. Even wee Cecilia has grown . . . though she seems to have misplaced her teeth," he added, grinning at the little girl with the long brown braid who sat between two of her brothers. Cecilia smiled and Catriona saw that she was indeed missing two teeth. She felt a bit concerned for the lass, but no one else, even the girl, seemed to notice her dangerous position.

Lina filled Catriona and Tayg's trenchers with a perfectly roasted bird each.

"Ceci misplaces many things," another brother said, "like my hornpipe."

"I did not!" the lass said, then stuck her tongue out at the lad. "You gave it to Annag at the gathering. I saw you. Sim wants to marry Annag. I saw him kissing her."

Sim went scarlet, nearly matching his brilliant red hair but instead of reaching across the table and yanking Ceci's braid or some other painful action as Catriona's brothers would have done, the family broke into loud laughter and Sim took his sister's jibe good-naturedly. Or so it seemed. Catriona would make a point of sticking close to the lass after dinner to make sure Sim didn't come back to exact his revenge later.

"He can have Annag," another brother said. Catriona turned to look at the new speaker and realized he was Sim's exact copy—twins—and by the look of them just coming into manhood. Those two must surely cause trouble for Lina and Gair. "Annag is sweet enough, but I'll take her cousin Maggie."

Loud laughter followed this, and Niall said, "As if she would have you, Kennon."

"Neither of you will be taking anyone yet," Lina said. "Not till I say 'tis time for you to take a wife. I've not tamed ye enough to turn ye over to another woman's keeping. I would not do that to either of those lasses." She winked at Catriona. "It takes a lot of training of you lads before ye are fit to live with."

"I shall never want to marry," the last brother piped up. He could not be more than ten or eleven and shared the twins' bright hair and copper freckles. "Why would anyone want to kiss a lass?" He screwed up his face in disgust, then dug into his dinner with all the abandon of a hungry young boy.

Gair laughed. "Perhaps our guest would like to explain that to you, Pol."

All eyes, including Catriona's, turned to Tayg. He looked flustered for a moment, then she watched as his familiar cocky grin broke out.. He turned to her and raised his eyebrows as if to challenge her.

She was up to the challenge. She grinned back at him and was gratified to see concern fill his eyes, though his grin remained in place.

"Ah, Pol," she said, snuggling close to Tayg and resting her head on his shoulder, "'tis very nice to kiss, especially when 'tis someone you love you are kissing." She stretched up and kissed Tayg's mouth chastely.

'Twas Pol's turn to blush. "Oy, I hate that kissy stuff!"

"That hardly counts as *kissy stuff*," Niall said, grinning at Tayg and Catriona. "Show him how a proper kiss is done, Tayg."

"Aye, 'twas not a proper kiss for a new bride," Gair added.

The table erupted in a chant of "kiss her, kiss her" and

Catriona felt her heart kick as she realized he was indeed going to kiss her, here, in front of everyone. 'Twas only right to convince their hosts that they were who, and what, they said they were. 'Twas part of pretending and she would show him that she could do this and keep her wits about her. She would show him that he had no effect upon her, body, mind or heart.

The family added the stomping of their feet to their chant. Tayg leaned close, taking her face in his hands. "You brought this on yourself," he said just loud enough for her to hear.

He kissed her then, soft and gently as if she were the most delicate of China porcelain. Catriona grasped his forearms but she wasn't sure if she did it to hold him away or to pull him closer. The family whooped and Tayg deepened the kiss. Catriona closed her eyes and was swept away by the passion pouring into her, the need and desire that sang through him and into her—the burning want.

"A-hem! There are weans present, lad."

Catriona wasn't sure who spoke. She opened her eyes and became vaguely aware of the raucous whoops and the odd jerky movement of Tayg's body where the older brother was slapping him on the back.

"I think we'd best get supper out of the way and done and let these two have some privacy," Lina said, her eyes twinkling. "'Tis clear we should not keep them longer from their bridal bed."

More laughter, but Catriona could not take her eyes from Tayg's, where desire was plain but something else, some deeper emotion, also reigned. Whatever that emotion was it reached out and wrapped itself about her heart, making her wish that this evening were true and not an accidental fabrication.

Pain wrenched her at the thought, for this moment was just what she yearned for: a happy family, a loving husband, a simple life where she felt cherished and desired. She broke Tayg's hold on her gaze and looked about the table. She sat here in the circle of a loving husband's arms, surrounded by people who accepted her, celebrated her supposed good fortune and wished her happiness. Perhaps, just for tonight, she could imagine it was true.

She could.

Just for tonight.

She snuggled closer to Tayg, his arms around her still, and happily played her part.

Tayg held as tightly to his raging emotions as he held Cat in his arms. She was killing him, torturing him, daring him and he could do nothing but help her along. She had set up this farce and now she made it all too real. And damn her, he wanted it to be real. Never had he felt the way he did when she was in his arms. Never had he experienced desire so strong it twisted in his gut until he could barely think. Never had he wanted anyone so much—and not just physically—though that was his most pressing desire.

He looked down at her contentedly leaning against him, a smile playing over her full lips, a twinkle of happiness in her eyes. She laughed at something Niall said to one of the twins and the sound was like the grandest music he had ever heard. She turned to say something to the friar and he felt a pull of jealousy at the hand she laid upon the man's arm. He pulled her tightly to his side before he could stop himself, earning a surprised glare from her that quickly changed to a heated look as she lightly placed that same hand upon his cheek and kissed him.

The look that passed between them made him tremble with its openness. There was no pretense there, no calculated glance, nothing but a lass in love. The knowledge rocked him as he recognized its mate in his own heart. He loved her and not in spite of, but because of, her sharp tongue, her rapid temper, her passion and the way he came alive in her company. She would bring that same passion to all aspects of her life and he could imagine no less in his own.

He wanted her, and not just for this night, but for all the nights to come and the days, too, for the days were as exciting in her company as he was sure the nights would be. They would be a grand match and they would start right here, right now.

Cat laid her head on his shoulder and wrapped one arm around his waist, wriggling just a little so that her hip was close against his and the side of her breast pressed against his ribs.

Tayg's breath caught in his throat and he heard a chuckle from the friar.

"Shall we have a wee dram of John's aqua vitae?" Gair asked. "'Tis the best whiskey in all of Scotland, or so he tells me."

"Aye, 'tis. The brotherhood of Auskaird Abbey has made this for over a hundred years." He pulled an earthen jug from his saddlebags that rested in a corner of the room. "We have perfected the recipe to give only the finest, smoothest, most potent"—he grinned at his cousin—"whiskey in all of Scotland. The king himself requires our whiskey to be served at his table."

"Och, you're blowing a hot wind there, my cousin," Gair said, "but I have tasted your brew before and I agree, 'tis a fine drink." He pulled five small wooden cups off a shelf and handed them down to the friar. When the adults each had a cup Lina raised hers.

"To Cat and Tayg! May they live long and happy and bring many a bonny bairn into this world!"

Tayg raised his cup. "And to our fine auld"—he looked at Gair—"and new friends who have helped us celebrate the occasion!"

"And to the king's health!" the friar added. At an odd look from Gair he added, "Well, 'tis his whiskey we are drinking."

Everyone laughed, saluted each other with their cups and drank of the friar's offering.

"'Tis fit for the king," Cat said. "'Tis where you are heading, is it not, friar?"

Tayg tensed at the turn in the topic. He did not want Cat with her sharp mind putting anything together. She still did not know his true purpose for taking her to the king and the less said about politics the better as far as he was concerned.

"Aye, lass. I am bound for the wedding between Princess Maude and the Earl of Ross's heir. 'Tis not a sight I wish to miss."

"We should excuse ourselves, wife," Tayg said.

"Finish your whiskey, lad," the friar said, his eyes twinkling. "I'll not bore your lass here to sleep, I promise you. The doings of the king and his Highland chiefs is far from boring."

"Aye, 'tis true, but Cat is tired from our journey and would seek our bed." Tayg looked at Cat and noticed the pale blush stealing up the length of her lovely neck. He knew how to distract her from thoughts of kings and royal weddings. He leaned near and nuzzled her neck. "Though I dare say she is not thinking of sleep," he said so quietly he thought only she heard but the friar erupted in laughter.

"Aye, lad, I daresay she is not." He winked at Cat and Tayg had to smother that strange jealous twisting in his chest.

Cat said nothing, keeping her eyes demurely downcast when Tayg wanted to see the snap of anger there, the sharp spark of temper.

"I am tired," she said, glancing at him out of the corner of her eye.

He saw challenge there and heat. Fire sparked, but he did not think it was temper that fanned the flames, but rather something deeper, darker. Something that reached out and sang through his bones, rushed through his blood, raked over his skin. Desire pulled him to his feet, dragging Cat with him. He wanted to sweep her off her feet and carry her away, but he was not yet healed enough to do so. He would have to satisfy himself by keeping her tucked close to him.

"We would bid you all a good night," he said, desperately trying to control the trembling that threatened to show itself in his voice. "The meal was excellent, Lina, and we thank you most humbly for your hospitality, but we are . . ." He glanced down at Cat who stood with her arm around his waist and a slightly dazed look upon her face.

"We are tired," she finished, never taking her eyes from his.

"Oof!" Gair rubbed his ribs where Lina had apparently elbowed him. The weans snickered at their father. "I am reminded that I must need talk with you a moment, young Tayg," he said, though his glare was at his serenely smiling wife.

Before either Tayg or Cat could cry off, Gair had let the cold wind in through the doorway as he disappeared into the night.

Tayg squeezed Cat. "I shall be but a moment . . . wife." He kissed her forehead and slipped through the door into the cold.

Gair awaited him, standing near the corner of the cottage in the lee of the bitter wind.

"You need not scowl so," he said as Tayg joined him.

"You cannot see my face in this darkness."

"Aye, but I know where ye wish to be. I ken well what ye're wantin' right now."

"Then why are we out here?" Tayg couldn't keep the

impatience from his voice. As far as he was concerned
this was his wedding night, 'twas only left for him to inform the bride.

"Easy, lad. I would but counsel you to go slowly with
the lass. Do not rush her. I know you are anxious, but you
must woo her even as you no doubt have done these last
weeks or months. Just because she is your wife now does
not mean you have left behind the lass you wooed."

"I will endeavor to go slowly," he said. "Nights are
long this time of year and we have plenty of time."

"Aye lad, 'tis true. The mattress was newly stuffed on
St. Aidan's Day and still smells of fragrant heather so
'twill be a bonny spot to pass this night. Go slowly with
the lass and ye shall have all that you could wish for in a
wife."

The man's advice was sounder than he knew. Tayg took
a deep breath of the cold air and told himself that nothing
must happen this night. He must not rush her. She would
realize the feelings she held for him soon and that they
must wed, then all would be complete. But he must give
her time to come to the idea herself. The cold wind cut
through the wool of his trews and whipped his hair around
his face. Aye, the cold was good. He took another deep
breath and felt a quiet calmness seep into him.

"Are ye ready to go in?" Gair asked.

"Aye. Thank you for your advice. I shall heed it."

Gair hmphed but Tayg could not tell his intention from
the sound. "Let us go in where 'tis warm."

Tayg opened the door and found everyone still gathered
around the table except for Cat. She was gone. Panic
raced through him.

"Where—"

"Be calm, lad," Lina said, her smile broad in her round
face. "Your bride awaits you above." She pointed at a ladder in the far corner that led to the loft. "The weans shall

sleep down here this night so you have all the privacy you need."

Tayg's blood quickened at the woman's implication and his earlier resolve vanished. He managed not to run to the ladder, but 'twas a near thing.

He wanted Cat, and he wanted her now.

chapter 14

$\mathcal{L}$

C atriona took her leave of the family amidst much
whispering and giggling. She climbed the ladder to
the loft then stood, staring at the simple box bed pushed
into the corner. An oil lamp sat on a shelf, illuminating the
cozy space with its tiny flickering flame. The bed, tucked
under the eaves, pulled at Catriona.

Soon Tayg would climb the ladder and join her here, in
this intimate space. The thought of his long body stretched
out next to hers in that bed had every nerve singing and
heat gathering, curling through her until her heart raced and
her breath came fast and shallow. God help her! She
wanted to share that bed with him, wanted to feel his hands
on her, taste his mouth again. The man was like a fine wine,
making her muzzy-headed and foolish and yet she craved
another taste. 'Twas lust, she was sure, but somehow it was
deeper, darker, earthier than lust. The man had invaded her
thoughts, rousing disturbing desires with his kisses.

That kiss at the table had changed everything. Raw desire had poured through her, tempered by the strength of Tayg's tenderness, his gentleness, the way he grinned afterward as if he were embarrassed at his display of feeling.

They had played their parts too well, but 'twas no longer a game. She wanted him in truth, and though she was not well versed in these things, she was certain he wanted her as well.

Heat flashed through her as it had the night by the fire in their travelers' hut—the night he had raised a firestorm within her to rival the gale that had whistled outside.

She heard laughter from below and remembered how he had laughed along with the family at the evening meal. He was a rare man—charming and kind, funny, strong, caring, protective, more than pleasing to look upon and even a bit jealous, if his behavior tonight could be trusted . . . and it could, she realized.

She trusted him. The sudden knowledge was sweet, simple, true. She trusted him as she had never trusted anyone before, with her life, with her heart. With her body.

The heat pulsing in her veins ignited to a roaring fire at the thought of the two of them twined together on the bed. He would be a passionate, tender lover, she had no doubt. And he desired her as much as she wanted him.

If only . . . Nay, there would be no "if onlys" tonight.

She trusted this man. She loved this man. Nothing else should matter.

The truth sank in, filling her heart with a wonder she had never before experienced. It was calmer, subtler than desire, but just as potent, just as fierce.

She loved Tayg, and the rest would work itself out, somehow. They would figure out a way to help her clan. Together there was nothing they couldn't overcome. She wished to be his bride and so she would be . . . if he would have her.

A moment of doubt threatened to quench her exhilaration. Would he have her? She had felt his desire, his passion in his kiss, had seen his heart in his eyes though she had only just recognized it for what it was.

She stopped her pacing and began to loosen her hair with trembling fingers. 'Twas not what she had said she wanted, to marry a bard, but he was the man her heart yearned for. She loved him and she was certain he loved her. All else would sort itself out in time.

Tayg's voice carried from below. Catriona's heart leaped as fiery desire swept through her once more. She smiled. They would not be the first pair to celebrate the wedding night before the wedding.

Tayg *stood at the top of the ladder in the low-ceilinged* loft. She was there, waiting for him, the light from a single oil lamp casting a golden glow over her. Her eyes were big, her hands clasped in front of her. She had loosed her hair from its braid and it cascaded over her shoulders in dark waves.

He couldn't move, couldn't force his feet to close the distance between them. The need of his body warred with the logic scrambling through his head.

He wanted her and not for just this night. But would she have him once she knew he'd lied to her about who and what he was? Would she have him if she believed him an inept bard? The look on her face and the heat of her kiss downstairs told him she would. Soon though, very soon, he would have to reveal the truth to her.

But not now. Now he could only think about her and what she did to him.

Slowly, he moved to her, holding her gaze with his own. He could not tell what she was thinking, what she was feeling. He stopped in front of her and reached out to run his hand over her silky hair. She closed her eyes and leaned into his touch. His heart ached with the simple act of acceptance.

"You are the bonnyst lass I have ever known," he said, his voice more earnest than he intended. She opened her eyes but said nothing. "I must ask you something most serious."

She blinked slowly, then rose on her tiptoes and placed a sweet kiss upon his lips.

"I must tell you something first," she said, taking his hand and leading him to the bed. They stood there, silent for a moment. Catriona could not look him in the eye, did not know how to tell him.

"What is it, lass?" He brushed her hair away from her face, tucking it behind her ear in a gesture that both calmed her with its simple familiarity and burned her as her mind swept to other things his talented hands had . . . could . . . would . . . do to her.

She raised her eyes to meet his worried gaze and smiled a shy smile. "I wish to tell you . . ."

She stopped, unable to form the words that would leave her open to hurt from this man if he did not return her feelings.

"Aye, lass?"

Catriona chewed on her lower lip for a moment and looked away from his distracting cinnamon eyes. She must tell him. "I did not mean to . . . What I mean to say is . . . I never meant for this to . . ."

She glanced up at Tayg, hoping he would say something that would rescue her from her stammering. He only cocked an eyebrow at her and waited. That irritated her just enough to lend courage to her tongue.

"I never meant to fall in love with you, but I have. There, I've said it. I love you, Tayg."

A huge grin burst from him and he swept her up in his arms and swung her around before setting her back on her feet. He kept her in the circle of his arms and she held him close. He kissed her as he had at the dinner table, and Catriona knew she had not judged his feelings wrong.

"I love you, too, sweet Cat." His kiss was like fire to tinder, catching ablaze within her and burning away all thought save the feel of his mouth upon hers.

"I know that there is much yet to learn about one another, but there will be time enough for that later. I must ask you something most serious. I have thought much about my future in these last days."

He kissed her again until her head was spinning and she feared her knees would collapse if he did not hold her so tightly.

"I would have you be part of my future," he said quietly, "our future. Indeed I cannot imagine any future without you."

Catriona had never seen Tayg so serious, not even that first day when they were caught in the storm.

"Will you be my wife?" he asked, his lips still against hers, still wreaking havoc on her senses. "Cat?" He pulled away far enough to rest his forehead against hers, but no farther. "Tell me you will be my wife, for I cannot bear to hear otherwise."

She kissed him slowly, then smiled up at him. "Aye, Tayg, I will be your wife. I have given you my heart, 'tis only fitting that my body follow in its path, but do not make me wait for my wedding night." She grinned at him. "I fear I will be naught but ashes if you do not take me to your bed this night, indeed this very moment."

He laughed and hugged her so fiercely she feared for her ribs, but she laughed with him, sharing a happiness she had never known, had never hoped to know.

Raw need quickly burned through Tayg's relief at her acceptance. He pulled her close and kissed her, releasing all the mixed-up feelings of the last hour, indeed of the last days.

She tasted of smokey whiskey and the subtle herbs of the meal. He deepened the kiss, wrapping his arms around her until she was pressed firmly against the length of him. He ran his hands over her back. She moaned, low in her throat, and his blood surged, hot and needy. She pulled him as close as she could, moving against him, driving him mad. They needed each other and he was sure they would fit together perfectly.

He kissed her again, reveling in the feel of her against him. He showered kisses over her perfect skin and down the long column of her neck. He slipped his fingers through the heavy silk of her hair. Never before had he felt this hunger, this burning need for a woman that overwhelmed all rational thought.

Catriona knew what heaven was like. The sensations running through her wherever her body and Tayg's met could only be divinely created. Heat traveled through her veins and over her skin. Where their mouths met and danced there was fire, and somehow everything he did, every place he touched her seemed to feed the flames that threatened to overwhelm her.

Indeed, the heat of his mouth on her bared breasts made every thought vanish until there was nothing but the feeling of his lips on her flesh, his mouth tugging at her and somehow all of this feeding the fire low in her belly. She could feel her own moistness and wondered at the way her body seemed to know what to do when her mind was hazy and overwhelmed with sensations.

She tugged at the belt that held his plaid about his lean hips. She needed to feel his skin, taste him as he was tasting her. Needed. Wanted. She wasn't sure how but suddenly they were both standing in a puddle of discarded clothing, naked for each to see.

But seeing wasn't enough.

She heard his groan as he pulled her close, pressing her to him. She could feel him, pressed against her belly, branding her with his heat and his desire. She wanted that branding. She cared for naught except the feel of his mouth on her, his hands traveling over her body, even as she explored him with her own.

She moved her hands over his back, letting her fingers trail over the muscles his winter clothing concealed so well. She moved lower, daring to brush her palms over his buttocks, the skin there surprisingly smooth. Slowly, with her eyes closed so she could concentrate on what she was feeling, she moved her hands around, over his ribs, gentling her touch as she moved over the tender spot where he'd been injured, until her fingers threaded through the springy hair on his chest. She rubbed her breasts against his chest, too, wanting to feel the coarse hair against her sensitized flesh.

"Cat." He ground out the single strangled word as he shifted from statue-still to a man in motion.

His hands cupped her breasts, lifting them, caressing them, then he dipped his head and tasted them again. He laid her back on the bed, kissing her until her head swam and her body yearned. He moved down her, leaving a trail of branding kisses along her neck, over her breasts and down her belly. He kissed her inner thigh, urging her legs apart. The soft bristles of his whiskers tickled and she gasped as he kissed her there, where the fire burned brightest, until she thought she would cry with wanting. She reached for him, pulling him to her until he lay in the cradle of her thighs. She didn't know why but she needed to rock against him.

Tayg stilled her hips with a hand.

"Cat." He rose onto his elbows and framed her face with his hands. She was the most beautiful woman he had ever known, the most interesting, the most challenging. Her temper forced him to act. Her vulnerability pushed him to protect, a need no other woman had ever drawn forth in him. And yet he did not wish to protect on this night. He wished to make her his own.

"Are you sure you want this, sweet Cat?"

"Aye, Tayg, I do." She moved under him, sending flames racing over his body. Her hands were on him, urging him forward. Her passion was as strong as her temper, dear God!

He kissed her and stroked into her, breaking her maidenhead in one quick thrust.

Her breath hitched and he held very still, letting her get used to the feeling of him inside her. He kissed her again, quickly fanning the flames back to a raging inferno. When she started to whimper and move beneath him, he held still a moment longer, then let the force of his passion take over.

They exploded against each other, as if they had waited their entire lives for this one moment, each lost in the other and the exquisite feelings their joined bodies created. He heard his name, then heard his own voice whispering words of encouragement and endearment.

They moved with each other, against each other, over and under each other until at last he could not hold back any longer. He pinned her under him, his hands capturing hers and stroked into her, long and fast and hard. She wrapped her legs about his waist and a moment later a high keening sound came from her. He released his last hold on sanity and lost himself in her.

C at woke to the extremely pleasant sensation of Tayg's body curled against her back, cradling her against his chest, his thighs snugged against hers and her bottom tucked neatly into his lap. Thinking of his lap brought the events of last night rushing back and Catriona found herself wishing to experience that joining all over again. She closed her eyes and remembered, sinking into the feelings that had swept over her, the joy, the overwhelming tenderness, the desire to touch and to be touched. She squirmed a little to get closer to Tayg, needing to feel his skin against hers. His arm tightened around her waist. His hand moved over her ribs and up to cup her breast and the newly sensitive nipple he had been so attentive to the night before.

"If you keep wiggling against me, love, we shall have to repeat last night's activities."

She could hear the grin in his voice as she rolled in his arms to face him. He greeted her with a kiss that had her mind reeling and her body aching for his touch, which he quickly supplied. Catriona let herself wallow in the sensations of his hands and his mouth on her, then satisfied her own curiosity by exploring his well-muscled body with her own hands and mouth. When they were both breathless, he kissed her deeply once more and slid into her. She was sore, but he was gentle with her, moving slowly until she could not stand the pace a moment longer. They moved together, faster, urging each other on until there was nothing but white-hot, fiery pleasure.

After a while, Catriona opened her eyes to find Tayg staring at her, his nose mere inches from her own. He propped his chin in one hand and stroked her cheek with his other.

"You are truly a remarkable lass."

"In spite of my tart tongue?"

"I'm rather fond of your tongue at the moment," he said, leaning forward to kiss her lightly.

'Twas odd that such a simple chaste kiss could make her feel so desired, so loved.

"I think we should be married as soon as possible," he said. "I do not want to wait to make you my wife. You do remember saying you would wed with me, do you not?"

She smiled at the question. "I will be your wife, Tayg. 'Tis practically a done deed already." She stared at him a moment, drinking in the sight of all that sinewy strength, remembering the night they had spent, and the last hour. She would be content to stay here in his arms, safe from the world forever. But the world would not let them.

"Where is your family? Culrain, did you not say? We should go there and seek the blessing of your chief."

He nodded slowly, his expression serious. "To Culrain. 'Tis little more than a day's ride, perhaps two with the snow so deep. I think I can wait that long."

She pressed one hand to his cheek, then leaned forward and kissed him, letting all her love pour into it, into him. When she pulled away his eyes were dark and full of passion.

"Mayhap you can," she said, "but I am not sure that I can wait that long."

He grinned at her. "Some things need not wait," he said, pulling her on top of him and kissing her senseless.

Tayg grabbed his clothing and quickly dressed, never taking his eyes off Cat. A sharp possessiveness sank its claws into him equal to the fierce tenderness he felt as he watched her move about the loft dressing.

He must tell her who he was, explain the whole complicated mess to her, but he did not want to ruin this first bright morning of their life together. She would ride tucked within his embrace this day and he would tell her the tale from start to finish, or at least to the present, for the end of this tale was yet to be determined. She would no doubt display her fine temper when he told of his deception, but she loved him, fiercely, passionately, and eventually she would see that it mattered not what name he used nor who his kin were. All would be well.

"Hurry down, love. I would prefer to spend the day in this bed with you"—he kissed her—"but alas, we must make haste to the king."

"Aye, you must deliver your report and we must think of a way to protect my clan from Broc's folly, too."

Shame had him reaching for his pack to avoid meeting her eyes. "We will, lass. 'Twill be but a small matter once we find the king." He grabbed her and kissed her again, unable to keep his hands from her.

"Go!" She giggled and shoved him toward the ladder. "I will be down soon."

Tayg skipped the last few rungs of the ladder and jumped to the floor, pleasantly surprised when his jarring landing didn't pain his ribs anymore. The Friar, Gair and Lina sat at the table, talking quietly. Tayg cleared his throat to announce himself.

"Good morn to you, young Tayg," the friar said. "I trust you and your bonny wife are *not* well rested this morn?"

Lina smacked the man's shoulder as she rose from the table but the friar and Gair still grinned at Tayg and he could not help but grin back.

"Aye, we are not well rested, thank you very much," he said.

Lina served a bowl of porridge from the black kettle hanging above the fire. She handed it to Tayg with a spoon.

"Where is your lady?" she asked as she returned to her seat at the table.

"She will be down in a moment," Tayg said. "I thank you for your kind hospitality, but we must be on our way as soon as she has broken her fast."

"What is your hurry? Stay another day," the friar said. "You have not entertained us with song and story yet. Surely my cousin's hospitality deserves as much?" He winked at Tayg.

"My talent is but little," Tayg said with a grin. "Gair and Lina's hospitality deserves much more than I can provide. I promise I will send a more talented bard to visit here—and you, good Friar, will have songs and tales a-plenty while attending the wedding festivities in Dingwall."

"Besides, 'tis winter," Gair said. "'Twould be best for you to take advantage of the clear weather today, though your bride may not wish to sit a horse so soon." Gair grinned.

Tayg nodded. "I will pad the saddle for her if I must, but you ken well why we must hasten to the king."

"The king?" the friar said. "Och, 'tis no need to hurry then. The wedding in Dingwall is still ten days hence and 'tis but three days' ride at most. The king rides between his northern supporters until then, gathering new men to the cause of Scotland's freedom and gaining vows of allegiance from those who have not tendered such before. He should be at Linsmore or Culrain by now. He is said to work his way south to Dingwall arriving but a day or two before the wedding, which shall take place on Hogmanay."

"You did not tell me this news, John," Gair said. "Tayg,

'twill be even easier for you to find the king if he bides in your father's hall at Culrain."

"Your father?" The friar narrowed his eyes. "Me thinks, cousin, that you, too, have not been forthcoming with all you ken."

"Nay, John—"

"This is no bard," the friar continued as if Gair had not spoken. "'Tis braw Tayg of Culrain." A huge grin broke over the friar's face and Tayg felt the moment spin out of his control.

"I am not."

"Aye, 'tis why you seemed so familiar to me when we met upon the trail yesterday. I met you and your brother once when you were but wee lads and I have heard many a tale from Gair, and songs from the bards, about your exploits on the battlefield."

"Please, Friar, Lina," he added when he realized the woman stared at him, her mouth a hard line. "There are reasons for the deception. I would ask that you keep this knowledge to yourself—"

"Cat does not know, does she?" Lina asked quietly, her eyes now focused on a point behind Tayg.

Hair rose on his neck and he turned.

Catriona stood frozen at the foot of the ladder, her face ashen.

"I think we should leave these two alone, again," Lina said, shooing the two older men away from the table and out the door. "Give him a chance to explain, lass," she said to Cat. "'Tis sure I am, 'twill be a good tale."

Catriona stared at the stranger standing across the room. He looked like someone she knew, and yet, if what she had heard was true, he was a stranger. Tayg of Culrain, not Tayg her bard. 'Twas impossible.

"Cat, I can explain."

"Is it true? How can it be true?"

Tayg stepped towards her, but she held up a hand, stopping him before he could get close enough to touch her.

"You are a bard. I have heard you play."

"Though you yourself agree I do not play well."

Catriona's knees threatened to give out on her. She felt blindly behind her for something to sit on, finally lowering herself to sit upon the cold floor.

"Cat? Are you unwell?"

She shook her head, still trying to fit the Tayg she knew, the Tayg she had traveled with, bickered with, made love with . . . oh, God. What had she done?

"It cannot be."

"Aye, love, 'tis the truth. I am sorry I could not tell you sooner."

"You did not tell me now!" Pain flickered to life in her gut as she realized the full import of what had just happened. "You took me to your bed without ever telling me who you truly were." She had the odd thought that her voice sounded as if it came from someone else, someone quiet, breathless, afraid. "Did you laugh all night long at how gullible Catriona was?"

She raised her gaze to meet his but could not see him clearly for the tears gathering in her eyes.

"Nay, Cat, 'twas not so—"

"Tayg the Charmer of Culrain has taken yet another lass and this time he did not even have to dangle his reputation to get her to throw herself in his bed." She swiped at her eyes, determined not to let the tears fall.

"'Twas not like that, Cat. You know it."

"'Twould seem I know nothing. I am but an ignorant, gullible, stupid git, so easily duped that I did not even ken I fell in love with a guiser." The depth of his betrayal made the admission so much harder, the pain so much greater.

"Cat, please, I did not want to hurt you. I did not lie to you about my feelings. I love you. Could you not feel the truth last night? I love you, Cat. I wish you to be my wife, to spend your life with me. There is no reason that cannot be. I am Tayg of Culrain. I am the man you said you wished to marry all along."

She looked up at him, unable and unwilling to disguise the anguish that ripped through her, the shame. " 'Tis too late now," she said. " 'Tis too late."

Slowly he moved to her and crouched before her. "When we met I was already traveling as a bard and saw no reason why you should need to know otherwise. Later, 'twas too late, and I was a coward. I did not wish to challenge the tender feelings that were growing between us with my secrets."

"Secrets? Are there other lies? Other tales yet to be told about poor, stupid Catriona?"

"Aye." He winced. "Nay. Not about you, and neither are you poor, nor stupid." His voice held a hint of exasperation but she did not care.

"There is more then?"

Tayg held her gaze for a moment, then looked to the floor and seemed to make a decision. He settled himself in front of her as if they still sat in their little travelers' hut amidst the storm—only this storm was of a different making and she didn't think she would survive it.

Whether it was a moment or a day later, Cat couldn't say, but when Tayg finished his tale of Dogface's plot against the king, her clan's part in it, and her own status as a hostage, she was sure the world had ended. She had nowhere to turn, not even the comfort of Tayg's strong arms. She had nowhere to go. She had nothing.

In the space of time it took to tell the tale, her world had crumbled until there was nothing left.

As she stared at the stranger before her, a vast emptiness opened up within her, extinguishing the fire that had been Catriona.

chapter 15

"Catriona?" *Tayg's gut clenched. She was so still, so silent.* This wasn't how she was supposed to react. Where were the sharp words, the angry glare? "Cat? Lass? This changes naught important. I love you. I want to marry you. 'Tis better for your clan that you marry Tayg of Culrain, not Tayg the bumbling bard."

He expected a smile or at least a snide agreement with his description of himself, but she continued to stare at his chest, not making eye contact, not reacting in any way. He reached out and she didn't even flinch or tell him not to touch her.

Fear crawled out of his gut and strangled his heart. "Cat, please, look at me. I never meant to hurt you, never intended . . . any of this. But it has happened and I—"

The cottage door burst open and a grim Gair scattered snow as he rushed to Tayg's side.

"'Tis a rider, coming this way in a great hurry. Pol saw him from the ridge. You must away immediately." He looked from Tayg to Catriona's stricken face and the concern on Gair's face deepened. "Lass, the lad meant well . . ."

"Leave it, Gair. She knows it all now."

This was his doing and he'd not have her pushed for his mistakes. The lost look on her face had him tied in knots. If she'd scream, throw something, he could understand that, but the silence, and the look of despair, was something new. 'Twas as if she had gone from a finely forged sword to the most delicate of glass goblets—an empty glass goblet ready to shatter at the slightest touch.

"Cat? I'm sorry lass, but we cannot risk capture. I'll not let your brothers have you—and we must warn the king."

She blinked slowly, as if waking from a dream. "What?"

"We must away now. Someone comes."

She rose from the floor, refusing the hand he offered. "My bag . . ." She looked up at the loft and he knew from the pain etched about her mouth that she could not return to the place where she had given him so much of her heart and her self.

"I will fetch it, Gair,"—he turned to the man—"will you help her with her cloak and have the horse brought round?"

"The horse is already sent for," Gair said, grabbing Cat's cloak from a peg by the door.

Tayg was back before Gair had finished settling the cloak on her shoulders.

"My thanks, Gair, for everything, and my apologies for getting you involved in my troubles."

"'Tis an honor to get into trouble with you, Tayg. You keep that lass safe and give her some time. She loves you, 'tis clear, only you have given her a bit of a shock. She'll come round when she realizes she's captured the brawest lad in all the Highlands. Now go. Quickly. Give my respect to your da when you see him."

Tayg nodded and reached for the door just as it opened.

The brightness of the morning sun glinting off the ice-
crusted snow blinded him for a moment, then Pol stepped
into the dim room.

"We've another guest, Da, and he's looking for Tayg
and Cat!"

Tayg stepped in front of Cat as a larger form blocked
the doorway. He squinted, trying to make out the features.

"'Tis quite the merry chase you have given, sister."

Tayg's head pounded. 'Twasn't enough that he had hurt
the woman he loved this day, but now her future was doubly in jeopardy.

Ailig MacLeod had found them.

"H*ello, Triona," Ailig said.*
    Catriona seemed to be swimming through mud.
Every movement took more effort than it should. Voices
seemed distant, muffled, separate. Words didn't make
sense unless she concentrated very hard. So when she
heard Ailig speak, 'twas hard to believe he was really
there, even harder to drag herself from her misery and respond. Tayg said something, his tone harsh, but it took her
a moment to understand.

"What do you want? Where are the others?" That was
Tayg's voice and he sounded . . . worried?

He was worried, but not scared. He should be scared.
He had not fared well with her brothers the last time they
met. Her mind raced away from the memory. She did not
want the concern that threatened to cast a light into the
misery. She listened hard, swimming up from the black
pit, determined to understand, to avoid the memories.

"I wish to speak to my sister, bard," Ailig said. "The
others are not with me. Triona, do you now let others
speak for you?"

He spoke to her. She must reply, but words were difficult when she could feel nothing.

"Triona? Are you well?"

"Her name is Cat," Tayg said, his voice possessive.

She stepped around Tayg's bulk to stand beside him. She made herself look Ailig in the eyes and was surprised by the concern she saw there.

"I do speak for myself," she said, her voice more quiet than usual, "but only when I have something to say." She swallowed, struggling against the black pit that beckoned to her. "Go home, Ailig. Leave me be. I am weary of so many men manipulating my life." She roused herself enough to glare at both men for a moment before the numbness stole over her again.

"I have things to say to you, sister. I would know what has happened to you and why you travel with such as this bard."

She sighed and rubbed a spot over her left eye that had begun to throb. "You know very well why, and the rest is not your concern. 'Tis between myself and Tayg."

She glanced at Tayg and saw a glimmer of hope blossom in his face, shining from his warm brown eyes. For a moment, he held her gaze and her heart. For a moment she would have given up everything to be with him, to fall into bed with him again and have the world disappear, leaving only the two of them to revel in each other. But she would not love again—not him, not anyone—for love led to weakness and betrayal and pain and she would rather live the rest of her life numb than to have her heart ripped out ever again.

How quickly joy had changed to pain, love to . . . She sniffed. She wanted to hate him, needed to hate him, for that was her armor against the pain, but she could not find the hate. Hurt, disappointment, betrayal, all of those rose from the dark pit and wound round her heart, but she could not lock them into place with hatred as she had done with Broc and Dogface all these years. She broke the gaze and purposefully looked Ailig in his icy blue eyes.

"At least my b . . . he . . . helped me. No one else would." She moved to a stool and sat. "Go home, Ailig, and prepare the clan for the wrath of King Robert for 'tis surely deserved and 'twill be swift, no doubt, once we inform him of the plotting against him."

"Wheesht, Cat," Tayg said, but he did not take his eyes from Ailig, who had gone very still at her words.

"Explain," Ailig said.

Cat looked first at her brother and then at Tayg. She had tried to lean on both, trusted both, yet both had failed her. She felt something shift, a strange sensation as if the world slipped out from beneath her feet, and she feared the new strength she had found in these last few days with Tayg might disappear. Her armor was brittle with betrayal and in danger of shattering altogether.

But she would not let that happen.

No matter what happened with Tayg, she'd not let her brother see the ravages her heart had wrought upon her. She tried to remember how she had been before she met Tayg: tough, self-sufficient, lonely. 'Twas difficult, though, when all she wanted to do was curl up and have the world leave her to her misery.

"Triona, I would have an explanation. Why will the king's wrath be ours?"

A sad smile drifted over her lips and she shook her head. "Do not you play me for an idiot, too. I have had enough of that for a lifetime." She glanced at Tayg but found no comfort in the wound her words caused. She turned back to her brother. "The truth, Ailig, you owe me at least that." She spoke the words but could not muster any force behind them. "What part do you play in Duff's plan?"

Ailig's eyebrows drew down and confusion filled his

eyes. "His plan to get the king's blessing for the marriage between you and him?"

"But—" Pol began.

"Let us sit and share a drink," Gair said, interrupting his son. "Tayg, this one cannot harm you with all of us around," he said. Catriona realized suddenly that all of Gair's family surrounded them, forming a circle around Ailig, protecting Tayg and Catriona from him. "It sounds as if there is a story to be shared," Gair continued. "I'm thinking perhaps the storyteller should spin this tale. Perhaps many things can be explained at once?" Gair looked from Tayg to Catriona, but she could not answer the question in his eyes.

"Do I have your word, Ailig, that the others are not following you?" Tayg asked.

"You do. I did not wish to have you beaten to death before I could determine Cat's wishes." He watched her for a moment. "Though by the way she looks at you I would say she cares not what happens when Broc and the others find you."

Alarm sliced through her. She surged to her feet. "You will not harm him, Ailig! Nor will you allow the others to."

"Hmm, that answers one of my questions, but opens the door on so many more." He loosened his cloak and one of the twins took it. "Let us enjoy these good people's hospitality while we discover a few truths."

Lina bustled around the fire, building it up while Gair got down the friar's whiskey once more.

"I always say a story goes down easier with a little whiskey to help it along," Gair said.

Ailig sat next to Catriona and Tayg sat across the table from her, leaning forward on his elbows. She tried to ignore the determination radiating from him. She would not be swayed by his tale. She could not allow herself the weakness that opening her heart to him had been. She must be strong, as she always had been, only it had been so much easier to be strong when she had someone to be strong with her.

"Gair, this tale is not for weans." Tayg glanced at the rapt faces of the children.

"Aye. Lads, go, take your sister. There is firewood to be hauled and chopped. Niall, you stay." They waited as the children left the room, grumbling about being left out of the excitement.

When the door closed behind them Tayg began. "Do you know who I am?" he asked Ailig. "What my errand was? What business of the king's I travel on?"

"You are Tayg the Bard and you have a missive you were to have delivered to Broc from Duff. I know nothing of the king's business."

Tayg took a deep breath. "I am Tayg of Clan Munro of Culrain, warrior of King Robert, son of Angus Dubh and next chief of my clan, though God willing, not for some time to come."

Catriona felt a stirring in her gut, a tiny flicker of pride, at the way Tayg explained himself but Ailig's face was impassive, unimpressed.

"And what is this business of the king's?" he asked.

"Where do you stand—you Ailig, not your clan, nor your chief, nor your brothers—where do *you* stand where King Robert is concerned?"

All eyes were raptly focused on Ailig.

"Has Triona told you that I spent time in Edinburgh?" he asked.

Tayg nodded. "*Cat* has."

"While I was there studying I found myself frequently in the company of lads who had witnessed the Bruce in battle or had met him in gentler company and knew him to be well-spoken, intelligent, and despite his father's interference, a supporter of Sir William and the fight against the English. I came to understand that he fought for all of us in Scotland, not just the nobility, but even the Highlanders whose allegiance he could not guarantee.

"I have great respect for this man and for all that he strives to accomplish for Scotland. I am bound by my clan's chief in my public actions, but I am the keeper of my own conscience, and in that I firmly believe the future of Scotland lies not with the power that gathers with the MacLeods of Lewes in the isles, nor with Edward of England, but in the hands of our own king. Were I chief of Clan Leod, King Robert would have my allegiance."

"Cat was correct when she said you were the intelligent brother," Tayg said. He fished in the leather sack at his waist for the documents that would accompany the tale he was about to tell.

A short time later, after a fortifying round of whiskey, Tayg refolded the documents and returned them to the safety of his sack. He tried to ignore the shocked faces around the table and concentrate on Ailig, who appeared to be rather pale, his blue eyes fevered. He stared at the place on the table where Tayg had carefully shown him the documents as if they were still there.

"I am a horse's arse," Ailig finally said, his voice tight.

Catriona rather agreed, but said nothing. She was appalled all the more with this second telling of her clan's culpability in the plot against the king. How could she have been so selfish as to ignore the wider implications of an alliance between the two clans?

"I should have seen this betrothal for what it really was," Ailig said. "I knew the alliance was Duff's motivation, but I had no idea how far his delusions ran, nor how deeply Broc was involved in them."

"'Twould seem that Broc knows well which siblings will trouble his conscience the most, aye?" Tayg glanced at Catriona then back to Ailig.

"Broc has no conscience, nor a lick of sense," Ailig said. "This is clearly a trap he and Duff have set for you and Triona. And I have played right into their hands, finding you for them. Surely Broc was counting on that."

"No doubt. And I would think also a trap for the king, as he is known to be traveling these parts before his sister's wedding. So what shall we do about it? Do we warn the king or stop the conspirators?"

Catriona noted the color rushing back to Ailig's face.

"I would stop the conspirators," he said, "then turn them over to the king to do with as he may, but I fear we are outnumbered."

Surprise rushed through Catriona and suspicion. Only moments before these two had been prepared to battle each other and now, after Tayg's wee tale, they were allies?

"I must agree," Tayg said. "We must learn the king's location and ride hard to his side."

Gair cleared his throat and Catriona jumped. She had forgotten that the others listened to her clan's shame.

"You will not be outnumbered, lads," Gair said. "We will be seven—the two of you, John, myself and my three oldest—to their five, and if we can use surprise to our advantage."

"And me," Catriona said. "I'll not be left behind."

"And Cat," Tayg agreed.

Gair nodded. "'Twill be short work with so many. I have no fear that Cat can stand against her brothers and this Duff—"

"Dogface," Catriona said, her blood starting to run again at the thought of facing the man instead of running from him.

"Dogface, then," Gair continued, "but can you, Ailig? Can *you* stand against your brothers?"

"Aye. I have stood against them one way or another my entire life. 'Tis only to do so more openly now. We must protect the king and in doing so 'twill protect my clan and Triona from the ill that Broc would serve to us. But we cannot drag you and yours into this, nor my sister," he added.

"Do you really think she will stay here meekly and let us slay her dragons for her?" Tayg asked. "Do you think we can keep her from her part in protecting the king?" He held her gaze for a moment and she was surprised to see hurt there. "She wishes the king to find her a husband after all."

"But she is already married to you!" Pol's voice piped up and all eyes turned to where his head hung down from the loft. "You did all that kissy stuff last night at dinner. I saw it!"

Ailig surged across the table at Tayg, pure fury on his face. Tayg jumped back just in time to dodge Ailig's blow, toppling the bench.

"Stop!" Catriona grabbed Ailig's tunic and hauled back hard on it. He staggered and turned his glare on her.

"You are married?"

"I would speak to you in private, brother." She glanced at Tayg who was standing, grim-faced, watching them.

"What have you done, Triona? What were you thinking?"

Catriona felt anger spark to life within her and she hugged its heat to her. "Do not take that tone with me, Ailig. If you will come outside with me I will explain to you."

"I'm coming with you," Tayg said.

"Nay," Catriona and Ailig said together.

"Aye. You cannot stop me. I am a part of this whether either of you like it or not."

Lina clucked her tongue and smiled at the glowering men. "Come, mine, let us be about our tasks and let these three sort through the rest of the tale without our ears privy to their secrets. Pol, come down from there, you imp, and take yourself out to the byre. There is mucking needed there to be sure and you have earned that task this day with your eavesdropping."

"Ma!"

"Do not *Ma!* me or I shall haul you out of here by the back of your shirt."

The woman quickly shooed even Gair and the friar out of the cottage leaving Tayg and Ailig to glare at each other and Cat to ponder what to say next. When the door closed behind the last of Lina's brood, Catriona crossed her arms and glared the two men back into their seats.

"We are not married. Nothing has happened between us except a bit of mummery to keep our identities secret while we traveled," she said, daring Tayg to contradict her. When they both started to speak, she held up her hand and shook her head. "I'll not listen to either of you about any of this for neither of you can be trusted."

"Cat, I did not mean to hurt to you."

"Aye, but how could you not? You are just like all the others after all. My mistake was in believing you were different—that I was different with you. 'Twould seem that I am just as stupid now as I was at twelve, trusting you, believing you were so much more than my brothers, than Dogface."

"Cat—"

"Nay, there is nothing more to say. I am going outside. If you still wish to kill each other, please do. I'll not stop you again, but know this: I shall go for the king with you or without you. 'Tis the only way to prove to him that not all our clan are against him." She pinned Ailig with a harsh look. "Not all of us are daft."

She forced herself to walk to the door without looking back. She slipped out of the cottage and fled for the woods before anyone could see the tears coursing down her face.

• • •

"What did you do to my sister?" *Ailig asked. His* eyes were hard but they were nothing compared to the confusion in Cat's eyes as she left the cottage.

"I lied to her about who I was and why I traveled. I did not lie to her about aught else but, with good cause, she does not believe me."

"Triona does not trust easily. She sees only your betrayal, not the reasons for it." Ailig watched him for a moment and Tayg tried not to squirm under the harsh consideration. "Do you care for her?"

"I love her."

"I thought as much. You are very protective of her."

"I have asked her to wed with me."

"And her answer?"

"'Twas aye, though I doubt not that she will change her mind in light of today's revelations."

"Today's? Surely she did not just learn the truth as you told it to me."

"Nay, but not long before, and not the way I would have had her find out. I have made a mess of it and I fear she will not give her trust to me again. 'Twas hard enough won the first time."

"She has not had an easy time, but then she does not make it easy for the rest of us either."

"Are you saying 'tis her fault she is treated so poorly by her own family?"

"Peace, man. I know only too well that her sharp words and quick temper are her armor against careless treatment at our brothers' hands. And yet she is strangely quiet, subdued even. She loves you, does she not?"

It was more statement than question but Tayg nodded anyway. "At least she did."

"Will you fight to win back her regard?"

"Aye. Do not think to stand between us for I'll not let you."

"I will not. I do not know all that has passed between

you, but if she let down her defenses long enough to fall in love with you, then you are surely her best hope for happiness in the future. You will not let the king choose another for her, will you?"

"I will not."

"And you will humble yourself in whatever way she requires to regain her trust and win her acceptance of your marriage proposal?"

"I will. Whatever I must."

"Then I am convinced that she will be happy with you. And an alliance with you and your clan will only serve to strengthen our position against the MacDonells."

"What of the MacLeods of Lewes? They are against the king. Are you not bound to them?"

"Aye, but we will approach that difficulty when we must. For now they seem content to tend to their own affairs and leave us to muddle through without their help or direction, which is all very well as far as I'm concerned. I must act to do what is best for my clan and my sister. She has had a difficult time and I would see her happy."

"As would I. I will do everything that I may to keep her happy, Ailig. This I swear."

"Good, then let us turn our attention to the more immediate problem of keeping the king safe from my brothers."

Tayg glanced at the door where Cat had disappeared. He knew Ailig was right. Protecting the king was the pressing need but his heart pulled at him to follow Cat and settle this between them.

With reluctance, he shoved his heart's urgings away and concentrated on what Ailig was telling him of Broc's plan.

chapter 16

❦

Before long Tayg had gathered up their belongings and was settling them on his horse. He had not seen Cat since he and Ailig completed their plan, yet every moment was filled with thoughts of her, thoughts of things he should have done, should have said, days ago if not when first they met. He played every scenario over and over in his head yet all save the one he had taken seemed destined to keep him apart from Cat. Every other path he could have taken—physically or verbally—would have resulted in the shrew keeping him from Cat. Only by disguising himself as someone who did not threaten her was he able to coax her into shedding her bristly armor, into showing her true self.

And her true self was a marvel to behold. He had been so proud of her when Isobel had declared her friend, when Cat had fought through the night and the storm to bring him safely to their travelers' hut. He had been humbled by her passion at Gair and Lina's cottage and intrigued by the flashes of quick humor and intelligence she revealed over and over again.

And yet, the very path that had led him to know her so well and so very intimately now led her away from him, back into the dangerous realm of Dogface and her brothers.

He checked the cinch on the horse. Ailig thought they could get to his brothers and Duff in time, yet Tayg could not be sure if the man was to be trusted. He seemed truly surprised and appalled by the plot Duff and Broc had devised, and yet, if he had known of it would he have acted so very differently?

If he did lie, Cat would be devastated. Ailig was the last man she trusted. If he lied to her, she would feel she had no one. If she felt the last person had betrayed her, she would never again trust any man and nothing Tayg could say would change that. He sent a fervent prayer up that Ailig was exactly what he seemed, for Cat's sake, and for the sake of any future Tayg could hope to have with her.

But just in case he wasn't to be trusted, Tayg wanted Cat on his own horse, whether she liked it or not. At least that way he could insure her safety if trouble found them.

He sighed, made sure his horse was ready, checked to see that Gair, John and the lads were almost prepared to depart, then he went in search of Ailig and Cat. They must leave immediately. The sooner they finished this task, the sooner Tayg could turn his attention to convincing Cat to give him another chance.

A very short time later they were all mounted and set out upon the road to Linsmore. They traveled single file with Tayg and Cat, who sat in front of him, in the lead, followed by Ailig, Gair and the others. He did not like having Ailig behind him where he could not keep a keen eye on him and his actions, but Gair would see the man behaved.

When they arrived in Linsmore, they stopped briefly at

a tavern to inquire if the king was present but rumor had him arriving in Culrain that day. As they passed out of the village of Linsmore the midday sky was bright, the sun blinding off the snow. Tayg could hear the sound of the river where it rushed under the Linsmore bridge not far ahead in the glare.

Tayg slowed his horse, scanning about him for any signs of danger. The brothers were to meet farther down the trail and several hours hence, just outside of Culrain, but he was feeling wary. Catriona too seemed restless, as if his own unease carried over to her.

"'Tis sorry I am, lass," he said quietly, his mouth near her ear. "I would not have withheld my true identity from you had it not been important."

She took a deep breath but said nothing, not to him nor to Ailig, not a word since she had left Gair's cottage. Nothing.

They rode in silence a few more minutes. The road rose over a small hill and the river came into view, the bridge a pale swath across the rapid rush of water. Tayg stopped and surveyed the area. The shadows were heavy where the brilliant light could not penetrate the thick trees. Anything could hide along the road and 'twould take someone with far keener sight than he held to see into the depths of the shadows.

"I will lead," he said, as they approached the bridge. "Gair, you will bring up the rear."

Gair fell back behind his sons and the friar. Cat's brother just nodded and fell into place behind Tayg. He seemed as alert as Tayg, whose every sense was on edge as they neared the river's bank.

Tayg's horse made hollow clopping sounds as it moved onto the bridge. Ailig's was next and before Tayg had reached the far side Gair, too, had ridden onto the wooden structure. He started to think about relaxing just as a shout came out of the deep wooded shadows ahead of them. An answering shout rang out from behind him.

"You son of a—" Tayg bit out as he glanced back. "Gair! Behind you!" He cursed as he could not draw his sword with Cat sitting before him.

"Ailig?" Cat's voice was uncertain.

"I swear I did not know," Ailig said. "I swear it."

"Ho, there, brother." Broc MacLeod stepped onto the far end of the bridge, blocking their retreat. The other three brothers, Callum, Gowan and Jamie, stood in front of Tayg, grinning up at him. "I see you found Triona and the bastard who took her. I knew you could woo their trust where I could not. Well done, Ailig. You are good for some things after all, 'twould seem."

Tayg desperately wanted to look at Cat, to see how she was faring, but he dared not take his eyes from the brothers. Her silence was ominous and he feared this latest betrayal would seal his fate.

"Why are you here, Broc?" Ailig asked. "We were not to meet here."

"Aye, 'tis indeed what I told you, but you see, I am not as stupid as you would believe. You are not the only master of manipulation in our household."

Tayg glared at the sheep, then turned his head just enough to let his voice carry without taking his eyes off the bulk of Cat's brothers. "And where is your master, Broc? Where is Duff MacDonell?"

"I have no master but myself," Broc growled. No one said anything and after a moment Broc added, "He is watching the king."

"Ah, so he sent his minion to deal with the troublemakers . . . and perhaps to secure him an unwilling bride that will bind your clan to his." Tayg grinned at the sheep and lowered his voice so only they would hear his next words. "Did you know that Broc intends to give over your clan to the likes of Duff MacDonell?"

"Nay, he does not," one of them said.

"Do not listen to him, Jamie," Broc yelled. "Get off your horses." Tayg could hear him moving up the bridge.

"Take your hand off my horse," Gair said, his voice low and dangerous.

"You have used me for the last time, Broc," Ailig said.

"Aye, for any brother who would aid Triona in disgracing her clan is not deserving of the regard of his kinsmen. You are no longer welcome in Assynt, Ailig. Nor you, Triona, unless you agree to wed Duff. Do not dishonor me any further in this business."

Cat twisted to face Broc. "I would slit your throat before I would wed Duff MacDonell, my brother," she said. Never before had Tayg heard the words *my brother* sound so contemptuous, so filled with . . . not hate . . . nay, 'twas disdain. 'Twas as if Cat thought Broc the lowliest form of dung. He grinned and took the chance of glancing at her face.

'Twas a mistake, for in that instant one of the sheep leaped forward and grabbed Tayg's leg, yanking him from his perch behind the saddle and tumbling him hard to the slippery wood decking of the bridge. A similar fate must have overtaken Ailig, for Tayg heard a familiar-sounding thump followed by a lively string of words to rival Cat in one of her more inventive moments. A scuffling told him that Gair and the others were joining the fray. Tayg shook his head and sat up, only to find a dagger aimed at his chest. He leaned back on his elbows.

"Fine, I'll stay put, but do not hurt the—"

Before he could get the word *lass* out, a shout went up from Ailig, followed by yet another bridge-shuddering thump. The brother standing over him glanced up and shouted Cat's name. Tayg struck the man's forearm with his own, knocking the dagger from his fingers and launching himself at his attacker. From the corner of his eye he saw Cat's horse flying off the bridge, heading into the woods, away from Culrain.

Relief surged through him. She was away and traveling in the wrong direction. Duff would not find her and he would see that Broc and the other brothers did not either. He reveled in the moment by landing several punches into the gut of the brother who had dumped him on his arse. A shout went up from the other end of the bridge, but Tayg was too busy paying back the MacLeod brother for the beating he had taken at Duchally for the words to make sense. Another punch and another, then suddenly someone was pulling him off the other man and shouting his name.

"Tayg, stop! Stop! The twins have him. Cat's gone and so is Broc. We've got to go after them!"

Tayg shook his head, trying to clear it of the battle lust that had gripped him, fueled him. At last the words began to penetrate.

"She is away, into the forest," Tayg said, "but not in the direction of Culrain."

"Aye, but Broc went after her," Ailig answered.

Fear slithered along Tayg's spine and he ruthlessly shoved it aside.

"'Tis no problem, that," one of the sheep said from beneath the ample weight of Friar John who sat atop him. "The lass could not find her own way out of a room with but one door." The friar settled his weight a bit more and the brother groaned. "Broc will find her quick enough. Get off me, man!" The friar grinned but did not budge.

"Aye," Tayg said, rising to his feet. "But Broc must not find her."

"He will not hurt her," another of the sheep said, this one was held in Gair's strong grip.

Ailig looked from Tayg to his brothers. "I do not think that is what Tayg is concerned about."

"The lass has had about all she will take from men,"

Tayg said. "I would not wish to be Broc should he catch up with her."

"Go after her, Tayg," Ailig said.

"He will not," the three sheep said together, each struggling against their captors.

Ailig stepped closer to his brothers. "This man has kept our sister safe. He has helped her where none of us ever has. Go, Tayg," he said over his shoulder. "Keep Broc from finding her before you do."

"Nay, Ailig. She does not wish to see me. You go after her. She is your sister. I must ride for the king before Duff finds him and brings harm to all of us."

"How may he bring harm to us?" one of the sheep asked. "He but seeks the king's blessing on his marriage to Triona."

"*Cat* will never marry the bastard," Tayg said. "She would kill him first—if I did not beat her to it."

The sheep surged but did not break free. Ailig drew his sword and aimed it at the belly of the largest brother.

"You would side with that bard over your own brothers, Ailig?" the man asked.

"Aye, Callum, I would, even were he but a simple bard." He glanced at Tayg and Tayg nodded. "He is Tayg, the heir of Munro, late of His Majesty King Robert's army and traveling on the king's business. Duff does not seek the king's blessing. He and Broc seek to harm the Bruce and bring ruin upon us all."

There was an uproar amongst the brothers, but Ailig just waited. Tayg waited, too, but less calmly. Duff only awaited the arrival of the MacLeod brothers to spring Broc's ambush upon the king and Cat was somewhere in the woods feeling betrayed by every man she had ever known, with Broc on her heels determined to bring her to Duff. By the time Tayg could find and warn the king, Broc would have found Cat, who would—who already had—as her brother so eloquently pointed out, get lost and require finding. He had no doubt she could hold her own with Broc, but he had doubts about her if they should also meet up with Duff.

"We have no time for this!" he yelled at the brothers, effectively silencing them all. "Ailig, you must go after Cat. I must ride for the king, and these . . . Gair, will you ride with me to see them safely to the king's keeping in Culrain?"

"Aye, Tayg. 'Twill be a pleasure," Gair said, scowling at the brother he still held captive.

"Gair and his can see to my brothers, but let me ride for the king, Tayg. If I take the truth to him, he is more likely to feel lenient towards my clan, if not my brothers." He glared at them. "You must go for Cat."

"You cannot let him go, Ailig," the smallest of the three said.

"I can, Jamie, and indeed I must or our sister will be destined to a fate she does not want and will not accept. She loves this man and he loves her. He is the only one she will listen to at this point."

"I do not know about that," Tayg muttered just loud enough for Ailig to hear.

Ailig glanced over his shoulder at Tayg. "She will not trust me after this. She certainly will not trust that lot." He stabbed a thumb in the direction of the muttering sheep. "She may be disappointed with you, lad, but you can change that with time."

Tayg nodded. "Aye, but the king—"

"The king will hear the full tale from my lips. You heard Broc. I did not lead you into an ambush on purpose, though Broc will never get away with such a ruse again, you may be certain. I am loyal to the king and Gair will be there to ensure I tell your tale well. Go now, quickly. Cat needs you."

Tayg was torn between his duty to the king and his need to see Cat safe.

"When were you to join Duff?" he asked the sheep.

"At midday today," the shortest one said.

Alarm raced through Tayg. He glanced at Ailig, then made a swift decision. He reached into his pouch, pulled out the two missives and handed them to Ailig. "If you cross me in this I will see that you and every one of your brothers dies a painful death. Gair, keep those wee idiots with you but do not look to their comfort. Ride fast to the king. Find out from them"—he stabbed a finger towards the sheep—"where Duff is and avoid him. The king's guard can find him once the king is warned. I must find Cat."

"Go!" Ailig said. "I will not fail you."

Tayg raced off the bridge following the trail Cat had taken. Ailig was yelling something to the brothers and Tayg found himself praying that his trust in Ailig was justified. His king's life hung in the balance, as did his love's. He only hoped Broc had not had a horse on Cat's side of the bridge.

C atriona leaned low over her horse's neck but held the horse back, riding fast, but not so fast her brothers could not catch up with her. She purposely made as much noise as possible, praying that at least some of her brothers followed her. She had made the decision when Jamie pulled Ailig from his horse, and Callum pulled Tayg from his, to draw as many of the brothers away as possible. Gair's lads were strong, but only half the girth of any of the MacLeods. Gair and Friar John were not young, and Tayg would never survive another confrontation with Broc and the sheep and no matter how much her heart ached, she'd not let them kill Tayg. If she was to insure his survival, she must push aside the hurt, the betrayal, at least for now, and focus on the trail ahead. She had turned upstream, knowing 'twas in the opposite direc-

tion from Culrain in the hope that she would draw the
brothers away from the road and let Tayg and Ailig race to
the king.

In Linsmore 'twas said the king was in Culrain. Tayg
had said this road led to his home . . . his home, not the
clan he entertained, his clan, his family. His home. Nay,
she could not think on that. She must draw the sheep
away, let Tayg and Ailig warn the king, save her clan from
Dogface's treachery, then she would contemplate her future—a future that was all the bleaker for her clan's dis-
grace.

Perhaps she would return to Lina and Gair's. She sat up
and the horse slowed. Nay, she would never return to their
pretty cottage. She had given her heart and her body to
Tayg the Bard in that place, only the bard didn't exist. She
had been Tayg of Culrain's hostage . . . a willing hostage
it would seem. Embarrassment flooded through her. He
must think her the most silly of wenches, giving herself to
a man she never knew. He must think her little more than
a whore, though the only coin he had need of was pretty
words and a twinkle in his eyes.

If only the bard had been real. That man she could
gladly spend the rest of her life with, laughing and arguing, loving . . . and making bairns. Oh dear God, what if
she was with child? She could not be. 'Twould be too
harsh a judgement for her folly.

Tears blinded her for she found more than anything she
wanted her bard's bairn. The man may not have been real,
but her feelings for him had been. A bairn at least would
prove that her feelings had existed, even if they had not
been truly returned. The man had even asked her to marry
him. Hah! What would he have done if she had?

He would have mocked her, left her behind somewhere
to fend for herself . . . but no. He would not. The honest
answer pushed through from her bruised heart. He would

not abandon her, would not mock her, would never leave her like that.

Her horse shied, nearly toppling her off his back had she not had her fingers firmly twined in his mane.

"I see 'tis the shrew at last," a deep voice rumbled.

She settled her horse and hastily swiped the tears from her eyes. "Damn."

Dogface MacDonell sat on his horse, blocking the forest trail, close enough to her horse that he reached out and grabbed one of the reins, yanking it free from her.

"You do have a way with words, wife." He smirked at her.

"I am not your—"

"Where are your brothers? Your . . . escort?"

Her breath hitched as she realized the full breadth of her danger.

"You have left them behind? Even your erstwhile lover?" He urged his horse closer to her, grabbing her arm in his steely grip when she made to dismount. He pulled her so close she could feel his sour breath upon her face. "You will never see him again, do you understand? If ever I lay eyes upon him he will die. You will be my wife."

Anger coursed through her, sharp and welcome, pushing aside her morose thoughts. "Nay," she said, yanking her arm from his grasp. "I will be no man's wife. If you think to force me you will find a knife in your heart, and I do not speak figuratively."

"The lass speaks the truth, I fear." Dogface and Catriona jerked their glances behind her. Broc sat his horse, a smirk on his face. "She is the devil's own spawn, Duff. 'Tis doubtful she keeps her virtue, even. Are you sure you want her?"

Dogface looked her over carefully, his expression grim. "I have no choice, as well you know."

Broc's horse brought him to the other side of Catriona and she did not know which man to keep her eyes on.

Each was dangerous, but she suddenly felt the power in the situation shift subtly from Duff to Broc. Surprised, she found herself studying Broc.

He grinned at her. "You did not think he wanted you for your bonny form, did you my sister? 'Tis only daft bards that would want such from a troublesome woman."

She felt as if he twisted a knife in her gut, but she forced herself to think. "What does he gain . . ." It hit her, everything falling into place. Her tocher—his clan—the alliance between the clans. All would benefit the Mac-Donells, not the MacLeods. All would put the Mac-Donells at Broc's feet, deep in his debt.

"He is not the instigator of this betrothal, nor of the plot against the king, is he Broc?" she said.

"You are not usually so easily led, sister."

She glanced at Duff. "'Tis the tocher, aye, the bride's portion? 'Tis said your clan is getting rather desperate. What did Broc promise you? Food? Livestock? Enough to get you and yours through a harsh winter?" She turned back to Broc. "And in return you get rid of me, but why the king? Why would Dogface go against King Robert? Why would you, Broc?"

It was Dogface who responded. "My name is Duff." He glared at her. "'Tis for power and respect. The MacLeod of Lewes gives his respect and support to many clans in the west, but not to us, and not to your clan, who are his kin. He looks down upon us both as mere Highland barbarians of little use to him—and of little concern."

"So you seek to gain his respect by bringing down the wrath of the Scottish king and his army upon our clans?" she asked. "Are you daft?" She looked back to her brother, sitting smugly upon his horse. "The MacLeod of Lewes was wrong to disregard the two of you. He should have killed you both when you were but wee pups."

Broc backhanded her so hard she fell sideways from her horse, landing first against Duff, then falling hard to the ground as his horse danced away from her. Her face throbbed and she tasted blood. She lay for a moment in the snow, assessing if aught was broken and letting her vision clear. She had to escape these two, but she must also distract them long enough to allow Tayg and Ailig to reach the king. They must get to the king to warn him. Ailig must tell him that all of Clan Leod was not so treacherous as her brother, to beg his mercy upon their people before Broc's idiocy brought his wrath down upon them all. Duff's folk were doomed, for they had chosen him for their chief and would live or die by his actions, but Broc was not yet chief. There was hope, but only if Tayg and Ailig could convince the king. And she *must* give them the time to do so.

Dogface grabbed her arm and roughly pulled her to her feet. Stars danced before her eyes.

"I say we return to Linsmore. There is a priest there. We can seal the bargain at last."

"Nay, the king first," Broc said.

"The king will be at Culrain another three days. We can take care of this wee problem"—he gave her a shake that sent the stars shimmering again—"and still arrive at Culrain in plenty of time to take care of our business there, unless . . ."

Dogface pulled Catriona around the back of the horses until they stood facing Broc. "Unless you never intended to give her to me, to give her tocher to me."

Broc smiled, a knowing, mocking smile that Catriona had never seen before. 'Twas as if the Broc she had always known fell away, revealing a truer self that had lain hidden all these years. No longer was he a bumbling idiot. The man before her now was clearly more clever than anyone had ever given him credit for being and she must not forget that.

"You played into my little scheme quite well, Triona, and you, Duff, though your obsession with that bard

nearly upset everything when you went haring off after
him. I nearly had that taken care of, too, if that woman
had not stopped us in Duchally."

" 'Tis too bloody bad you did not finish me off then and
there."

Catriona gasped at the words and the voice that filled
her with relief and alarm. She turned to find Tayg leaning
lazily against a tree, his arms crossed as if he had nary a
care in the world, though his eyes glittered dangerously
and his face held none of the humor she so often found
there. He was supposed to be for the king. She glanced
around but neither saw, nor heard, anyone else. She turned
her attention back to Tayg and tried to ask what had become of Ailig and the sheep with only a questioning furrow of her brow.

Tayg watched her but he gave no answers. Concern
washed briefly over his features, but was quickly replaced
with a hard cold anger when he shifted his attention to her
companions. Catriona sucked in her breath and took an in-
voluntary step backwards. She did not know the angry
man before her. Her move, coupled with Dogface's surprise at Tayg's appearance, released her from his grip. She
took one slow step backwards, then whirled and ran into
the thick forest.

chapter 17

Tayg was surprised at Cat's rapid disappearance into the darkness of the thick wood but he grinned at her quick thinking. Before Broc's cry of "Get her, you dolt!" faded, Tayg had pelted after her. He had to get her safely hidden away and then he would figure out how to stop Broc and Duff, at least long enough to let Ailig get to the king. He only hoped the king would honor Gair's plea to hear Ailig, for the MacLeods were not a clan known to honor the king with their fealty.

Though they were known for their clever daughter. She was running almost silently, but not quite. He veered to his left and found her tracks in the crusty snow. He did not want to cry out her name, lest Duff and Broc be close on his heels, so he ran on, despite a burning that was beginning in his chest. After another minute or two he glimpsed the movement of her cloak flapping in the wind. He veered right, leaving the deer trail she was following and cutting through the trees. He burst from between two oaks and collided with her, catching her in his arms and cushioning her fall to the ground with his body.

"Hello, love." He grinned at her.

She just stared at him as if he were a stranger. Her eyes grew bright as if she fought tears and she abruptly scrambled off of him.

"You should be on your way to speak to the king," she said, her voice low as she brushed snow from her clothing.

"Ailig is away with Gair and the others, including your brothers—" He held up a hand before she could get a word out. "He will get the news to the king. I gave him the missives as evidence."

"But the sheep—"

"They are well in hand. They did not seem to know about Duff's plot."

"'Tis Broc's plot."

Tayg stared at her, trying to make sense of what she had just said. "Broc's?"

"Aye," she glanced around and Tayg heard the noise that had drawn her attention. "We must delay them long enough for Ailig to get to the king."

"'Tis my own thought," he said. "Let us find you a hidey-hole and I will take care of them."

"Nay, this is my battle, too, Tayg. You will not set me aside—"

"I would never set you aside, Cat," he said, reaching out and running a thumb lightly over the bruise rising on her cheek. "Who did this?"

She shrugged. "It does not matter. We should let them glimpse us, then you go that way, I'll go this. Perhaps they will split up. I suppose we'll have to knock them out and tie them up."

"Or we could just kill them."

"Broc, despite his daft schemes, is my brother, and I'll not see him killed."

Tayg nodded. 'Twas no time for argument. Besides, the king's justice was likely to be less fleet and less forgiving than Tayg's swift dagger.

"There they are," she whispered. "Leave me be!" she said, startling him with her loud words. "Farewell!" she said, more quietly again and she turned and ran down the deer trail once more.

Tayg grinned after her. She was a cheeky lass with more courage than many a man he'd fought beside. He glanced back into the forest gloom and saw the two men on foot, swords drawn, sprinting toward him. He hesitated another moment, wanting them to get a good look at him, then he dashed back into the woods.

Playing right into Cat's plan, Broc went after Cat and Duff turned to follow Tayg.

*C*atriona glanced over her shoulder and found the unmistakable bulk of her eldest brother following her. Good, 'twas exactly as she had hoped. She skidded to a halt in a small clearing, found a large tree at its edge, continued across the clearing on the deer trail, then circled the edge of it under cover of the trees. She hid behind the ancient tree, caught her breath for a moment, then quickly prepared her ammunition.

Just in time, she peered around the bole of the tree, cocked her arm and let her snowball fly. It caught Broc squarely in the side of the head with a hollow thump.

"Triona!" he bellowed as he rubbed his temple. The rock she had packed her snowball around seemed to have done its job, dazing him just enough for her to scurry in the shadows to hide behind another tree. Broc turned towards her.

"That wee slap will be as nothing compared to the beating I shall give you if you do that again," he said, shaking his head.

Catriona let another snow-encrusted rock fly, hitting his shoulder with a splash of snow and a grunt from Broc.

"Treeee-oooo-nnnaaa!" he yelled as he charged towards her.

She cradled her supply of snowballs in the fold of her cloak and ran deeper into the woods.

Tayg heard the bellow, as did Duff, though since Tayg sat atop the other man there was little Duff could do to aid Broc. Tayg winced at the sound of the other man's voice. The lass had done something to provoke him beyond a simple chase through the woods. Part of him wanted to go and cheer her on, but the other part, the newer part of him that she had awakened, wanted desperately to protect her from any more abuse at her brother's hands.

"I've need to go," he said to Duff as if they were having a simple conversation instead of the fight they were actually engaged in. Tayg grabbed Duff by the front of his cloak, cocked back his right hand and landed a knuckle-splitting punch to the other man's jaw. There was a crunching sound and then Duff's eyes rolled up in his head. Tayg dropped his grip and stood. He had no rope to tie the man up with but he could not leave him here to recover and attack again. Tayg grabbed the hem of Duff's cloak and using the man's dagger cut several strips of wool from it. 'Twas a pity to destroy the garment, but he had no choice. Quickly he rolled Duff onto his stomach and tied his hands behind him, then he tied his feet and lastly he tied the final strip of cloth from the bindings about Duff's hands to the bindings about his feet.

"That should hold you."

Duff groaned but his eyes did not open.

"Good," Tayg said, looking about for his dagger that had been knocked out of his hand during the fight. Another bellow came from deeper in the woods followed by a surprised scream. Tayg ceased his hunt for the dagger and raced in the direction of the voices. If Broc hurt Cat, Tayg would see him dead, no matter what her wishes were. Tayg would survive her tongue-lashing but she would not survive the kind of revenge her brother would visit upon her for this. The stakes were too high in this game and he had no doubt Broc would suffer no more interference from his troublesome sister.

*C*atriona zigged and zagged through the trees so Broc could get no clear line of sight on her. She would stop just long enough to launch another missile at him, hitting him sometimes, but more often not. Broc had more experience dodging her missiles than Tayg did. She did hit him in the face once more, this time full in the mouth. Blood spouted and he bellowed and ran after her, true rage in his eyes. Cat sprinted away. She would be in peril if he caught her now, so he would not catch her. She had been dodging him for years.

She glanced back over her shoulder just in time to see Tayg come flying out of the woods to tackle Broc. Damn him! She had Broc just where she wanted him, but Tayg the Hero had to come racing to her rescue. She didn't need rescuing. Didn't need him. Let the two of them beat each other to a bloody pulp for all she cared. She rested her fists on her hips and sighed.

The two men were rolling over the snow-crusted undergrowth calling each other names. She quickly added the inventive epithets to her repertoire and was about to go in search of her horse when Tayg grunted and Broc let out an unmistakable shout of victory.

"Nay!" she yelled as she ran back to where the two battled. She grabbed a dead branch laying along the trail and raised it over her shoulder.

Broc straddled a dazed Tayg, his dagger poised to plunge into Tayg's heart. Before she realized what she intended, she swung the branch just as Tayg flung Broc from him. The branch whistled through the air, missing Tayg by the smallest of margins.

"Tayg!"

Broc launched himself at Tayg. Tayg sidestepped and grabbed the branch from Cat's grip. He swung, catching Broc in the side of the head. He flew sideways, landing in a crumpled heap next to Cat, his dagger still in his hand. She stepped on his wrist, not trusting him to be unconscious, then grabbed the dagger, ready to use it on him if she must.

Tayg tossed the branch aside and took the dagger from her. "Remind me never to make you angry, love," he said, giving her the crooked grin of her bard. "Did he hurt you?"

"Nay, he only hurts daft bastards who don't know when to leave well enough alone," she said, unable to take her eyes from Tayg. He had a large lump forming on his forehead and his lip was bloody.

"I could not."

"Aye, because you are a hero, a warrior."

Tayg wiped blood from his lip with the back of his hand. She noticed his knuckles were battered, too. "Not because I am a warrior, though that is part of who I am, lass. Nay, I could not leave well enough alone because I could not let him hurt the woman I love. I will never let him hurt you again."

He reached for her and she stepped back. Confusion flooded his eyes and she had to look away. Her own heart was confused and his touch would only cloud it further.

"We must get Broc and . . ." She looked about. "Where is Dogface? Did you kill him?"

"Nay," he said, still watching her intently. "He is back along the trail, trussed and ready to be taken to the king."

She nodded. "Then let us do the same with this one. We will need the horses to carry them."

"I will bind him, then we can return for the horses." Tayg grabbed Broc's cloak and began tearing strips from it.

"I shall go."

"But you'll get lost."

She looked at him for a moment, then listened to the woods around her. Off to her right she could hear the roar of the river. "I crossed the water and turned right, upstream, so if I follow this deer trail, keeping the sound of the river on my left I shall come to the horses." She cocked an eyebrow at him, daring him to say she was wrong.

"You came this way a-purpose," he said, surprise on his face. "You knew you turned away from Culrain."

"Someone had to draw these fools away. But you were supposed to go to the king with Ailig. There is little hope the king will forebear to hear Ailig's tale without his valiant warrior, Tayg of Culrain, there to speak for Ailig's good intentions."

She saw him flinch when she said "valiant warrior." 'Twas good. 'Twas what he was, no matter what he said to her. The bard had never existed and she would be a fool to trust him, no matter how much his crooked smile and the twinkle in his eye made her ache for his touch, for his humor, for his hard-won words of praise that had come to mean so much to her. Nay, she could not weaken in her resolve. She could not allow such weakness ever again, for even if she did find a way to trust him, his clan would never allow a future chief to burden himself with the daughter of such a treacherous clan. She would see Duff and Broc delivered to the king. After that . . .

"Cat—"

She turned her back on him and trudged down the trail to the horses.

•   •   •

Catriona led the horses back up the deer trail. It had taken her longer than she had expected to find them; somehow she'd passed them in her concentration on keeping the river on her left and had to double back. But she had found them and she was proud of herself for it.

"Cat!" Tayg's voice came from somewhere off to her left. Had she missed the clearing? "Cat!" he called again and she saw him loping towards her through the trees. "I moved Broc to where I left Duff. Follow me," he said, untying the rein that linked the second and third horse and taking the first two from her.

He turned back the way he had come and she followed, silently fuming that he had said nothing about her finding the horses, though perhaps his confidence in her was such that he had no doubt she would fetch them. That thought pushed the momentary hurt from her, but she did not dwell on it long, lest she let the warm feeling it created soften her towards Tayg of Culrain.

"Well, lads, your mounts have arrived and 'tis up to you how you shall ride," Tayg said.

Catriona stared at the two men trussed and sitting, arms behind them, knees bent from the tether connecting their hands and feet, leaning against separate trees far enough apart that they could not speak quietly with each other.

"We ride nowhere with you, Culrain," Broc said, a sneer darkening his voice.

"You shall ride with me, then," Catriona said. "And you shall explain to the king that 'twas you behind this plot. You shall explain that 'twas none of the rest of us." She looked at Dogface . . . Duff. He looked a pitiful shell of a man at this moment, resentful and angry, but no longer a threat. "And you shall explain that Duff's part in this arose out of need. Mind you I shall never wed him, but perhaps the king can find some way to win the fealty of Clan Donell if he knows the truth behind Duff's part in this."

"Aye, I shall be pleased to explain the circumstances to the king," Duff said. "I shall be pleased to explain how Broc lied and manipulated until my clan was so desperate I would agree even to take the Shrew of Assynt into my house in order to assure the survival of my clan."

"Watch your tongue, MacDonell," Tayg growled.

"Aye, mind your tongue, Duff, or I shall be required to cut it out," Broc said.

"Fine words from a man trussed like a fine, fat cow," Catriona said.

"Sister mine, do not provoke me."

"I shall provoke you all I like. 'Tis what I have done my whole life, is it not?"

"Aye, you were ever a thorn in my side, Triona."

"My name is Cat."

Tayg grinned and she grinned back before she could stop herself. She realized with a start that she was Cat now, no longer Triona the Shrew. She had changed and, except for the fact that 'twas her weakness for Tayg had led her here, she liked who she had become.

"From the moment you could speak you have gainsaid me," Broc snarled at her. "From the moment you could form a sentence you have done all you could to thwart my authority over you or anyone else. 'Tis so even now when I am so close to fixing our place in history, our place in the Highlands. When I have accomplished this feat, all will seek our support. The MacDonells are just the start."

"Nay, we shall never more seek anything from the treacherous, untrustworthy MacLeods," Duff said. "I would not trust you in my own house, and I would not trust your integrity even were I offered your hospitality. I would rather see my clan starve than to submit to such as you."

"I am the salvation of your clan." Broc spat in Duff's direction. "The MacDonells are nothing without the support my clan will bring to you."

"*Nothing* is a better fate than to be saddled with you."
Duff turned his attention to Tayg who stood, a small smile
on his lips, arms crossed across his broad chest, watching
the exchange. "Take me to King Robert. I shall tell him all
that Broc plans . . . all!"

"You will not!" Broc said, suddenly surging up from
his place by the tree. He charged across the open space, a
dagger held over his head. He launched himself at the
trussed Duff, who rolled to his side just as Tayg smashed
into Broc, knocking him aside. Broc landed in a heap a
few feet away.

Duff struggled to sit up again, his eyes wide. "Untie
me! Untie me now before the man comes at me again!"

Cat walked slowly over to her brother, who lay face
down, unmoving. She looked at Tayg as he came closer,
reached down and shook Broc's shoulder. The other man
did not move. Tayg grabbed his shoulder and rolled him
onto his back. The dagger stuck up to the hilt from between Broc's ribs.

"'Tis sorry I am, Cat."

She shook her head, still trying to take in the vision of
her brother, the man who had made life one long trial,
lying dead at her feet. A small part of her mourned the
loss; he was her brother, no matter how little good there
was between them, but a larger part just felt cold and distant, as if the man at her feet were a stranger.

"You had no part in this except to defend a man who
could not defend himself," she said.

"I did. 'Tis my dagger. I lost it in the fight with Duff."

"Aye, and Broc found it when you sat him by that tree,"
Duff said.

Tayg glared at the man. "You knew he was armed and
yet you goaded him?"

"No one ever said Duff was smart," Cat said, her voice
oddly hollow, even to her own ears.

"I should have let him at you," Tayg said to Duff. He

took a blanket from his bags and spread it out on the snow next to Broc. He pulled the blade from the man and cleaned the blood off in the snow. Carefully he rolled the body into the blanket, tied it and at last loaded it over the saddle of Broc's horse.

Swiftly he released Duff's feet long enough to sling the man into his saddle, then he quickly tied his feet again under the horse's belly. Cat mounted, and Tayg swung up behind her. It was comforting to be there in the circle of his arms, but she would not let herself lean back against him, would not take that solace. He tied the reins of Duff's horse to the saddle, as he had tied Broc's to Duff's, then silently they left the blood-stained scene behind them.

Surely Ailig was almost to Culrain by now. They must get there as soon as possible for she feared Gair would not command the king's attention as Tayg would. The king would not heed Ailig's tale. Ailig needed Tayg, trusted warrior of the king, to vouch for him lest he and their clan be blamed for Broc's ill-conceived plan. The king would throw Ailig into the gaol or worse, and Catriona had no wish to lose another brother this day.

chapter 18

𝒟❤

It was dusk before Tayg led the way into the village of Culrain and through the cottages to the hall house. No shouts of welcome greeted him this time; indeed, the village seemed deserted, which meant that everyone was gathered in the hall awaiting the king's response to Ailig's tale—if he had listened to Ailig at all.

He glanced back over his shoulder to make sure Duff was still there, as he had done so many times on this journey. Cat had said nothing to him since they left the clearing. Duff had tried to explain himself as they rode through the wood, but Tayg's quiet promise to follow through on Broc's threat to cut out the man's tongue—in spite of any useful information he might bring to the king—finally seemed to dampen Duff's need for conversation.

Tayg stopped near the steps and tied his horse to a post there. He went back to help Cat down, but she seemed to be in a daze, not noticing him standing at her knee.

"Lass?" he said, touching her calf lightly.

"We must tell Ailig about Broc."

"Aye, there is much we need to tell Ailig, and the king, but we cannot do so out here." He reached up, grasped her about the waist and helped her down.

She stood, still as stone. He tipped her face up though she did not raise her eyes to his. He ran a finger lightly over the vivid bruise on her cheek. "I am sorry for what happened."

She shook her head. "Nay, do not be. Broc brought his fate upon himself." She looked up into his eyes. "I find little sorrow in my heart for him. I am truly the cold-hearted shrew he always said I was."

Tàyg folded her into his arms and was relieved when she wrapped her arms about his waist and burrowed into his embrace. "Nay, lass. You are soft-hearted when given half a chance to be. You have warmed my heart as no one has ever done before." He kissed the top of her head, then laid his cheek against her soft hair. "You have little sorrow for him because he never gave you reason to care. Do not let him win by making you doubt yourself."

He pulled back and cupped her face in his hands. "I love you, lass. You have made me love you with your warmth and your humor and your stubbornness." He grinned at her. "And your way of winning friends—your way of winning me."

He kissed her then, letting all that he felt for her pour into that moment. She kissed him back, quite desperately, and he pulled her close.

"We have much to do," he said, resting his forehead against hers. "But I would finish this . . . conversation . . . as soon as we may, for there is much to discuss, much to explain."

"Nay."

"Aye, there is, but first we must see the king and see that Ailig and your other brothers are safe."

She stepped out of his arms and pulled her cloak about her. "To the king, then."

Tayg released Duff's feet and helped him to the ground, too. "What, no tender words for me?" Duff asked. "She was to be mine, despite her sharp tongue. She was always meant for me."

"You wanted only what the lass could bring with her."

"And you want less?"

"Nay, I want more," Tayg said, shoving the man towards the steps. He looked at Cat, capturing her startled gaze. "I will have her heart for my own. Nothing less."

She took a shuddering breath and he glimpsed a crack in the wall she had built around her heart. Perhaps there was hope for the two of them yet.

He shoved Duff through the doorway into the noisy hall, yet no one seemed to notice their entrance. He looked around noting that his parents and the king were nowhere in evidence, yet the door to the "bear's den" was closed and Duncan stood guard there. He pushed Duff, his hands still bound behind his back, in that direction. He grabbed Cat's hand and pulled her along. As they moved through the hall silence puddled around them until the ripples of their movement quieted the entire gathering. Duncan nodded at Tayg, then knocked on the door and opened it, stepping out of the way to let the three enter.

The king sat in his father's accustomed chair, his richly embroidered crimson mantel pooled about him. His dark hair and close-cut beard framed steely eyes cold with barely controlled fury. Angus Dubh, Tayg's father, Gair and Friar John ranged behind the king. Ailig and the other brothers stood opposite facing the king like pawns on a chess board and soldiers ringed the room. Ailig was mid-sentence but stopped at their entrance.

"Sire, here is Tayg," Ailig said. "Let him tell you in his own words all that he has discovered."

The king rose and accepted Tayg and Cat's hasty bows.

"This is the lass who has caused so much chasing about?" the king growled.

Catriona flinched, but stood her ground. Tayg wrapped his arm about her waist and pulled her close. "Aye, sire. This is she and were it not for her, your life would be in grave danger . . ."

S everal hours later Cat lay on the bed in the chamber that had been given to her. 'Twas a large chamber and the bed was broad and stuffed with feathers. She was tired, sore from days of traveling and Broc's toppling of her from her horse. She wanted to sleep, to escape all that she had heard in the last few hours, all that she had witnessed, to escape the knowledge that Tayg was not the person she had imagined him to be.

For she was sure she had imagined the bard. How else could she explain how the man she had watched eloquently argue for her clan could ever have been mistaken for a charming, bumbling bard? Tayg had been every inch a warrior, clearly in the king's favor, when he presented his case to save her clan, to save Ailig, the sheep, and she had realized belatedly, herself, from the king's all too evident wrath. Ailig had stood silent, allowing first Tayg, then, when questioned, Duff, to verify the tale he had already told the king before their arrival.

At last the king had sent all but Tayg away, placing Duff, Ailig and the others under guard. Only when Tayg whispered something to the king did he release her to Tayg's mother's care with Cat's promise she would keep to her chamber until summoned back to the king's presence. She gladly gave it. The woman who led her away from the crowded chamber to this comfortable one had looked at her oddly, but said little beyond pointing out the tub and the clothing that had been provided for her comfort.

Cat had sat in the tub until the water was too cool to be comfortable. She had dressed, first donning a beautifully made linen shift, then a gown more beautiful than any she had worn before. It was made of finely woven woad-blue wool, like the gown Isobel had offered her, and was soft and warm, with an intricately embroidered decoration in a line down the length of each sleeve. The embroidered trim was studded with tiny grey and white freshwater pearls. A similar decoration edged the neckline. The rest flowed simply and gracefully over her hips, nearly, but not quite reaching the floor, as if it had been made specifically for her. A plaid in shades of crimson shot through with saffron and black served as a wrap.

She had combed out her hair and dried it in front of the fire. She had left it loose, braiding only the front sections, then looping them back and fastening them together with a bit of leather. Now she waited, wondering if she had dressed thusly for her execution.

A soft knock came at the door. Her breath caught as she sat up. Would she learn the destiny of her clan now? Would she learn her own destiny?

"Come in," she said.

The door swung open and Tayg stepped into the chamber. He had not changed his clothing . . . Broc's blood still stained his tunic. Cat stood. Sitting on the bed was too intimate, reminding her of things she wanted and things she could not have.

Tayg stared at her. He licked his lips and looked about to say something but stood silent. He shook his head and took a step towards her.

"You are even bonnyr than I knew," he said.

Cat looked at her feet, unable to answer the question in his eyes. "'Tis the gown."

"Nay," he said, lifting her chin with his finger. "Nay, 'tis you."

"Am I summoned to the king?" she asked, afraid to ask more.

"Soon. He wishes us to attend him at the evening meal."

She nodded and lifted her chin to release herself from his touch, for it was meddling with her mind, as was the look of need in his eyes.

"You need not worry, lass. The king is fair. He has not yet decided the fate of the MacLeods and the MacDonells, but I do not think harm will come to any save those who knowingly went against him."

"And the rest of us will be exiled from our lands and our homes?"

"You shall always have a home, lass, if you will but marry me."

Tears burned her eyes and clogged her throat. "I cannot abandon my clan to secure myself a soft future."

"I do not ask you to abandon them. I ask you to join with me."

"'Tis the same thing. I do not know you anyway. You are so much more than my bard."

"Cat, I—"

"Wheesht, let me finish," she said, laying her finger on his lips. 'Twas a mistake, that, for all she wanted to do was to place her own lips there and forget everything in the sweetness of his embrace. She wanted the forgetfulness and the total focus that had come in the same moment when she had lain in his arms. She wanted the feelings of love and acceptance, of safety and sweet good humor. She wanted that and so much more. But she would not have any of it. Could not, thanks to Broc.

"I cannot marry you, Tayg. Were you but a bard 'twould be different, for then the black stain upon my clan's name would matter little, but I cannot ask Tayg of Culrain to do the same. I do promise to do whatever I may to insure my clan does naught against the king, indeed, if

Ailig and I can do so, we will sway the clan to declare fealty to King Robert—though whether they will listen to either of us after this remains to be seen. They may banish us all and choose another to lead the clan. My father will be mortified, as well he should be, and there is little I may do to change any of that."

Tayg stood silent, devouring her with his gaze. At last he asked, "Will you do as the king bids you?"

"I can do no less."

Tayg nodded and turned to leave. He stopped, his hand on the latch, and turned back. "Do you love me?" he asked. "The truth, Cat. You owe me that much."

Tears filled her eyes, but she would not let them fall. "I do love you, Tayg, with all my heart. I understand now why 'twas necessary to keep your identity hidden—and all the rest. But the rest is why I cannot saddle you with the taint of my clan. You are bound for great things, 'tis clear. 'Twould break my heart to see you fall because of me."

His eyes were dark and determined but he said nothing as the door closed behind him.

*A*n *extra table had been added on the dais in the hall* to serve the king's folk and Tayg found himself seated near the end of it, Duncan to his left and his parents on his right, nearer the king's still empty seat. The bard played near the fire, just as he had a fortnight before. How could everything change so quickly?

Just a fortnight past he was unwilling to consider marriage. Now he was ridiculously morose because a difficult bonny lass had declined his proposal with an all-too-logical argument. 'Twas an argument worthy of Robbie, but he wasn't Robbie and neither was Cat. The lass wasn't culpable in her brother's plot. She had done all she could to stop it. Did that not make her a worthy bride for a warrior of the king and the future chief of the Munros of Culrain?

"Daft lass."

"Aye, they all are," Duncan said, considering Tayg in a way that reminded him of his mum when he was a wee lad and had gotten into the sweets. "But no more daft than a lad in love. Is there one in particular you are brooding over?" he asked with a smirk.

Tayg glared at him. "You know there is. She will not have me."

His mother chuckled from his right. "'Tis somehow just that you should finally find a lass you want and she will not have you."

"It has little to do with justice," he said. "She thinks her brother's treason makes her unworthy."

"And does it?" she asked quietly.

Tayg looked at his mother, considering his answer carefully. "Nay. She is a most worthy lass. She is loyal and I would—indeed I have—trusted her with my life. 'Tis not her doing that her brother is a fool."

"Aye," his father said. "From the tale told 'twould seem she risked much to keep her clan from falling prey to her brother."

"And for many a year," Tayg said, almost to himself. "She has been a thorn in Broc's side for many years and were it not for that he likely would have tried something like this sooner. Certainly the MacDonell would have supported him sooner."

"She sounds like a noble lass, despite her reputation."

Tayg snorted. "Her sharp tongue is but a defense. She is a sweet lass, a strong lass, beneath that armor."

His mother smiled a knowing smile.

"What makes you smile, Mum?"

"You, my lad. 'Tis clear Catriona is the lass for you, yet you sit here as if the world had ended and there is naught left to be done but watch the destruction."

"She will not have me. She says she will not taint me nor this clan. Robbie would have agreed with her."

"Aye, but Robbie could be a-right shortsighted at times," his father said.

Shocked, Tayg did not know what to say.

"You are not Rob, my son," Angus continued. "Rob was a good man and would have led the clan well, if without imagination. You have handled this situation with the MacLeods and the MacDonells with imagination and discretion. You managed to keep the king safe while still preserving the dignity of as many of the people involved as possible. The Munros will follow you, not Rob, God rest his soul. You must lead in your own way. You must lead as much with your heart, Tayg, as with your head, and the two will balance well. Catriona will make sure of it."

"She will not have me."

"You are not thinking, Tayg," Duncan said. "'Tis clear you love her, and if I am not mistaken, the lass has proved her love of you, has she not?"

Tayg refused to blush at his friend's implication, though 'twas true. Even before she had said the words to him he had known by her body's reaction to him just how she felt about him. "She says she loves me. She says were I truly the bard she knew instead of the heir to Culrain . . ."

"Then find a way. You are still the bard she met, are you not? 'Tis but a part of you. Were you less yourself with the lass just because you took the guise of a bard?"

"Nay," he shook his head, considering his friend's questions. "Nay, I was more myself with her than ever before. I was no longer trying to be Robbie, nor was I trying to live up to anyone else's expectations, save my own."

"Then you have but to show the lass that you are the same man she fell in love with. She loves you, aye, but she needs a wee bit of convincing."

Images from their travels flashed through Tayg's mind.

That first night in the cave, her standing beside Dolag while he sang that awful . . .

He grinned. "I know just the thing. Excuse me," he said, rising from his seat. "I must speak to the king."

Cat sat on the bed, exactly where she had sat when Tayg had left her. Somehow she knew this was his chamber, the bed his bed. She wanted both to throw herself across the bed and cry her heart dry and to leave the room and think no more of the dark-eyed man who had worked his way through her armor and made a place for himself in her heart. Her heart ached and she was sure nothing would ever stop that pain. Everything she had wanted was here in her grasp, had been offered to her, and yet she could not take it, could not pull Tayg and his family into the black morass that was the plight of all MacLeods thanks to her brother and that idiot, Dogface.

There was naught for her here. She could not take it, so it might as well not exist. If only she had never left Assynt. Never met Tayg. Never come to love the irritating man.

But she had, and if she was honest with herself, she knew 'twould have been worse for everyone had they not met, had they not worked together to thwart Broc and Dogface, had they not worked together to warn the king. 'Twould have been worse for her, too, for she would now be wed to Dogface and that was an even bleaker future than the one she now faced.

A soft knock came on the door.

"Come in."

The door opened and her heart leaped for a moment, thinking Tayg had come back to beg her to change her mind. But it wasn't Tayg. 'Twas Ailig.

"We are summoned to the hall, Cat," he said.

Startled, she looked up. "Why do you call me that?" Her voice was quiet and she cringed at the wobble in it.

"'Tis a fitting name," he said gently. "You have teeth and claws aplenty, and yet, as I have been told, you are sweet and gentle and protective of your own."

"I am not."

"Aye, lass. For all that you are angry with your bard—"

"He's not—"

"He is yours, Cat, whether you can see it or no, he is yours and you are his. Do you not see how you have changed under his care and influence?"

"I have changed, that I cannot deny, and 'tis sure he had some hand in it." Her traitorous body remembered only to well how his hands had been upon her. Her breathing increased and panic welled up in her. She could not forget that he had lied to her, betrayed her. Used her. He took her as a hostage, not to help her. Lies, all lies. Aye, but lies for a greater purpose. Not lies to hurt her.

"We must go," Ailig said, gesturing to the door.

She nodded and rose, settling the beautiful gown about her, then preceding him out of the room. The corridor was cold, but they had only to cross to the turnstile stair and descend a floor. They stepped from the stair directly into the hall. It was crowded with people, far more than when she had arrived with Tayg a few hours ago. A fire burned along one long wall and two long rows of trestle tables filled the space. The chamber where she had met the king was at this end of the hall but this time the king sat at the table, raised above the rest, at the far end.

Ailig placed a hand at the small of her back and steered her along the wall where an aisle had been left.

"Why do you think the king wishes to see us?" she asked Ailig in a whisper.

"I do not know, sister-mine. Do not fret. I am sure 'tis simply a formality before he sends us back to Assynt, or perhaps he wishes us to stay in his . . . care . . . as hostages against the good behavior of our kinsmen. Keep good hold of your temper, no matter what happens."

She narrowed her eyes at him. "If you think to goad me so I will not be afraid 'twill not work. I have learned the value of holding my tongue . . . at times . . . and of keeping a tight rein on my temper."

Ailig smiled at her. "You are a remarkable woman, Cat. Tayg is a remarkable man."

Catriona looked down at the floor. "He is."

Another moment and they stood before the king's table. Ailig bowed and Catriona curtsied, though she could not bring herself to look up at the table. She did not want to see Tayg, could not meet his eyes again lest he see the shreds her heart was in. She would not give him any reason to believe she was not at peace with her decision. She would give him no reason to play the hero to the heartbroken lass.

"Ailig of Assynt," the king's voice boomed out over the crowd, startling her into looking up. His eyes were on the two of them. His voice was firm, his expression . . . unreadable. She started to shake and Ailig took her hand and squeezed it. The contact gave her courage. Together they would face whatever the king deemed just.

"I have considered the information you brought to me this day. I have conversed with each of your surviving brothers, your sister,"—he gave a slight nod of his head in her direction—"with the MacDonell and with my loyal man, Tayg of Culrain."

Catriona held her breath, knowing that her own fate fell close to her brother's.

"I find your loyalty to me to be remarkable and greatly appreciated. I also find the death of Broc MacLeod of Assynt to be a boon, leaving the future leadership of your clan in some disarray." He stopped and watched Cat and Ailig for a moment. She struggled not to squirm, though 'twas difficult under such scrutiny.

"Ailig, though you are the youngest son of your father, I find you to be a man I can trust, a man who will be loyal to me and to the greater good of Scotland. Will you swear fealty to me, here and now?"

"Aye, sire," Ailig said without hesitation. He drew his dagger, placed it on his palms and presented it to the king. He went down on one knee and bowed his head. "I do swear it though it may cause me to be cast out of Assynt. I swear fealty to you, Robert, King of Scotland."

"Rise."

Ailig did and the king returned the dagger.

"The MacDonell will accompany my guards to Dingwall where the Earl of Ross will host him in his dungeons that he may do no further harm to his clan. I command the three, Gowan, Jamie and Callum of Clan Leod of Assynt to serve in my army until such time as I deem their duty finished. Ailig, I charge you with bringing your clan into the community of Scotland."

"But, Sire—"

"A good chief should have no trouble in this task."

Cat thought it was a rebuke at first, then realized the implication of the king's words. She glanced at her brother and found his face serious; worry filled his eyes. This was just what she had wanted, and just what Ailig had not.

"I will do what I must, Sire. Clan Leod of Assynt will serve the King of Scotland."

Cat knew 'twas easier said than accomplished, but Ailig would find a way.

"As it should," King Robert said. "As for you, mistress," he said, turning his attention to Catriona. "What boon would you seek for your loyalty?"

"I ask for naught," she said, startled by the unexpected question, "save to return to my home with my brother."

"I was given to understand you undertook the journey from Assynt in search of me to make a certain request."

Catriona tried to hide the pain such words caused. She swallowed, lifted her chin and looked the king in the eye. "Nay, sire. I did not. 'Tis my place to return to Assynt and to leave you and the good people of Culrain to see to the future of Scotland."

The king shook his head. "There is one who would have otherwise."

"I cannot, sire. He deserves better than the cast-off daughter of a disgraced clan."

"Hmph. Is she cast-off, Ailig?"

"Nay, lord, never."

"Is your clan disgraced?"

Ailig did not say anything.

"It is not," the king said. "I am satisfied that those responsible are accounted for and will, or already have, paid for their part in the conspiracy. So, you are neither cast-off, nor disgraced, Catriona. Even so, 'twould seem a mediocre bard would not quibble over such."

A drum beat began, unsteady but strong. Catriona turned to find the crowd, so thick when she entered the hall, had parted down the middle between the tables to reveal Tayg, seated on a stool, his drum on his thigh and a grin on his face. A very pregnant lass rose from the near end of the tables and took Cat by the elbow and began pulling her down the hall.

"Bard," the lass said loudly.

"Aye, Mairi?"

"Will you not make up a song for this lass, here? She is the bonnyst I have seen in a very long time."

"I am not good at such things," he said and Cat found herself smiling in spite of the weight in the pit of her stomach.

"'Tis sure I am that you can spin a fine verse. There is much to be said about this lass, aye?"

Tayg's gaze locked with Cat's. He picked up the beat

and Mairi dragged her forward, the crowd closing behind her, cutting off any hope of escape.

He whistled the tune to the song he had made up for Dolag and Cat shook her head. "Do not . . ."

"A lass, known as Cat, she is loyal and true." His voice rose over her objection. "Her hair made of ebon, her voice like a flute."

Cat put her hands over her mouth, desperately trying not to cry, not to give in to Charming Tayg.

"She is soft, sweet and bonny, my own love, 'tis true. And she is never, no never, ever a shrew."

He stopped and the hall was absolutely silent. Catriona couldn't breathe, couldn't think. Tears trickled down her cheeks.

Tayg handed the drum to someone and rose, slowly moving towards her.

"You see, Cat," he said, grasping her hands and pulling them toward him. He held them, lifted them to his lips. A shudder ran through her at the soft touch of his mouth on her skin and she could not take her eyes off his. "I am the same man I was when first we met . . . nay, I am a better man, and 'tis your doing. I cannot live without you. If you will not stay here in Culrain, then I have asked and gained the leave of my liege to follow you to Assynt where I will serenade you daily until you can stand it no longer and you take pity upon me and become my wife. For I will not rest until you are mine, love.

"Will you marry me, brave Catriona? Will you be my wife, with all that entails? There will be strife and turmoil and hardship and happiness and laughter and love. God willing we'll have bairns with your good looks and my easy temper," he grinned at her then, the grin of her bard, her Tayg, the man she loved, the man who made her a better person than she had ever been, who taught her to laugh, to play, who made her heart, mind and body sing, despite his poor efforts at verse.

"Say yes, lass," he said, more with his eyes than his voice.

"Say yes!" the crowd yelled.

Catriona looked about at the beaming faces surrounding her. She glanced over her shoulder at the dais and found the king, Tayg's parents and Ailig all grinning at her. Ailig nodded at her. Tayg's mother did the same; even the king was grinning and nodding.

"Say him yea," the king boomed out.

Tayg took her face in his hands and kissed her, softly, gently. "Say you will be my wife, Cat. The king deems you worthy of the exalted heir of Culrain," he said with a grin. "Will you not marry me?"

"Aye," she said, kissing him lightly on the lips as joy lifted her heart. "I will marry you."

Tayg grabbed her about the waist and swung her around, whooping and hollering to the cheers of the crowd.

"Wait!" Cat cried. "Wait!"

Tayg put her down and looked at her quizzically.

"There is one condition I require," she said, trying hard not to grin at the concerned look on his face.

"Anything," he said with complete seriousness.

"I will marry you but . . . you must promise never to make up any more songs."

Tayg's expression stayed serious. "I do not know if I can make such a promise."

Now 'twas Cat's turn to look worried.

"If we have a wee lass, I may have to make one up for her." He grinned then and Cat's heart blossomed. He was her Charming Tayg, now, and always would be.

Laurin would love to hear from her readers.
Please e-mail her via her website at
www.Wittig.com/Laurin